The Monkeybars of Life

Ted Pittman

iUniverse, Inc.
New York   Bloomington

iUniverse books may be ordered through booksellers or by contacting:

iUniverse
1663 Liberty Drive
Bloomington, IN 47403
www.iuniverse.com
1-800-Authors (1-800-288-4677)

Because of the dynamic nature of the Internet, any Web addresses or links contained in this book may have changed since publication and may no longer be valid. The views expressed in this work are solely those of the author and do not necessarily reflect the views of the publisher, and the publisher hereby disclaims any responsibility for them.

ISBN: 978-0-595-46462-3 (sc)
ISBN: 978-0-595-90760-1 (ebook)

Printed in the United States of America

iUniverse rev. date: 04/19/2010

For Motherdear.

Namaste.

Acknowledgements

I want to thank my family and friends for their loving support throughout my life. I also thank those who presented challenges which forced me to grow and learn about myself and the universe.

Special thanks to the following people for patiently reading, critiquing and encouraging me during the writing of this book.

John Casey
Karen Dawson
Myheir Hill
Kimberly Johnson
Pearl Jackson
Alea Kalae
John Morse
Gina Nurse
Ricky Nurse
Margaret Talevi

www.monkeybarsoflife.com

Contents

Main Characters

Aron Balsam	Mechanical engineer for Emmi
Art Chavez	Antagonist at MicroStep Corp
Beatrice Niles	Nate's lover
Bill Davis	Co-inventor of Gamma engine
Brandon Allison	Lena's grandson
Claudette Thomas	Sister
Colonel Abrams	Mossad special agent
Dave Nichols	CEO of Nova Medical Systems
Del Adams	Inventor of arcade games
Darryl Wilson	Boss at Shirotronics
Douglas Thomas	Brother
Ernest DuPree	Technical partner
Eva LaChae	First wife
Gabriel Morris	Programming partner
Henry Harris	Best friend
Jeanette Ramsey	Lover, mother of Nate's son
JimmieMae LaChae	Mother
Lena LaChae	Second wife
Marcus Ryan	European boss
Marilyn Wilkenson	Lena's daughter
Mario Messina	Friend and European co-worker
Mr. Cassell	Emmi customer in France
Naomi Boatwright	Cousin and confidant
Nate LaChae	Protagonist
Nate LaChae Sr.	Father
Paul Brown	Prolific inventor and friend
Peter Eastlund	Boss at KMS and inventor of Emmi
Reggie Overton	Buddy and co-worker
Russell Taggart	FBI special agent
Sheila McKnight	Friend
Willy Raymond	Antagonist at MicroStep Corp

Prologue

The flight from New York to Chicago was Nate LaChae's second flight. Eleven years before, when he was sixteen, he won a Navy award at the school science fair and was flown up to Boston. That flight was on a noisy prop-plane. Now he was gliding along at 530 mph over Pennsylvania. He wished he had the seat by the window, but even from the middle seat, he could see the clouds reflecting the setting sun.

He removed his mother's letter from his briefcase and read it again.

---

841 Eastern Parkway
B'klyn. N.Y. 11213

My dear son,

    I frequently, just get in my car and take, what I term, therapeutic drives. I call them therapeutic because they seem to do me - a world-of-good. One of my favorites is driving from Brooklyn to Harlem. I passed the playground in Mt. Morris Park - off Madison Ave. - and went immediately on a nostalgia trip. I saw a little four or five year old boy (you) climbing to the top of the 'monkey bars', while Mom and I watched and prayed somewhat uncomfortably, until you reached the top. A little boy or little girl might have got gotten into you path, your way, but you would go around them, sometimes over them and would always reach out and make it. Little did I realize then [I had

---

not studied - Child Psychology & Development at that time] that you were setting your pattern for life.

Now my son, Mom and I still watch and pray for you (we never stopped), while you deal with, while you climb those 'giant monkey bars' of life. I'm keenly aware of many things, huge things, incidents that have gotten in your way, in your path. I have watched you rise above them all. Gee! Those 'giant monkey bars' must seem almost insurmountable at times, but 'you made it' on those bars at Mt. Morris Park, and you were only four or five years of age.

Love you –
Motherdear

Nate idly rotated the gold ring Beatrice had given him, remembering her saying, with her Caribbean accent, "This was supposed to be your birthday gift; but now I don't know if I'll ever see you again."

"Don't worry", he told her, "I'll be back. I'm just going to meet my father's side of my family."

After the stewardess served drinks, Nate's thoughts turned to his best friend. *Henry will never have this kind of opportunity, of being plucked out of the ghetto and flown to another city where his father will be waiting for him.*

Location: Bedford Stuyvesant, Brooklyn / New York

It was late and the family was still sitting around the dinner table.

MommaMary reached over and squeezed her daughter's hand, "JimmieMae, you did the right thing sending Nate to live with his father for a while. Otherwise he might have lost his mind and done something bad."

JimmieMae looked up, with her big round eyes, "I know, Momma, I just hope they don't turn him against me."

"Ain't nobody gonna do nothing like that." MommaMary said.

Sam finished chewing his bread pudding and then said, "He shouldn't have quit his job. He been there seven years and they liked him too. You should never leave a good job where they like you."

"He wasn't thinking right." JimmieMae said, "He told me he didn't have any reason to work there any more. Nate's biggest mistake was giving up that apartment after Eva walked out."

"Why'd he do that?" Sam asked in his deep voice.

"He said she asked him to do it, because she had some illness that could be contagious. And he said he didn't want to be living there anyway, with all the rooms empty." JimmieMae shook her head, "They should have never let her marry him in the first place. He could've got an annulment after what she told him about her childhood."

MommaMary sucked on a fishbone. "Way back, I told you he was too crazy 'bout that girl. And it was plain to see she didn't feel the same way 'bout him. She even kept him from taking those scholarships and from going to the Air Force too. That whole family just saw Nate as a clean young man who would make a good husband and father. Why you think they use to let him stay 'till all hours of the night."

"Now, Momma", Sam said, "Nate only did what y'all taught him. He married her when she got pregnant and stayed with her through everything. Look how he took care of them babies. And he never came back to us for money like I thought he would."

"He's too proud for that." JimmieMae sipped her tea.

"What I want to know", Sam said, "is how the court sided against him."

JimmieMae turned to her brother, "I told you, because he didn't get a lawyer or defend himself. Eva accused him of abusing her and not giving money for the kids and the judge believed her."

"Everybody knows he always took care of his kids-," Sam said.

"Everybody except the judge. And Nate didn't have any receipts."

"Didn't he say anything about her abusing the kids and the tragedy?"

"Not a word."

"Why would he do that?"

"I'll tell you why"," MommaMary said, "cause that hussy done bewitched him. Y'all can shake your heads all you want, but they done taught her how to put a spell on him and he's so confused he can't see it. It won't be the first time that happened in our family." She rolled her eyes at her son.

Dispirited, Sam went to the refrigerator for another beer.

"Momma, that's not right for you to say things like that." JimmieMae said, "What happened to Sam was altogether different from what happened to Nate."

"Your brother suffered because that singer put a spell on him and now your son is suffering in the same way."

"Well, spell or not", JimmieMae said, "Nate will be away from New York for a while. I couldn't stand the thought of him staying up there in that abandon building, in Harlem. He wouldn't survive the winter."

Location: Bedford Stuyvesant, Brooklyn / New York

Henry loaded more Soul music on the stereo and turned the volume up. Meanwhile his wife, Margie, refilled three glasses with the wine Naomi had brought.

"Your cousin sure is something else." Henry said, "We had some real good times together. Here's to Nate."

They clicked their glasses together.

"Those two fools used to get so drunk", Margie said, "I'd have to drag them up the stairs."

Naomi smiled and took a drag on her cigarette.

"We go way back, you know." Henry continued, "He was always building some science project and asking me to come see it."

"So, tell me", Naomi said, "What's going to happen to the Cervaza Kings social club now?"

"Shit, I don't know. Frank is dead, and I heard Sonny moved to Louisiana. Me and my cousin Johnny are the only ones left now. Maybe the Juniors will take over one day. Douglas wants to take Nate's place now, but he's too young and he ain't been through enough shit yet."

The music stopped and a gloomy silence followed.

"I sure hope Nate comes back."

"Me too." Naomi said, "But, his mother told me a lot of people are looking for him right now. He owed money and the courts want him to pay child support." Naomi shook her head, "It's still hard for me to believe he quit his job at the Port Authority over that."

"Ha!" Henry flipped the records over and restarted the music. "That's because you don't really know your cousin. He ain't gonna let nobody *make* him do nothing.

I remember when I first met Nate; we were teenagers. I saw a crowd and I went over to see what was going on. This real tough boy name Calhoun was picking on a guy with a bad leg and Nate stepped in and took up for the guy.

Calhoun jumped on Nate and they started going at it. Calhoun was winning and he told Nate to say, 'A cripple ain't shit'. Nate wouldn't say it and they kept on fighting. When I saw Nate wasn't gonna say it, I was scared, but I jumped in and helped him anyway. When we heard the police coming, everybody ran.

After the fight, I asked Nate why he didn't just go ahead and say what Calhoun wanted him to say. Seems like that would have been better than a ass whippin'. And guess what Nate told me."

"What?"

"He said he wasn't gonna let nobody be his master." Henry laughed, "And would you believe, he got that shit from one of his mother's poems.

So, that's why I know Nate ain't gonna give in to his wife or the courts or anybody else. Not after all the shit he done been through with her and her family. They lucky he ain't hurt nobody."

Naomi looked at her watch, "Hey, I got to get going. Nate's mother just wanted me to tell you not to give any information to anybody that might come around asking questions about Nate."

"She should know we ain't gonna say nothing." Margie said.

"Yeah, she just wanted me to remind you."

Location: Jamaica, Queens / New York

Eva LaChae brushed her hair back from her forehead, "I'm afraid of being in that apartment alone."

Her mother continued glancing at the soaps on TV and folding her laundered clothes. "Don't Walter come around?"

"No, I've asked him to stay away ... in case Nate might see him again."

"Nate got better sense than to be stalking you. He knows the court will lock his ass up if he tries something."

"You don't know him like I do, Mother. He can be real mean when he's angry. I wish the court would have made him turn over his hunting equipment. He still has those rifles and that pistol."

"He ain't crazy." Eva's mother said, "We can get guns too. I'm telling you, you don't have to be scared of that man. Look at me, I ain't scared and he gonna be bringing or sending that money over here. He just tried to be too smart for his britches, that's all. I told him he gonna pay the same for each of the children like all the other parents, of kids I keep."

"But, I didn't know the judge was going to tell him he couldn't see them."

"Eva, he brought it on himself. Besides, what did you think the court was going to do?"

"I figured they'd make him pay more money. But, when I told how Nate had treated me, the judge acted like Nate had been a bad father too."

"Girl, quit whining. You did what you had to do. You can take the kids over to his folks, in Brooklyn, sometimes and he can see them then.

You said you was through with him; now, get on with your life. I like Walter; he's got real business sense. Not out there building rockets and science junk like Nate.

When is Nate supposed to bring the first payment, anyway?"

Location: 125th Street, Harlem / New York

"I still don't see why Nate had to leave." Douglas said.

Ernest DuPree looked over the equipment piled on the old desk and then said "Your big brother is going through changes he never expected; they tried to take away his soul. He needs time and a place where he can get himself together again. It's not gonna be easy."

Douglas shook his head, and then he reached into the pile and picked up a rocket nozzle. "I thought aluminum would melt-"

"Yeah", Ernest grinned, "see the inside? That's a graphite coating, to stand the heat from the exhaust gases."

Satisfied, Douglas put the nozzle back on the pile, shrugged his shoulders and then said, "At least he got to work on the Lunar Module. I never understood why he didn't stay with that company."

"Grumman?" Ernest said as he leaned back in his chair, "I think Nate felt guilty about his son dying at the same time he got the Grumman job. Maybe, he couldn't feel happy at such a sad time in his life. That was before we met and started the MiniLab and Aerospace Innovations, Inc."

"What's going to happen to A.I.I. now?"

"That's a good question. We were trying to get a contract to use your brother's tracking system to monitor the sway of the World Trade Center's buildings when they're finished."

"Oh, wow! You mean it's that good? I thought it could only detect things like the moon."

"That good?" Ernest laughed, "Nate's tracking system has detected the planet Venus in the daytime. We were trying to get enough money to build three more. Now, I don't know what will happen."

"Can't you go on without him?"

"Not really. That was his project. I'm working on my own stuff. Let me tell you what's really going on, Douglas. Nate's tracking system is like a toy to us. He discovered a way to use a gyroscope to reduce gravity itself. He built a toy car that ran using nothing but two vibrating gyroscopes.

Now, the smartest guy I know lives over in New Jersey. Bob Jones works, part-time, over there at Picanny Army base. He can get parts the rest of us amateur rocketeers can't get. I interviewed him and wrote an article in Space World magazine when I was an editor. Bob Jones had proven, theoretically, that a gyroscopic engine could be built that would reduce gravity.

When I introduced Bob and Nate they went into an orgy of technical talk about inertia, Coriolis forces, centrifugal force and stuff. You should have seen them. I just got out of their way and watched. Bob wrote equations on the board and Nate showed his photos and tests results. At the end of the day, they agreed to publish a report together."

"So, what happened then?"

Ernest sat back in his chair, shook his head, and grunted, "Nobody believed them."

"What about those guys that helped you set up A.I.I.? You said they have PhD's in science."

"That's the worse part. They came, saw Nate's car running, and even saw the gyros. But, they said it must be working on some other principles than what Nate thought."

"Didn't they read the report with Bob Jones equations?"

"They did. And they said it violates Newton's laws."

"So, what?"

Ernest rubbed his hands through his Frederick Douglass-styled hair. "You still don't get it, do you? Your brother and I are impossible! We're not here! Nobody in the world believes ghetto black men can possibly do the things we're doing.

"Nate told me the guys that helped you incorporate were all aerospace guys." Douglas said, "I don't see why they wouldn't help you more."

"Oh, our partners", Ernest exaggerated the words; "They invited us to dinners and meetings and even made us honorary board members of one of their aerospace clubs. But, when I asked them for $3,000,000 their eyes got big and they balked."

"You really asked them for $3,000,000?"

Ernest laughed, "Yeah, I did. And your brother's eyes got big too. But, that's what's needed to do a meaningful program. Those guys, eventually, told us they wanted us to buy real estate in Harlem for them. They didn't really give a damn about our technical abilities and projects."

And, Douglas, I haven't even mentioned my own projects like exploding bridge-wire technology. I've corresponded with people all over the world. And I got more responses outside this country than within it. I'm about ready to work with whoever will help me; I don't care who it is anymore."

Douglas didn't respond.

Ernest stared out of the third floor window, of the dilapidated building in Harlem, cracked his knuckles, and then said resolutely, "I mean it."

Zemit Radio

Nate awoke as the flight was landing at O'Hare International airport. As soon as he exited the gate, he spotted his father who was a big man that stood six foot three. There were two young men standing with him. Nate and his dad hugged. Then he was introduced to his brothers. He grinned and shook both their hands warmly. Stan had the prominent family nose and Nate saw the resemblance. Greg was bigger, had a beard and was tougher looking.

They let Nate sit with dad in the front of the car. Stan told Nate how they had heard about him for years. Nate admitted he didn't know anything about them. But, he was happy to learn that he had three brothers and two sisters.

They didn't go to his dad's house in Gary, Indiana. Instead, he was taken to meet his Aunt Lil. He remembered meeting her once when he was 20 years old. She and some other relatives had visited New York.

Aunt Lil greeted him as if she had known him all his life. She went right past the others and gave Nate a big hug. Once inside, he met other relatives. Everyone greeted him warmly.

Aunt Lil's cooking was as good as he had heard it would be. The dining room was too small for everyone to eat together, so people were eating in the living room and kitchen.

After dinner, some family members left and things settled down. Nate's dad explained that arrangements had been made for Nate to stay at Aunt Lil's house. Nate Sr. explained that his own house was too crowded and Nate would be more comfortable at Aunt Lil's. Nate was disappointed, but felt he should trust his father's judgment.

Later, after Nate unpacked, he wrote a postcard to Beatrice saying how comfortable he felt and that he loved her. He promised to send a letter soon.

On the weekend, Nate Sr. and Stanley came to bring Nate to Gary, Indiana to meet his other siblings. During the hour's drive, Stanley told stories about their dad and Nate began to understand where he inherited his sense of humor from. When they got to the house, Nate was met by smiling faces. Two sisters (Margaret and Sabrina) and a little brother (Terry); Greg was there too. Nate was introduced to his stepmother, Jewel. She smiled, but the warmth wasn't there on either side. "Now y'all let Nate catch his breath." Jewel said as she went into the kitchen.

Sitting in the living room, with Terry right by his side, Nate heard Stanley say, "I heard that you play chess."

"Yeah, I play a little." he replied, smiling.

"Oh boy!" Terry exclaimed and jumped up to get the chessboard.

Once the game got started, Margaret, Sabrina and Terry all rooted for Stan. So, Nate decided to be diplomatic and let Stan win the first game.

No need to burst their bubble and embarrass Stanley, he thought.

Nate maneuvered into a position where Stan was able to checkmate him. While the siblings cheered, Nate was busy setting the board up again. That's when Nate's father came into the room and asked, "Who won?"

"Stanley did", Sabrina said.

Nate Sr. replied, "I knew he would, that's my boy" and walked out of the room.

At that moment Nate promised himself, Stan would never beat him at chess again.

*   *   *

Nate was surprised how comfortable he felt at his aunt's home. Her husband, James, was mildly tolerant of Nate. They didn't have any real conversations when Aunt Lil wasn't there. They'd try to eat enough of her huge meals, so she wouldn't fuss at them when she got home from work.

James was always reluctant to discuss the work he did at Argonne Nuclear Labs. "It's government work", is all he'd say.

"I used to work at Grumman Aircraft Company." Nate explained, "They did government contracts too. So, I understand about security clearances and not discussing your work."

James responded quickly with, "Yeah, you understand."

*   *   *

Nate offered his services to Operation PUSH, The DeSable Afro-American Museum and the Illinois Institute of Technology. Each of their responses was negative.

He found a help wanted ad, in a Sunday newspaper, for a technician at Zemit Radio Corp. He called a recruiter the next day arranged for an interview, and sent his resume.

Wednesday, Nate went to Zemit and met Ed Reardon, who shook his hand and ushered him into an office cluttered with papers. A photo of a P-51 Mustang airplane hung on the wall. Nate couldn't tell if the pilot in the photo was Reardon or not.

Reardon read Nate's resume, and then said. "Why don't you tell me a little about yourself? Do you know anything about transistors?"

"I understand the basics and I made a transistor amplifier for my tracking system. Beyond that, most of my work has been in aeronautics." Nate was quick to add, "And, I took physics and math in college."

"How much math have you had?"

"I took pre-calculus at Hunter College. This notebook has some photos and awards that I've won for my projects."

Reardon took the notebook. "Have you flown any of your rockets?"

"Yes, I flew small ones at parks in New York. I fired a larger metal rocket at Camp Pickett Army artillery range in Virginia."

"Really. How high did it go?" Reardon asked.

"We calculated that one went over 17,500 feet." Nate said, "We heard a sonic boom when it came down out on the range. We didn't try to recover it."

Reardon opened Nate's notebook and started examining its contents. He grunted a few times as he turned the pages. He looked up and then said, "This is very impressive, Nate. I'm not sure the job we have available would be challenging enough for you. The duties are for performing routine testing of transistors and diodes. It's not exactly rocket science."

"I understand that, sir. My astronautics work has been mostly on my own. My jobs have been electronics technician most of the time. That's what I'm good at."

"I see." Reardon ran his hand through his grey hair. "I want to arrange for you to speak with some other people. Can you come back next week?"

"Yes, sir. That won't be any problem."

*   *   *

Saturday morning, family members started arriving at Aunt Lil's house. They brought kids and parents. They came in all colors and sizes. Some knew Nate when he was a baby. They hugged him and pinched his cheek. He was relieved when his dad arrived with his siblings, which he, at least, knew for a few weeks.

Everyone heard Bobby's arrival with his wife and kids. After hugging his mother, Aunt Lil, he turned to Nate. "So-o-o, this must be my long, lost, cousin." He hugged Nate. "You know how to play bid-whisk?"

"A little ..."

"Good, 'cause we're gonna be kicking some butt today." Bobby moved on toward the backyard. It seemed the music got louder as soon as he arrived. The smell of food barbecuing drifted across the yard.

Aunt Lil's daughters Mae, Myheir and Frances came over and kissed Nate on the cheek. They teased him about an earlier episode when he didn't realize saying *grace* was the same as *blessing* the table.

"Are you seeing somebody now?" the younger one asked.

"Yeah, she's from Barbados."

"Oh-h-h", Frances said, "you like them exotic women."

"She's not all that exotic", Nate said, "but she's very sweet. I wish you could meet her."

Sam LaChae came over with two beers.

"Want a cold one?" he said, "I'm your second cousin."

"Yeah", Nate took the beer, "Thanks, Cuz."

"The stronger stuff is in the kitchen", Sam said.

Nate's dad came over and put his arm around Nate's shoulder.

"Well son, how does it feel to be around your family?"

"It feels great, dad. Everybody is so friendly."

"Come on over here, somebody wants to see you."

Nate walked over to a group of older women sitting under a tree."

"Come on over here boy and give your Aunt Mattie some sugar."

Nate did as instructed by the stranger.

"You don't remember me, do you?"

"He can't remember," Nate's dad said, "he was only two years old."

"I bet he remembers to do what I taught him," she said laughing. "Don't you Nate?"

"I ah … I don't know."

She laughed again and then said softly, "I taught you to shake your thang when you finish peeing."

Nate was embarrassed as the group of women and his dad laughed. LaChae senior tugged at Nate's arm and pulled him away. "Don't pay her no mind, Mattie's like that."

Nate followed his father toward the back of the yard where an old man was sitting alone. He wore a white shirt, pants with suspenders, and black boots that laced up above his ankles. Nate couldn't tell if the man was frowning or squinting from the sunlight.

"Uncle Chae, this here is my oldest boy, Nate Jr."

The man stared, as if he hadn't heard Nate's dad. "Come closer boy, so I can see you better. Yes, you're a LaChae for sure. You got our nose. How you doing, boy?"

"I'm doing fine, sir. I'm very happy to be here."

"How's your mother and grandmother and your uncle?"

"They're doing well. They live in New York."

"I know where they live. We came there to visit one time when you were a little fella. Don't you remember?"

Nate tried, but couldn't remember.

"How's your kids?"

"They're fine."

"They safe now?" the old man asked.

Nate looked at his dad, and then at Uncle Chae, "Yes sir, they're safe."

"That's good; we don't need to lose any more babies like that."

Nate felt a knot form in his stomach. "No, sir."

The elder addressed Nate's dad, "You bring him around to my house sometime so we can talk, you hear."

Nate Sr. promised he would.

Aunt Lil called out above the music, "Y'all come on and get your plates."

Bobby and his wife beat every pair that dared play Bid-Whisk against them. He came out to get a beer and saw Nate talking with Sam. He popped the top of the beer can.

"There's my city-slicker cousin. Somebody told me New Yorkers can't play cards. Is that true?"

"Some can't." Nate said.

"Well, get yourself a partner and come on and let me see which kind you are." He motioned for Nate to follow him.

"Sam, want to be my partner?"

"I don't play cards, Nate."

Great. Now who can I get? Nate thought.

His cousin Frances came over and then said, "I'll be partners with you, Nate, but I don't play all that well."

Buoyed by the beer and the spirited atmosphere, Nate grabbed her arm and charged after Bobby.

The next morning, Aunt Lil woke Nate. "Breakfast is on the table and you got two pieces of mail."

Nate's cousins made room for him at the table and one said, "I'll bet it's from Beatrice."

"Y'all mind your own business", Aunt Lil said, "and let your cousin eat in peace.

As Nate sat, he said, "Please excuse me; I can't wait to read this one, it's from my mother."

"Sure baby," Aunt Lil said, "we understand. That's from your mother. I'd do the same thing."

"I thought it was impolite to read at the table," Mae teased.

"You keep on reading, Cuz." Bobby reached for more chicken, "I'll take care of the food."

"Oh wow! She's coming here," Nate said, "next month."

"She wants to make sure her baby is okay." Aunt Lil said, "That's the way a mother is. She knows you never lived on your own before."

Nate filled his plate, "I'm twenty-seven years old."

"That don't matter, Honey. Us mothers always see y'all as our babies."

*   *   *

While Aunt Lil did everything to make Nate feel comfortable, he sensed James didn't want him there. Once Nate overheard them talking. "...he likes it here," James was saying. Nate couldn't hear his Aunt's reply. Shortly afterward, he was asked to move down to the basement room. Aunt Lil explained it was because Uncle Chae was coming for a few days and he had a hard time with stairs. So, she wanted him to have the guest bedroom.

Nate found the basement room to be bigger and more to his liking. He wasn't used to getting all the attention he got upstairs. Every visitor seemed to either know him or wanted to meet him and they were all strangers to him. His new room gave him space to think.

Without a job, or money, he could only make plans; and to keep from getting bored, he started planning the next phase of work on his Gamma engine. He didn't know when, where or how he'd get started again, but he knew he would – someday. He bought a whiteboard and started making calculations on it.

Again, Nate overheard Aunt Lil and James talking about him. "I don't care! I want him out of here." James said, "Next he'll be moving furniture downstairs. He brought that board in here without asking anybody." James voice sounded accusing, almost angry.

Aunt Lil's response was too muffled for Nate to understand.

"Well, you better tell him, or I will. Two more weeks and that's it!"

Nate strained but couldn't hear his aunt's reply.

Later that evening, Aunt Lil knocked on his door and then said she had some hot tea for him. Nate opened the door and pretended he hadn't overheard their conversation. She sat two cups of tea on the nightstand.

"Are you alright, Nate?"

"Sure, I'm fine." Nate sipped his tea, "Thanks."

"Do you mind talking with your Auntie for a little while?"

"Not at all, Aunt Lil."

"I heard you talking in your sleep the other night."

Nate didn't know what to say, "Really?"

Aunt Lil pushed her glasses up on her nose and then said, "Nate, I'm not one to meddle in other people's business, but I love my family and can't sit quiet while any of y'all are hurting. Honey, I know some of the things about your life and I believe you have done the best you could. You're a grown man and that's your business.

I just want you to know that both your mother and father love you so much that they started talking to each other again after twenty-five years. Your mother called your father and then said she felt you needed a vacation from New York for a while. She was very worried after you and your wife broke up.

Now they don't know I'm telling you this. I thought you should know they are wondering if you are going to go back to New York or stay in Chicago. Whatever you do must be your own decision and I don't believe you will do anything that will hurt your family."

Nate looked down at his teacup and then said, "I'm not going back to New York, Aunt Lil. I don't want to talk about all the things that went on, but it's best for everybody that I stay away from there."

"Lord knows, sometimes that is best." She paused, "Do you pray?"

"Sometimes."

"It helps, especially when we need to make decisions. When we listen to the little voice in our heart, it tells us what to do."

Nate wanted to tell her about the voice in his heart that was full of anger and hurt. He wanted to tell her about his dreams, but didn't.

"I understand everything you've said Aunt Lil. It's just hard for me right now. I never, ever, thought about living life without my family and now the court said I have to. And it's not my fault. I can't prove it and everybody thinks that I chose to leave my family." His voice started to break and he sipped some tea.

"I don't know what happened, Nate, but I believe you tried your best. Your mother used to call from time to time and tell me how you were doing. Everything we heard about you always made us proud. When your son died, your father said you should have brought the other kids here then. We all heard how you stayed and kept things together."

"Aunt Lil, it was very hard for me. But, I thought that was what I was supposed to do."

"It was, Honey, and you did good. So, you go ahead and get on with your life. Whatever you decide, I'm on your side." She paused, and asked, "Do you sleep well?"

"Yes, this bed is very comfortable."

"I mean, do you dream?"

"Oh, yes sometimes I dream. Why do you ask?"

"Cause sometimes things in life make us have bad dreams. But, prayer can change that and answers can come in dreams." She got up and touched Nate's head. She gathered the cups and then said, "You get your rest, Honey. Everything is going to be all right. You're with your family now."

Morning came and Nate was joined by his father for breakfast.

"Here, Nate, have some more pancakes." Aunt Lil said as she plopped two on Nate's plate.

"But, I'm almost full."

"You look like you could use a few more pounds." Nate Sr. said, "And this is the best cooking in town. That's why I drove over here so early."

"It is delicious." Nate said, "I don't usually eat so much."

Aunt Lil came over and put her hand on Nate's shoulder.

"You're at your Auntie's house now, Honey," she kissed him on the forehead, "and you don't want me to have to throw food away, do you?"

"No ..."

She turned and stirred the grits.

"Dad, my appointment at Zemit Radio isn't until 1:30. I didn't expect you here so early."

"I thought we could spend some time together this morning. Maybe, go over to the Museum of Science and Industry?"

"Hey, that's fine with me."

"That's something you surely got from your father." Aunt Lil said, "He's been tinkering around with things ever since he was a boy. That's how he got to be the first black manager at Standard Oil Company."

Nate looked at his dad and then said, "I didn't know that."

"Oh yeah, Nate," Aunt Lil continued as she did the dishes, "where do you think you got all them brains to do science stuff?"

"Well, my mother told me she got straight A's in Chemistry and Math. I always thought I inherited it from her.

"I'm sure you did get some from her, Honey; I'm not saying you didn't. I'm just telling you about your father. Out of all his children, you're the only one that's been building rockets and things. Ask your father to tell you about the time he made a steam train from old tin cans."

Nate looked at his father in amazement. "Really? How did it work?"

Nate's dad smiled, "It only ran for a few minutes. Come on, I'll tell you about it on the way to the museum."

By lunchtime, Nate was amazed at his dad's knowledge of engineering. His dad was equally impressed with Nate's knowledge of astronautics.

At the museum's exhibit of the Grumman Lunar Lander (LEM), Nate said, "I almost got into one of these, dad."

"How'd you do that?"

"I was working at Grumman and there was a finished LEM in one of the hangars. One day somebody left the door open and I walked over to the LEM and just stood there looking up. I didn't touch it because I remembered oil from our hands can change the surface finish of metal."

"So, what happened?"

"The guard came in and then said HALT!"

"Did you get in trouble?"

"No. Luckily, my supervisor came by and he kept me out of trouble."

"At least you can say you were there."

"Yeah, I was."

They stared up at the LEM together.

*   *   *

The second round of interviewers at Zemit Radio were impressed with Nate and an employment offer came the next day. Nate accepted over the phone. He didn't care much about the salary; he rejoiced at having the title of Technician once again.

The Components Engineering lab consisted of a diversified group. A dozen people sat at workbenches that had test equipment and cables scattered everywhere. Nate smiled as he was introduced to his supervisor. Edwin Casey didn't return the cordiality.

"So, you're the rocket guy?" Casey said.

"Yep, that's me."

"You have any experience with transistors?"

"I've worked with them a little; I built an amplifier."

"Un, huh." Casey said, "And how much beta did you get out of it?"

"I didn't measure the gain, but it worked well enough to detect stars and airplanes when it was attached to my telescope."

"Un, huh. You have any more experience with electronics?"

"Just the other parts of my tracking system, I-"

"Okay, okay. So, we can say your knowledge is limited. Right?"

"Yeah, that would be right."

Casey turned and called to another worker, "Hey Reggie, come over here for a minute." The black man who approached was well built and intelligent looking. He stared over his glasses at Nate.

"This is Nate; he's going to join our group." Casey said, "This is Reggie Overton; he'll show you what we do." Casey returned to his papers.

Reggie smiled, "How you doing, Nate." His handshake was firm.

"Great. It's good to be back into electronics again."

Casey glanced at Nate, but didn't speak.

"Come on, let me introduce you to the guys," Reggie said.

* * *

Using a loan from his dad, Nate got an apartment in Hyde Park. James drove Nate to his new apartment and waited in the car while Aunt Lil went inside and inspected the little kitchenette.

"This is nice, Nate. You even have a stove and all, but where's the bed?"

Nate laughed and then said, "Stand back and watch this." He open a closet door and swung an upright bed around and down. It descended slowly on springs.

"Lord have mercy, what will they think of next?" Aunt Lil said.

"Now you be sure to put that food away in the frig and here-", she shoved some folded money into his hand.

He tried to refuse it, but she hushed him up.

"Now, you be sure to call me every day?"

"Okay, Aunt Lil."

He walked with her to the car. They hugged and she left.

Back upstairs, Nate thought, *I'm alone again, like I was back in Astoria after Eva and the kids were gone. Hope those dreams don't start again.* A chill went through him. *I've got to keep my mind occupied. I'll start designing another Gamma engine.*

He turned the radio to a jazz station and opened a bottle of beer.

* * *

The train station was crowded. Nate navigated around people, as he peered through the windows of the New York Express, searching for his mother. There she was. A gentleman was taking her suitcase down from the overhead rack. Nate waved and got her attention. Her smile brought joy to his heart. The gentleman carried his own bag and hers off the train.

Nate rushed up and hugged his mother, and then he turned and thank the man.

"Whew, that was a long ride." she said. "You've gained weight Nate."

"That's Aunt Lil's cooking, she fixes really big meals."

"How's she doing?"

"Very well; we can go by there whenever you're ready. But first, let's take a cab to my place. Do you remember Hyde Park?"

"It's over by the university, isn't it? The science museum is there; I know you've been there, haven't you?"

"Several times." Nate opened the cab door for her.

Once inside, Nate asked,

"How's Mom and Uncle and Douglas and Claudette?"

"They're all fine. Your sister sent you a card."

Ms. LaChae watched the scenery go by. "Everything looks so different. The train station used to be on the other side of town, by the stock yards."

"When was the last time you were here, Motherdear?"

"Not since you were almost a teenager. Don't you remember?"

"Vaguely. I didn't know anyone back then."

She looked at Nate, held his hand and then said, "Most of the people you met then were my schoolmates. But, now you've been meeting your father's family, haven't you?"

"Yes, I have. There was a family reunion at Aunt Lil's house and everybody was so friendly. Some of the people knew me when I was a baby."

"I'm glad. I wasn't sure how you would feel around them."

"It's been wonderful so far; they treat me like they've always known me."

The taxi turned off ML-King drive and drove along Washington Park.

"Look over there. That's where you were born Nate, Provident Hospital."

"Dad said Joe Louis' daughter was born across the hall from me. Is that true?"

"Yes it is. Some reporters came and took pictures of you and started asking me all sorts of questions about how proud I must be. I told them 'Yes' I was very proud of giving birth to my son. The next day, one of the newspapers showed a picture of you, the caption read 'Joe Louis' new son'. That's when your uncle started calling you Champ."

*   *   *

"I like your little kitchenette apartment, Nate. And this furniture was already here?"

"Yes, Motherdear. Not bad, huh?"

"It reminds me of the first place me and your father had."

"That reminds me", Nate said, "we're being taken to dinner tonight."

"Let me guess by whom." Mrs. LaChae said.

"Dad said he'd be here at six o'clock."

"Maybe that wife of his won't let him come."

"Aw, Motherdear, it's only six-thirty. He's probably stuck in traffic."

"Uh-huh."

The doorbell rang and Nate pushed the buzzer. Nate opened his door and saw his dad looking sportier than ever. He had on a white cap, white sport shirt, dark blue pants, with a crease that could cut butter, and dark brown shoes that shined like new.

"Come in, dad." Nate tried to hug him as he came in.

"There's my dream girl." He stopped with his hands on his hips.

"Hello, Nate." She stayed behind the kitchenette counter.

He removed his cap. "Come on out here and let me see you."

"I thought, maybe you weren't going to make it."

"I got the car washed when I stopped for gas."

She came into the main room and they held each other's hands for a moment. Then they hugged, her face pressed against his chest, her eyes closed. She pulled away and composed herself. She returned to ironing her blouse. He followed her into the small kitchen and stared.

"How have you been, Nate?"

"I've been fine. I see you still got your figure."

"Don't try teasing me. We're too old for that."

"This'll be just like old times when I used to take you out."

"Only, you're a married man now and our son will be with us too."

Nate Sr. turned toward his son, "She had a few words to say about me being late, didn't she?"

"Yeah, a few words. And you know what? You two are acting just like my generation. I thought your older generation knew all about handling relationships, but the two of you are behaving like it's your second date."

Before they could respond, Nate held his arms out and then said, "I just want to say, I sure am glad to be here."

Nate turned the radio up as he heard Sly and The Family Stone singing: *Thank you For Letting Me Be Myself Again.*

His mother looked up at Nate Sr. and then said, "Bet you still can't dance, can you."

"I can hold my own. But I'd rather hold you."

"Will you please move out of the way so I can get dressed?"

"You got to kiss me first."

"Now you talking crazy."

"How about on the cheek?"

She pecked him on the cheek, "Now, move please."

Nate Sr. cruised up to Flukey's Lounge. Duce-and-a-quarters, Cadillacs and Lincolns were double-parked near the entrance. He found a spot in the next block and parked his black Cadillac Deville.

Nate saw his father slip money into the doorman's hand before they were escorted, through the crowd, to a booth in the center of the lounge. Flukey's was exactly the way Nate had heard it to be – Black people with money having a good time. The music was old-school and smooth. The women were elegant and sexy. Several men smoked cigars and all were dressed down.

Sitting across the table from his parents, Nate saw his father had his arm around his Mother. He couldn't hear their conversation above the music. His mother leaned forward and then said, "Sorry, you're not in the conversation."

"Sorry?" Nate Sr. said, "What about me? I was here before him."

They were laughing as the waitress delivered champagne.

The next day, Mrs. LaChae was chiding Nate about his kids. "They're your children Nate and you should try talking with Eva again."

"Talk?" Nate paced the small room, "There is nothing more to talk about. She's got them a new daddy and all she wants from me is money. Besides, you're the one that told me the kids should stay together."

"When are you going to see them, if you stay here in Chicago?"

"Motherdear, the judge said I-can't-see-them." Nate pronounced each word carefully, "I couldn't even get my things out of my own apartment."

"You should have never given up the apartment in the first place."

"I told you - she said she was still sick and asked me to let her stay there, without me, so she wouldn't have to go back into the hospital."

"Why didn't she stay at her mother's house?"

"She said she was having fevers and couldn't be around anybody."

"Did she say what she was in the hospital for?"

"Something; I don't remember. I just know I ran into her boyfriend for the second time there."

"What did he have to say?"

Nate stopped pacing, turned toward his mother and then said, "I convinced him to leave."

"Did you two fight?"

"No. He left."

"How do you know that was her boyfriend?"

Nate gritted his teeth.

"Listen, Motherdear I don't want to discuss this any more." Nate said. "I'm going for a walk."

"Nate, you come back here. Don't you walk out when I'm talking-"

Nate left and walked four blocks to Lake Michigan. He heard drums as he approached The Point, which jutted out, into the lake. One of the brothers was getting up and Nate took his place at a big conga drum. He turned down an offer for some smoke, closed his eyes, and began his message of passion and anguish. Through his hands, Nate fought all who opposed him. The others followed his lead and amplified his message. The men took turns telling their powerful and beautiful stories through the drums.

When Nate returned to his apartment, he was no longer angry. "Hello, Motherdear."

She was packing. "You won't have to leave your own apartment any more. I'm going home in the morning."

"Aw, Motherdear. I'm sorry we argued, you're always welcome here. You don't have to go, unless that's what you really want to do."

"I was going to leave in a few days anyway. I've just decided to go tomorrow instead."

They were silent for a time. Then Nate asked,

"Want to play some Gin-Rummy?"

"No, I'm going to find something to read."

"Come on, Motherdear. Are you scared I'll beat you?"

Her smile told him it was okay to set up the card table. They spent the rest of the evening playing cards and reminiscing.

Later, before he fell asleep on the couch, Nate came over to the bed and kissed his mother on the cheek.

"I love you, Motherdear."

"And I love you, Nate, you'll never know how much."

The next morning, as they walked to The Pancake House for breakfast, Mrs. LaChae said, "I saw you have a stack of letters from Beatrice. You been writing her a lot?"

"Yes, and we call on weekends." Nate said, "I wish you knew her better."

"She seemed like a nice girl."

"She's wonderful, Motherdear. I know you probably don't approve, but we really love each other."

"My concern is with the children, Nate. You shouldn't let anything interfere-"

"Beatrice doesn't interfere with anything, Motherdear. I didn't even meet her until after Eva and I had broke up."

They reached the Pancake House and waited, silently, in line to be seated. As they were finishing their meal Nate said, "Motherdear, I want to ask you about something you've never answered."

His mother sipped her tea and glanced around the crowded room. "Wouldn't you rather wait until we're outside?"

"Yes, okay, but promise you will answer me."

Ms. LaChae smiled, "I will, if I can, Nate."

Nate hailed a taxi immediately upon leaving the restaurant. As they rode along Lake Michigan he asked, "Please tell me why, when I was a little boy, you used to say, if I came to visit my family in Chicago, I could never come back and live with you."

Ms LaChae didn't answer right away. Then, while still looking at the lake she said, "I told you that because I felt you would want to stay with them and I didn't want you to leave me. It might not have been the best decision, but you asked me to tell you, so now I have."

"But, Motherdear, I would have come home."

"I was afraid to take that chance, Nate, and I was young. When you're young you see things differently."

Nate saw his mother take a handkerchief from her purse and dab her eyes. He fought back his own tears and then said, "All you would have had to say, to get me to come back, was that you had bought me that football you promised to replace."

"Kids always remember the toys they didn't get, don't they."

Their tears mixed with their laughter as the taxi arrived at the train station.

Soon, she was on the train and it was pulling out of the station. Nate watched until it disappeared into the tunnel.

At least she still has Douglas and Claudette at home with her, he thought.

*   *   *

At Zemit Radio, during lunch, Nate said, "I noticed all the guys have slide rules. They whip them out like cowboys drawing their guns."

Reggie laughed and finished chewing, "Yeah, that's to see who gets the correct answer first."

"What kind do you have?"

"Mine's a Pickett-N515"

"You know how to use all those scales?"

"Not really, but it's the slide rule the engineers use and I'll be needing it for school."

"What are you studying?"

"Electronics, at DeVry."

"Hey, I heard that's one of the best schools for electronics."

"It is, and my G.I. bill is paying for my courses."

"What did you do in the service?"

"I worked on Air Force radar systems."

"Then why are you going to DeVry?"

"Believe it or not, the Air Force equipment was old. It used vacuum tubes mostly and everything in the future will use transistors. That's why I'm here learning all I can about transistors."

"So, how was the Air Force?"

"It was good most of the time."

"I heard they give a lot of tests and certifications."

"Yeah. That's how you move up."

"Are the tests hard?"

"I was worried that they were and I studied so much, to get my E5, that I came out number one on the list.

"You mean for your whole class?"

Reggie looked over the top of his glasses and then said, "For the whole Air Force."

"No shit?"

"No shit." Reggie laughed, "I was surprised myself."

Reggie went on to relate some of his experiences in the Air Force. When he finished Nate asked, "Can I see some of your DeVry lessons when you're finished with them?"

"Why don't you just take a course?"

"Nah. I only need to know enough to finish a project I'm working on."

"What kind of project?"

"It's something I've been working on for years. I need to figure out how to measure the frequency of some spinning disks that are hitting on a long shaft." Nate said, "Here, let me draw it for you."

"Show me later, Nate; we better be getting back."

Reggie took a short cut, through the production area.

"What's this all about?" Nate asked, stepping over tracks.

"They move finished parts on these tracks. You'll see some carts in a minute."

The cart Nate saw didn't have television parts on it. It had a five-foot sign that read:

> ## SUBMIT YOUR SUGGESTION
> ## AND WIN UP TO
> ## $25,000

"Is that for real?" Nate asked.

"Yep, they pay money for ideas that improve production."

"Has anybody actually won twenty five thousand dollars?"

"I don't think so. But, a lot of people have won fifty or a few hundred dollars."

As they exited the production area, Nate glanced back at the cart with the $25,000 sign.

*   *   *

One of Beatrice's letters arrived in a large manila envelope. It contained a letter from Ernest DuPree.

> Hey Brother Nate,
>
> I'm here sweating it out in Harlem and wondering when you're coming back. Some of the brothers have gone stone crazy with their greetings. I saw two, dressed in African garb head-to-toe, do a special handshake and then they touched elbows. After that Nate, you wouldn't believe it but one of them turned around and the other one tapped on his back in what looked like Morse-code! I said to myself right then, if I have to do all that to be black then count me out! But, so much for mundane trivialities!
>
> What I'm really writing about is to tell you that I've perfected a Turf Wagering System to a point where you can't lose money using it! That's right – CAN'T LOSE MONEY! Those so called experts, all the way back to Pittsburg Phil, have been missing the point, they can't see what's right under their noses. I read their books and corresponded with many of them. Now I've made their theories obsolete!

The Daily Racing Form is all that's needed to review each horse's past performances and then to reduce the Value-Field to no more than three contenders. Once these contenders are identified, you only need to wait for the odds to be in your favor and then you bet all contenders. The spread guarantees a return on your money most of the time.

Nate I've been researching this for months now and I can tell you it's a sure thing. I know you're one of the few people who understands anything is possible. That's why I became partners with you in the MiniLab. And I have thought about that too. Our problem was that we didn't go after the money first! Not from the SBA or those other front organizations who can't see beyond liquor store and laundry shop loans. We should have applied our scientific knowledge and analysis to making money itself!

Now I'm offering you a partnership in a sure-fire way to raise money for all our future projects. Be aware, this is not a short-term project. It is a way to have a net-income all year around. Just look at the projections on the graphs I have included. While it does not show the full theory I've developed, you will clearly see that Overlay-Projections can increase income in a non-linear fashion!

What we need now is to get at least six serious people together who will not only invest in this project, they will have to go to the track on a regular basis so that opportunities are not missed. The profits will make it more than worth their while.

Check out the math Nate (chart-1). I'm sure you will be convinced, as I am, that lots of money can be made with this system. I am still refining it even more so that the techniques can be used with specialty races – where the profit can be ASTRONOMICAL! (See chart 2).

So, write me as soon as you can and let me know your thinking on this important project."

E.C.D.

Nate didn't respond immediately, but he wondered if Ernest was on to something.

*   *   *

Nate spoke of Beatrice so much that her visit to Chicago surprised no one. She was exactly as he had described her, dark and lovely with a quick, dimpled, smile. The surprise was Nate's when Beatrice said, "Nate kept me downtown in a hotel all yesterday." The female cousins giggled and Nate's dad said, "I would have done the same thing."

"Well, you just make yourself at home, Beatrice", Aunt Lil said, "while I heat up some food. You must be starving."

"I have to admit", Beatrice said, "I'm ready to taste some of *your* cooking."

"Come on Beatrice", the girls said, "let's take some pictures. Then we want to hear your side of the story of how you and Nate met."

During Beatrice's remaining two days, Nate took her around Chicago in a rental car. He showed her The South Side, the planetarium and museums along the lakefront, The Loop, Grant Park, and the North Side. They strolled through Washington Park, hand-in-hand.

Evening time found them, sitting in the car, admiring Lake Michigan. "Now I hope you see why I don't want to go back to New York." Nate said, "I wish we could be together here."

Beatrice sat, snuggled in his arm and then said, "I'm glad to see how comfortable and happy you are here. I was so worried about you living in that old building in Harlem."

"I wish we could be together here." Nate repeated.

"Nate, you know I love you. But, what can we do? We don't have any definite plans."

"We would do what we've been doing, love each other. We haven't been following anybody's rules before and we've been happy, haven't we?"

"Yes, but I want to have a family."

"So, do I. We have to take things one step at a time. I miss you so much sometime I feel like I'm going to burst. That's when I write letters to you."

"I read every one of them, over and over, Nate and I always write back right away."

"You cry too, don't you?"

"Sometimes."

"I saw the stains on the letters." Nate said, " It doesn't make any sense for us to be apart."

"No, it doesn't." She turned to him, they kissed and then made love in the car.

Three weeks later, Beatrice returned to Chicago to stay. They bought English-Racer bikes and tennis racquets and loved each other, according to their own rules.

*   *   *

Nate was at his Cousin Myheir's house playing chess with her husband, Chuck.

"Hey you guys," Myheir called out, "come and eat."

Nate brought some papers to the table.

"What's all that?"

"My friend, Ernest, has come up with a plan for beating the race track."

"I thought you told me he wrote you about some plan for giving stamps to shoppers or something?"

"Yeah, that was a way to get people to come back to a store and eventually they'd earn enough stamps to get free things. Now he's saying he knows how to beat the racetrack."

"Do you believe him?"

"Well...it is Ernest and he's one of the smartest guys I know."

Chuck chewed his food, then he asked, "How much has he won so far?"

"It's not like that. He needs a group of people to do it."

"So, what are you going to do?" Chuck asked.

"I don't know. I was thinking of mentioning it to our chess group."

During dinner, Nate and Chuck discussed the possibilities of Ernest's plan, then they returned to their chess game. They were evenly matched as chess players. Neither one able to get more than two games ahead. But, today Nate surprised Chuck.

"Mate in two."

Chuck took a long drag on his self-wrapped Turkish cigarette.

"Where'd you dream that move up?"

"Funny you should ask that question that way." Nate laughed, "I did dream it up ... the other night."

Chuck smiled and looked at Nate with dreamy eyes that always made him look like he was high, and he was, most of the time.

"No, really, man," Nate continued, "I dreamed I was the size of a chess piece. I was standing at King's-bishop-five and saw I could mate in two moves."

"That reminds me, I know a guy you've got to meet, Nate. He's into mind stuff like you are. His name is Ted Ray. Man, sometimes he's way out there. He says another personality takes over his body at times."

"Does he play chess? You should bring him sometime."

"No, he don't play games, not the kind we do. He uses real people. He and my brother were trying to hypnotize some women into doing stuff for them. They gave some LSD to one of the women."

"Did it work?"

"I don't know."

They even built a six-foot isolation pool in someone's basement and the water pressure burst it. Luckily, no one was in the tank or seriously hurt.

"Yeah man", Nate said, "I'd like to meet this Ted Ray."

Nate did meet Ted Ray and, before long, they and Ken Davis, from work, met regularly discussing ESP. At one of their meetings, Ken looked through his bulbous glasses and asked the others, "Have you ever heard of Silva Mind Control?"

"No. What's that?"

"It's something you should look into, that's all I'm going to say about it. They give a free introductory talk once a month where they describe the course they give. It's another whole level of mind functioning."

"What do you mean another level?"

"Nate, you have to experience it; I can't adequately describe it. When you're ready, I'm sure you will experience it."

*   *   *

Back in the lab at Zemit Radio, Reggie explained to Nate how suppliers sent samples of their transistors for Zemit to consider using in television sets.

"We test them on the TI-745 before and after we run them through environmental chambers." Reggie said. "These data sheets are the measurement values from the suppliers. If their transistors stand up to our testing, we pass them, otherwise we fail them."

"But this TI-745 only gives a red or green light at the end of a test," Nate said, "You don't really know how well the samples did; they might be marginal."

"That's all it can do, Nate, until they come up with something better."

As Nate got into the routine of using the TI-tester, he noticed Casey always answered his questions in a curt manner.

"What's with Casey?" Nate asked Reggie.

"What do you mean?"

"He's always trying to talk down to us."

"Yeah, that's just the way he is."

"He has the same title that we do. So, why is our group called Casey on all the documentation?"

"Aw, come on, Nate, that's just because he used to be the only one in the group."

"Yeah, well to me it's like we're invisible or something."

Reggie smiled, "It doesn't matter."

"It does to me." Nate said

"You want to speak to Mr. Reardon about it?"

Nate thought for a moment and then said, "Yeah, I think I will."

He headed off toward the front office as Reggie cocked his head and stared.

Mr. Reardon listened and sympathized with Nate. Casey remained stoic when the group's official name was changed to ETG (Environmental Testing Group).

Reggie was impressed. "What did you say to Reardon?"

"The same thing I said to you."

"I don't think Casey liked it."

"Did he say something to you about it?"

"He mumbled something about you trying to take over."

"Give me a break." Nate said, "There's nothing to take over.

Listen Reggie, I went down to personnel and asked about the suggestion system. They told me nobody has won $25,000 yet and they gave me a copy of the actual rules. Here read this part."

'For suggestions that result in substantial annual savings, the awarded amount shall be 10% of the net savings resulting from implementation of the suggestion.'

"That could be some serious money." Reggie put the document down slowly, "What do you have in mind, Nate?"

"Somewhere inside that TI-745 a comparison is being made to the programmed values we input … right?"

"Yeah … and?"

"That means, at some point the TI-745 has an actual measurement. If we can find out where that is and read it …"

Reggie finished the sentence; "We could generate datasheets like the ones sent in by the suppliers."

"Exactly." Nate exclaimed, "No more guessing whether transistors are marginal or not. I went a step further, Reggie. I 'm gonna ask Ken Davis, in the computer department, whether he can plot the two datasets for us."

"Wait a minute, Nate." Reggie said, "they're not going to let you-"

"Not me, us."

"Have you mentioned it to Casey?"

"No, but I will."

"I don't know Nate. That's the only TI-745 they have."

"I think we can do it, Reggie … and think how much money it would save Zemit ."

When Reggie grinned, Nate knew he had won him over.

Casey's response was, "Even if it could be done, Reardon isn't going to let anybody mess around inside the 745."

"We've made repairs to it before," Nate insisted, "and we have all the technical manuals."

"The 745 is so old you probably won't be able to get parts for it if you screw it up."

"Look Casey, I'm going to ask Reardon for permission. Are you going to help us or not?"

"No, I'm not and you won't have time to waste on it either."

"We'll do it on our own time." Nate turned and headed for the front office.

To everyone's surprise, Reardon gave the okay for Nate's project. They had to promise to restore the TI-745 to its standard configuration after their experiments, so it could be used during normal working hours.

As the project progressed, Ken Davis got swept up in Nate's excitement. "I'd heard rumors somebody was trying to do this; I didn't realize it was you. And you've already got analog measurements from the TI-745?"

Nate held up a Teletype tape, "Right here."

"Then, it'll be a simple matter of inputting the tape and using programs that are already in the computer to get all sorts of graphs."

"That's great!" Nate stood and then said, "Of course we'll share the suggestion award with you."

Ken waved his hands, "No. That's not necessary. I won't have to do much; you guys have done all the work."

"Are you sure?"

"Yeah, I'm sure. Tell me how did you come up with the idea in the first place?"

Nate was asking questions about computer programs when Reggie walked up and then said, "Hey, man, I been looking for you. Casey wanted to know what happened to you."

"Oh, yeah. I got caught up with Ken Davis here." Ken and Reggie shook hands, "He says we'll be able to get our printouts and graphs too."

"All right!.." Reggie said.

"Can you run the TI-745, in it's modified mode, right now?" Ken asked.

"Sure can." Reggie said, "That's what I came to tell you, Nate. The latest supplier's data sheets includes some graphs."

The three of them headed to the ETG lab.

*　　　　*　　　　*

At home, Nate continued working on his gyro-engine project. One day he brought his small teststand to work. Reggie had promised to try and measure the frequency of the disk hitting the shaft.

"What the heck is that?" Casey asked when he saw them attaching an o-scope.

"It's mine." Nate said, "It's not part of the 745 project."

"What's it for?"

"I want to measure the frequency of this disk", Nate pointed, "hitting this shaft."

Casey twisted his mouth to the side. "Lunchtime is over in another twenty minutes."

Instead of replying, Nate turned the electric motor on and Reggie adjusted the scope. After several attempts, they weren't able to synchronize or measure the signals they saw on the screen. As lunchtime ended, Reggie asked Nate, "What will you do now?"

"I've got another plan." Nate said.

During the ride home, on the bus, Nate went over his new plan to fly one of his gyro-disks into the air.

I'll build a Gamma engine with four spinning disks that will counter balance each other. The engine will slide down onto a powerful electric motor and be clamped there. I'll spin the electric motor up past the disks' resonant frequency and then I'll release the engine. As the motor slows down, the engine will pass through its resonant frequency and it should slide up off the motor's shaft. That'll prove it's generating lift.

One cold morning everything was ready. Nate's dad and Beatrice were there to witness the flight-attempt in Washington Park. They nearly froze, waiting for Nate to spin up his Gamma engine. There was a problem with the release mechanism.

At the other end of the football field, someone launched a model rocket that parachuted safety mid-field. They approached Nate's group.

"Hey, what you got there?"

Nate grinned at the man and the boy, "The next step after rockets."

"What? Do you expect that to fly or something?" the man asked.

"Yep. You better stand back out of the way."

After a while, everyone saw Nate was having a hard time pulling the release mechanism free. The rocket man came to him and then said, "Here, put some grease on it. It's not pulling free because it's too cold."

Nate's nose had frozen mucus on it. He turned toward the stranger and accepted the tube of grease without comment. Nate cautioned everyone to stand back as he started the electric motor. The Gamma engine gave one loud click as the four disks locked into position due to centrifugal force.

Nate cut the juice to the motor and waited while holding the release cable taut. As the motor slowed, the disk began to vibrate and Nate pulled the release latch free. The disk clattered against their plastic shafts for a time, and the motor slowed below the disk resonant frequency and stopped. The Gamma engine was still sitting on the electric motor.

Nate repeated the experiment two more times before one of the plastic shafts broke and the entire stand fell over. He rushed up to examine the damage. Squatting, Nate looked up into the other cold faces and then said, "There won't be any more testing today."

The stranger said, "The shafts need to be made of steel and you should grease the shaft between the electric motor and your machine."

"Thanks for the advice." Nate said.

"How's it supposed to fly without helicopter blades?"

"It's not aerodynamic."

The rocket man stared at Nate as the significance of the statement sunk in. Then he said, "I'm a machinist, I can help you."

Nate extended his freezing hand and then said, "My name is Nate LaChae."

The stranger took off his glove and shook Nate's hand, "I'm Bill Davis. Pleased to meet you."

*   *   *

At Zemit , Nate's and Reggie's project became the talk of the lab. They stayed after work exploring the innards of the TI-745. They borrowed test equipment from other departments and even got an outside company to loan them an A-to-D converter. They promised to buy the converter if their suggestion was implemented by Zemit .

One evening they took some newly arrived samples and measured them on the modified 745. The results were printed out on a Teletype and punched on a paper tape roll.

"YES!" Nate yelled as he compared their printout to the supplier's."

Reggie got excited too, "They're almost identical Nate. WE DID IT!"

Ed Reardon was working late and came out of his office.

"You boys made that old 745 give up its secrets?"

"We sure did." Nate said, "We used this A-to-D converter, fed it through an ASCII converter and it prints out on the Teletype."

"Look here, we'll run another sample through right now so you can see."

They ran another test and watched for Reardon's reaction as the Teletype printed the results.

Reardon read the printout, peeped inside the 745. It had its guts open and wires clipped on critical points. He stepped back and rubbed his chin with his thumb and forefinger.

"Yep, sure looks like you got something here."

"Next," Reggie said, "we can take this output tape to the main computer room and they'll plot graphs for us."

"First there's one more thing." Nate said as he reached into a bag. "Would you mind taking a picture of us in front of the 745."

"For your scrapbook?" Reardon asked.

"Yes, sir."

"You boys better submit your suggestion soon. It's going to take time to get the engineers' evaluations." Reardon paused, then said, "I'll be retiring soon, you know."

"We're pretty sure we'll get their support," Nate said, "because they've been complaining about the lack of precise data all along."

"What about Casey?" Reardon asked, "Did he help with this too?"

"No. We asked him if he wanted to help, but he chose not to."

"I see." Reardon said as he turned to leave, "Congratulations. You boys have done a fine job."

Alone again, Nate and Reggie stared at the TI-745.

"We did it."

*   *   *

Everyone in the chess group wanted to hear more about Ernest DuPree's horse racing scheme; it was decided to send for him.

Nate and Ted Ray met at a diner on Chicago's West-side and discussed making accommodations for Ernest.

"Then it's settled" Nate stood, preparing to leave, "Ernest will stay at your grandmother's house for a couple of months. By then the project should be generating rent money for him – okay?"

"Of course, all this hinges on the group's approval of the project." Ted Ray said, "Otherwise, he's welcome to stay just for the weekend."

"Oh, don't worry. Unless he's changed an awful lot since I left New York, I can guarantee we'll all want Ernest DuPree to stay. I'll wire this money for his ticket tomorrow."

Ted Ray closed his day-planner and remained seated. "And I'll stop by Purvis Staples place and pay for a meeting room for this coming Saturday."

Ted chewed on his coffee stirrer. "This could be historic you know!"

"Yeah, bet they never had a meeting like this over there before."

"You never mentioned whether Ernest has an interest in ESP."

"No. He doesn't." Nate said, "At least, not like we do. He's a very smart guy, but he seems to think only a few people have the gift of ESP. He called it hocus-pocus one time, so I left it alone."

"Just remember, it'll be a triumvirate; Ernest, you, and me will make final decisions."

"Right." Nate looked at his watch again, "Hey man, I've got to get going. See you on Friday."

Ted Ray stood and shook Nate's hand; Nate headed out the door. Sitting back down, Ted Ray motioned to the waitress, who had been watching from a discreet distance.

She refilled his coffee cup and asked, "Was that the guy you told me about?"

Ted Ray swooshed the coffee around with his chewed-up stirrer. He looked through the rain-stained window and saw Nate running to catch a bus.

"Yeah. That guy and his buddy are either geniuses or con men and I intend to find out which."

The waitress put one hand on Ted Rays shoulder, laughed and then said, "A genius would've thought to bring an umbrella."

Ted Ray grabbed the waitress' wrist firmly and squeezed. "I didn't bring an umbrella either." he said through clenched teeth.

The waitress winced, "Sorry baby, I didn't mean you too. I wasn't thinking-"

"That's your problem Cynthia, you never think. Do you?"

"You're right Baby … you're hurting me."

"That's what I do darling," he said, "I hurt stupid people."

Still gripping her wrist, he turned and puckered his lips. With tear-filled eyes, Cynthia leaned forward and kissed him. He let her hand go, stared out of the window again and then said, " …Stupid people and con men."

*   *   *

Nate looked at his friends around the conference table and smiled.

"Gentlemen, before we start, I'm going to ask each of you to introduce yourselves and tell us why you're here.

Will you start us off Reggie?"

Reggie tapped his pen on his pad, smiled and looked down the table, "I'm Reggie Overton, and I've been hearing a whole lot about Ernest. I'm here to get the details about Ernest's money-making plans."

Next was Chuck, Nate's cousin's husband and his chess partner.

"Charles Walker. I'm interested in any way I can make money. From what Nate told me, Ernest knows how to do that, so that's why I'm here."

"My name is Paul Walker and I invest in anything that I feel is sound and profitable. When my brother told me about this, it seemed like it was in that category."

Nate prompted Bill Davis, "Go ahead, Bill."

"I'm Bill Davis and I've known Nate for a while now. Like you guys have already said, he talks a lot about how he and Ernest formed a company in New York and all. So, I believe they are probably on to something and I'm glad to have a chance to be in on it."

Ted Ray was next. He stood, walked to the front of the room and put his hand on Nate's shoulder. "This man is the only person I've found, besides myself, with enough imagination and intelligence to attempt things other people call impossible. I'm Ted Ray and, among other things, I'm an entrepreneur. I'm here to make history with you." He shook Nate's hand and returned to his seat.

"I'm Johnny Coleman. I've done some investing in real estate and I'm always looking for legitimate ways to make money. To me, the race track seems like the perfect equalizer, because there's no middle man or bank you have to pay. So, Ernest, I'm all ears."

Ernest said, "Glad to hear it."

Herb was the last one to introduce himself.

"Hey man, I just work for a living," Herb said, "and I ain't never going to retire rich just working. To me, life is just like a chess game and most people are pawns. All their lives, they just move ahead, without much power and hope one day they'll be bigger and powerful. The chess players around the table know about castling. You do it to protect yourself just in case the going gets rough. I'm ready to castle in real life 'cause my going is already tough as a black man."

"Amen to that brother." Ernest said, "I believe it's my time now?"

Nate turned to Ernest and then said, "Yes it is, Ernest. Yes it is."

Ernest looked better than Nate had ever seen him. He started with, "Avon, The Muslims, your church, General Motors. What do they all have in common?" He paused and looked around the table.

"They're all out to get your money. They all promise you something for your money. Their ads even tell you how much money you will save by buying their product or that you will save your soul by paying their church. And, even though I don't play chess, Herb was right – you're not going to retire rich just working all you life. The cards are stacked against you. You all know or suspect that is true, that's why you're here tonight.

Gentlemen, the racetrack is about as even a playing field as you can get. Sometime there are only five horses running; you don't have to bet unless the odds are in your favor; the time between investment and return is minutes; and like Johnny Coleman pointed out, there's no middleman. Sure, you pay a small track fee and taxes, but that is fixed and known. There's no fine print or catches to get you after you've paid twenty-nine years on a thirty-year loan."

Moving around the table, Ernest continued, "Now, don't be mistaken – handicapping horse races is like gambling. You are guaranteed to lose sometime. Most people lose most of the time. Some fools lose all the time. A few people win most of the time. Nobody wins all the time. But a black man who knows what he's doing, can make just as much money as anybody on any day or night at the track."

Back at the head of the table, Ernest flipped the chart page and drew a huge dollar sign and a percentage sign.

"Right here, tonight, I'm going to show you how you can minimize your losses and maximize your wins. You can start taking notes if you want."

Ernest proceeded to explain the ins and outs of horse racing in America. He mentioned jockeys, owners, trainers and handicappers he had studied. He spoke of correspondences he had with some of them. Then he produced a copy of *The Daily Racing Form* from his briefcase and pointed out various charts and data available therein. On his last chart, he showed potential winnings from parlay betting. The amounts went into seven digits.

"That's the basics. If you join me, I'll teach you the rest of it."

When Ernest sat, everyone was spellbound.

Nate got up applauding and everyone else applauded as well. Once things quieted down and everyone was seated again, Nate asked, "Are there any questions?"

Paul Walker said, "I thought you were going to give some examples of your system using real races that you have won."

"I didn't get into specifics tonight on purpose, but here …"

Ernest slid *The Daily Racing Form* newspaper across the table to Paul.

"You pick a race."

"You don't have to prove anything here tonight, Ernest." Nate said.

"No, Paul wants to see the real thing. That's okay, I brought the next day's Racing Form because it has the results in it."

Paul chose the fifth race and slid the paper back to Ernest.

They all crowded around, as Ernest started scribbling on his pad. In minutes, he chose three of the twelve horse field and announced,

"I'd bet these three to come in second and I'd only bet if all three had odds of two-to-one or better."

He turned the paper around for everyone to see and then said, "Now, someone look at the results in the next day's Racing Form, here."

Johnny Coleman picked up the newspaper and started turning to the results. One of Ernest's picks won the race and another came in second. Johnny passed the paper around.

Reggie Overton looked at Ernest, "So, how much would you have won?"

Ernest did some quick calculations and then said, "Three times whatever I had bet and that takes into account the loss on my third choice."

"Very impressive, Ernest." Ted Ray said, "Very impressive."

"I think we're almost out of time for this room." Nate said, "Whoever wants to be in on this project, call me tomorrow because we'll be starting Ernest's classes next week."

As the meeting ended, everyone was either reviewing the two Daily Racing Forms or shaking Ernest's hand.

*   *   *

On June 5, Nate and Reggie's suggestion was formally submitted to Zemit. It described their modifications to the TI-745 and the results obtained. They included an estimate of the time that would be saved and emphasized the increased accuracy of their method.

Nate read the reports of past Suggest Awards and found no one had ever won more than $500. He was sure that was about to change. Copies of the suggestion were circulated to department heads for evaluation. Part of the evaluation process called for a demonstration. The modified TI-745 performed perfectly and Nate and Reggie were congratulated. Casey was, conspicuously, absent during the demonstration.

Days went by and Nate called down to the suggestion board office.

"We are still collecting the engineer's evaluation forms, Mr. LaChae."

"When do you expect to have them all?"

"We can't say. It's up to the evaluators to return their forms."

Nate couldn't wait. He went to the engineers, whom he knew by name, and inquired. All but Donald Paget had returned their evaluations with favorable recommendations.

Paget told Nate, "We've invited the GenRad Company to give a demonstration of their semiconductor tester next week. I'll send my form back afterward."

The GenRad demo was a flop. Their big, expensive machine failed to produce accurate results and damaged some of the test samples as well.

"Reggie we're in." Nate said "They tried and failed; that'll be the end of the story – right?"

"I don't know, if they fix whatever went wrong, the engineers might give them another chance."

"Aw, man, surely the suggestion board will make a decision before then."

*   *   *

It was the third meeting of the Turf Project group. Everyone had joined, except Bill Davis. Ernest used *The Daily Racing Form* to explain how speed, distance, condition, class, pace, age and weight contributed to a horse's potential for winning a race.

Everyone sat around Nate's living room, staring intently at their racing forms, when Ernest said "Okay, it's five minutes to post." He pointed, "Herb, you're the man at the track. One of your horses has odds of 9-to-5. What do you do?"

Ted Ray knocked at the door and Nate let him in. Ernest glowered at him. "We start at seven pm Mr. Ray, not CP time."

"It was something unavoidable, besides I'm here now."

"That's not the point." Ernest shot back, "This project needs the full commitment and dedication of everyone involved; no exceptions."

No one spoke as Ted Ray took off his jacket and then said, "Why don't you just go on with what you were saying?"

"I was saying, it's crucial that everybody's here on time."

Nate interceded with, "Herb? I'm waiting to hear what you're going to do."

"Hey man, I woulda made my bet while Ernest and Ted were jabberwockin'. At five minutes to post, I got in line. When I got to the betting window, there was still one minute to post and the odds were the same. So, I let one person ahead of me in line and waited. Cause you know when they announce 'THEY'RE AT THE GATE' you really have another minute or two to bet. I watched the tote board make that final change and my three picks all had odds better than 2-to-1 so I bet them all to place and went and had me a beer and a hotdog."

There were a few chuckles, then Ernest said, "You did good Herb, except for-"

Herb interrupted, "It was a root beer Ernest ... a root beer."

Everyone laughed, even Ernest.

Ernest continued, "I'll assume everybody understands the importance of avoiding distractions of any kind. You'll be at the track for one purpose only – to conduct business. You will not be gambling; because my formula works. You'll be there to take information and collect our money. Anything that interferes with that is our enemy. Any questions?"

"I have one." Paul spoke up, "I understand our trip tomorrow is for reconnaissance and that's why you don't want us to bet yet. But, you already know all this stuff and I propose that we put together a separate kitty just for you to bet with. That way we can start making money right away."

There was a moment's silence.

"Yeah, that's a good idea." Johnny Coleman said.

They all agreed and dug into their wallets.

"Now, you guys understand," Ernest said, "I'm at a different level than you, so my betting strategy will be a little different from yours. Some of it will be experimental."

This time Chuck spoke up. "Hey man, as long as we're making money, I don't care what you do with the second kitty. Go ahead and develop the system as much as you can. That's research and development."

There was a murmur of agreement and heads shaking up and down.

"Okay then," Nate spoke up. "Maywood Park opens at noon tomorrow and the races start at 1:30, so let's meet at 12:30 at the main information booth."

The meeting adjourned and Nate asked Ted Ray and Ernest to stay behind. Once the others were gone, Nate said, "Everybody's doing pretty well so far, don't you think?"

"That's was only our third class" Ernest said.

"How many more classes do you think they'll need?"

"They still need to learn parlaying and specialty betting."

"And how long will that take?" Ted Ray asked.

"Until I think they're ready."

Nate leaned forward, "I think we just need a number Ernest, so we can work out a schedule."

Before Ernest could answer, Ted Ray said, "And we need to decide how much money will be used for R&D too."

Ernest snapped around, "That money is for whatever I decide to do with it."

Ted Ray waved his hand from side to side and shook his head. "No, no, no. We already agreed it takes at least two of us to make decisions." Ted looked at Nate.

"Well, yeah," Nate scratched his head, "but that shouldn't apply in this case."

"And who's going to decide when the rules don't apply?" Ted Ray asked.

Ernest got up to leave. "If you don't trust me, then you can do your own turf project."

"Wait a minute, Ernest." Nate said, "Sit down; let's discuss this."

"There's nothing to discuss. The second kitty is mine by group decree."

"But, Ernest we just need to know what you're doing, that's all."

"Oh, it's WE now?" Ernest stopped at the door. "Nate I'm not going to slow down enough for you and him to understand what I'm doing. When I get it perfected, I'll explain it to you all."

Nate walked over to the doorway. "Are you saying we have to wait until whenever that is?"

"That's exactly what I'm saying." Ernest opened the door and left.

Nate closed the door slowly, turned and looked at Ted Ray. "I warned you, Ernest can be difficult sometimes."

"Yeah, and that can be dangerous." Ted said.

"Let's just concentrate on making some money. We knew all along that we weren't going to agree on everything."

"Nate, that's why we set up the triumvirate."

"I know." Nate acquiesced. "We need to stay focused. Besides, the checking account requires two signatures."

"Checks and balances, huh?"

Nate thought for a moment, "Yeah. Checks and balances."

*   *   *

It was Friday and Nate stopped and got two orders of barbeque ribs on the way home. Once there, he opened a cold beer and started reading his mail. Something was wrong with the bank statement for the Turf Project. There should have been seventy-three hundred dollars in the account, but the statement showed a withdrawal of almost all the funds, dated two days before.

"This can't be right. Nate dialed Ted Ray's mother's house and got a bigger surprise.

"Ernest is gone." Ms Ray said, "He left with his sister two days ago. They didn't look none alike at all. Yeah, he brought her right up in here and introduced her as Susan. But, I heard him keep calling her Cynthia."

"Yes, but Ms. Ray," Nate said, "what makes you think Ernest is gone?"

"I'm telling' you, he done pack up everything he had and took it with him. I ain't seen him since."

"Ms Ray, if Ernest does come back, would you please tell him to call me right away."

Nate hung up and his mind raced. He wanted to find some answer other than the obvious one, but he couldn't.

I'll have to call the others.

Nate called Ted Ray first and suggested they meet at the diner. He went into his closet, got something he thought he might need out of a box, and then took a cab to the West Side. Ted Ray was sitting in the rear of the diner by the window.

"So", Ted said, "Ernest and Cynthia flew the coop with our money."

"Yeah, it sure looks that way."

"And what do you propose to do about it?"

"What are WE going to do about it, is the question."

"Nate, I told you that nigger was dangerous all along." Ted spat, "But you kept talking about how smart he was."

"Look man, that's not the point now. First we need to find out how he managed to get the money when two signatures are needed."

"Forgery perhaps?" Ted said sarcastically.

"Ted, I didn't come all the way over here in the rain to argue with you. We need to figure out how to handle telling the others."

"You put this together. You tell them what happen to our goddamn money."

Nate got up, "Is that how it's going to be between us?"

Ted put money on the table for the check, "I'll walk out with you."

It stopped raining and water was dripping everywhere.

"I'm going down to the train station." Nate said, "I can get a cab there."

"I'll give you a lift."

"That's alright. I can walk."

"Come on, Nate. I was upset about Ernest; I have to go past the train station anyway."

They didn't talk for the first few blocks. Ted pulled up to a store, a few blocks from the station, and then said, "Got to get some cigarettes."

When he returned he opened the trunk and got something. A coldness came over Nate. He hadn't felt it for years, but it was familiar. He knew in the next few minutes he might have to kill or be killed. Nate's hand was in his jacket; he prepared himself.

Ted got back into the car and Nate asked, "You remember where I grew up?"

"What the hell are you talking about now?"

"I asked you if you remember where I grew up. That's what the hell I'm talking about."

"New York City, so what?"

"Whatever it was that you got out of the trunk, needs to go into the glove compartment right now."

"I don't know what the fuck you're talking about and you better back off."

There was silence. The car window fogged up. They stared at each other for another moment. Then Nate pushed the muzzle of the .38 into Ted's ribs and then said, "If you think this shit is worth somebody dying over, now's the time."

"You ... you're tripping Nate. I didn't take nothing out of the trunk."

"Take-it-out-of-your-pocket and lock it in the glove compartment."

Ted Ray's eyes filled with water.

"I always carry a piece; but I wasn't gonna do anything to you. I swear Nate. I always have it on me. You know how it is over here on the West-Side."

Nate pushed the muzzle harder into Ted's ribs.

"Listen, man, I'll put my piece in the glove compartment if it'll make you feel better. Just be cool alright?" Ted Ray slowly removed the .32 caliber revolver from his pocket with two fingers. He leaned across Nate and put it into the glove compartment.

"Lock it." Nate said and Ted did so.

"You fucking with me, right?" Ted asked, "That ain't no-".

Nate removed the .38 from his pocket, carefully released the hammer and put the safety back on. Ted watched him tuck it back into his jacket.

"He's not worth us killing each other." Nate said as he got out of the car. "I'll call everybody tomorrow. It might be a good idea if we conference call each one of them. Let me know tomorrow."

"Yeah man, we can talk to them together." Ted said through the car window, "Nate, I was just gonna try and scare you to see if you were in on it with Ernest, that's all."

Nate leaned on the car and Ted's eyes got big.

"Notice how I didn't suspect that you were in on it with Ernest?"

Ted Ray looked down at the steering wheel.

Nate walked away, wary of turning his back to Ted.

*   *   *

Ed Reardon retired from Zemit Radio and was replaced by Howard Jackson, a black man whom nobody in the lab knew. He stayed in his office most of the time and attended meetings with other managers. He barely acknowledged the blacks in the lab, so they nickname him: Oreo. The one time Nate asked him about *the suggestion* he answered, "That was before my time."

A week passed, then another, with no word about their suggestion. One day Dan Walton, head of Research & Development showed up at the lab and invited Nate and Reggie to lunch. He congratulated them on their successful demonstration and invited them on a tour of the Zemit's R&D lab in Skokie, Illinois.

"I have a test this afternoon," Reggie said, "at DeVry."

"In that case, I'll give this to the two of you now. It will clarify the status of your suggestion."

He opened an envelope and gave them the consensus evaluation of their suggestion. The last page read:

'While these young men should be lauded for their efforts, it's doubtful that their approach represents the optimum solution for Zemit 's long term interest. Alternative solutions, which have been in the planning stage, should be explored before any final decision is made.'

Nate looked at Reggie and then said nothing.

"I guess this means we have a long wait?" Reggie asked.

"Something like that, yes." Walton replied.

Nate turned toward Walton and then said, "Even if Zemit uses an alternative approach, won't it mean our suggestion was implemented?"

"I understand your concern Nate, but it doesn't work that way. Company suggestions are explicit and do not cover similar solutions. Besides, we've been considering replacing the TI-745 for some time now. I'm afraid it was an unfortunate case of timing, that's all."

Nate gritted his teeth, but said nothing.

Reggie looked at his watch and then said, "I've got to get going. Thanks for the lunch."

Nate thought about declining the tour invitation, but couldn't think of a good excuse. For the rest of the afternoon he nodded, commented and went through polite motions during the tour. In his gut, he wanted to scream.

The next day Nate called Paul Riley, the recruiter that had sent him to Zemit, "Do you have any electronics jobs?"

Without hesitation, the reply was, "I've got an opening at Copyrex for a Field Service Engineer. They'll train you and give you a company car. You interested?"

"Yeah. When can you set up an interview?"

One week later, without giving notice, Nate quit Zemit Radio and went to work fixing copiers for Copyrex Corporation.

Reggie finished his courses at DeVry and quit Zemit also. Lorrell Systems hired him as a Field Service Engineer, servicing their minicomputer office systems.

Lorrell Systems

Nate shook his head from side to side. "I almost killed that girl today, driving that damn car Copyrex gave me."

"But you didn't." Beatrice replied; "You said she wasn't hurt."

She was crossing in front of a bus and I couldn't see her. When I decided to pass on the right-hand side of the bus, that girl ran into the side of my car. I'm telling you, something is wrong with that car because when I step on the gas it jumps into passing gear all by itself."

Beatrice massaged Nate's shoulder and neck muscles.

"It's over now, Honey. Relax, come and eat your dinner."

Nate washed his hands and came to the table. Beatrice poured two cups of Mourby.

"Tell me what your first day at Copyrex was like."

"Everything was cool, actually," he said while chewing, "I remember thinking how lucky I was getting a car on my first day and the fact that they're going to give me tools. I think I might be able to borrow an o-scope on weekends. That's one thing me and Bill need desperately for our work on the Gamma engine. We're building a teststand in one corner of his basement and we're setting up a control console too. "

"Does he have room for all that in his basement?"

"Oh yeah, we've got more room now than I had in my lab in New York. You've really got to come down and see it, Bea."

"I will, Honey, but tell me more about your job."

"I'll be going through some training here for one week then I'll work with another Field Engineer for two weeks. After that, they're sending me to Massachusetts for more training. They said the sign-on bonus will be paid-out after 90 days. Then we'll be able to move to a bigger apartment, like we've planned."

"What am I supposed to do while you're gone for weeks?"

"Aw, Honey, it won't be so bad. You can call Myheir or Aunt Lil if you need anything and I'll call you every day. If you get your driver's license by then, you can drive the car too. I've already put your name down as a second driver."

Beatrice sipped her Mourby. "Are you sure you want to drive that car back to work, Nate? It's dangerous."

"I'm used to it now; I'll be alright. They'll give me a different one."

*   *   *

The office atmosphere at Copyrex was exciting; everybody was busy. Nate approached an older black woman who was standing alone, in the break-room. She was tall, good looking and shaped like a model.

"Hi, are you one of the secretaries?"

She smiled, glanced down at her coffee and then said, "No I'm not a secretary, Nate."

"Oh, sorry, I just thought – hey, how'd you know my name?"

"It's my business to know all the people working in my territory." She shook her head to throw her hair back from her face, "I'm the N.P.C. for the Midwest."

"I still don't know your name."

"Sheila McKnight."

She extended her hand. Nate grabbed it and felt the coolness and softness of her skin; then he remembered to let it go. Sheila's eyes were bright as she waited for Nate to speak.

"And what does N.P.C. stand for?"

"I'm in charge of new product coordination; I deal with customer's technical issues."

"That's fascinating," Nate said, "I've never met a beautiful woman that knew a lot about technical stuff."

"I'll take that as a compliment, Nate. But, equating someone's appearance to their intelligence is what kept both of us out of companies like this," she made a sweeping gesture with her hand, "for so long in the past."

Nate shook his head from side to side. "I didn't mean that the way it sounded. Maybe, I can make it up to you somehow."

Sheila looked him up and down and then said, "Maybe."

There was a moment's silence and then they both laughed as another worker came in for coffee and left.

"Can I ask you one more thing." Nate said. "What's with the black Field Service Manager? He seems confused all the time."

"He is. They put poor Fred Woodland into the Field Service Manager's slot without any preparation or training. They have a habit, around here, of taking a minority employee and sticking them somewhere highly visible. It can be a formula for failure.'

"Why didn't Fred decline the offer?"

"Are you kidding? Would you turn it down?"

"Maybe. If I thought I couldn't handle it."

"Nate, at Copyrex people are either moving up or moving out. The business is exploding. You either ride with the wave or you drown." She looked at her watch, "We better be getting back, don't you think?" Without waiting for an answer, she said, "I enjoyed talking with you, Nate. Maybe I'll see you down at Playboy Towers some Friday evening."

"You can count on it."

That Friday, Nate and Reggie sat at Playboy Towers in suits and ties.

"Didn't they used to have a big ballroom next door?"

"Yeah" Reggie said, "Now it's only open for special events. And ... Damn! Looks like a special event just walked in."

Nate turned and saw Sheila and two other women. He stood and waved to them. Sheila recognized him and headed his way.

"I'm glad you made it, Nate. This is my cousin Ceretha, she's visiting from Virginia and this is my girlfriend Terry."

Reggie didn't wait, "My friends call me Reggie, but you can call me Reggie."

They laughed and all sat. Nate ordered a round of drinks and asked for more popcorn.

"So, is this where you hang out?" Nate asked Sheila.

"This is one of the places, yes. I'm surprised I haven't seen you guys here before."

"We're usually at The Other Place," Reggie said, "down on 75th Street."

"Where's all the black folks?" Ceretha asked.

The drinks arrived and Terry offered a toast.

Here's to the bee,
that stung the bull
and started it to bucking.
Here's to Adam and to Eve
who started the world to ...
eating apples.

"I heard, that you like to invent things, Nate." Sheila said.

"I build things from time to time."

"Then, you should meet Del Adams. He's an inventor of arcade games; his father invented the automatic bowling-pin setter.."

"Really?" Nate said, "Yeah, I would like to meet him."

"I Iυιι, I'll write down his number for you."

Ceretha was on her second Long Island Ice Tea. "Where's the action in this town. I'll be back in my boring hometown on Monday. I want some action!"

Sheila smiled at Reggie and then said, "I don't know if these boys are ready for the kind of action we like."

"Boys!" Reggie faked indignation. "You girls ain't never partied, until you have partied with us."

Nate looked at Reggie with raised eyebrows.

"Ceretha wants to have a memorable time in Chicago." Sheila said, "Think, we can give her what she wants?"

"You're always so direct." Terry said.

"You only live once," Sheila countered, "might as well have fun doing it."

"Yeah," Ceretha slurred, "Doing it, that's what I'm talkin' 'bout, y'all."

"Let's get out of here," Nate said.

"Where we going?"

"I know a place." Sheila said, "Whose credit card can we use?"

Forty minutes later, they were in the Sunset Motel and somebody lit a joint.

*   *   *

Nate didn't reach Del Adams until the following Tuesday. They arranged to meet at Del's workshop. When Nate arrived, the door was open to the storefront and he heard jazz music. Beyond the front wall, a huge workbench was covered with pinball-machine parts. There were machines in different stages of assembly and other mechanical gadgets all over the place. The workbenches were pulled together forming one large working area. They took up the center of the room, leaving barely enough space to walk around by the walls. A canvas covered one end of the workbench.

Del seated himself at the head of the workbench, on a tall stool and then said, "So, how do you know Sheila?"

"We work together; I mean, we both work at Copyrex. She told me that you're an inventor and gave me this address."

Del didn't look at Nate, instead he looked down at a wiring schematic and then said, "She's one fine sister."

"Yeah, she sure is and very smart too." Nate said, "So, are these some of your inventions?"

Del rubbed his hands over his scalp and then said, "Most of this is old stuff." He pointed across the workbench "That's a baseball game that I've had on the market for a couple of years. And over there's a hockey game that came out this season. I'm working on some new stuff for this Christmas."

"This is neat. I've never really seen the insides of arcade games like this."

Under the playing surface, there were motors, gears, solenoids, springs, cams and dozens of light bulbs. Nate couldn't help notice how little electronics there was. He was tempted to tell Del about the lab down at Bill's basement, but decided against it.

"So you're into computers?" Del asked.

"Yeah. I've done a lot of programming, but, most of my inventing has been with rockets and electronics. It must be great having a father who's an inventor. Do the two of you work on these games?"

"No, he used to help around here." Del sat back and wiped his hands across his head again. "This is my thing now." He got out of his chair and moved around the workbench and picked up a relay board, "I invented this sequencer that's used in several games. It's patented and Balley Gaming has approached me for licensing it for use in their games." He handed the circuit board to Nate.

"The sequencer determines which bulbs will be on or off, based on the player's selections and a random timer. The bulbs are my main problem right now. Even though I run them at low voltage, they burn out too soon. With the top on the game, it's like a player disappears for an instant when a bulb doesn't come on. People don't like that and they won't play the game again." He went in back to a coffee pot and offered Nate a cup.

"What about video games?" Nate asked.

"I know they're coming out with all that computer stuff. But, these games are still in demand for two players. People like the big playing field. It gives them the same effect as if they were sitting at a stadium. It also has the pinball feel. People like that too. A fortune can still be made, If a way can be found to keep the bulbs from burning out so soon."

"Really." Nate said, and his mind started looking for a solution.

Inspiration hit Nate, on his drive home. In his mind's eye, he saw that a projector, built like a computer disk drive, could show pictures. He saw it could project images in sequence or randomly, and be used for arcade games.

He phoned Del Adams and described his idea. Nate was shocked when Del told him, "You stay away from my wife, you hear."

"What are you talking about?" Nate asked.

"I only wanted to see your face." Del said, "That's why I let you in here. Even though me and Sheila are separated, she's still my wife and I'm telling you to keep away from her."

"Hey, I didn't know, Man."

"You know now." Del said and hung up.

*　　　*　　　*

When Nate phoned his mother, to tell her he found another job, he sensed something was wrong.

"I know you can't talk long." His mother said, "Nate, your sister needs to hear from you."

"What's up, Motherdear?"

"She thinks she's grown now and doesn't want to stay in school."

"I thought she was all set to go to college next year."

"She doesn't want to listen to me any more. I think you two need to talk or write to each other. Maybe you can get through to her, she worships you. She's not here right now or I'd put her on the phone."

"Tell her to write me." He gave his address.

"How's Douglas?" Nate asked.

"Douglas is Douglas. He's living with an older woman, named Helen; they have two kids. He comes by sometimes. I never know when."

"My money is about to run out, Motherdear. Tell me how you have been."

"I've been in for a few tests, nothing to worry about. I'll write to you about it. Otherwise, I'm okay."

"Been writing any poems?"

"As a matter of fact I had started writing again, but I stopped because of all this confusion with Claudette."

"We'll figure it all out, Motherdear. I've got to go. Love you."

Nate found his sister's letter amusing. He recalled his own adolescence and some of the difficulties he and his mother had. His nineteen-year-old brother, Douglas, quit school and now, his sister was bumping heads with his mother.

Dear Nate,

How are you doing? Tell Beatrice I said "Hello."

Everyone here is doing fine except for cousin Cozette. She has been in the hospital for two weeks now and they are still not sure how to cure her. Nobody has told me what she has. They only say it's female problems. I visited her last Sunday, she smiled a lot, and we talked.

Anyway, the main reason I'm writing you is because of MD.

She's on my back about everything lately. I am almost 18 now and I know I won't have to keep putting up with this much longer. She doesn't want me to stay out late even when I give her the telephone number where I'll be. And none of my boyfriends measure up to her standards. I even dated one guy who was an honor student and she didn't like him either.

Now, don't get mad when I say this, but I am a strong black woman too and neither one of us likes to give in when we disagree. All I want is to live my life the way I choose. My role models are modern black women, like Shirley Chisholm, who make a difference in the world.

The latest disagreement is over which college I'm going to attend. I don't want to get into all the details with you. Basically, she wants me to choose my major before I'm even a freshman. In today's world, the women I admire have more than one degree and multiple careers. But MD can't accept that.

I hope you can get her to expand her ideas a little bit. She has to see that I am not like her and that's simply the way it is. Sorry if I sound angry, but I think you know how it can get around here sometimes. Please tell me what you would do in my situation.

Hope to hear from you soon and please write Motherdear too.

Love,
Claudette

Nate imagined how disappointed his mother must be. Claudette was the baby girl of the family and had always done whatever their mother wanted. Now she was rebelling like the boys had done.

Motherdear's not going to give up on any of her children, especially her last child, he thought, *but, I can't tell Claudette that.*

He stared at the blank writing pad in front of him and rotated his pen between his fingers.

Beatrice came into the kitchen, behind Nate's chair, and put her arms around his neck.

"What's bothering you, honey?"

"I'm trying to figure out what to tell my sister."

"Tell her what's in your heart. Tell her you love her."

"Yeah, she knows that. She needs something to help her cope with my mother."

"You told me she was your mother's pet."

"Not any more. The pet has a mind of her own now." He turned to Beatrice and asked, "How did you and your mother get along when you were a teenager?"

Beatrice came around, straddled him and they kissed. "My mother is different from yours and our customs are too."

"I know all that. But how did you two resolve arguments?"

"I didn't argue with Stacey and she wouldn't argue with me either. We would both have our say and then go our way. I always understood where the line was and the consequences if I crossed it."

"You mean you always gave in?"

Beatrice smiled at him, shook her head, and then said, "I'm here, aren't I?"

They laughed and kissed again.

"Tell her what's in your heart, Nate."

A few minutes later Nate started writing.

Dear Claudette,

Sorry to hear about your troubles with Motherdear.

I remember she and I started having communication problems when I became a teenager. Only, in my case MommaMary was like an instigator. She would tell MD what she thought was the reason I came in late and then MD would accuse me of all sorts of things that were not true. As soon as I got home (late), she would say "I know where you been and I know what you were doing." Then I'd get a whipping or a long lecture. My buddy Henry, from across the street, went through the same thing with his aunt. Sometimes, when MD was making me promise to get home early, I wanted to say, "Would you please just give me a whipping now, because I'm going to be tired when I get home late." So, at least your troubles are different from what mine were.

I understand what you said about being your own woman, but you need to think again about role models. I've been out here on my own for ten years now and I've learned something about people. The Bible 'says the battle goes not to the strong, nor the race to the swift'.

And I translate that to mean there's more to winning at life than what seems obvious.

The women you admire for their independence and achievements all had mothers. I'll bet their mothers played a major role in who they became. Even if they wanted to be the opposite of their mothers, that was still a motivating factor. Having a lot of education or money or fame shouldn't automatically make somebody worthy of our admiration. We need to also look at the people who got them there. Those people are often not educated or rich or famous.

Our mother is one of those special people. That's why we are not in jail or on drugs or doing harm to people or in the nut house. That's why we are healthy and can think for ourselves. That's why we know we are just as good as anybody else. We didn't become who we are automatically you know. It was Motherdear's planning and love and hard work and sacrifice that made us who we are today!

So, Motherdear should be our number-1 role model. She may not save the world, but she has saved us from a lot of misery and pain already. The fact that she took the time to teach us and guide us, when she really didn't have to, shows the kind of person she is. Nobody is perfect, but she is a whole lot better than anybody else is when it comes to being a mother.

When I hear some of the stories from my friends about their parents it makes me real glad we had the ones we got. So, when you and MD have differences, listen carefully to what she says (and then do what you think is best).

As far as college, it seems to me that you can do both what she is suggesting and what you want to do. Pick one major and then get as many degrees as you want in whatever subjects you like.

I hope this letter helps.

Love,
Nate
P.S. Beatrice says hello.

*   *   *

That night, Nate awoke shortly after midnight. He had the dream again. He went through his ritual of checking that Beatrice was asleep and taking the phone into the hall closet. He dialed Eva's number; it rang several times.

"Hello?" she said groggily.

"It's me." Nate whispered.

Eva said, "I don't want to-"

"No, wait; I didn't call to argue. I wanted to tell you something."

"What do you have to tell me at 2am, Nate?"

"I'm going to start sending saving bonds for the kids and-"

"Those things don't mature for seven years-"

"Will you wait a minute?" Nate raised his voice. "That's right, they don't mature for seven years. That's part of the reason I decided to send them. They'll be in the kids' names and not anybody else's."

"What do you want me to say?"

"Nothing. This is just my way of sending money for my kids."

"This won't change anything."

"Well maybe, when you see that I'm serious about this, I'll be able to see my kids sometime."

"You can visit them now, you know."

"Yeah, right. And get arrested for coming within 50 yards of the house, huh?" Nate paused, "I don't think so. Anyway, I just wanted you to know I'll be sending the bonds."

"Well, now I know. Was there anything else?"

"No. That's all. Goodnight." He said.

"Goodbye."

*　　　*　　　*

Saturday, as Nate shut off the power to his engine's teststand, Etta shouted down the basement stairway, ""Bill! What are you doing down there?"

Bill walked over to the base of the stairs, "What? What's wrong?"

"The TV picture started messing up."

"Honey," Bill said patiently, "We just started up the engine that's all. We're going to put a shield around it and the TV won't mess up again. Relax, will you."

54

"You sure that thing ain't dangerous, with the girls coming down there to do laundry and all."

"No, Honey. It's not dangerous. We know what we're doing."

"I hope so," she closed the door – not too gently.

Bill walked back to the teststand. Nate was frowning with his arms folded. "I didn't expect that."

"Didn't you get effects like that in New York?"

"I don't know. I never had a TV sitting nearby."

Bill folded his arms and asked, "This means something is being given off, doesn't it?"

"That's for sure," Nate said, "and I think I know what it is. Bob Jones' theory predicted entropy waves would be given off."

"What's entropy waves?"

"The engine works by pulsing the gyro. Right?"

"Yeah, but the pulses are so small."

"Right. But, when the gyros are at resonance, the pulses can build up."

"I don't see what you mean." Bill said, "A pulse comes and then it's gone."

"True, but-." Nate pointed one finger upward, "Think about when you're in a tub of water. Have you ever swayed back and forth to make waves?"

"Sure, when I was a kid."

"And what did you do?"

"I used to see how big a wave I could make."

"Exactly, you were amplifying the wave, even though you didn't sway any harder each time. If you did it just right, you built up a lot of wave power with a small steady rocking motion."

"So, you're saying the engine can amplify these entropy waves Bob Jones predicted?"

"I think so."

"Do you think entropy waves are dangerous to our health?"

"I hope not. But to tell the truth, I don't think anybody knows. And that's all the more reason for us to shield the teststand."

It took eight months of Wednesday evenings and Saturday mornings to complete the teststand and console. Bill and Nate got to know each other pretty well. They talked about everything. Most of their talk centered around what it was going to mean when they succeeded in making the Gamma engine fly.

"It's going to change the way a lot of people think, both black and white, when they hear about the engine. And you should get the Nobel Prize."

"I don't know about the Nobel Prize and all that, Bill." Nate looked up from his printouts, "But, it's sure going to erase some of the stereotypes that they have about us."

"I really mean it, Nate. Why shouldn't you get the Nobel Prize? This is going to open up all of outer-space to the world. I remember what you told me when I met you in the park. You said the engine would make rockets obsolete. I thought you were some kind of a nut."

"And now you know, huh?"

"I didn't believe you were serious until I saw your notebooks and how long you'd been working on this. All jokes aside, this is great stuff, Nate. You are a genius."

"Thanks, Bill. But they won't give a Nobel Prize to somebody like me."

"And why not? You beat all those guys with their PhDs and stuff."

"Because I don't have a degree from one of those prestigious colleges. Besides, I still can't explain the Gamma principle in mathematical terms. We just know how to make it work."

"Yeah, and we're getting better at it too."

*   *   *

Nate took his key out of the door and saw Beatrice on the phone. He grabbed her from behind and kissed her on the neck.

"Honey-y-y, wait a minute. Reggie is on the phone."

"He will understand." Nate turned Beatrice around and they kissed. Then he took the phone. "Hey, Regg. What's up, man?"

"Lorrell approved a requisition for another Field Service Engineer."

"You're kidding. Why didn't you tell me they were looking for someone?"

"I wasn't sure we'd get the requisition approved. The job is yours if you want it."

"IF … I want it?" Nate exclaimed, "You know I do. This is great! When can I start?"

"Hey, slow down" Reggie said, "They'll want me to interview several people, but you'll get the job Nate. I can almost guarantee that."

"Almost?"

"They'll run a background check …"

"I'm clean."

"You're gonna need a car. Lorrell pays for business miles and gas." Nate was silent.

"Nate? Did you hear me?"

"Yeah, yeah, I'll have to figure something out because my credit is shot."

"That's important Nate. It's a requirement."

"I understand, Reggie. I'll rent a car if I have to."

"I have an application here."

"Okay, I'll stop by in the morning and get it. Thanks, man."

Nate hung up and sat staring at the wall.

"What's wrong, Honey?"

"Reggie has a computer job for me, but I'll have to buy a car."

"Do you have enough money to buy a car?"

"No. I'll figure that out later. Now it's time for us to have a little meeting."

"About a partnership?"

Inwardly, Nate cringed, "Sure, about our partnership."

"I mean our permanent partnership." She put her arms around his neck.

"I know what you mean."

*   *   *

In Copyrex's Human Resources office. Gavin Jacobson tapped his finger on Nate's resignation. "I have to say, I'm not totally surprised by this. I remember asking you if you would be satisfied repairing copiers."

"I've been happy here, but I want to work on computers."

"You're scheduled for training on our new Model-3600 series; we have computers in those. Nate, you haven't been with us for a full year yet." He paused and slid the resignation back across the desk. "I think you would be making a mistake by leaving us now; I've been setting goals for your advancement."

Like the goals you set for poor old Fred Woodland, Nate thought.

"Mr. Jacobson, I have goals of my own."

Nate slid the resignation letter back across the desk.

$$* \qquad * \qquad *$$

Two weeks later, Nate arrived at the Lorrell office in time to see Reggie balancing his breakfast sandwich and coffee as he unlocked the door.

"Morning, Nate, you look all clean and ready to go. But, get rid of the tie please."

"You want a hand with that door?" Nate asked.

"No, I got it." He turned the handle. "It sticks sometimes."

They entered the sparse central room and Reggie switched the lights on. He went to his office, opened the windows, and pointed to another office. "That one's yours."

"Where's my window?"

"Man-n-n, you better get some posters of mountains or something."

Nate entered the office and flipped the light-switch. Darkness.

Reggie called to him, "You'll need to change the florescent bulbs."

Nate sat behind the metal desk and examined the empty drawers. The room had a metal bookcase and filing cabinet.

At that moment, the third member of the team came puffing through the front door. He too, was carrying breakfast, coffee and an overstuffed briefcase.

"Reggie, we need to do something about that door." As he passed Nate's office, he said, "Good morning. So, you're here." He was huge; his passing by the doorway was like a total eclipse.

"Yes, I'm here." Nate replied, "Morning."

"Let the newest guy fix the door." Reggie said, "It can be his initiation."

Nate walked over between his coworker's offices and then said, "I don't do windows, floors or doors."

Brutus was sweating. "Why do you have the windows open Reggie? We should turn the air conditioning on. You know how it gets in here on weekends."

The phone rang and Reggie said, "Here we go. I'll bet its Margaret down at Montgomery Wards."

Brutus picked up the phone. "Lorrell field service. Yes. Good morning to you too Margaret. Yes … Yes … It did? Okay, one of us will be on our way shortly. Yes … Within an hour. Right. Bye.

Your girlfriend says the system is down. You gonna take Nate down there or shall I?"

"You take him. I promised Hudson Insurance I'd be there first thing this morning." Reggie closed his attaché case and came out of his office. "You'll like Margaret," he told Nate, "She's your type a woman."

"Yeah, I can tell."

Reggie said, "I'll catch you guys later." and he was gone.

Brutus started devouring his sandwich while reading the Wall Street Journal. He looked up at Nate and then said, "I'll let you know when I'm ready."

Nate returned to his own office to install the florescent lights. He sensed a change in Brutus' demeanor after Reggie left.

During the ride to town, Brutus kept the AC on high and it annoyed Nate, but he didn't comment about it.

"You know, Nate, after all those projects of yours we saw during your interview, maybe I should stand back and watch you do your stuff when we get to Montgomery Wards, huh?"

"No. I don't think so. I don't know anything about your systems yet."

"It's basic stuff." Brutus smiled, "Nothing as advanced as the Lunar Module."

Nate thought Brutus was joking until they arrived. They brought the toolbox and o-scope upstairs and Brutus introduced Nate to Margaret. She was huge and had an attitude.

"You call this 'within an hour'?"

"We ran into some traffic on the way down here." Brutus lied.

"I had my girls take another break while waiting for you. How long you going to be?"

"Nate here is going to get started while I go downstairs and get some parts from my car." Brutus walked away without looking back.

The way Margaret looked at Nate made him wish he had kept his tie on.

"Well?" she said with arms folded.

"Oh ... yes." Nate took his jacket off, folded it and placed it on a chair. He walked over to the control console and removed the covers. He stacked them in a corner and hoped for Brutus quick return. Margaret walked away, shaking her head from side to side.

Soon, the returning young women sat at their terminals and watched Nate. Hoping to impress them, Nate turned on the o-scope and adjusted it for his Outer-Limits trace. Instead of ou-ou-ou's and ah-ah-ah's the young women busied themselves chewing gum and doing their nails.

Nate got down on one knee, behind the console, like he was examining something inside.

I sure don't want to screw anything up. I'll put the o-scope's probes here ... like that ...

He adjusted the o-scope and stared at it. He rubbed his chin and opened the toolbox. He took out a small screw driver and pretended to make an adjustment in the rear of the console.

Still no Brutus. How long has it been? A half-hour? An hour?

Nate turned the main breaker switch off and back on. To his surprise, the console lit up and he heard the fans running. Keeping his cool, Nate came around to the front and pushed the start button. He prayed no smoke would appear.

Margaret returned as the sixteen workstations came on, displaying their Logon screens.

"Got it going, huh?"

Nate wanted to laugh, but didn't. "Yes. I made an adjustment."

Margaret turned like a sergeant and clapped her hands, "All right ladies, break time is over."

Nate was putting the last of the covers on when Brutus returned with several circuit boards. He stopped when he heard the fans and asked, "What did you do?"

"Just a little rocket science," Nate said, "Where's the men's room?"

Wait until Reggie hears about this one. I didn't do a damn thing.

For the next two weeks, Nate accompanied Reggie on service calls. Nate learned some customers were afraid to touch their machines when anything went wrong. Others insisted their machines be repaired immediately.

*   *   *

When Reggie got called out of town, Nate and Brutus took care of the local service calls. Nate was pleased that Brutus didn't assign him to any difficult tasks. Nate accumulated a lot of mileage on his rental car driving between Des Plaines to Chicago and managed to keep Margaret happy at Montgomery Wards. The young ladies got in the habit of staying close as he fixed their workstations. Some would remain seated, with their legs crossed, while he replaced fuses under their desks.

It was almost five o'clock when Brutus called one time.

"What's up, Brutus?"

"It's what's down that matters right now. DataScribe called, both their systems went down when that storm passed through Indiana. Think you can go over there and get them going again? The problem is, most likely, a blown fuse."

Nate knew thirty-two operators would be sitting idle until the systems came back up. And, he needed the overtime pay.

"Give them a call, would you? And get them to sign your service report as soon as you arrive; this will be a billable call."

"Okay, I'll be there by six-thirty."

Nate crept along in the rush hour traffic on the Dan Ryan Expressway and arrived at DataScribe at six forty-five. He gave his greetings, smiled at the women and went to work. The newer system came up right away; it had circuit breakers instead of fuses. The supervisor applauded when the main computer came to life and she ordered the ladies to get busy.

The second system resisted every effort Nate made to power it up. Hours went by; at nine-thirty he phoned Brutus at home.

"Sorry to bother you, but I can't get the power going."

"Have you checked the fuses?"

"Of course, that was the first thing I did."

"Okay tell me what symptoms you have."

Nate described the dormant state the system was in. Brutus asked Nate to try another outlet and instructed him to examine connections.

"It sounds like a fuse to me. Check them again and call me back if you need to." Brutus hung up.

That's just a waste of time. Nate thought, *I've already looked at them twice. Only one was discolored and I changed it already. Brutus doesn't know what's wrong, that's all.*

Nate examined all the fuses one more time. None of the glass fuses were burned and the big paper-wrapped fuse wasn't discolored either. He thought of swapping the power supply with the other system, but that might have resulted in two dead power supplies.

It was after eleven when Nate called Brutus again and explained that he had made no progress.

"Listen, Nate, I've looked at my schematics. That system should come on."

"Yeah, I've looked at the schematics too and the system is down."

"Aw, hell," Brutus exclaimed, "They already signed for the work, I'll have to come down there."

Nate said nothing. He could see the supervisor, across the room, staring at him.

"Stay there." Brutus said, "I'll be there in an hour and a half."

Nate used what charm he could muster and explained the situation to the supervisor.

"You don't expect us to pay for all this time, do you?" she said.

"We'll adjust the time on our report." Nate replied.

The storm had returned and Brutus arrived soaked. He all but ignored Nate, as he huffed over to the computer cabinet. He opened the power supply door and took out his multimeter. Nate, immediately, got an empty feeling in the pit of his stomach. He hadn't used his multimeter to check the fuses. Brutus measured the resistance of the fuses, one by one. When he checked the big paper fuse, he looked up at Nate with killer-cold eyes, but said nothing. He replaced the paper fuse and the system hummed to life. He tossed the fuse at Nate.

"It wasn't discolored." Nate pleaded, "I assumed it would look burnt if it had blown."

Brutus slammed his tool box shut and left without saying a word.

Nate heard the supervisor say, "All right girls, let's see if we can get caught up."

Nate took the fuse and taped it to the inside lid of his tool box. He never checked a fuse again without using a multimeter.

The day Nate left for Lorrell training in Boston, Reggie teased him, "Be sure to ask them how to check fuses."

"2Q plus 2Q, Reggie," Nate replied.

*   *   *

On the first day of class the instructor, Ray Stout, asked, "Anyone here that does not have minicomputer experience?" Of the nine students, Nate was the only one who raised his hand.

"What experience do you have?"

"I've taken basic computer classes and I've worked on automated testers." Nate said.

"I see," the instructor was peering over his glasses, "in that case you may find this class a bit challenging. You understand there will be very little time spent on the basics?"

"Yes sir, that was explained to me."

"Alright, we'll start with the overview shown on page one of your booklets."

By lunchtime, the instructor and students had made so many unfamiliar references that Nate was in a state of internal panic. But, outwardly he kept cool.

He was waiting in the lunch line with his tray.

I'm not taking notes fast enough; I can't build on ideas that I don't understand. He's not giving me enough time to figure out how things work together. The notes I brought from Reggie's DeVry classes are not going to be enough help.

"NEXT," the server roused Nate out of his daydreaming.

"Oh … , Give me a well-done hamburger and fries please."

He paid the cashier and sat with some of the other students. One of them said, "Aw, hell" and got up and moved to another table. Nate had noticed the guy looking at him in class.

"Was it something I said?" Nate joked to no one in particular. There was no response and everyone kept eating without looking up.

Back in class, the instructor continued making references that were alien to Nate. He struggled to understand the new information. He used graph paper to draw concepts and connect them like a flowchart. He decided he would buy a mini-tape recorder as soon as possible.

At the end of the day, the students were told they would be sharing rental cars and hotel rooms. Nate was given one of the car keys. The two fellows from Nate's lunch table, and the third one that had moved from the table, were assigned to his car. The third fellow was obviously displeased.

Nate was stopped in the hall by an older black man he'd seen earlier.

"Glad to see you young man. You're the first black student I've seen come through here."

"Thank you, sir." They shook hands., "How long have you been here?"

"Almost five years now. I was here when they started."

"Hey, I got to run right now." Nate said, "I'll see you later."

When he got outside, his car doors were open and he saw impatient faces. He took the driver's seat and started the car.

"You two freedom riders finished your meeting?" the third guy said.

Nate looked in the rearview mirror and then said, "What's that suppose to mean?"

"You know what it means."

Nate didn't turn around, "No I don't. Why don't you explain it to me?"

"Aw come on, Nate," Hal said, "let's go on to the hotel."

Not wanting to have an incident and lose his job, Nate cooled down. But that didn't stop the third guy. During the ride Nate heard him say, "I don't buy all that 'peaceful demonstrations' crap, not for one minute."

Nate kept his eyes on the road and thought about how far away from home he was. There would be no help coming if the shit hit the fan out here. The tall guy quieted down and they all checked into the hotel without incident. Nate went back out and bought a mini-tape recorder. He practiced using it while he and Hal had pizza in the room they shared.

"You handled Festus really well, Nate." Hal said between bites.

"I don't know what his problem is with me" Nate said.

"He's from Louisiana that's all. He says demonstrators are stirring up trouble."

"Yeah, but I'm not one of them."

"Racists don't have to make sense, Nate." There was a pause while they ate, then Hal pointed toward a book in Nate's open suitcase.

"What's that book about?"

"It's 'The Center of the Cycle' by John Lilly. He's the guy who did studies with dolphins and the mind."

"I heard about him; didn't he say dolphins were intelligent?"

"Yeah, that's why he refused to continue studying them in captivity."

"Didn't he also do studies about ESP?"

That question triggered a discussion that kept Nate and Hal up past midnight discussing ESP theories and UFOs.

In the days that followed Festus continued to simmer, but kept his comments to himself. Nate taped everything Ray Stout said and reviewed it in the evenings. At last, it all started making sense.

One evening Hal told Nate, "Your head is going to explode if you don't take a break from that stuff. Why don't you come on down to the pool and rec-room?" Hal stood by the door in his swimming trunks.

Drained, Nate agreed "You're right. I need a break." He put on his swimming trunks and joined Hal. The rec-room wasn't crowded and he heard some of his fellow students splashing about in the pool. Nate played a game of pool with Hal before going outside. He sat in a lounge chair finishing his bourbon and soda. His courage built up as the guys were leaving the pool.

"All yours, Nate" Hal yelled to him with a raised bottle of beer.

Just as well, Nate thought, *since I can't swim.*

He moved around the edge of the pool, took a deep breath and dove in and glided across the width of the pool. He was working on his technique when his breath gave out before he reached the other side. He came up for air, reached for the side of the pool and got a mouth full of water before going back down. The next time he came up, he glimpsed Festus inside the game room staring at him. Nate refused to call out for help and went down again. He was tiring when he came up the third time.

Something hit him on the head. For a moment he thought it was Festus trying to drown him. Instinctively, he grabbed the object and felt a strong tug. Hal had thrown a life preserver and was reeling him in.

"The trick is to swim on the top of the water, Nate."

Nate coughed up water and then said, "Now you tell me. Thanks." He looked toward the game room and didn't see anyone at the window. In that moment he realized, *Festus would have let me drown.*

Back in his room, Nate phoned Beatrice and told her he was going to stop in New York when the class ended. Afterward, he dialed Eva's number.

"Hi, it's me."

"Yes, Nate, what is it?"

"What? Are you in too big a hurry to talk? Got a date?"

"The kids are downstairs waiting. What do you want?"

"I'm going to be in New York for a few days and I want to see the kids, if that's alright with you."

"When?"

"This weekend."

"You should speak to them first, they've changed."

"Oh, you saying they might not want to see me?"

"I don't know, Nate. It's up to them. Call back on Thursday, okay?"

Nate hesitated. "I assume you've been getting the savings bonds."

"Yes, I got them. I've really got to go now."

"Then go; I'll call back on Thursday."

Nate dialed his buddy, Henry.

"Hey man, I'm coming to New York"

"Nate! When?"

"I'll be there next week. I'm taking a train from Boston."

"What are you doing in Boston?"

"School. My company sent me for three weeks."

"Beatrice with you?"

"No. She's in Chicago."

"Okay, cool. So, when do you want to get together? Margie wants me to ask you to come over here Saturday and we'll have a party." Henry cupped the phone and whispered, "Hey man, I'd rather for us to go and hang out."

"I'll come Saturday and we'll do - whatever."

"You got it, man; it'll be like old times."

"Sure will; see you then."

Nate put the phone down and took a deep breath. Next he dialed his grandmother.

"Hello," she said in a tired voice, "Who is it?"

"It's me Mom, Nate."

"Hey Baby. How's Momma's big boy? Where are you?"

"I'm in Boston, Mom. I'm coming to New York this weekend."

"You gonna come by here?"

"I sure am. You going to fix some bread pudding?"

"I'm gonna fix some black-eyed-peas and corn bread too, if you coming."

"I'll be there Sunday, Mom. I can't wait to see you."

"I want to see you too, Baby. I love you, you hear?"

"Yes Mom, I love you too. Is Motherdear there?"

"No, she's over at SammyLee's house. But, Sam is here, you want to speak to him?"

"Yes, sure Mom. Let me speak to Uncle for a minute."

Nate heard his uncle's deep voice, "Hey there, Champ, how you doing?"

"I'm fine, Uncle. I'm coming to New York this weekend."

"Oh, yeah? I heard Mom say she's going to cook dinner. You know she don't cook every weekend any more."

"Well, I can't wait to get some more of her food. How have you been?"

"Oh, they still trying to drive me crazy down at Lord & Taylor's, but I'm hanging on."

"You been playing the piano any?"

"Not since Christmas, I just practice sometimes after work. You still playing the drums?"

"I go down by Lake Michigan sometimes and play bongos with the guys."

"That must be nice, down by the lake. I remember how it was back when I lived in Chicago."

"I think it's still the same, Uncle. Bea and I ride our bikes, along the lake, on the weekends."

"I didn't know Beatrice was there with you."

"Yeah, she came a few months after I did."

"That girl really loves you, Nate."

"I know. I'm trying to get a divorce, so I can marry her, but Eva won't give me one."

"Probably because of the kids."

"I can't see what good it does her for us to stay married."

"She wants to hang on Nate, some women are like that."

"Yeah, but she has another man and all."

"That don't matter none; she's got your name and your kids."

The operator interrupted requesting more money into the pay phone.

"Hey, Uncle, I've run out of change for the phone. Be sure to tell Motherdear I called."

"Okay, I will and we'll see you on Sunday."

When the training ended, Nate was Ray Stout's biggest success story. Most of the training staff had heard about the student with the tape recorder.

After the final tests Ray Stout gave Nate his certificate and then said, "You did real good, Nate. For a time there, I didn't think you were going to make it."

"Oh, I was going to find a way. I had already decided I was going to be working with computers."

"Keep up the good work" Ray said, "And erase those tapes; you don't need them any more. I'm not sure I want every word I said heard again."

"Okay Ray, you got it."

*   *   *

Nate's train arrived at New York's Penn Station at noon. He rented a Buick Electra from Hertz.

If Lorrell complains, I'll use the argument that they aren't paying for my hotel this weekend, he thought.

He parked the car at Mt. Morris Park, in Harlem, walked to the playground and remembered how dangerous the monkey bars used to be. Sometimes someone tried to push him off, to the concrete below. Sometimes a very daring boy would stand atop the highest part of the monkey bars, swaying in the wind like a flag.

Nate always carefully picked his way to the top. Avoiding the bullies and sometimes climbing over slow-pokes that were in his way. He remembered gripping tightly with one hand while waving to his mother and grandmother.

The day was beautiful and the local people were his; so were the smells and the music.

Chicago is nice, but it's no New York, he thought, *this will always be my home.*

He drove past his deceased buddy, Frank Jr's, neighborhood in Queens. He saw the house, the bar, the handball court. He slowed as he passed Hazel's house. They had almost hooked up, once. She had kept two of his kids for a few days, when he and Eva broke up. That was, until his mother convinced him to let his kids stay together. He thought about ringing Hazel's bell, but couldn't think of what he'd say.

He drove pass his in-laws' neighborhood. Some of Eva's cousins were sitting on the stoop. The Buick's dark tinted windows obscured Nate from them. He didn't stop.

On Grand Central expressway he continued pass his motel, almost to the Triboro Bridge. He told himself he had to see the MiniLab where he and Ernest DuPree had toiled so long and so hard to have an aerospace company.

He was drawn the extra three miles to the Astoria Projects where his family was. It was getting dark and he double parked with his parking lights on. He saw the second floor lights in the kitchen. He remembered sitting, parked in the same spot, with his rifle - the bolt action one that had a scope on it. He remembered wanting to shoot out the windows.

He knew it wouldn't have changed anything, but, he wanted her to feel his rage.

He sat for a while remembering … trying to put up a tent, with his sons, in the snow, playing on the handball court with his tennis racquet, drinking vanilla egg-creams at the ice cream parlor with his oldest son, being summoned home from his job for an emergency, seeing his infant son motionless, the police in his apartment, running behind the paddy wagon, not recognizing his son at the funeral hall, visiting his wife in Creedmoor, standing in front of the judge years later, hearing Eva lie about his not supporting his kids. Now it seemed as though it had all happened at the same time. The memories replayed like an old film strip; their nine years of marriage compressed into a few frames. Feeling empty, he turned the car around and headed for the motel.

Meanwhile, 150 yards away, inside the apartment, Jeff was telling Eva, "It's probably better if Nate doesn't know I'm staying here."

"I was thinking the same thing, Jeff." Eva said, "I'm having him pick up the kids at my mother's house."

"You've painted a totally different picture of him. I always thought you two had an almost perfect relationship."

"That was the front he puts up when other people are around." Eva poured more coffee and called out to the kids, "If I keep hearing all that noise, I'm coming in there."

Jeff stared at his cup and Eva asked, "What's bothering you?"

"You know, I had started wondering about Nate and Ernest's plans."

"What do you mean?"

"A bunch of us devoted our time and money to their projects. I don't know about the others, but I looked at it as an investment in something that could be spectacular. Then they got incorporated and offered us only six-percent of the stock."

"What excuse did they give you?'

"Some cock-and-bull story about having to save most of the stock for their 'backers'. I suppose that meant their new college professors and lawyer friends. I told them to keep their stock, if that's all I was going to get."

"See, I told you." Eva said as she got up, "Just when you think you're into something with him, he's all for himself. That's the way he is." She went to check on the kids.

Jeff stared at his empty cup and thought, *One day somebody's going to show Nate how it feels.*

*   *   *

Saturday, Nate picked up the kids in front of his in-laws house. He had promised to take them to dinner anywhere they chose. He ignored his mother-in-law when she waved from the window.

Two of Eva's cousins sized up the big Buick. "They say only pimps and pushers can afford cars like this."

"Yeah, well they're wrong," Nate said, "Computer technicians have them too."

"Yeah, rental." the cousin laughed and slapped the other's hand.

"I'm in this one." Nate said, "What do you drive?"

Nate's son, Malcolm, came and challenged him to a race. Nate gave it all he had and was pleased that he didn't lose by much. "It's been a long time since I ran on my high school track team."

The kids piled into the car and they went to the local buffet.

"Daddy, are you going to come home now?," Charlene asked.

Nate was prepared, "Mommy and Nate are not going to live together any more."

"I told you already." Darnell said, "What did you have to ask for?"

"I want us to be together, Darnell." Nate said, "but we can't. When you get older you'll understand. Let's get some dessert, okay?"

"I don't want any." Darnell folded his arms.

Malcolm and the girls headed toward the food counter.

"We'll still see each other, Darnell."

"No we won't. You live far away." He was on the verge of crying.

The others returned with three scoops of ice cream each.

"Here, let me help you with that. In fact, let's put it in a cup and take it with us."

"They don't let you take food out of here." Malcolm said,

"Okay," Nate said, "we'll eat it here. Come on, aren't you going to help us, Darnell?"

"I don't want no ice cream." he almost shouted.

"You told me you were going to be a big boy about everything and take care of your brother and sisters."

"I am a big boy. That's why I don't want no ice cream."

On the ride back to the house the girls were quiet. Darnell sulked while Malcolm asked questions about the car. As soon as they arrived, Darnell jumped out and went into the house. Malcolm stayed for a while as Nate reassured the girls he'd see them again. They hugged him and Nate was about to leave, when Eva came out.

"What's wrong with Darnell?"

"He didn't want no ice cream", Malcolm said, "and he got mad at daddy."

"He's old enough to see what's happening," Nate said, "but not old enough to understand."

"Oh, he understands." Eva retorted, "He don't want to accept it."

"I know that feeling." Nate said and turned and hugged the girls and Malcolm.

"Bye, daddy."

"Bye, daddy."

"Bye, daddy."

"I'll call you tomorrow." Nate said and got into the car.

*　　　*　　　*

The rest of Nate's Saturday was spent with Henry. It was as if he had never left New York; they got drunk Saturday night, laughed a lot and passed out. Margie dragged them onto the two living-room couches, took off their shoes and covered them.

Sunday, his grandmother's meal included pork chops, black-eyed peas, cornbread, rice, collard greens, candied yams, and bread pudding. Nate blessed the food and thoroughly enjoyed the evening with his mother, uncle, sister and grandmother again. All efforts to contact his brother, Douglas, had failed.

After dinner, everyone went to watch TV in the living room except Nate, his sister and his mother. They stayed at the dinner table.

"Claudette, will you excuse us, darling?" JimmieMae asked, "Nate and I have some things to discuss."

Nate's sister frowned and left the room.

"She idolizes you." Nate's mother said.

"Yes, I know."

"Nate, have you thought about your family?"

"Motherdear, I don't want-"

"All I asked was have you thought about them, Nate. You don't have to get upset. Can't we discuss any topic?"

"Yes, Motherdear," he squirmed in his chair, "but does it have to be that topic?"

"Nate dear, I don't know when we'll see each other again and I want to know what you're planning on doing."

"Motherdear, Beatrice and I love each other. We have an apartment in Chicago and we're happy. I just want to go on with my life and do something."

"What about your responsibilities here in New York?"

"I'm sending Savings Bonds for the kids. Nate spoke through clenched teeth, "Eva has her boyfriend and her mother is taking care of the kids."

Mrs. LaChae paused to let him cool down. "You shouldn't have given up that apartment." She quickly added, "But, that's water under the bridge now. I think you can still get your family back if you tried."

"I don't want her back. Can we please change the subject? How's your landlord behaving?"

"What about your children, Nate?"

"Maybe I'm just like my father." Nate said angrily, "He didn't live with me either. You ever think of that?"

"Nate, you don't have to raise your voice."

"Then, let's discuss something else, please."

"Alright. Since you asked, my living conditions have actually gotten worse. My neighbors play their music loud and they watch when I go out and come in. I've called the police on them twice."

"Why don't you move?"

"It's hard to find an apartment and landlords want a big deposit too."

"You ever think about moving to Chicago?"

"It has crossed my mind. In fact, your father offered to buy me a house there."

Exasperated, Nate asked, "Well, why don't you take him up on it?"

"I'm not going to be his 'other woman'."

Nate shook his head and stifled a laugh.

"Do you think that's funny?"

"No. It's not funny, Motherdear. I just realized how both our situations, with our spouses, reminds me of one of your poems."

"Which one is that?"

Nate reached across the table and took his mother's hand, smiled sympathetically and then said, "You Can Not Be My Master. Now, can I please have some more of that gingerbread you made?"

The phone rang and Claudette told Nate it was for him.

"Hello, Nate."

The nasal sounding voice couldn't be mistaken.

"Hey, Jeff, how'd you know I was here?"

"I saw Eva and she told me you were in town."

"How's Wanda and the kids?"

"Wanda and I have broken up. I've moved in with a friend for a while."

"You and Wanda gonna make up?"

"Not this time. It's over for good."

"What about your son and Wanda's daughter?"

"Josh is with me and Debbie's staying with Wanda."

"Hey, man, I'm sorry to hear it."

"What about you? Still working on your engine?"

"No, none of that. I just finished training for a computer job."

"So, you're going to be working with computers again."

"Yeah, there's only one catch. I've got to get a car and my credit is all screwed up."

"Does it have to be a new one?"

"Not really."

"I have a friend who can get you one for $1,200."

Nate laughed, "Jeff, I need something that I can use everyday for work, not a jalopy."

"I'm serious Nate. The car might be only three or four years old."

"Is it hot or something?"

"Luke warm."

"What does luke warm mean?"

"You get registration and ownership papers with it."

"Are they warm too?"

"Not too warm to get insurance."

"I don't know ..."

"Look, if you have the money, we can deliver a car in two weeks."

"Can someone bring it to Chicago?"

"Yeah, but you'll have to pay for the gas."

Nate thought for a moment, then said, "Let's do it."

"Alright, I'll speak to my friend and get things in motion."

"Hey thanks, Jeff. I really need this."

"Glad to help you out again."

"I was so busy telling you my troubles that I didn't think. Let me know if I can do anything for you."

"Your buying this car will help me in ways you can't imagine."

"Good," Nate said without hesitation.

Later, he pondered Jeff's curious choice of words."

⸎   ⸎   ⸎

Having returned to Chicago, Nate stepped out of another rental car and grabbed his attaché case full of certificates for his office wall. The cool air invigorated his spirits. Brutus was standing in the doorway to Reggie's office when Nate came in.

"Well, well, well. The prodigal son returns," Brutus said.

"How are you doing, Brutus?" Nate opened his coffee and approached Reggie's office. "Hey Regg."

"All r-r-right," Reggie lifted his coffee cup toward Nate, "our troubles are over."

Brutus said, "I doubt that" and walked away.

"Don't mind him," Regg said, "He just got back from Minneapolis late last night."

"What's going on up there?"

Regg bit into his breakfast sandwich and spoke with food in his mouth, "Creditek called this morning; they're getting CRCC errors again."

"Oh, that."

Regg stared at Nate for a moment and then asked, "What did they teach you about CRCC errors, Nate?"

Nate felt Reggie was testing him, so he described how to fix CRCC problems. When he was finished, Reggie said, "Yeah, that sounds like Ray Stout's class. The problem is caused by the disk drive getting bumped during shipment. The platters shift off-center. If you open the drive case and re-center the platter, everything is honkey-dory again."

"You're kidding right?" Nate asked, "You don't, actually, touch the platter do you?"

Reggie slowly shook his head up and down.

*   *   *

One week later, Jeff made good on his promise.

"Wake up, Honey," Beatrice shook Nate again, "It's Jeff; he's downstairs at the front desk."

"Huh? What? He's here now?" Nate asked, "What time is it?"

"It's almost midnight. I told him you would be right down."

"Good." Nate said as he jumped into his pants and shoes. He put a tee shirt on and headed for the door.

Beatrice put her robe on and asked, "Are you going to bring him up here?"

"Of course, Honey. First, I want to see the car they brought."

Jeff seemed the same as ever, but Nate didn't get good vibes from Jeff's two friends. They were restless; one of them kept pacing in the lobby.

"So, where is it?" Nate asked.

"We parked both cars a block away." Jeff said, "You wanna see it now?"

"Yeah. Let's go."

"I got to pee" the pacer said.

"Okay," Nate said, "let's go upstairs first."

No one spoke during the elevator ride and Nate assumed his guests were tired from their trip. Jeff smiled when their eyes met. Once they were in the apartment, Nate showed the pacer to the bathroom. Beatrice had the bedroom door closed. The other guy looked out of the window with his hands in his pockets while Nate and Jeff talked about the car.

After handing over the registration and ownership papers, Jeff said, "We want to head back to New York tonight. So, if you can give me the cash now ... here's the keys."

"Oh, well sure, Jeff," Nate opened his attaché case, "Of course, I'll want to drive the car before you leave."

The pacer joined them and remained standing as Nate counted out the money. Jeff handed the wad of cash to the guy at the window who counted it again.

"Let me get my jacket and tell Beatrice I'm going."

The Dodge Coronet was in good condition and drove well. Nate waved to Jeff and his buddies as they accelerated past him on Lake Shore Drive. Now that he had the car in his hands, Nate's curiosity peeked.

I wonder how they managed to get the registration if the car was stolen. They must know a good forger or something. If I didn't trust Jeff, I'd never try something like this. I'd have to give up the job since I can't afford to keep renting cars.

Nate had no trouble getting the registration transferred and getting insurance for the car.

Good old Jeff. I could always count on him, Nate thought. *Wonder why they were in such a hurry to get back to New York?*

*   *   *

Brutus stayed busy in Illinois and Minnesota while Nate and Reggie drove all over Michigan and Indiana fixing Lorrell's machines. Nate surprised himself by fixing everything he touched – occasionally, with help over the phone. When Nate and Reggie's paths crossed, out in the field, they would share stories over dinner.

"Regg, I'm telling you man, I've developed a sixth sense for avoiding the highway patrols. But, it also gave me an excuse to drive faster. Then one night I realized I had been asleep with my eyes open. I drove over into a ditch and barely missed hitting a telephone pole."

"You think that's something?" Reggie said. "I worked late over at Elkhart Center one night and as I was coming out of a rear exit with my o-scope and tools I heard a voice say, "Don't move and keep your hands where I can see them."

"I froze" Regg said, "and I told him I wasn't going to move. I asked him to let me explain, but he was already calling for backup. Nate, man when he did let me turn around and I saw how much that old security guard was shaking, I thought it was all over."

"So, what happened?"

"Some cops came and after some very nervous moments and a couple of phone calls, the guard put his gun away and apologized.

"Damn," Nate said, "That was close."

Reggie drank his beer, "Too close. I'm not working late like that anymore."

*   *   *

One Monday, after weeks of constantly traveling, Nate and Reggie found themselves in the office doing expense reports.

"What's all those parts in the corner?" Nate asked.

"Those are spare parts that the home office doesn't know about" Reggie said, "It's how I'm able to diagnose problems with certainty." He smiled and added, "It's also how I can promise a babe, at a customer site, how long it'll be before I return."

"What do you mean?"

Reggie walked over and picked up a circuit board. "See this memory board? It works for three weeks and then fails intermittently."

"So, why don't you send it back?"

"You're not listening, Nate. This is how I can get to go back to a customer whenever I want to."

Nate's eyes got big and he opened his mouth, "You mean …?"

"Yep, three weeks if I install this one. Plus or minus a couple of days."

"Are all these parts defective?"

"Nope." Reggie laughed, "I almost have enough good parts to assemble a system right here in our office."

"Oh man, that would be great! If we had a computer of our own we could analyze the races at Maywood Park and make more money than we did with Ernest DuPree's method."

Brutus came in huffing and carrying his bags.

"Hey, Brutus, Nate thinks we could use a computer here in the office to make money."

Brutus threw his bags down and then said, "I've been trying to tell Reggie that all along. There's a ton of money to be made in stocks if we could analyze the data fast enough."

Reggie laughed, "So, which is better horse racing or the stock market?"

That set off a debate that lasted almost until lunchtime. In the end there was a consensus that a computer system, in the office, could help them make money - one way or the other. Nate and Brutus still disagreed over which method would be better. Reggie remained neutral and seemed to enjoy the bantering between his coworkers.

Nate said, "I've already got two keypunch girls at our accounts that are willing to input past racetrack information for me. I want to input a whole season of Maywood Park racing forms."

"A whole season?" Brutus said, "That would take months."

"So, what? It'll be worth it." Nate retorted.

"If you're so dead set on getting a computer system in here, you should go out to General Insurance Company in Cincinnati. The owner has a bunch of old Viatrons just sitting there-"

"What?" Nate blurted out.

"Last week, Mr. Goldstone asked me if I knew how to interface a Viatron to his Lorrell system. He even said he'd give me one if I did."

Nate was ecstatic, "You mean he'd *give* you a Viatron for free?"

"That's what he said," Brutus headed toward his office, "but I didn't waste my time on it."

Reggie leaned on his desk and lit a cigarette. "Would one of you guys mind telling me what a Viatron is? Sounds like something out of a Flash Gordon movie."

"Oh man, Regg," Nate said, "Viatron was the cheapest computer ever made. It had a screen, keyboard and two cassette tape decks."

"It wasn't really a computer by definition" Brutus cut in, "because it only ran programs stored in its Read-Only-Memory. So, it's very limited in what you can do."

"Yeah, but you can probably substitute your own ROM somehow."

"Now you're dreaming," Brutus said.

Reggie walked over and put his hand on Nate's shoulder. "Guess who called last night wanting service?"

Nate's mind was focused on Viatrons, now he tried to refocus on Reggie's words. "Who?" Reggie smiled and Nate's eyes lit up as he and Reggie said together, "General Insurance Company!"

That evening Nate was so excited he could hardly eat his dinner.

"Bea, do you realize what this could mean? A Viatron could not only be used to analyze races, me and Bill could use it down at the lab."

"How long will you be gone, Honey?"

"Just a few days; maybe all week at the most. Wait until Bill hears about this."

"There's something else we need to discuss Nate"

"What, Honey?"

Beatrice hesitated, "When you finish eating."

"Tell me now. I don't like suspense."

Beatrice got up and walked to the window, turned back around and then said, "Nate, it's been almost two years now and you still haven't gotten a divorce."

"I will, as soon as I can."

"That's what you always say."

Nate got up and walked toward Beatrice, but she moved around the table, keeping her distance. He stopped by the window.

"I mean it Nate. If I'm good enough to be your woman, then I'm good enough to be your wife."

"You know I love you, Bea."

"That's not enough. What about children. I don't want my children to be bastards." She continued before Nate could collect his thoughts, "I'm giving you until Christmas, Nate. I'm not going to wait forever while you procrastinate."

Her words stung him. He was disturbed by the thought of loosing Beatrice. He didn't want to be all alone again either.

If she leaves, the dreams will surely start again, he thought.

He walked to her slowly, took her in his arms and held her.

"I love you, Bea."

Beatrice pulled back and looked him in the face, "Do you think I'm asking for too much?"

"No, Bea. You deserve more, much more."

"Have you spoken with her?"

"Yes, more than once. I need more time, Bea."

"What did she say when you asked for a divorce?"

"She said she'd think about it."

They stood there silently embracing each other for a long while.

Nate awoke in the middle of the night, closed himself in the walk-in closet and called New York.

"It's me, Nate. Were you asleep?"

"Yes, I was. What do you want?"

"What I want is a divorce. Don't you think it's about time?"

"No, I'm not giving you a divorce. Not until you pay all the money you're suppose to."

"Look, you see I've been sending the savings bonds. Nobody told me to do that, and I'm going to continue sending them. But, I can't pay all that money the court ordered me to pay. I wouldn't have enough money to live on."

"That's not my problem. If you want a divorce, then you have to take care of your kids. I'm having a hard time getting aid and we need the money."

"I always took cared of all of you. Now you see it's not so easy, is it? But, I'm not going to live in some old abandoned building and have no money to eat with. And I'm never going to pay for you and your boyfriend to lay up in my apartment, with my kids."

"Walter doesn't live here-"

"I don't give a damn, where he lives! We'll stay married forever before you and your mother get any money out of me, you can believe that."

Eva didn't respond.

"If you don't want to be with me", Nate said, "why keep my name?"

"I'm not ready for a divorce yet."

"Why not?"

Eva didn't respond.

"Why not?" Nate repeated.

Eva exhaled heavily, "Because, maybe someday you will get past all this anger."

"And what? Come crawling back home on my knees? Listen, after all I went through with you, I will never trust you or anyone like you ever again. I don't know what you expect to happen."

"So, that's it then?" Eva asked.

"Yeah, that's it."

Neither of them suspected someone was listening-in.

*   *   *

The next day, as Nate drove to O'Hare airport, he felt as if someone was watching him. And, in fact, he was being followed by a black Chevy that had been shadowing him for weeks. F.B.I. agent Russell Taggart was hoping Nate would lead him to Ernest DuPree.

Arriving too early at the gate, Nate went to the men's room. He sensed something when a tall man in a trench coat came in and used the urinal on the end. Nate washed his hands and felt he had seen the man before but couldn't remember where. As they washed their hands, Nate saw the man was wearing a ring with a military insignia and a red stone in the center.

This guy is from the F.B.I. and he's following me, Nate thought. *Wow! I should say to him "You guys really do wear trench coats, huh?" No, I better leave him alone.*

Agent Taggart blended into the crowd and Nate didn't see him again until they were collecting their baggage in Cincinnati. After leaving the airport, Nate pointed the rental car west on highway-22 and thought, *I don't see anyone following me; maybe it was just my imagination.*

The plump secretary at General Insurance Company looked like Ruth Buzzi. She was all smiles as she led Nate to the owner's office.

Glenn Goldstone stood and extended his hand, "Glad to see you."

"Thank you."

"Any idea how long this will take?"

Nate hated it when a customer asked him that question before he had an opportunity to examine their machine.

"Maybe two days … unless I have to order a part."

"We can't stand for the system to be down very long." Goldstone sat, "Let me know if you need anything."

"There is one thing," Nate smiled, "Where's the system?"

The three of them laughed.

"Of course. Janice, please show Nate to the computer?"

Two hours later, Nate isolated the computer's problem and replaced what he thought was the offending part. But the signals were still inverted and the disk drive wouldn't work. He went deeper into studying the schematics and became oblivious to his surroundings.

At 6pm, Mr. Goldstone walked in and startled Nate, "How's it coming?"

"Oh, I'm getting there," Nate said, "Should be fixed by tomorrow."

"Good, because there's another matter I want to discuss with you."

"What's that?"

Nate's heart jumped for joy as Mr. Goldstone described the Viatrons and his desire to interface them to the Lorrell system.

"I'll be glad to see what I can do, once I get this fixed."

"See you tomorrow then."

Nate sat on the floor, lotus style, dialing Reggie's phone when he heard Janice say, "Hi Nate." She was standing in the doorway with her coat on.

"Hi."

Janice sat on the desk with one foot on the floor. "You look like the kind of guy who likes to party."

He looked at Janice big shapely legs and then said, "I do my share."

"Me and my girlfriend Rita go to the Holiday Inn on Thursdays; they have live music there. I thought you might want to join us."

"Sounds good to me. That's where I'm staying anyway."

"Good," she stood, "then it's a date?"

"Yeah, Thursday. I'll look forward to it."

Janice smiled, "We will too." She turned and sauntered away.

Nate called Reggie and tried to resolve the system's problem, but couldn't.

"You better call California." Reggie said, "It's only 4pm out there. Talk with Justin, he's the expert."

"Will do." Nate replied, "Later, man."

Two days later a new disk drive arrived and Nate tried everything he could think of to make it work. But, the problem persisted. Nate's boss instructed Brutus to fly out the next day. Mr. Goldstone no longer greeted Nate in the mornings and merely grunted when Nate told him Brutus was coming.

Nate sat in his hotel room that night, staring at the TV. It was too late for dinner; he had a bourbon and soda instead.

That's all I need, for Brutus to come out here and find something simple that I overlooked. Why didn't they send Reggie? ... Shit!

I can't believe this. I really can not fix that disk drive. I've tried everything they suggested and followed the instructions in the manual. The damn thing still won't run right. And I don't even have a clue why not. I could modify the design and make it run, but not now.

Motherdear must have been right. I should have stayed in school and gone on with an academic education. I thought I had a knack for this stuff. This could be the end.

Damn!

Nate kicked the desk chair over, on his way to the bathroom.

The next day, in spite of himself, Nate was glad to see his coworker. "Hello, Brutus. How was your flight?"

"Got yourself in pretty deep this time, huh?" He was almost out of breath.

Nate ignored the quip, "The new disk drive behaves the same as the old one."

"I brought some diagnostic tools that should help."

Brutus went through the same procedures Nate had been doing and got the same results Nate had got.

"Hum, either there's an error in the manual or they're putting the wrong chips in these drives. Look here."

Nate followed Brutus observations and saw that he was right. The parts didn't match the schematics.

The manual is wrong. It could never have worked this way. I'm saved, Nate thought.

"We'll have to modify the circuit to get this thing to work."

"I know how to do that, Brutus, but I didn't think I should have to redesign the drive to fix it."

Brutus didn't look up, "There's a first time for everything, Nate."

An hour later the system was running and Mr. Goldstone listened to Brutus' explanation.

"This was one of those occasions where our supplier screwed up royally. They're gonna have to send upgrades to all their customers once we tell them what we found."

"I'm just glad you got us going. I appreciate your efforts." Then Goldstone added, "Will you fellas be here tomorrow?"

"I've got an early morning flight," Brutus said, "But Nate will stick around and make sure everything is okay."

"Good."

After Goldstone left, they were clearing up their tools and Nate said, "I want to thank you Brutus for helping me out today. Can I buy you a drink or something."

Brutus looked at Nate, "I would take you up on that, Nate, but it's late. How about a six-pack when we get back to the office?"

"You got it." Nate said.

He looked at his watch and remembered Janice's invitation. *It's too late for a lot of things.*

The next day, Mr. Goldstone described his Viatron problem and Nate worked all day trying to interface a Viatron to the Lorrell system. He told Janice he'd meet her at the bar later. But he ended up working on the Viatron until midnight. He stayed Saturday and worked without taking a lunch break.

"You don't have to push yourself like this, Nate," Mr. Goldstone said.

"You don't know what one of these Viatrons means to me."

"I'll tell you what, Nate, you take one back with you and when you figure out how to interface it, call me with the instructions?"

"Really?"

"I'm confident you'll figure it out." Goldstone smiled, "Besides you've earned it."

Nate looked up and grinned. He called Reggie with the news. "You know what, Nate?" Reggie said, "I was going to call you. I think your interface problem might be HTL tristate logic."

"What's that, Regg?"

"It uses plus and minus fifteen volts for its binary ones and zeros."

"But, I thought digital logic was based on plus five and zero volts."

"That's only TTL logic, Nate. Remember how old that Viatron is. Engineers were trying different kinds of logic back then."

Nate thought for a moment, "That could explain why it communicates in only one direction."

"Sure, whenever the HTL signals go above or below TTL levels, the Lorrell would interpret it as ones and zeros; but the signals from our system never reach both of the HTL levels."

"Then all that's needed is a level-shifter circuit."

"Bingo." Reggie said.

"Thanks, man. I've got to get to the electronics store."

He got the parts and assembled a 'black box' that allowed Goldstone's Lorrell computer to communicate with the Viatrons.

Nate was on the 10:30 flight back to Chicago. His Viatron was boxed, in the cargo hold, with his luggage.

*　　　*　　　*

When Nate got home, he knocked on the door instead of using his key. Beatrice opened it and saw his out stretched hand and the bouquet of flowers. She smiled, reached up and kissed him, "Thank you, baby." She hurried back to the kitchen.

"Something smells mighty good in here," Nate said, "and I'm hungry too." He put his case down and took off his leather coat.

"Nate, come and meet Volley, we work together."

Nate entered the kitchen and saw a young, attractive, European-looking woman; they shook hands.

"Nice to meet you, Nate. I've heard so much about you." She spoke with an accent.

"Volley's joining us for dinner tonight." Beatrice said.

The toilet flushed and a small, blond, round-faced boy came out. He wore an embossed blue jacket, grey tie and eye-glasses that made him look intelligent. He walked over to Volley.

"Geisley, say hello to Mr. LaChae."

"Hello, Mr. LaChae."

"Hello, Geisley. It's nice to meet you."

They shook hands and Geisley turned around and climbed on to his mother's lap. He appeared to be four or five years old.

Volley has asked us if we'd baby-sit Geisley while she and Anar go out tonight.

"That would be fine with me." Nate said, "Do you play checkers, Geisley?"

"Yes," Geisley replied shyly, "but chess is better."

Nate grinned, "I see we're going to get along just fine."

"Anar is studying for his doctorate in physics, over at the University," Beatrice said, "You two might have something in common."

"Oh?" Nate said.

"Beatrice told me you work in physics too?" Volley asked.

Nate finished chewing. "Yes, I've been working on a gyroscopic engine for several years now. I published a report about my work a few years ago. Maybe, your husband could read it and give me his opinion."

"I'd be glad to give it to him. But, I have to tell you, he's very busy with his studies."

"I can understand that. Ask him to mark-up the report whenever he has time."

They enjoyed their dinner while discussing events at their jobs.

After Volley left, Beatrice asked, "Would you let Anar see your engine and equipment?"

"I don't know. That depends on what he says about my report. Besides, I want to meet him first."

That night Nate went to bed thinking, *Maybe, now the Gamma effect can be explained once and for all ... by a physics professional*.

Three weeks later, after reading Nate's report, Anar agreed to see Nate's Gamma engine.

Bill's basement felt damp and cold as the control console came to life with a hum. The different colored indicator lamps flashed like Christmas tree bulbs. The scene always looked surrealistic since Bill had installed a blue 60-watt light bulb in the ceiling.

"We have about an hour before Anar gets here."

Bill had one elbow on the console and was staring at Nate through thick eyeglasses. "Aren't you afraid that this Anar guy might steal the Gamma idea?."

"Not really. We'll just show him that the engine works and not let him touch anything. Besides, he's already read my report. He marked it up like a teacher grading a paper. Most of his notes said that he didn't believe this or that. That's the main reason I invited him down here to see it for himself. You and I have made a whole lot of progress since that report. So, even if he tried to copy our work, it would take him a lot of time."

Seeing Bill wasn't convinced, Nate added, "I'm hoping he'll take over the math explanation of the Gamma effect where Bob Jones and the guys from NYU left off. We know how to make the engine work, now we need a mathematical explanation of why it works."

"Will you, at least, get him to sign some kind of paper saying that he witnessed the engine?"

"Yeah, I thought of that too and what I'll do is ask him to sign our log book. I'll tell him that we always have people sign it when they witness one of our tests."

In the hour and a half that followed Nate and Bill brought everything up to a state of readiness and ran the engine briefly.

Upstairs, the doorbell rang. A few seconds later Etta opened the basement door and announced Anar's arrival. Nate and Bill met Anar as he descended the wooden spiral staircase. He looked like Thor Heyerdahl with his beard and thick wool coat.

Nate was exchanging introductions when Etta called down "Anyone want coffee or hot chocolate?" They all gave their preferences and headed toward the console.

Bill noticed that Anar showed no emotion as he approached the console.

"I'm glad that you came, Anar." Nate said, "As I told you, my math skills are not as good as my hands-on skills. Bill here is a machinist and has been able to machine the disks that we've needed. Sometimes he's even made parts I hadn't realized we needed."

"I see," Anar said, "You have complementary skills."

"Exactly. This is our control console where we monitor and record different parameters of each test. In the earliest tests, that I did in New York, the disk had a habit of breaking free and bouncing off the walls. So we decided to build our teststand behind this brick wall over here." Bill resisted an impulse to block the door as Nate led Anar toward the test pit,.

Squatting near the teststand, Anar concentrated as Nate described what they were seeing.

Anar's first question was, "Why do you need all the cinder blocks on top?"

"The disks generate a lot of centrifugal force and vibration. The blocks keep the teststand still."

"Can you isolate the extraneous vibrations from the measurements you want?"

"Oh yes, we've solved that problem." Nate rose, signaling it was time to leave the test pit.

Nobody noticed that Etta had brought hot drinks and set them on a workbench.. Bill was sitting at the console.

"Okay, Bill, let's run the engine up to resonance mode."

"Roger." Bill responded."

Minutes later, Nate said, "There, you see the pulses are starting to synchronize." He motioned for Anar to come over to the view port window.

"We're at resonance." Bill shouted over the noise.

"You can see that the disks are almost touching the lift arm now."

Squinting, Anar shook his head agreeing.

"Okay, Bill, give us some lift please." Nate stepped back.

Anar fixed his gaze on the gyrating disks.

Bill set the controls as high as he could without chancing another broken coupling.

"Now, If you will come over here ..." Nate motioned to Anar, and continued his descriptions.

Anar looked at Nate for a few seconds and then said nothing. Then he looked at Bill at the console and went back over to the viewing window. Nate looked at Bill in the blue light and winked. Bill smiled, nodded and began the shutdown sequence.

Nate walked over to the view port and then said, "Well, what do you think? Will you help us with the math equations?"

Anar seemed to be angry. He walked over, picked up his briefcase, turned and then said, "Now I've seen it, but I still don't believe it."

He went up the stairs while Nate and Bill stared in astonishment. They heard the front door close and wondered if Etta had had time to show Anar out.

Stunned, Nate said, "I don't believe it!" and started toward the stairs. Bill grabbed his arm gently and then said, "No, Nate."

"What?," Nate pulled free, "What are you doing?"

Bill said in a soft voice, "You don't get it, do you?"

Nate struggled for comprehension, "Get what?"

"Anar will never believe it, Nate; he can't."

"But, we showed him." Nate protested. "He's got to believe his own eyes."

"That guy has done years and years of studying", Bill said and now he's about to get his Ph.D., right?"

"Yeah." Nate sat, dumbfounded.

Bill continued, "He's never going to accept that, two black men without college degrees, proved that some of what he's been taught isn't right."

"But he's from Iceland. I didn't think racism mattered to him."

Etta came downstairs and then said, "How'd it go with your guest?" She looked at the untouched cups and added, "You guys let the drinks get cold?" Sensing the gloom, she asked, "Did something go wrong?"

Bill looked at her and then said "No, Etta, Anar had to choose between our engine and Isaac Newton laws."

They never heard from Anar again.

After the disappointment with Anar and a letter from the US Navy saying Nate's Gamma car merely hop-scotched across the floor, Nate began to doubt that he could ever convince anyone that the engine works. He became deeply depressed and managed to hide it from everyone, except Reggie.

They were getting high one evening and Reggie said, "Nate, I'm telling you, Sheila keeps bugging me about you. She's left her old man and been living with her sister, only two miles away from you."

"So?"

"Aw, come on, Man. Why don't you, at least, give her a call? I been over there and met her stuck-up sister."

"And?"

"Ain't nothing happening there, man. She must be into women or something. All I know is I don't qualify in her book, 'cause I don't have a university degree."

"Yeah, I met Joan once, down at The Towers. She seemed just the opposite of Sheila."

"Look man, I'm only the messenger. But, if it was me ... "

"I get the picture, Regg. And I appreciate where you're coming from. Right now I need time to think."

"Cool.." Reggie said.

"Thanks anyway, man."

*   *   *

Nate and Beatrice went to the Lorrell Company Christmas dinner and saw the play, Fiddler on the Roof. Nate drank more than he should have and all the way home, in the snow, he talked about how he wished he could have joined the performers on stage.

Beatrice pointed, "Watch out for that ice."

Nate searched for a parking space. "Looks like we got lucky; a car just pulled out at the corner."

Going up in the elevator, Nate sung " ...If I were a rich man ..." He smiled at Beatrice who shook her head and rolled her eyes at the ceiling.

Their apartment was chilly and they were in bed in no time. Hearing a sound from the street below, Nate's last thought, before he passed out, was: *That car sounds just like mine when I try to start it.*

The next morning Nate's hangover made him forget where he'd parked his car. He looked in his usual spots and even his alternate spots. Then, as the cold Chicago breeze began to seep through his clothes, he remembered, *I parked at the corner. And now my car is gone!*

He remembered hearing someone trying to start a car that sounded like his. *That must have been MY car! Oh, no! My company tools and parts and o-scope were in the trunk. I'll have to report this to the police. I sure hope my registration is good or I'm screwed.*

He called Jeff, who didn't sound surprised and assured Nate the paperwork would fool anybody. The forged documents proved to be "real" enough for the police report.

Nate called the headhunter, Paul Riley, again. He was assured a computer field service job could be found that didn't require a car. Meanwhile, Nate used the last of his savings to rent a car. He deeply regretted having to tell Reggie he was going to have to leave Lorrell.

*   *   *

One evening, Nate answered his phone and heard an official-sounding voice ask, "Is this Nathaniel LaChae?"

"Yes."

"Would you please verify your social security number?"

"Who is this?"

"This is the F.B.I. calling. I need to verify that you are Nathaniel LaChae. You can call me back if you need to authenticate this call."

"What's your number?" Nate asked.

Holly shit! Is this about Eva, or the Port Authority, or my creditors, or something Ernest has done, or what?

He returned their call and identified himself.

"Your car was found in New Jersey. Mr. LaChae. "It has been stripped." The speaker paused, then asked, "Do you know anyone in New Jersey?"

Nate thought of Bob Jones and, immediately, dismissed the thought.

"No, I don't."

"We traced the sale of a Tektronix-453 o-scope to your police report. Do you know anyone in the immediate area of New Jersey?"

Nate got a chill - *Jeff!*

A remote possibility flashed though his mind. *They must have stolen the car back from me! Why would Jeff do that?*

"Mr. LaChae? I asked if you know anyone in the New Jersey vicinity."

"Ah ... , I grew up in New York City. I know lots of people there."

"Do you know anyone that would want to steal your car?"

"No, I don't."

The agent thanked Nate for his cooperation and gave him a case reference number. "You can get a copy of the report for your insurance company. You should contact us if you have any further information."

Shit! That's all I need – to have my name up on some F.B.I. screen.

"Who was that?" Beatrice asked.

"The police; they found the car in New Jersey. I think Jeff and his friends must have stolen it back from me."

*   *   *

Nate returned his rental car and took a taxi to work. His phone rang and it was his cousin Naomi.

"Hey, Cuz. How did you get this number?"

"I have my ways." Naomi said, "How have you been?"

"Things are a little rough, but I'm making it. Where are you, you sound close?"

"I am; I'm at O'Hare, on my way to San Diego. My flight's been delayed overnight and they put me up in the Marriott hotel, by the airport. I thought maybe we could get together."

"For sure!" Nate said, "I'll come out there."

Nate called home and left a message saying he'd be late, then he took a taxi to the Marriott.

Naomi was waiting in the lounge. They hugged and kissed lightly on the lips. They pulled back and looked, knowingly, into each other's eyes.

"Hey, Cuz. This is really a surprise."

"It's so good to see you, Nate. I hope you haven't had dinner yet; I'm starving."

"No, I haven't. What do you have a taste for?"

"Let's see what they have here at the hotel." Naomi grabbed his arm and they headed for the dining room.

Naomi proceeded to update Nate about the family in New York and Alabama.

"What about you, Nate?"

Nate finished his wine, and their server, immediately, refilled their glasses with Chardonnay.

"To tell you the truth, it's been a little rough lately. My car got stolen and I may lose my job because of it."

"What? Was it a company car?"

"No. That's the whole point. I'm required to have my own car. I had rented one, but I can't afford that any more.

The other thing is, Beatrice is pushing me to get a divorce. She has given me until the end of December. She wants to have kids and says she don't want them to be bastards."

"So, will your wife give you a divorce?"

Nate swirled his wine around and then said, "Naomi, that whole mess with Eva is about money. My money. I'm not going to pay as much as she and her mother want, and she's not going to give me a divorce."

"Sounds like you two are at a standoff."

"Exactly. And I don't want to hurt Beatrice; she had nothing to do with my troubles."

Naomi lit a cigarette and blew smoke toward the ceiling. "I can tell you what to do, but you won't like it."

"Tell me anyway."

"If you really love Beatrice, you have to set her free. Nate, that's the only way to be fair to her. If you're not going to marry her, then let her get on with her life."

Nate turned sideways and put his arm over the back of the chair. "How come, lately, *if I really love someone, I have to let them go?* When

I took two of my kids to be with me, my mother told me to let my kids stay together. And now you're telling me to let Beatrice go if I love her. How can I be showing love when I have to give up people I care about."

Naomi leaned across the table and then said, "Cuz, I'm a woman and I'm telling you, if you don't pay the money and get the divorce, you'll be hurting Beatrice even more."

"I'm not gonna pay it!" Nate shouted, "I can't!"

"Hey! I'm on your side."

"Sorry. It's just that nobody understands what's been going on." Nate's eyes were full of tears. "It's like Eva wants to put a noose around my neck – and for what? Because she got herself some new boyfriend."

Naomi put her hand on his. "Listen to me, Nate. I know a lot of shit has happened to you. And I understand you want to move on with your life. But, dragging Beatrice along with promises you can't keep, is not going to help anyone in the long run. Can't you see that?"

"To tell you the truth, I don't want to be alone again."

"I believe you, Nate." Naomi patted his hand, "None of this is easy. I believe Beatrice loves you, but she's not going to hang around forever waiting." The server poured the last of the Chardonnay into their glasses.

"I hear you, Cuz. It's not like I don't send any money for my kids. But, that's not enough for that … ". Nate stopped short of saying the "B" word.

"Let me tell you this," Naomi said, "If you do decide to break up with Beatrice, you can't half do it. You'll only keep breaking her heart, if you let her think you might get back together again. I know because I've been there." Naomi stared into her empty glass.

"Hey, enough of all that." Nate said, "Tell me about your fiancé, what's his name?"

"Freddie." Naomi held up her hand, "See my ring."

"Yeah. That's a big diamond. You always liked fine jewelry."

"Never had anything this fine before. He brought it from France."

"So, how did you meet him?"

Naomi grinned and told Nate about her Marine beau and her engagement plans.

At home, that night Nate lay awake, next to Beatrice, thinking, *Eva's never going to give me a divorce. I'm never going to give them all the money they want. When Beatrice leaves me I'll be alone again. I'll have no one. Those dreams will start all over again. I don't want to be alone …*

He dozed off for a moment, then awoke with a start.

If I pay the money, Bea and I won't have enough to live on. As soon as the creditors discover where I am, they'll garnishee my check and I'll have nothing. Me and Beatrice can't live like that. And I don't want to have more kids if I can't live a normal life with them. Why is all this shit happening to me?

He wished for a drink or a joint, but didn't have either. He got up in the middle of the night and took a taxi to Sheila's place.

"Nate, is that you?" her voice came from the intercom.

"Yes, Sheila."

She buzzed him in, past the security guard. After they embraced at the door Nate took off his long coat and he was still in his pajamas.

"I don't know why I'm here," he said.

"I'm glad you're here, Nate. She took his hand in hers and they walked to her bedroom. Soon they were devouring each other in passion.

Afterward, Sheila asked, "What really made you come here tonight?"

"I just need to stop thinking for a while." Nate finished the wine in his glass and turned onto his stomach, in the darkened room. "To tell you the truth Sheila, it's like every fucking thing is going wrong."

"Don't let it get to you, Nate." She sat on his back and massaged his shoulders.

"I won't … I just need a break sometime … a time-out … ," he started snoring.

Sheila stroked his back and then said softly, "I'm what you need, but you're not ready for me yet."

When Nate got home Friday morning, Beatrice had gone to work. He phoned Reggie. "Hey, man, I'm moving out of my apartment."

"What about Beatrice?"

"That's over with man."

"Hey, man, are you sure?"

"Yes, Reggie. I need you to help me move some of my things in your car. Can you come over?"

"Well, okay, Nate. But what happened between you and Beatrice?"

"I'm going to tell her when I get there."

"You mean you haven't told her yet?"

"No Reggie. Listen man I need your help. Either way I'm moving this evening. Are you going to help me or not?"

"Yeah, I'll come over after work. Where are you moving to?"

"I'm moving in with Sheila and her sister for a while."

"Damn, man. I didn't know you were going to do all that."

"I'll see you after work."

On the train ride home, Nate thought about how to tell Beatrice that his wife was never going to give him a divorce. He remembered his Cousin Naomi's advice.

When Beatrice arrived Nate asked her to sit down in the living room. "Bea, I've got some bad news to tell you." he paused. "I think its time we moved on with our lives."

"What do you mean 'move on with our lives'."

"Bea, it's over between us. I'm moving out today."

Beatrice was quiet for a moment. She stared at Nate waiting to see if this was one of his jokes. She kept her composure and then said, "The other night, when you called your wife, I overheard every word the two of you said, Nate."

"What are you talking about?"

"I borrowed another phone and plugged it into the old outlet in the bedroom."

Nate stared at her and then said, "I'm glad you heard both sides."

There was a knock at the door and as Nate answered it, Beatrice went into the bedroom and closed the door.

"Where's Beatrice?" Reggie asked.

"She's in the bedroom. Give me a minute and I'll finish getting my things together; I'm only taking my clothes."

"You're really serious about this, aren't you?"

Nate didn't answer; he took clothes from the closet and put them on the couch. Reggie grabbed them up and then said nervously, "I'll take these down to the car."

Nate went into the bedroom and saw Beatrice standing by the window. "I'm sorry Bea. I didn't want to hurt you. If there's anything you need, let me know."

She turned and then said, "Don't worry about me, Nate; I don't need anything from somebody that don't want me."

Nate wanted to hold her one more time. Instead, he turned and walked out of the room. He put his key on the living room table, and was about to leave when Beatrice came out of the bedroom. She walked toward him; he could see tears in her eyes. For a moment they were frozen, a few feet apart, staring into each others eyes.

Beatrice said, "If you ever get your life together, come and find me."

Nate swallowed, bobbed his head, and walked out.

*   *   *

Meanwhile, in conference room 1201, of the Chicago office of the F.B.I, Section Chief Weitz listened to one of his twelve agents seated at the table.

"You want to clarify that statement, Taggart."

"I said, we should reclassify subject-373."

"On what grounds?"

"I ran his potentials through the computer and got a spike."

Weitz took his glasses off, "How the hell did we get a spike from a low-level subject like LaChae?"

"Sir, when all his potentials are factored in, there is a 13% chance he could go rogue."

"Taggart, this guy is a loner, didn't graduate high school, poor and black on top of that." Weitz turned toward the only Afro-American at the table, "No offense intended, Johnson."

"None taken, sir."

Taggart persisted, "Still, the computer showed-"

"All right, all right. Enough about that damn supercomputer. Soon, it's going to either put us out of work or turn us into puppets." Weitz put his glasses back on. "Continue your investigation, Taggart. But, if someone like LaChae can produce an antigravity machine in a Chicago basement, we're all in trouble."

"The first fission reaction was produced in a Chicago basement," agent Johnson said.

Everyone turned toward him, but no one spoke.

Weitz stared over his glasses and then said, "Let's move on, shall we?"

* * *

Nate's dad visited him once at Sheila's condo. He was angry about the breakup and didn't care if the sisters in the next room heard him.

"Beatrice was in your corner," dad groaned. "She's the kind of woman you need. You should go back to her."

"It's over, dad."

"You're making a stupid mistake, Nate. That's all I have to say about it." With that Nate's dad left without saying goodbye to anyone.

Nate walked to the living room window and watched his dad drive off. Sheila walked up behind him and asked, "Are you alright, Nate?"

"No, I'm not," he said, "but I'm gonna be." *As soon as I get access to a computer system,* he thought. "I heard Nationtech Computer Systems has some openings; I'm going down there tomorrow and fill out an application.

Nationtech

This is the moment I've waited for, Nate thought. Today he was starting as a Field Service Engineer (FSE) at Nationtech Computer Company. He would be doing on-the-job-training (OJT) with Alan White,

Two weeks prior to that, Mr. Neidermeyer told Nate about Clarence Brown, an Afro-American, superstar FSE. The company had recently flown Clarence and his family from Europe to Japan. "That Clarence", Neidermeyer said, shaking his head, "he can fix anything we have. That's the kind of opportunities we offer here at Nationtech."

Neidermeyer examined Nate's notebook of projects and certificates and then said, "So, do you think you would like to join us?"

"I sure would. I've wanted to work on mainframes for quite a while now."

"If we made you an offer, when could you start?"

"Right away; I have no other obligations right now."

"In that case, Nate, you'll be hearing from us soon."

Nate stepped up to the automatic doors of Nationtech's immense data center in downtown Chicago. It hummed from the sound of hundreds of fans. Rows of tall blue cabinets sat along the back wall. In the center of the room a dozen high-speed printers devoured green striped paper. On another wall, huge tape drives whirled to their own beat. Long loops of tape played up and down in glass chambers below the tape reels.

Nate stood in awe thinking I'll have to fix all this when it breaks?

A half dozen people were busy in the data center, tending the computers, like priest in a monastery. Nate approached one of them, "Can you tell me where I can find Alan White?"

"Sure thing, he's working on one of the disk drives."

"Thanks." Looking around, Nate realized he didn't know where the disk drives were. As he turned to ask, the operator pointed and then said, "You must be the new guy."

"Yes, today's my first day. Thanks." Once Nate crossed the room, he saw a row of shorter blue cabinets. He counted six rows and six columns of disk drives. One of the cabinets was open, with a toolbox next to it. Nate peeped behind the open cabinet and saw a man sitting cross-legged on the floor staring intently at an o-scope.

The man looked up and then said, "You must be Nate Lachae."

"That's right. You're Alan White?"

Alan got up slowly and shook Nate's hand. He turned and pointed at his work. "We've been getting intermittent errors on these three drives in the corner here. This one is the worst. You have any experience with disk drives?"

"Not large ones like this. The ones I've worked on had only two platters."

"These babies have 12 platters with read/write heads on both sides. We finished installing the last four a month ago. Come on I'll show you where our cubicle and parts storage are. It's about time for some coffee anyway."

Over coffee, Nate told Alan about his background and asked about the OJT training.

"Mostly, you'll be tagging along with me on PMs and service calls until you go to the training facility in Boston."

"How long is the training?"

"That depends on how many modules you're scheduled for. Plus, I hear the training department has a new program they'll be starting. You'll probably be out in Boston anywhere from eight to twelve weeks. Hope you like seafood."

For the next two weeks, Nate worked with Alan learning the basics of Nationtech's computer systems. His mornings began at the Nationtech office where three other black FSEs had been hired.

The tallest one, Dave Johnson sat cross-legged in the break room. He wore a tailored double-breasted tan suit that fit his six-foot-three frame. The red stripes in his black tie topped off his appearance. "Man, you know the black secretaries have already divvied us up in their minds? Harold took his pipe out of his mouth and looked over his glasses "Looks like we don't get to choose around here." Harold resembled a college student with his argyle vest and tie.

Tom, with his devilish grin, looked toward Nate and then said, "Yeah Nate looks like you get the skinny one at the front desk. What's her name again ... Minnie?"

Nate shook his head and almost spilled his coffee on his herringbone sports jacket. "No way man!"

"Hey ..." Tom said, "they've already decided!"

Dave and Harold chimed in with "Yeah, man."

Nate responded with, "I got my eye on somebody else, and I'm not going to say who it is."

*   *   *

One month later, the new FSEs were on their way to Nationtech computer school for three months. On their arrival at the training center, the brothers from Chicago, and four other students, were handed a stack of forms. Soon they were ushered into a classroom and told to put their baggage in the rear and wait.

Bryan Scott came in and introduced himself. "I'm the class facilitator" he said, as he gave out more forms. "I'll be making sure you get your manuals, tests and other documents. Please let me know if you need any other supplies. I'll put my number on the board. You should know, starting with your class, we're having a new program of audio training. Gordon Murphy, the director of training, will explain it to you. It's experimental and you guys get to be our guinea pigs."

The Chicago guys glanced at one another.

"First, I'm going to hand out a little test. It's not a pass or fail type test. It's just to see where you're at as far as the basics. Take your time; I'll be back in twenty minutes. There's coffee and Danishes on the table in the back. Any questions?" There were none.

Nate quickly scanned over the test, then he glanced around the room at his competition. He assumed he had as much technology experience as the brothers from Chicago. But what about the other guys? There was a Hispanic who seemed pretty calm; he wrote studiously on his answer sheet. The other two were white and one of them was staring back at Nate with his arms over the back of his chair.

One of those Stuyvesant-High-School types Nate thought. At least this wouldn't be like the Lorrell class was; where all the other students had years more experience than me.

Gordon Murphy stormed into the room with Bryan Scott behind him. He barely acknowledged the presence of the students before he began speaking, "You fellas will be the first class to go through our new audio course. Each of you will be able to progress at your own pace. The lessons start with the basics and progress through all that you'll need to know. Your training applications indicate that some of you have computer experience. That's good; the first few lessons will be a refresher for you. As for the rest of you, you'll find all the information you'll need In the manuals. Once you pass all the tests, you can advance to the lab part of the course. We haven't scheduled any class for this afternoon so you can check into your hotels. You are to be here, in the classroom, tomorrow at 0-900. Are there any questions?"

Harold raised his hand, "Am I to understand, we won't get any hands-on until we finish all the tapes?"

"That's correct," Gordon Murphy snapped back. Tom raised his hand. Gordon Murphy put his hands on the table and leaned forward, "Yes, what's your question?"

"I just want to know, where the men's room is."

There were chuckles around the room. Gordon Murphy wasn't amused. He turned and left the room.

"I'll show you where the rest rooms are", Bryan said, "then I'll take you to your hotel. In the morning, there will be two rental cars for you to share. First, please sign these papers, so I can give you these checkbooks. Every week you will be expected to turn in an expense report and you can sign a traveler's check for that amount. We've found this system is better than giving an advance and having you wait for the approval cycle before being reimbursed." All the guys liked that idea and gathered around for their packet of traveler's checks.

That night the Chicago brothers gathered in the hotel dining room.

"Hey man, can you believe this shit about the checkbooks?"

"Yeah! I counted mine and there's $3,000 worth of checks in the pack."

"Let's split right now, I know a joint on the South-Side ..." Everybody was laughing as the waitress came to take their order. Dave asked in his most proper English, "Would it be possible to get an order of Chitterlings?"

When the waitress asked "How do you spell that?" the guys roared with laughter.

The next morning, Bryan Scott came in and asked the guys to follow him to the audio training room. It was a room they would come to know as The Dungeon. Two rows of four partitioned booths filled the room. The tops of the partitions were five feet high. Each booth had a reel-to-reel tape recorder and a set of headphones. The cushioned chairs had wheels but couldn't roll well on the carpeted floor. There were no windows, just florescent lights above. The light olive green walls were intended to have a calming effect.

"These are your workbooks," Bryon said, "They will tell you when to turn your tapes on and off. When you have all completed each lesson I will give you the tests." Groans were heard around the room.

"Exactly, how many lessons are there?" Harold asked.

"There's twenty-two in all. The first ten cover basics that can be applied to all Nationtech computers. Then there are ten lessons on the Series 200 systems."

Without waiting, Tom asked, "And what about the last two?"

"They cover diagnostics and troubleshooting." Bryan quickly added "All the lessons were prepared by an outside firm. So, if you find any errors or have any comments, please let me know. The success of the program depends on you." Bryan paused and glanced around the room.

"Okay, you should get started. I'll be back in one hour. You know where everything is and if you need me dial 3749 on the phone on the wall."

When Bryan left, Dave said, "If the success of this audio tape project depends on me they can hang it up right now."

The guy they nick-named Einstein had his headphones on and was eagerly turning the pages in his workbook. Nate opened his workbook as he heard the voice in his headphones say, "Lesson One … Binary Numbers. Please turn to page 3."

Day after day, the brothers followed their routine that included going into Boston each night. Back in the classroom, Harold got permission to smoke his pipe. The ventilation system did little to dissipate the sweet Cherry Blend smell; no one complained. Meanwhile, the tests grew more difficult as the students progressed. Each of the students fell asleep at some point, except Einstein; he was three lessons ahead of everyone.

One day, they had settled in when Einstein shouted, "Hey! Who turned my tape around?"

Everyone stood and looked over their partitions. Einstein went over to the wall phone and began dialing. The guys chuckled and looked questioningly at each other. For a moment, Nate and Eric's eyes locked and Eric winked. Tom went and put Einstein's headphones on, "It sounds like space people talking. The words are being pronounced backward." Everyone roared with laughter.

During their fourth week the hotel receptionist had mail for each of the Chicago students. Each envelope was marked "Personal." Inside Nate found another sealed envelope with a note that said, 'Hope this helps'. It was from Skinny-Minnie and it was the answers to all the tests. When Nate called her, at the office, she said, "Now you owe me, don't you?" He had to concede that one. Tom, Harold and Dave received similar packages from the secretaries back home. The Chicago student's test scores were excellent after that; they wisely avoided getting 100% every time.

One morning, there was a notice on the blackboard. It read: "ALL STUDENTS WILL REPEAT TEST-107 AGAIN."

Dave was the first to comment, "This is bullshit man."

"They don't believe our test scores." Tom said as he glanced toward Einstein.

Nate went to the blackboard and started composing:

'From all across the country they came,

Computers were their game.
They were the smartest and the best,
And it showed on their tests.'
"O.K." Tom exclaimed, "I got something."

He took the chalk and wrote.

'The big Bear growled and snapped all the time.
But they refused to respond or breakdown.
They knew if they stuck with it,
everything would be fine.
And they would be free of this clown.'

Tom turned around and held the chalk out, "Anybody else?."
Dave rubbed his chin trying to think of something witty.
Harold shook his head, "You really going to leave that like that?"
Kurt said, "Let me add something."

'They survived the audio in the windowless room.
Knowing that this suffering will be over soon.
They mastered Boolean, octal and hexadecimal code.
And yet the big Bear increased their load.

By now, all the guys were gathered at the blackboard. Even Einstein was smiling. Dave added his finishing touch as Bryan Scott came in. It read:

'Now they were mad as hell
and thinking about walking out the door.'
'If they can't go to the lab,
they weren't going to take it any more.'

Bryan Scott walked slowly over to the blackboard and read. He chuckled, turned around and then said, "I'd change clown to town, if I were you."

Tom quickly complied. The guys took their seats at their cubicles. Bryan Scott gathered a stack of papers and handed them out. It was Test-107. Without looking up, he said, "He'll want to know who wrote that."

Kurt responded with, "We all did." Everybody looked at Einstein to see if he was going to protest; he didn't.

They took test-107 again and everyone scored 100%. Just before lunchtime, Gordon Murphy arrived with another man. They read what was on the blackboard and the other man smiled. Gordon Murphy turned toward the cubicles and saw everyone studying with their headphones on. He looked at Bryan Scott, then left the room.

*   *   *

In the evening, Nate came down to the hotel lobby and found Tom reading a newspaper. Tom said. "Dave was talking about going into the city for dinner. What do you think?"

"Hey man, I don't know." Nate flopped into one of the cushioned chairs. "I always have a hard time getting up in the morning after that trip."

"Yeah, and we have another test tomorrow too."

Nate reached over and grabbed the newspaper. "I was thinking about going to a movie after dinner, if I can get the car."

"The movies turn out late," Tom said, "You get there about 7 – 7:30 and it's over at 10."

Nate didn't respond. He thumbed through the pages looking for the movie section. An ad with a drawing of a human head got his attention. The ad read, "Learn to Use More of Your Mind. Come to the free introductory seminar on Thursday …" When he saw it was from Silva Mind Control (SMC) he remembered Ken Davis, back at Zemit Radio mentioning it.

It had been years since Ken told him that one day he'd take the SMC course. Ken's confidence had impressed Nate. Ken hadn't tried to persuade him and that enticed Nate even more. But the price of the course turned him off. Ken had said, "When you're ready, you'll take it." Now, Nate realized, he had the extra money and the time.

Tom noticed Nate's intent interest and then said, "I'll bet you're looking at that Silva Mind Control ad."

"Yeah, you read it too?"

"That's what I was thinking about checking out tonight."

"Hey, Tom, I didn't know you were interested in mind stuff."

"Yeah, I dibble and dabble in a lot of things. I've read Psycho-Cybernetics and some other books like that.

The two of them started exchanging book titles. They didn't notice when Harold and Dave got off the elevator.

Overhearing one of the titles, Dave said, "I don't suppose either of you used your power of positive thinking to come up with a good restaurant for us tonight."

"Not yet." Tom said, "We're thinking about going over to New Bedford."

"You guys going to that Silva thing, aren't you?"

"Yeah." Nate said, "We thought we'd check it out."

Dave turned back toward the elevator. "Let me know what it's about. I'm gonna have room service and call some of my women."

"I'm staying in too." Harold said, "I'm burned out."

Nate and Tom didn't have much trouble finding the Holiday Inn where the SMC meeting was being held. The receptionist greeted them and gave them paper badges for their names. She was friendly and Nate noticed her staring as he walked into the room. There were a dozen or so people in the room. They were of various ages and attire. A Catholic nun and an older couple sat by the window. A young hippie sat on the floor with his legs crossed. Nate followed Tom to a table that had handouts, books and audiotapes. They helped themselves to the free materials, then found seats in the middle of the room.

As the room filled, Tom leaned over and whispered, "We're the only blacks here."

"Are you surprised?" Nate said.

"Not really."

A tall young man walked to the front of the room and then said, "We're going to start now." He motioned to the young woman at the door, "Please tell the people in the hallway." The man waited patiently while everyone sat and quieted down.

"Good evening. Let me begin by thanking everyone for coming tonight. My name is Ken Cantrell. I trust that all you will find the information I'm going to give you tonight interesting and stimulating. For some of you tonight will be the beginning of a new life. Jose Silva says, "The greatest thing you can do before the SMC Course will be the least thing you can do afterward." Tom looked at Nate, but Nate was intent on every word Ken Cantrell was saying.

The next morning, while enjoying buffet at the hotel, Harold asked about the Santos lecture. Nate and Tom smiled at each other.

"They asked us not to discuss it until next week, Harold."

"Aw, come on man. This is ME. I almost went with you guys remember?"

Nate took a mouthful of home fries "We'll fill you in after we finish the course." Harold looked at Tom who nodded agreement.

Dave finished chewing, laughed, and then said, "Looks, to me, like they're already controlling your minds."

Harold shook his head "I don't believe it. You guys are really not going to tell me anything about it?"

Tom finished his orange juice, looked over his glasses and ended the discussion with, "Nope."

The next weekend, Nate and Tom completed the SMC course. After receiving their certificates, Tom looked at Nate and then said "Wow! Harold and Dave will never believe this."

"I'm not going to try to tell them anything." Nate said, "And I'm going to take the advanced course as soon as I get back to Chicago."

"Me too, Nate. That must be where we learn to walk on hot coals."

"Think I'll skip that part", Nate said as they laughed heartily.

*   *   *

Nate flew to New York City on the weekend and rented a car. An hour later he was at Henry and Margie's apartment drinking Walker's Deluxe bourbon and Collins mix.

"You know, you two are the biggest success story from our group of five." Nate said, "You stayed married and raised your kids. None of the rest of us succeeded at that."

Nate pointed to the wall, "Who won all those certificates?"

Margie brought hot pizza, "We call it our Wall of Fame."

"Yeah, and back when we had that fire, it was the Wall of Flame," Henry added. "That plaque is from two of the kids. They gave it to me for Father's day; it says Dad of The Year. The kids got the other certificates from school for sports and music."

Nate stood and was surprised how woozy he felt from the liquor, "What's the newspaper article about?"

"That's about Henry and me." Margie said, "Tell Nate about Mr. Bernstein, Henry."

"I met this white guy, named Peter Bernstein, at the kid's school. He told me he was a reporter and asked if he could come by the house and do a story on us. I asked him if he was going to pay us ... cause I don't do interviews for free."

Margie punched Henry in the shoulder, "Come on fool, tell the story right."

"Anyway, Peter came here and talked with the kids and us; he even had dinner with us. He said he was interested in printing our story because it was different. When he said that, I upped the price in my mind."

Impatient, Margie finished the story, "In the end Mr. Bernstein did two articles, one about me and the kids, it got burned up in the fire, and that one on the wall, about Henry. We were famous on the block for a month or two."

"Did you get paid?," Nate asked.

"Does shit come out a goose?," Henry said crying laughing."

"Hey, Man. I left a message on Sonny's phone to see if we can all get together tomorrow night and go out." Henry glanced at Margie as Nate continued. "I'm gonna call him again later. What do you say?"

"We'll see." Henry said coldly.

"That's it?" Nate asked, "We'll see?"

"I might not have anything to wear." Margie said.

"Aw, come on."

"She's right." Henry said, "Why don't you call us tomorrow. Here man, let me pour you another one."

"No, no. I got to drive back out to the motel."

"You can stay here tonight." Margie said.

"No, really, I got to go. I'll call you in the afternoon.

Saturday morning Nate contacted Sonny and arranged to meet him at the Audubon Club, in Harlem.

"I haven't seen or spoken to Henry for years," Sonny admitted.

"Why not?"

"I guess we just lost touch. I went around Frank's old neighborhood and asked for Henry's address or phone number, but nobody had it."

"Well, we'll be three Cervaza Kings again tonight!"

"Alright!, Diamond," Sonny used Nate's nickname.

Nate responded in kind, "See you around eight, Duke."

When Nate called Henry's house, Henry said that he and Margie couldn't make it.

"But, Sonny and his wife are going to be there", Nate said, "and they said that club is jumping."

"Yeah, I know. But we can't make it tonight Nate. I'm sorry man."

"Do you need a ride or something?"

"No it's not that. Margie's got sick with something and she's been in bed all day. She gets like this when she eats the wrong things and drinks. Hey Brother-Rat, have a good time!"

"Okay, Brother-Rat, tell Margie I hope she feels better. I'll tell Sonny you couldn't make it."

"Yeah. You do that."

It was late when Nate arrived at the club, so the introduction to Sonny's wife was made over the loud band noise. She smiled and shook Nate's hand. Nate and Sonny gave the Black Power handshake and patted each other on the shoulders.

The club was jumping and, that night, it featured a James Brown impersonator. The live band kicked up the tempo as Sonny shouted across the table, "Do you still drink bourbon?"

Nate nodded affirmatively.

Sonny lifted a brown paper bag from under the table and handed it to Nate.

He grinned, "Oh yeah!"

The band played until 3:00 AM. Nate drank the black coffee that Sonny's wife got for him and they said their good-byes.

Somehow, Nate made it to Zion Baptist church at 11:30 the next morning. He sat near the back of the little church, as the choir sang. Before long, the whole congregation was singing and shouting. One of the deacons got up from the bench and was doing a jig. Women raised their hands above their heads, clapped in praise and cried. It was as Nate remembered it, except Reverend Lowery's son was now the preacher. Nate tried to remember why his wife had never come to his church.

After the service, he had just enough time to get to the airport and return the rental car before his flight back to Boston.

*   *   *

Finally, the students finished their audiotape training and entered the computer lab.

"Oh, wow! So, that's a card reader?" Randy exclaimed.

The lab instructor, Mr. Hernandez stopped his tour, turned around, and spoke in his Hispanic accent.

"Yes, that's a 6620 card reader. Didn't you learn about them in class?"

"Yeah, sure, but I thought they were desk-size, that's all".

"I did too." Harold said.

Nate and Tom exchanged glances.

Mr. Hernandez reached into his sports jacket, got a pack of cigarettes, lit one and then said, "You fellas are supposed to know the basics."

Almost everyone responded at once. Tom stepped forward and pushed his glasses up on his nose. "Mr. Hernandez we got lots of the basics, but you can't know the size from the photos."

"Yeah," Harold added, "that's why they should have let us into the lab while we were still doing the tapes".

Mr. Hernandez stuttered, "W-W-Well, you guys are the first to use the tape training and t-t-they may make changes f-f-for later classes". Mr. Hernandez puffed on his cigarette, and calmed down.

Dave decided to light up a cigarette too.

"Come on over to the console," Mr. Hernandez said, "and w-w-we'll get started with some diagnostics."

As the weeks went by, the students became more skilled and confident. Mr. Hernandez would, occasionally, leave the lab, after putting bugs in the machines and assigning teams to troubleshoot.

Their confidence lead to a few pranks between the teams. On one occasion, Randy and Harold were squatting near one of the opened electronics chassis, tracing signals with an o-scope while Einstein read off the test points to them.

Dave and the others were standing behind the cabinet when Dave whispered, "Watch this". He took a piece of clear plastic tubing and stuck it through the back of the opened chassis. The other team, doing the troubleshooting, didn't notice. Then Dave, casually, blew cigarette smoke into the tube.

"OH SHIT!" Randy and Harold jumped backward onto the floor. Einstein's eyes were bulging and he said, "What did you guys do?"

"We didn't do anything ... ". Then they started laughing.

Another time, Nate programmed one of the computers to display: "Access Denied" no matter what password was entered. Soon after Mr. Hernandez left the room, he activated the program and pretended to be intent on his own work.

Einstein tried everything to gain access to the computer, then he called out, "Did you guys do something to our computer?"

"What? Every time you have a problem you think it's us?"

Einstein stormed out of the room. Harold and Randy decided to take a break, Nate went to their computer and pushed one button that erased the offending program and returned everything to normal.

No one admitted anything when Mr. Hernandez came in an entered his password without a problem. Randy scratched his head and Harold puffed on his pipe, Einstein stared toward Nate with beady eyes.

By the last weeks of the course, Nate and Tom had honed their SMC skills. They were discussing it at lunch.

"Man, oh man. You know how good we're going to be when we get back. They're always talking about Clarence Brown at the home office."

"You mean Super Nigger?"

"The same. Well, Nationtech ain't seen nothing' yet."

Tom paused and looked over his glasses, "Unless Clarence ... "

"Unless he what?" Slowly, Nate realized Clarence Brown might be a SMC graduate too, "I never thought of that".

On the last day of the Nationtech course the guys were in the break room having morning coffee when Dave said, "Has anybody been getting phone calls from any recruiters?"

"Yeah," half the group answered.

Kurt said, "They told me another company would pay 10% more than I'm making now."

"And give a company car," Harold added.

"It must be because of all the training we got." Dave continued, "I'm still surprised they would do something like that. I mean, ain't that illegal or something."

"You notice," Harold puffed his pipe, "they didn't put anything in writing."

"We better be heading to the classroom."

Gordon Murphy and Brian Scott came in together. "Are you guys ready for your final tests today? Mr. Hernandez is preparing the computers right now."

Nate responded, "Ready as we'll ever be."

Gordon Murphy said, "We have reviewed your suggestions and we'll be making some changes to the course. We have another class starting next week." Then he added, "Of course I won't be changing, because it's my job to piss you off."

Everybody laughed.

"That's just so you'll do your very best while you're here. I want to say, you have all done an outstanding job and I expect that to continue when you're out in the field. You've been trained on the latest equipment we've got and you'll find yourself ahead of some of the senior FSEs. Now, Brian has some books-" There were groans around the table.

"If you'll all hang on for a minute, you're going to appreciate these particular books."

Brian Scott started opening boxes and handing out fat little pocket-sized books. They were guides that had the critical test points, calibration values and shortcuts in them. Each student received one and an envelope containing their certificate.

Dave was first to say, "Hey, we wouldn't have needed all those loose-leaf manuals if we had had these."

Gordon Murphy said, "That's why you only get these now. First, we had to make sure you understood ..."

"THE BASICS!" they all said in unison.

Gordon Murphy shook his head and left the room smiling.

Everyone aced the final open-book test, with the help of their new pocket guides.

Before they left, the group came to Brian Scott's office and gave him a gift they had bought. They also gave him an envelope for Mr. Hernandez.

Brian said, "He can't accept money."

"Oh, it's not money", Nate leaned over and whispered in Brian's ear, "it's all the places we've put bugs in the training computer."

Brian leaned back in his chair, looked up at the ceiling and started laughing.

*   *   *

Returning to Chicago, Nate called his buddy while he was waiting for his luggage.

"Hey, Reggie, I'm back."

"How was it?"

"The school was great. They taught us about mainframes and the peripherals."

"No wonder you were gone for so long. How was Boston?"

"It was nice. I ate a lot of sea food, and got to see Les McCann and The Dells while I was out there."

"Sounds like you had a party."

"You got that right. Now, I'm waiting to get into these mainframes. What's been happening with you."

"I've been traveling a lot for Lorrell. Their customers are spread out and my territory is all the Midwest. Man, they keep me jumping. I put 3,000 miles on my company car so far this year."

"Don't you fly?"

"Some times. But with the o-scope, tool box and suit case it's easier to just drive."

"Yeah, I know what you mean. That's the only thing missing here at Nationtech."

"What?"

"A company car. They pay for me to take taxis, since all my customers are in, or near, downtown Chicago. It's a drag, but I guess I can't have everything. You been to the racetrack lately?"

"Not really. I figured I'd quit while I'm ahead."

"How's your memento?"

"You mean the T-Bird? Man, once I got my company car, my old lady took over the Thunderbird. She calls it her Blackbird."

"I can imagine her cruising around Maywood in it."

"You got the picture." Reggie said.

Nate took a cab to Sheila's sister's condo. No one was there and he found a note on the table.

My Dear Captain,

I didn't want anything to interfere with your computer training, so I waited to tell you that Delbert and I have decided to give our marriage another try. We've spent too many years together to throw our assets away now.

I think you'll agree that you and I are not ready for a deep commitment with each other. So, we should seek out those things and people that give us the best quality of life we can have.

I'm glad we were there for each other. I know you'll be alright, now that you're free and doing the things you enjoy doing.

I truly hope you get closure to the problems of your past.

I will always remain-

Your friend,
Wonder Woman

P.S.- Joan is not renewing her lease at the end of the month. She's in the process of moving in with mother. She agreed to let you stay for the remaining two weeks.

Nate poured a drink, sat and stared out the window until night came. Then he smiled and went to Chances Are restaurant and had dinner alone.

*   *   *

Monday morning, Nate walked into Nationtech's Chicago lobby and Skinny-Minnie was the first to greet him.

"Hello there, stranger."

"Hi. How have you been?," she looked better than he had remembered her.

"Oh, I've been surviving," she got up and came around the desk.

She had on a miniskirt that shamelessly showed her legs, Nate didn't know what to expect; she handed him a strip of paper with a phone number on it.

Does she really expect me to call her home?, Nate wondered.

"Wouldn't you say you owe me at least one drink."

"I'll buy you one after work Friday. Okay?"

"That will be wonderful."

Friday, Nate arranged for Sheila's friend Terry to join them at Playboy Towers. As prearranged, Terry brought the conversation around to such explicit sexual suggestions that Skinny Minnie decided to leave. Nate went outside with her and hailed a taxi. Before she stepped into the taxi, she kissed him on the cheek and handed him a small envelope.

"Thanks for the drink." she said, "Goodnight, Nate."

Nate returned to the table where Terry was sitting sideways with her legs crossed.

"How'd I do?," she asked.

"Too good, you were embarrassing me at one point."

Nate opened the envelope and found a card. It read, 'Dearest Nate, Thank you for whatever this evening brings us. Your friend, Minnie.'

Nate paused and then balled up the note. He looked across the table at Terry. "You want another drink?"

"One more bourbon and I'll screw your brains out."

"Waiter!" Nate called out.

*   *   *

Over the next six weeks, Nate did nothing but PMs on older equipment and no troubleshooting at all. The other, returning students, had similar experiences. One day, they were all sitting in the cafeteria waiting to go to a team meeting.

Tom said, "What's with all these PMs?"

Nate joined in, "I thought we'd be troubleshooting CPUs and memory consoles."

"It's bullshit," Dave said, "that's what it is. I could see how, when we first came back, we'd work with someone for a while doing PMs. But, since I've been on my own, I haven't been assigned to do troubleshooting even once."

"Remember when we started", Tom spoke with his lisp, "all that talk about Clarence Brown? Well, I don't see any career path for us to get to where he's at."

"No. That door was opened and Clarence went through it and now it's slammed shut. They just wanted to have a spook they could show off."

"Hey man, I'm going to check out some of those smaller companies."

"Yeah, me too."

*   *   *

Saturday, Nate and Bill finished making modifications to the Gamma engine teststand and were having lunch.

"You know, Bill, I've wanted to tell you something for a long while. You have never asked me about shares or anything like that. You offered to help me right at the park and ever since then we've been equal partners. You've made parts that I had barely described and that I could not have made by myself. You and Etta have opened your house to me and been very kind. Now, we both know the potential for the Gamma engine and I want you to know that I'm going to draw up some papers giving you half of anything we make."

"Hey man, thank you Nate. But, I don't deserve half. You were working on it for years-"

"Bill, half of what we're going to make will be more than enough for me. Besides, you DO deserve half. Because you believe in the idea that we can do it. Two black men without degrees in physics. We don't have arguments or let our egos get in our way. When we get this done it will inspire many people. They will see that we can do things that seem impossible when we work together."

"Hey, man, I feel the same way. When we first got started down here, I had to explain to Etta that what we were doing was very important. Not just for us, but for everybody."

Etta opened the basement door, "Dinner's ready. Are you going to eat with us Nate?"

"No, not tonight. But thanks."

Without another word, they put the equipment away and Bill turned to Nate and shook his hand firmly. Nate grabbed his attaché case and then said, "See you on Wednesday."

On Wednesday, Etta opened the door for Nate and then said, "Bill has gone to the store. You can go on downstairs, he'll be right back."

When Nate turned the lights on, his eyes lit up. There on the console were two gyro-disks Bill had machined. One was made of aluminum and the other was steel. Bill came downstairs, Nate complimented him on the workmanship and how quickly he'd got the disks made. Then Bill told Nate there was a bigger surprise. He reached under the console, took out something wrapped in paper towels, and gave it to Nate. "Check this out ..."

As Nate unwrapped the object, he noticed it was bigger and much heavier than the new disks. He was suddenly holding a disk like one he had only imagined. His mouth dropped open. Before he could speak, Bill said, "You've always said the disk should be more like a gyroscope so I cut out all the excess material between the hub and the outer rim. This is the largest size that I can make at my job".

"This is great, Bill! How much does it weigh?"

"23 ounces exactly."

"Man, I don't know if the teststand will be able to hold this one."

"That's why we got that brick wall between us and it."

They laughed as they remembered how some of the earlier tests ended when the gyro-disks broke free from the teststand and ricocheted off the walls before either of them could hit the emergency-off switch.

"This is absolutely great." Nate repeated.

"I figured you'd want a heavier disk next."

"You figured right and you certainly got the design right."

On the way home, on the bus, Nate was planning the next phase of testing. Having the new gyro-disk meant the measuring and recording equipment needed to be upgraded as well. They needed to be able to measure the frequency of the thrust impulses. Nate and Reggie had used an o-scope, at Zemit, to see the pulses of a disk. Now an o-scope was needed at the basement lab. It was essential and Nate decided he knew where to get one.

The next day he walked into one of Nationtech's data centers and picked up a Tektronix 453 o-scope that belonged to another service team. He casually walked pass the lounge, down the stairs, pass the police office, and took the o-scope to Bill's basement, on the bus. He'd never done anything like that before and was surprised he wasn't nervous. *Wait until Bill sees this*, he thought.

On Saturday, Bill matched Nate's 'surprise' by uncovering an ASR33 Teletype machine.

"You said we needed a printer for the computer output. This one was sitting in a corner, collecting dust, at my job, for months."

"Oh, shit." Nate said. "I don't believe you did it."

"And I don't believe you did it either."

"Man it would take us forever trying to get the engine done if we follow all the rules. Nobody's going to give us this kind of equipment for free."

"You got that right. I remember how I made my first science fair rocket by soldering tin cans together. And I'll never forget there was a kid named Rob Strom who exhibited right next to me at the fair. He had got permission to run his experiment at a real nuclear reactor." I won a third prize that year and he won a first prize. "I never got over the fact that he had access to such equipment to compete with."

"Now we can compete too, Nate."

"You got that right brother!"

The testing went quite well from then on. The heavy gyro-disk stressed the teststand to its limits. Nate devised a method for filtering out the unwanted vibration signals and was able to isolate the thrust impulses on the o-scope. Other parameters were fed to a tape deck and printed on the Teletype later. During the next few weeks, they gathered more information than they had in the previous year.

*　　　*　　　*

Nate and Tom didn't hide their frustrations about not getting opportunities to use their skills on tasks other than cleaning Nationtech's machines.

After Dave quit, the black secretaries lost their fascination with their brothers. Nate realized he missed Skinny Minnie's doting attention. Then, when Tom left, Nate felt increasingly disenchanted. He met Clarence Brown once. They didn't have time to chat and Nate hadn't seen him since.

So, when the recruiter's inevitable phone call came, Nate asked for a FSE job that included a company car.

"I've got openings in the medical field." Paul Riley said, "Would you consider one of those?"

"Only if I get to work with computers."

"Okay, Nate. I'll see what I can do."

Alan White approached Nate one day and then said, "I heard you were thinking about leaving."

Cautiously, Nate said, "Yeah, what about it?"

"To tell you the truth, I wasn't surprised when the other Afro-American guys left the company, but you ... "

"Me what?"

"You seem to like this stuff so much, Nate. Some of the guys spoke about how gung-ho you are. I can't understand why you would want to give it up."

"How long have you been here, Alan?"

"Eleven years."

Nate looked at him and then said, "That's why you can't understand."

With all the diversity hiring that was going on in the electronics industries, it didn't take Paul Riley very long. Nate accepted an offer from Serian Medical Company.

It'll be great having a company car and airline flights again, he thought, *it's time to celebrate.*

Nate dialed Terry's work number.

*   *   *

At the exit interview from Nationtech, Neidermeyer closed the door to his office and then said, "I wanted to talk to you about this resignation, Nate. What seems to be the problem? Did one of those smaller computer companies get to you?"

Nate ignored the second question, "It really boils down to your promotion policies. During my interview, you talked about Clarence Brown and the exciting things he's doing. That sounds good, but, in reality, there's no career path to get to where he's at. Some of the other guys I'm working with have been here for years and they haven't moved up very much. And then, I got all that training on the latest equipment, but only the senior guys get to do that kind of work."

"I see. You're frustrated with the pace of things around here. But that's the way large corporations work, Nate. I had expected you to give Clarence Brown a run for his money. You have a point about his career being special. But, have you considered all the benefits we offer here? And Nationtech isn't going to go away, you know; there's a degree of security here."

"Mr. Neidermeyer, I mean no disrespect, but I'm not looking for security; I'm looking for a place where I can use my talents and develop my skills to the maximum."

"Do you think you'll be able to do that better somewhere else, Nate?"

"I don't know; I just feel I won't be able to do it here at Nationtech."

*   *   *

Saturday, as Nate and Bill prepared their teststand for another run, they heard a knock on the basement window.

"Bill," Etta called out through the opaque glass, "I need help with the groceries." Bill headed up the wooden spiral staircase. Nate went up to use the restroom. When he emerged he had to step over bags of groceries that were piled on the floor. Etta came in with more bags and Nate said, "Can I help? Are there many more?"

122

"Hi, Nate. Yes you can 'cause I've got to get into that bathroom." She threw her coat over a chair and brushed past. Nate met Bill at the front door, grabbed the bags and Bill about-faced to get more from the car.

He returned puffing and then said, "This is the last of them."

"Man! You guys really like to eat."

"When you get paid just once a month you have to stock up. Etta saves all the coupons and we go to the food club and buy whatever's on sale."

Etta had the refrigerator open and was simultaneously putting food onto shelves above and below. She reminded Nate of a postal worker sorting mail.

"Bill, will you pick up the girls at 5:30 from their gym practice? I'm tired and I'll be fixing dinner by then."

"Okay, Honey, which gym did they go to? The one at the church or the one down at the school?"

"I told you on Saturday they go over to the church."

Nate excused himself , "I'll leave you two to your chores."

Bill called after Nate, "I'll be right down as soon as we get this food put away."

As he descended, Nate heard Etta saying, "Bill, you haven't been to any of the girls' games lately or any of their practice sessions."

Nate hardly noticed when Bill came downstairs because he was reviewing computer printouts. He had run Gamma programs on Nationtech's mainframe while he was doing a PM. He ran several projections of what he expected from the next Gamma tests.

Just then, Etta called down the stairs, "Alright you guys, I got sandwiches and french fries on the table." Etta joined them and Nate related an incident that happened a few weeks before.

"Some friends came over and they brought an African student with them. I asked him whether he felt there would ever be an African space program. When he said he didn't think so, I asked him why not. Then I went OFF when he said he felt The White Man had something special in his head that allowed him to invent things and go to the moon!

The reason I was so upset is that I believe the greatness of our race will not come from the USA. It will be from Africa one day. And to hear an African student say what he said just set me off. I told him, anybody that fills a thirty-five story rocket with liquid oxygen and hydrogen can go to the moon." I explained that the laws of physics work the same for everybody. Then I told him not to ever think or say what he said again. Even I was surprised at how I reacted. But we'll never even try things with the kind of thinking he had. I just want to show that God doesn't play favorites."

While still chewing Bill said, "Hey man, I agree with you 100%."

Then Etta added "That's what we teach our girls, that they can be anything if they put their mind to it. What about your kids Nate? Me and Bill were wondering if any of them are interested in science." Bill looked toward Etta with surprise.

"To tell you the truth, Etta, I don't know what they like."

Bill said "Hey man, if you don't want to talk about it ..."

"No, no. It's alright. I have wondered about the same thing myself. You see, my father was the first black engineering foreman at Standard Oil Company and my mother was good at chemistry and math in college. So, I figure maybe that's where I inherited whatever talents I have. I'd like to think that some of it got passed on to the next generation, but I just don't know."

"Did they ever see you launch some of your rockets or stuff like that?" Bill asked

"Oh yeah, I took them to the MiniLab sometimes. And before that, I was building everything at home. I remember when I was building the tracking system and working late at night, sometimes one of them would come quietly into the room and scare me. But, I haven't been communicating with them since I left New York. Its better that way."

"I don't know, Nate." Etta said, "I'd have to communicate with my kids no matter what. And it seems like they should know about the things you're doing. Where else are they going to find a role model who builds space engines?"

"I know what you mean. And you notice I haven't talked about my family in New York before ..."

"Was it because of Beatrice?"

"No, not at all. In fact, I met Beatrice after my wife and I had broken up. So I don't have any guilt feelings about that. It's just that the breakup was very bad. I loved my family and did the best I could."

Nate was staring at the wall as he spoke. Bill thought about stopping him, but didn't.

"My wife didn't think my work was important. She even told me I should have opened a taxi business instead of the MiniLab. At one point I saw how ironic everything was because I got a patent pending on one of the Gamma engines just one month after we broke up for good."

"So, what about all your equipment and notes at the MiniLab?" Bill asked.

"All of that stuff was moved to an old abandoned building in Harlem on 125th street, where me and Ernest lived for a while. I always kept my Gamma engine notebooks in a safe place. When I came to Chicago, they were the only technical stuff that I brought.

I tried to forget about the Gamma principle because everyone kept saying 'It can't work' and 'it violates Newton's laws'. But I knew that my experiments had worked and I believed what I'd told that African student ... about God giving ideas to anyone. Besides, I saw the Gamma principle everywhere; even when I looked at ceiling fans rocking back and forth. So, I slowly got started working on the engine again. Then I met a guy in Washington Park ..."

Bill finished with, "And the rest is history ... No, I mean *will* be history."

Etta put her elbow on the table and rested her chin in her hand, "But, why is it taking so long?"

"Tell her what you told me, Nate", Bill stammered.

"It's almost over, Etta," Nate said, "I finally realized we could keep on improving our designs and getting a little better performance forever. So, I've come up with a better plan," he paused and got up, "Hang on for just a minute, I brought it in my briefcase."

Etta said, "You two can go on back downstairs; I've got things to do."

Nate showed Bill the step-by-step script he'd written for the Pendulum Test.

Bill read it and then said, "I can't get over the fact that we don't have to actually fly the engine to prove that it works".

"That's the cool part Bill. The pendulum test cancels out the effect of gravity and it will show any net thrust that is generated. So, the

Gamma engine won't have to lift itself. All that it has to do is deflect the pendulum, and keep it deflected, in one direction."

"Well these four gyro-chambers on the new engine", Bill pointed to a drawing, "should cancel out the lateral translations."

Nate grinned and then said, "You're right about that."

"Come on man", Bill said, "what are you grinning about?"

"It's just that I remember when we started working together, you used to tease me about the technical terms I use, like "real-time" and all that. And now here you are talking about lateral translations instead of 'sideways motions'.

Bill laughed. "You're right. I've learned a lot these past years. You know it's been almost two years that we've been working down here. I bet nobody would believe that two black men would be this dedicated. I don't think we've missed a single Wednesday or Saturday."

"No, not one. I have to tell you though, there was one Saturday morning that I was in a hotel downtown with some broad, and I looked at the clock and told her I had to leave. I tried to explain to her that it was something very important that I was working on and guess what she said."

"She didn't believe you?"

"Not at all", she told me, 'Rush on back to 'her' if you must.'

"Well, you should have known," Bill glanced toward the stairs before continuing, "women ain't never going to think anything is more important than they are."

"And they're right - except on ... ", Nate paused.

Together they laughed and then said "Wednesday evenings and Saturday mornings."

Nate took a large drawing from his briefcase and spread it on the workbench.

"Now, here's what we need to do ... "

*　　　　*　　　　*

The night before the Pendulum Test, Nate tossed and turned for hours. He awoke in a sweat at one point. In the morning, he didn't remember his dreams, but felt there had been a lot of them. Not much light was coming through the shades, but the clock showed it was

10 AM. He got up and peeped outside at a cloudy gray sky. Nate became alert when he remembered what day it was; *this is the day of The Pendulum Test.* He reached under his bed and picked up a cigar box containing the disks that would propel his Gamma engine today.

He unwrapped one and marveled at the beauty of the precision-machined piece of metal. Until a few weeks before, these disks existed only in his imagination. Bill machined each disk at his job, during his lunch breaks. Nate weighed them at his job on a triple-beam balance. They were duplicates to within 2-grams.

It was cold and humid as Nate pulled out of his parking space. He drove pass North Western's campus and thought about the physics being taught there. As he headed toward Lake Shore Drive, he thought about Dr. Fox and Dr. Hoydash back at New York University. He wondered why the two professors hadn't got more excited when they saw his earlier engine running. They produced mathematical descriptions of the relative motions of the engine parts, but they insisted it couldn't work for the reasons Nate believed. They had no alternative theories.

As Nate drove through downtown Chicago he remembered New York patent attorneys Dierman & Bierman who had offered to patent his invention for free, if he could show it in action. They told Nate he didn't have to wait until he made it fly. "Just make it propel itself on wheels" they had said. Nate demonstrated that two days later. He had the propulsive disks enclosed in a shoebox, which was taped onto a toy truck. When he switched the engine on, the toy car wobbled across the floor, and even went up an incline. He remembered how the deal with the attorneys fell apart when they decided they wanted a fee after all.

Passing the Museum of Science and Industry, Nate thought of the time he and his dad had gone there. He had felt very comfortable examining and discussing the exhibits with the father he met when he was twenty-seven years old.

Going through the South-side Nate thought about his and Ernest's aerospace efforts: the MiniLab, PAE in Philadelphia, the black engineers at aerospace exhibitions who said they didn't think black people could ever do those things by themselves, and the winos in Harlem who said it hurt their heads to even think about such things. Statements like, "Why can't black people pull themselves up by their bootstraps?" echoed in his head.

A truck almost hit him as he merged onto the Dan Ryan Expressway. Soon he was cruising pass the Illinois Institute of Technology where he had applied for a job as an electronics technician and got turned down..

Now he realized, he should have taken Bob Jones' advice earlier and done a pendulum test earlier. But, he always felt getting a device to fly would be the ultimate test, and it wasn't until today that he could test a totally isolated engine. *All that is in the past,* Nate thought as he pulled into Bill's driveway. Bill was standing in the doorway; he wasn't smiling.

"Hey, man, I wish you had called." Bill said, "I desperately wanted to get in touch with you."

"What's up?"

"Come on downstairs, I have to show you something."

"Is anything wrong?"

"Well, in a way 'Yes', but in a way 'No'".

Nate struggled to be patient. He didn't want any glitches at this point. Once in the basement, Nate saw the Gamma-815 engine on the workbench; only it didn't look right. He walked over to it, looked at it from different angles, turned and waited for Bill's explanation.

"Nate, I tried and tried, but I couldn't get the upper gears to mesh right with the main drive shaft; the lower gears worked just fine, but the upper ones kept binding when I rotated them by hand. If I had more time … " Bill looked like he wanted to cry.

Nate's mind was racing. He knew if Bill tried and couldn't get it done, the gears just couldn't get done. Determined that nothing was going to stop the Pendulum Test that day, Nate said, "It's okay, Bill. I know you did your best. We'll just hang the 810 engine in a pendulum configuration."

"But the 810 engine uses heavy electric motors and you said the whole idea was to-"

"Yes, yes I know", Nate headed toward the teststand. "but any sustained deflection during the P-test will mean that we have a net thrust. Besides, with the 810 we can control both motors and keep them in the resonance range. The 815 would have quickly passed through resonance as the flywheel spun down. We can still prove that the engine gives a net thrust today!"

Hours later, they had the bulky engine suspended on 8-foot chains. The monitoring equipment was attached; all the preliminary teststand checks were completed; everything was ready. Nate entered The Pit and took two small vials of liquid from his pocket. He carefully placed them under the engine inside a cinder block. He packed dirt from the ground to hold them in place.

With Nate's approval, Bill's brother, George, was going to be filming the test with his 8mm-movie camera. He was to only film them working at the console. He was so enthralled, he barely heard Bill say, "Bringing Lower motor to 600 rpm", followed by Nate saying, "Starting the upper motor." Then Bill and Nate alternated in cadence as they read from their checklists:

"Lower motor steady at 600 …"

"Bringing upper motor to 25% …"

"I'm seeing pulses on the scope now."

"Upper motor at 50% …"

"II I pulses are starting."

"Upper motor at 70% …"

The humming noise in the test chamber, on the other side of the brick wall grew louder.

"Upper motor at 85%. We're almost at resonance."

"Turning on lift sensor."

"IH pulses coming into phase."

"I'm seeing a little vibration on the lift gauge."

"Upper motor at 90% …" Nate shouted over the pulsing noise.

Bill shouted back "The lift needle is still vibrating."

"Upper motor at full power! We're in resonance mode."

By now, it sounded as if they had a loud propeller engine in the pit. The metal clacking sound was gone; all the parts had synchronized and the engine emitted a loud hum.

Nate and Bill watched the instrument panel intently. George wanted to go over to the porthole and see the engine but he was riveted by the spectacle.

"DO YOU FEEL THAT?" Bill yelled.

"YEAH!" Nate said, "Vibrations are coming through the floor."

"Should we shut down?" Bill yelled.

"NO, KEEP IT RUNNING!" Nate said and jumped to the reinforced pit window. He was astounded to see the lower electric motor glowing yellow and the glow was spreading up the support chains as he watched. "HOLY SHIT!"

"What is it, Nate?"

"You got to see this, Bill." Nate called out, "George, quick, get over here with the camera!." As Nate turned to relieve Bill at the console, the engine tore itself apart. Instantly, Bill's hand slapped down hard on the emergency-stop button.

George stumbled and fell. Then he heard rotating metal screeching on metal; its frequency slowly decreasing.

Nate and Bill were going through their shutdown procedure.

"Tape recorders off."

"Scope off"

"Instruments off."

"DC off"

"AC off"

Bill jumped up and peered through the view port. "Must have been the couplings," he said.

"Yeah, that's what it sounds like. And those were the reinforced ones too."

"What did you see, Nate?"

"It was incredible, the rear motor was glowing yellow and the chains too!"

"The chains were glowing?"

"Yeah! Whatever was happening, made the glow creep up the chains."

"What does that mean?"

"Bill, I don't know."

It was only then that George was able to speak. "Man, that shit was awesome! It sounded like it was going to take-off. I thought the ground was shaking."

"Did you film that glow?" Bill asked.

"I fell, man and by the time I got up it was too late."

Nate unlatched the wooden door, and went into the small chamber. George started to follow, but Bill touched his arm and then said, "We don't allow anyone in there, but you can look through the porthole." George stepped aside. Bill entered the pit and found Nate staring at metal shards everywhere.

Just then, the basement door opened and Etta yelled down the stairs, "What the hell are you doing down there? It felt like the whole house was shaking."

"Everything's alright." Bill said, "Some parts broke loose, that's all."

"But, stuff fell off the dresser upstairs; that never happened before."

"I'm sorry Etta", Nate said, "the engine must be sitting on one of the beams of the house or something. We're all finished running it for tonight."

George asked, "Did it do what you wanted before it exploded?" Nate and Bill looked at each other and rushed over to examine the strip chart recorder. Nate rolled the chart-paper back past the jagged line that recorded the engine's destruction. Then he saw it; the needle had registered a small, sustained, positive deflection before the explosion.

He turned to Bill, who was looking over his shoulder and then said, "We did it" with tears in his eyes, "We did it"

Bill took the chart-paper from Nate's hands and stared at the ink marking.

"We did it. We, actually, did it. And we got the proof right here."

George started filming again and then said, "I thought it was going to take off."

Nate turned around to the camera, smiled and then said, "Not quite yet, George."

"What's next?" Bill asked after George left.

Nate looked at him and then said, "They're not going to believe us until we make a Gamma fly, Bill. And to do that, the mass ratio has to be an order of magnitude better than we've done."

"What do you mean?"

Tears were in Nate's eyes, "It's too heavy, man. It's too damn heavy with the gyros."

"Then we're done?"

"No." Nate smiled, "We've opened a new door, Bill. What I saw was a yellow glow in there before the engine broke apart and I think I know what it was."

"What, Nate, what was it?"

"Some sort of a plasma."

Bill sat for a moment, thinking, then asked, "But, why haven't we seen it before?"

"All the conditions must have been just right tonight. That Russian guy, Kozyrev, reported that his gyroscopes behaved differently at odd times too. I'll tell you what I believe ..."

Bill waited.

"When the engine swayed the pendulum and kept thrusting, something was given off that made the chains radiate. Energy was being transferred and given off, Bill!"

"That's great, but that brings us back to my question, What's next?"

Nate didn't feel comfortable telling Bill the truth, but he had too. "We've moved into a whole new realm. To do the next step, we're gonna need a backer ... somebody with big bucks.

I'm going away to computer class for a few weeks. That will give us both time to think."

When Bill went upstairs to the toilet, Nate examined the shattered teststand again. He moved debris out of the way and saw what he suspected – the vials, that had contained liquids, were empty.

Kozyrev was right, Nate thought, *oppositely rotating molecules.*

Searian Medical

Nate peered at the gray cloud layer, that blanketed Los Angeles, outside the window of the Boeing-737. It disappeared, as the airplane sank into it and got closer to the ground. Looking upward, Nate saw only blue sky. He felt a sense of excitement and remembered his dad saying he'd enjoy California.

During the cab ride from the airport, Nate realized he hadn't felt this way since leaving New York City. The sunshine, and the people he saw, invigorated him. The driver took Nate through Compton and Riverside, where Nate saw lots of his people.

At Searian's training center, there was the usual sign-in and introductions to other students from as faraway as Japan. The coordinator gave them info sheets with a map showing the locations of restaurants and their motel.

"You fellas will have to share hotel rooms", she said.

Nate was paired with a Lebanese guy, named Sammy Hassan. At dinner that night, Sammy proudly described his and his wife's successes at suing people.

"We like the American legal system", he said.

The next morning the students were introduced to their instructor – Ray Stout.

"So, we meet again, Nate LaChae."

"Yep. How've you been, Ray?"

"I'm well. I was surprised when I saw your name on the student list. Last I heard, you were with Lorrell."

"That's a long story. A lot has changed since then."

"I hope you're not going to tape record me again."

"Not this time, Ray. I've got some experience with computer systems now."

"Good." Ray turned, "Now what about the rest of you fellas."

Nate felt more comfortable as each of the students' described their backgrounds and experience. This time he wasn't a novice. There was another black student named Marshall Bell, who had been to L.A., several times, for training on other systems.

Sammy had the least experience of anyone there. He leaned over and whispered, "Nate, if you teach me about computers, I'll teach you about suing people. Okay?"

"Deal." Nate laughed and they shook hands.

Nate's experience with the Lorrell systems helped him whiz through the first days of the training. He quickly fell into the routine of getting up, having breakfast and riding to the plant with Sammy, Marshall and another student. On their fourth day, Nate drove out of the motel parking lot, turned onto Slauson Avenue and stomped on the breaks.

"Holly shit!"

"What?"

The students gasped in amazement as they stared down the road at mountains.

"I didn't see them any other morning."

"Me neither. And I don't remember there being clouds in the way."

Cars behind them began honking and Nate stepped on the gas.

"The smog must have obscured our view."

"But the sky was clear."

"L.A. smog is like that", Marshall said.

"You're saying, we've been looking into smog the past mornings and that's why we didn't see the mountains?"

"Well," Marshall said, "they didn't move 'em in last night."

During Friday's lunch break, Marshall said, "Hey Nate, You wanna hang out tonight? My girlfriend, Cynthia, knows some cool night clubs."

"You bet", Nate said.

That evening, Marshall drove with a lit joint in his mouth, "The thing I like about Cynthia is she looks exactly like my ex-wife."

"I would've thought that would be a bad thing." Nate said.

"No, man." Marshall said, "I get to have the best without the mess. My old lady was nuts; she threw a brick through my windshield one time."

"Damn."

"Cynthia doesn't behave like her, they just look alike. She and some friends are meeting us at the Rainbow Room."

Nate heard the music as Marshall drove pass the entrance and he saw bouncers patting people down at the front door.

Inside, Marshall spotted Cynthia at the bar. They joined them and Marshall introduced Nate. Cynthia introduced her girlfriend, Jeanette, who had a huge Afro. Her v-neck dress revealed her deep cleavage.

The music was so loud Nate barely heard Cynthia ask, "Where you from, Nate?"

"New York City."

"The Big Apple, huh?' Cynthia said, "Well, this is how we do it here, baby." She pulled Marshall onto the dance floor.

Nate turned and gazed at Jeanette, who was staring at the people on the crowded dance floor. Her high cheekbones and square jaw revealed Indian ancestry.

"You want to dance?" Nate asked.

"Not right now." Jeanette spoke in a deep voice, "How good is your aim?"

He looked into her almond eyes. "It all depends on what I'm aiming at."

She handed him a decorative lighter and then said, "Will you see if you can light my cigarette with this?"

The lighter had an opening, in its center, that was too small to insert the cigarette. And the flame didn't extend beyond the casing.

Jeanette picked up her glass, "I think you have to line the hole up with the cigarette and draw on it."

Nate managed to get the cigarette lit and passed it to Jeanette. He took the seat that became vacant next to her and waved his hand at the bartender.

"Thanks, Nate." Jeanette said, holding the lighter up, "This thing was a special gift."

"From that special someone?"

"No. Nothing like that." Jeanette smiled, "It's from a girlfriend."

"Oh?" Nate's raised his eyebrows.

Jeanette almost spilled her drink, "It's not like that either."

"All I said was 'Oh'." Nate replied as Marshall and Cynthia returned.

"You finally got that lighter to work, girl?"

"Nate helped me."

Cynthia eyed Nate up and down, "Fast work Nate. You just got here and you already lit a fire."

*   *   *

It had all started in Chicago, five months before, when Nate dialed Paul Riley's number.

"You found a computer job for me yet?"

"Nate." Paul always seemed excited, "I've been trying to get in touch with you. Don't you have a phone?"

"No. Not right now. What's up?"

"I've got something you'll be interested in." Paul said, "It's with a medical company and they use computers in their newest products."

"Is it Field Service?"

"Yeah, it's a Tech Support position with Searian Medical. They need someone to install their new body scanners in hospitals. There's only one position open, so you better call this number right away."

The next day, Nate sat in Larry Hughes' office. Larry's toothy smile could disappear as quickly as it could appear. His finely groomed hair swept down across his forehead. He leaned back in his chair, with his thumbs in his vest pockets of his expensive suit, and asked, "So, now that I've given you a tour of the PhoCon manufacturing area, do you think you would like the job?"

"It seems interesting. But I won't really know if I like it, until I try it."

"Let me put it another way then," Larry said, "What interests you the most?"

"The minicomputers."

"I see." Larry glanced at Nate's resume again. "You understand there will be a lot of travel? Some of it might be international?"

"Yes, that's no problem. I'd enjoy it."

"Part of the job will be training the local service guys too."

"That's fine with me."

"Well then, Nate, I believe this will be a good match up. You seem to be somebody I could depend on and that's very important. I'm determined to make this project a success. Do you have any questions?"

"Just one. Do you provide a company car?"

"No, but there is a car allowance that's enough to cover a car note." Larry paused, "Will that work for you?"

"Yes, sure," Nate replied, not knowing how he would buy a car.

Nate's counterpart, Victor Sagan, was out of town doing a PhoCon installation. So, Nate spent his first week with Phillip Hertz, a small man with a nervous laugh. All the women liked Phil for some reason that Nate couldn't fathom. Larry Hughes secretary, Denise, was the prettiest and the friendliest of the lot. She and Phil were always making references to private jokes.

Nate was the only one in the group, other than the managers, that wore a tie.

One day Phil said, "You sure like to dress up, don't you?"

"It makes me feel good."

Denise walked up behind Nate, "And it makes you look cool too."

"I, ah … thanks," Nate said.

"Don't listen to her," Phil said, "she used to be a truck driver. Anyone not in greasy overalls looks cool to her."

"Your jeans aren't greasy, Phil," Denise said, "and you don't look cool to me."

"That's 'cause I'm hot, babe."

"Yeah, so is Technesium."

Nate laughed. "What is Technesium, anyway? I keep hearing that word."

"It's a radioactive isotope." Phil said, "Come on, I'll show you how we use it for testing the PhoCons."

Phil glanced toward Denise, "Later, Babe."

"Stay cool, Nate." Denise said.

"I think she likes you, man."

"Thought you said she's married."

"She is." Phil smiled devilishly.

Out on the production floor, Phil picked up a square plastic plate that had tubes of red liquid inside.

"This is a Technesium source."

"And it's okay to hold it in your hand like that?"

"Yeah," Phil chuckled, "it has a half-life of only six hours."

Nate remembered reading that radiation dissipation is measured in how long it takes to diminish to half its potency.

"But, I wouldn't recommend sitting on it." Phil said.

"Show me how the computer works."

"You have a one-track mind, don't you?"

"I just want to get to the heart of everything."

"Okay, let's go into the lab."

Phil shared his knowledge with Nate. And by lunchtime, Nate understood the basic operations of the Photcon's computer and how it controlled the system.

"Larry wants us to come up with a way to run diagnostics on the system."

"Us?"

"Yep. Welcome to tech support."

Nate spent most of his time developing a paper-tape reader for feeding diagnostics into the system. He was pleased to see how Larry Hughes supported his efforts. At one point, Nate went to PhoCon's chief engineer, Norman Prescott's office to get circuit diagrams.

Prescott's premature balding head made him look older than his thirty-six years. He looked at Nate incredulously and asked, "You mean you're the one developing the diagnostic hardware?"

"No, I'm just making the interface for loading the diagnostics."

"Says who?"

"Says Larry Hughes." Nate cocked his head, "Why?"

"I'll take it up with Larry." Prescott turned away.

"What about the schematics I asked for?"

"I said, I'll take it up with Larry."

Nate wasn't sure what to do or say, so he headed for Larry Hughes office. Denise told him Larry was out of town, so Nate went to Phil's cubicle and described Prescott's attitude.

"Listen, Nate," Phil said, "You need to say that we're working on the paper-tape project together, okay?"

"But, we're not working together on that part of it."

"I know that and you know that. But if we're going to get this approved, the engineers want to deal with someone they know."

"That's not it and you know it, Phil."

"Nate, I'm on your side. Really I am. But if we want to get this done on time, we don't need to get into a pissing contest with Norman Prescott."

"It's not right." Nate said.

"Come on, Nate. We're not going to change that asshole's views anytime soon and we need to get this done." Then he added, "Larry knows you're the one doing it and he's the one that signs your bonuses."

Nate wrung his hands and looked around the cubicle as if an answer were posted on the walls. He felt hot; he took off his tie. Then he handed some papers to Phil and then said, "I need this information."

"I'll get it for you, Nate."

Denise came to the cubicle, "Anybody for lunch?"

"Be right with you, Hon." Phil said.

"You going to join us, Nate?" Denise asked.

"Not this time, Denise."

"Phil's buying, he just doesn't know it yet."

Phil opened his mouth and looked shocked.

"No, thanks", Nate said, "I'll take a rain-check."

Nate finished the paper-tape interface on schedule and got the diagnostics running before Larry Hughes returned. Phil made sure Nate got the credit for it and they never mentioned the Prescott incident again.

"You're doing good work, Nate." Larry said, "Phil holds you in high regards. I've already approved a pay raise for you."

"Thank you, Larry, I appreciate it."

"I want you to meet Vic in Texas on Monday. You two will be installing a system down there with the local service guy. Immediately after that, I've got you scheduled for training out in California. Is that going to cause problems at home?"

"No, Larry, I'm not married."

*   *   *

Vic met Nate at the airport and gave him a limp handshake. They walked, in silence, to the parking lot.

"Throw your bag in the back and we can get going."

"Shouldn't we put it in the trunk?"

"Doesn't make any difference. Just put it on the back seat."

"Did you start the installation yet?" Nate asked.

"The crates didn't arrive until yesterday, so all we've done is start unpacking. You haven't missed anything important."

"Good. Larry said this may be the only time we work together."

"Yeah", Vic lit a cigarette as he merged onto the highway, "It's pretty straightforward, you'll see."

"How long have you been doing this?"

Vic exhaled and leaned his head from side to side as if mocking Nate's inquisitiveness.

"I was hired six weeks before you" he said and turned the radio way up.

Glad I won't be working with this guy a lot, Nate thought.

They spent the rest of the day unpacking the crates containing the PhoCon system.

During dinner at the motel, they discovered their only common interest was technology and women. After several glasses of Merlot, they shared stories of their prowess with the fairer sex. They parted laughing after the waitress told them they were both "full of cow dung".

The next morning Bill Rourke, the local serviceman, met them at the hospital site. He was friendly, wore cowboy boots and spoke with a strong Texas drawl. The three of them got started immediately.

Nate tried to help a couple of times, before being instructed to do so by Vic, and was told, "Not that. What do you think you're doing?"

"Just trying to help out."

"I'll show you two what to do", Vic said, "Just watch me, okay?"

Nate and Bill looked at each other and stood back.

The rest of the installation went smoothly and when the PhoCon passed all its tests Vic said, "Now, watch this."

He de-tuned one of the circuits so the video image was slightly out of focus in one corner.

"That's so I don't miss my flight."

"What are you talking about?" Bill asked.

"You'll see." Vic called to one of the medical technicians. "You can tell the doctor we're ready for a patient."

The team waited while Doctor Schmerhorn's patient was scanned. When the film was developed, Dr. Schemerhorn complained about one corner of the image. Vic winked toward Nate and Bill and then said, "Let me see what I can do about that."

They watched as Vic re-adjusted the circuit.

"Try it now", he told the doctor.

The patient, still on the table, was scanned again.

"Now, that's much better." Dr. Schemerhorn said. "That's the quality we need. I'll sign-off now."

As Bill drove them to the airport, Vic explained, "You're going to find, a lot of doctors are finicky and they want a little more out of their machines. I learned the hard way, my first time. I tuned the machine perfectly and the doctor wasn't satisfied. I spent two hours showing him the image couldn't be improved. So now, I misadjust the damn thing on purpose. Then, when they want that 'little bit better image', I can give it to them and not miss my flight."

They drank beer at the airport and got to hear the servers singing "Cotton Eye Joe".

*   *   *

Nate and Vic traveled, separately, around the country installing PhoCons in major hospitals. They trained the local service engineers and met some of the country's top cancer doctors. Nate found the doctors to be friendly people who insisted their equipment be in tip-top shape. And he made sure each machine that he installed was.

After one installation, an elderly woman was lying on the scanner table waiting for the doctor. Nate walked by in his lab coat and the lady asked, "Are you a doctor?"

"No. I'm the man who makes sure this machine works right."

She turned her head away and then said, "Oh."

"You're not afraid, are you?"

The lady's gaze darted from one part of the machine to another, finally stopping on Nate.

"Yes", she said, staring into his eyes.

Nate held her hand and then said, "Don't be afraid. I've made sure this machine will take the best pictures for your doctor. It will show him exactly where the problem is."

Dr. Ryan came in. "Practicing without a license?"

Nate snatched his hand away, "Oh, no, I was just reassuring her about the equipment."

"That's fine, Nate. Mrs. Juarez is one of our best patients." The doctor leaned over his patient, "We've been waiting for weeks to have a scan on this new machine, haven't we?"

Mrs. Juarez shook her head, positively.

On the plane ride home, Nate thought about Mrs. Juarez. *I hope the PhoCon images help the doctor cure her. I really should practice my SMC techniques more often.* He closed his eyes and projected loving energy to Mrs. Juarez. He visualized her being bathed in a white light.

There was one doctor, in Utah, who called the plant and asked for someone to come and check on Nate's work. Nate heard about it from Phil Hertz and was surprised since the doctor had given him no hint of dissatisfaction. Larry Hughes never mentioned sending Vic, to pacify the doctor.

Nate reminisced about the first time he went to Jeanette's place. It was the same night Marshall Bell introduced them at the Rainbow Room nightclub. Nate was the designated driver and he had a contact-high by the time he dropped Marshall and Cynthia off at her place.

As they continued, Jeanette lit a joint and passed it to Nate. He dragged too hard on it and started coughing.

"Easy, Nate. Easy."

"That stuff is good, Jeanette. I played chess with some guys in Chicago that smoked, but I never did."

"My friend grows it in her back yard." Jeanette said as they pulled into the carport at her condo.

Nate parked the car and they kissed passionately until Jeanette said, in her deep sultry voice, "Let's go to the pool. It's never crowded this late in the evening."

"I don't have swimming trunks."

"I got some that'll probably fit you."

"What about your boys?"

"They'll be asleep, if the baby-sitter gave them their bath."

As they got out of the car, Nate asked, "Do you have a Jacuzzi?"

"Yeah."

They walked on a path that wound through, lush plants. The smell of lit fireplaces met them. Soon they were in their swimsuits, heading toward the pool. Nate walked behind Jeanette, admiring her toned body. It took some coaxing to get Nate out of the Jacuzzi and into the pool. He dove in and glided across the width of the pool under water.

"I have a confession," he said, "I can't swim."

"I figured that out already. Come on, it's easy. Watch me." She swam gracefully to the other side, turned and then said "come and get it." She waved her legs open and closed in the water.

Nate stroked, kicked and doggy-paddled himself across.

"See, I told you it was easy."

"I guess I just needed that extra incentive."

"Don't stop now, you're doing good."

"Can I get some more incentive?"

"Maybe later."

Back in the condo, they showered, then sat on the shag carpet eating pizza and drinking Sangria.

"I like your place," Nate said.

"I have to move out of here when the lease is up."

Jeanette passed a joint to Nate and asked, "Are you married?"

"No. Are you?"

"Yes, but we're separated. You have any kids?"

"Two boys," Nate said with a straight face.

"Why did you break up?"

"Basically, because we out grew each other."

"That's the same with me. I had his baby and helped him through college, then he decided he wanted out."

Nate poured more wine, "Why did you say had his baby?"

"Because Derrick's father is in Chicago. You want more ice in that drink?"

"No, I don't want you to get up."

Nate pulled her to him and they kissed long and hard.

"Stay with me tonight, Nate."

"I can't Jeanette. In the morning, the other students will need the car to go to the plant."

Jeanette got up and changed the music. She played the O-Jays singing 'Heaven Must Be Like This'. Then she started to dance and Nate joined her.

"Are you sure, your boys are asleep?"

"We don't have to worry about them. They'll sleep through the night."

After midnight, Nate headed back to his motel. He fell asleep at the wheel and bounced up onto the sidewalk on Crenshaw Boulevard. Two winos leaped out of his path as he stomped on the brakes and narrowly missed crashing through a storefront.

The next weekend, Nate rented a car for a month and spent every night with Jeanette. He quickly bonded with her young sons, Derrick and Dikeba, by taking them to the gaming arcade on Saturday mornings.

Everyone was comfortable with the arrangement, especially Jeanette's brother Dennis.

"Hey man, I'm glad to meet you." Dennis said, "My sister needs a good man and the boys can't stop talking about you."

"I heard about you too, Dennis, even heard you play a little chess."

Dennis rolled his eyes, "I know how to move the pieces around."

"We'll have to play sometime."

"If Cheryl, here, will let me." Dennis grabbed his wife in a neck lock. "Man, white women want all your attention."

Jeanette said, "What are you complaining about? You married her."

"Don't start with me Jeanette. You know I don't want nothing from a black woman. I been there and ain't going back – ever again."

Too soon, Nate was saying goodbye to Jeanette and the boys at the Airport. Despite Nate's assurances, Jeanette cried.

"I'll send for you soon. You'll see."

"I love you Nate."

"Love you too."

*   *   *

During the days that followed, Nate mused about Jeanette and her boys.

I can have a family of my own after all; with two sons that I can raise and teach and play with. Everyone will see what a good father I can be. All I have to do is not tell Jeanette that I'm still married. Neither of us want to get married again anyway.

After that, everything between Jeanette and Nate happened fast. He found an apartment in Oak Park, and sent for Jeanette. She and the boys arrived without mishap. But, when the moving company arrived with her furniture, the bill was twice as large as originally quoted.

"That was only an estimate," the mover said, "we didn't know, for sure, until we weighed the truck. Turns out there was a lot of heavy stuff."

"So, what do we do now? Can I make payments?"

"That's not our policy. We'll have to put your stuff in storage."

"Will there be a charge for that?" Nate asked.

"Yeah. We can hold it in short term storage for two weeks at the cheaper rate. After that it goes into long term storage."

"Can we get some things off the truck right now?" Jeanette asked.

"I'm afraid not, Miss. Everything is wrapped and boxed. You'll have to call the main office and make arrangements. Sorry."

For the first few months, while Searian paid for Nate to take limousines to and from the airport for his business trips, the family slept on rented cots and ate off a folding table. Nate had to get a loan from his credit union to pay for the furniture shipment; he had enough extra for a down payment on a car.

He took Derrick to Detroit to meet his real father who was in the music business. The three of them went to a softball game and toured a recording studio afterward.

At dinnertime, when Derrick went to the restroom, Donald said, "Nate, I want to thank you for taking care of my son. He seems happy."

"It's my pleasure Donald. He's a good boy, you can be proud of him."

"Do you have any kids of your own?"

"Yeah, in New York. It didn't work out with me and their mother."

"You too, huh?" Donald said, "Funny how things end up, ain't it?"

"It sure is, man, it sure is."

Maybe this is the way life really is, Nate thought. *I had a step-father and my mother and father didn't know their real dads either. I guess, we're suppose to take care of the kids under our roof ... wherever we are. I hope my kid's step-father is doing his job.*

By summertime, Jeanette had Derrick and Dikeba calling Nate "Daddy".

"Come on, daddy, they're having a block party in the alley. It'll be fun. All the parents are dressed up like the 1950s."

Reluctantly, Nate came out and was surprised by the friendly atmosphere. The kids were playing games and someone offered Nate a cold beer. Jeanette grabbed Nate to dance to one of the oldies that was playing.

When a drizzle started, a neighbor opened his garage and the party continued in there. Another neighbor snipped roses from his garden and gave each of the women one. Nate's faith in humanity was restored.

*   *   *

Nate's next PhoCon installation was at Houston General Hospital. Everything was routine and he finished up on Thursday. His flight home was delayed and he arrived home after the boys were asleep. Jeanette greeted him at the door with a warm kiss.

"Are the boys still up?," he asked, "I brought them a rocket."

"They wanted to stay up, but there's school tomorrow. And I wanted to tell you something …"

"First let me tell you about the Space Center in Houston. I saw Mission Control!"

"That's nice, but-"

"You don't get it, do you? I was at the place where they controlled the flights to the moon. Here, look … ," Nate unwrapped a long tube, "You can't buy one of these around here." It was a three-foot long model of the Saturn-V moon rocket.

Jeanette said nothing until Nate calmed down.

Jeanette sat on Nate's lap and put her arms around his neck. "I've got exciting news too. I'm pregnant."

Nate froze. "What?"

"I've missed my period for two months in a row now."

"But, you told me you were on the pill."

"I stopped taking them when my divorce came through."

Nate almost dumped her on the floor when he jumped up.

"You stopped taking them on purpose? After I told you I didn't want any more kids? Why would you do that?"

She came to him and he turned away.

"I wanted to give you something you don't have … a daughter."

"Jeanette-", Nate shook his head and walked into the bedroom.

She followed him, "I thought you would be happy."

"Come here, Jeanette and sit down, I've got to tell you something."

Nate told her he was still married and had four children, two of whom were girls. Jeanette stared at him for a moment, then burst into tears and ran into the bathroom.

"Is Mommy all right?," Derrick asked.

"Yes. She's just a little upset. You go on back and watch TV."

She refused to unlock the door and then said she was taking a shower.

Nate hoped she wouldn't do anything rash.

When she emerged, she asked, "When are you going to get a divorce?"

"As soon as I can," Nate said, still doubting Eva would give him one.

*   *   *

In time, Nate's attitude about Jeanette's pregnancy changed completely. He'd started thinking of the new baby as God's replacement for his son that had died. They moved to a larger apartment and Nate prepared a separate bedroom for the new arrival.

"This is one person who is going to be welcomed into this world," he declared.

When Nate's mother visited, the boys took to her right away and she to them; but Jeanette remained distant. Within days, Nate saw things weren't going well between the two of them. When their verbal exchanges switched to outright insults, he intervened.

"Will you two come here and sit down for a minute."

Jeanette said, "I don't want to sit with her." Simultaneously, Mrs. LaChae said, "Don't you talk to me like I'm a child, Nate."

"Please sit down for a minute, both of you!"

They sat at opposite ends of the long couch. Nate sat, facing them, in the rocking chair he'd bought Jeanette.

"I see that you're both having trouble getting along and I'm going to remind you how I was raised. I was taught that if you can't care about the people I love then you can't really love me and I believe that." He raised his hand when both women started to speak and he continued.

"Whether you like it or not, this is my mother", Nate said to Jeanette; then to his mother, "and this is the woman I love. That's not going to change. Now, I'm asking you both to please show respect for each other because you love me and because I love both of you. Now, I'm going for a walk." He walked out through the patio before they could respond.

Afterward, things seemed better until one morning Nate came home early and heard his mother calling out. Jeanette was out on the patio with the radio blasting. Mrs. LaChae was in bed and in a lot of pain.

"What is it, Motherdear?"

"I can't get up. Help me get to the bathroom."

Nate struggled to half-carry her down the hallway.

Once at the bathroom, she flopped onto the toilet seat. Nate was afraid to let her go as she seemed like she'd fall over.

"What happened?" he asked.

"I'm sick Nate, very sick," she said, "Ask Jeanette to come here."

Still holding his mother upright, Nate called out for Jeanette. He shouted at the top of his voice: "JEANETTE! JEANETTE, COME HERE!"

There was no response and he heard the radio get louder.

"Oh, Nate," his mother said, "I've got to GO right now."

Nate closed the door and then said, "Okay, Motherdear, I'll hold you."

"I'm so sorry, Nate." She began to cry.

"You don't have to be embarrassed." Nate said.

He spent that evening in the room with his mother with the door closed. She told him her cancer had returned after her mastectomy and that it was spreading.

"Why did you wait so long to tell me?"

Mrs. LaChae was laying back on her pillow, "Because, there's nothing that can be done about it and I didn't want you spending a lot of money-"

"Money is not the point, Motherdear. I work at hospitals all around the country installing and fixing equipment that's used to treat cancer."

"I know darling, but that doesn't mean we can afford treatment."

Nate took his mother's hand in his, "Listen to me Motherdear. I will get treatment for you. There are things I can do that you don't know about. But, it's very important that you keep a positive attitude about all this. Will you promise me that?'"

Mrs. LaChae turned her head to the side, smiled and then said, "Yes, Nate. I promise."

*   *   *

Nate walked into the Product Group meeting late. All the rest of the PhoCon team was there. A black man, Nate had never seen before, was sitting at the head of the table.

That must be the new Project Manager, Dave Nichols, Nate thought.

Norman Prescott tapped his pen on the table as he spoke. "This degradation in performance shouldn't be happening."

Larry Hughes frowned and shifted in his seat, "I've had calls from three of our customers in the past two weeks. They're all experiencing the same symptoms." He turned, "Tell them what you've seen, Vic."

"The problem is intermittent, that's all I know." Vic mumbled, "I never get a chance to troubleshoot it."

"Gentlemen," Dave Nichols said, "as you know, we plan to have a PhoCon at the Medical Equipment show in Europe in a few months. We can't afford to have the systems breaking down."

"They're not breaking down.," Prescott said.

"Okay then, failing," Dave Nichols countered.

"It doesn't matter," Vic said, "our new LFOV systems will have the best resolution in the industry."

"Oh, it matters, Vic", Dave said. "If doctors can't depend on any of our systems, they will tell others and we'll be in a world of trouble. Nate, do you have anything to add?"

"Only that most of the systems in my region are new and they haven't had this problem."

No one spoke as Dave Nichols lit a cigar. Then he said, "I've heard that some people, here in Searian, believe the PhoCon project is dead. I wouldn't have taken this job if I believed that; if anyone in this room believes that, they should leave right now."

Dave looked around the room and stopped at Vic.

"Good. Now, here's what we're going to do ..."

Dave outlined a plan that would keep Vic and Nate moving from one hospital site to another, hoping to catch the PhoCon's intermittent problem. Hospital technicians were instructed to pause any PhoCon that malfunctioned and leave it in its failed state. Dave told Norman Prescott to be prepared to go to any site exhibiting the problem.

Nate was impressed with Dave's take-charge attitude and his ability to get everyone's compliance. As the meeting ended, Nate went over and introduced himself.

"Sorry I was late. I was riding with someone else at lunchtime."

Nate noticed Dave had a wandering eye that made it hard to tell which way he was looking.

"Do you think I put some fire under their butts?" Dave asked.

"You sure did," Nate laughed, "Especially when you let them know you had heard the rumors about the PhoCon project."

"Nate, I took this project because nobody else thought it could work. Come on, man, it's not rocket science. With your help we can turn this around. Are you with me?"

"Yeah, Dave, you can count on me."

"Good." Dave picked up his folders, "Let's go to the production area. I need to know how to operate one of these things."

Three weeks later Nate was back at Massachusetts General Hospital speaking with Dr. Ryan.

"Yep, I caught it," Nate said, "watch when I tap on this detector."

Dr. Ryan peered at the computer screen, "Sure looks like you did, Nate. Can you fix it?"

"Not right now, but I've figured out how to make the problem appear. Apparently, there's some sort of flaking in the upper detector and, since it's upside-down, the flakes fall on the cathode. That's what messes up the image."

"That must be why we never see the problem on the lower detector."

"I'm pretty sure." Nate said proudly. "I'm going to call the plant right now."

"This will be a feather in your cap, Nate" Dr. Ryan said as he left the room.

After hearing all of Nate's details, Norman Prescott deviated from Dave Nichols's action plan and didn't go to the troubled site. Instead, he instructed Nate to gather information and return to the plant.

Dave Nichols called a meeting one month before the medical show.

"You're telling me that, even with Nate's data, you can't fix the problem, Norman?"

"It's not that simple," Prescott doodled on his writing pad, "I can't reproduce it consistently."

"I can." Nate said.

"No, you can't." Prescott countered, "It's multi-variant and, apparently, temperature related as well. You're both trying to oversimplify the problem."

Dave exhaled cigar smoke and smiled, "Are you saying there's a conspiracy here, Norman?"

Larry Hughes sat back in his chair and shook his head from side to side.

Prescott was sweating now, "I need more time to analyze the data, that's all."

"We're almost out of time. System-17 is shipping to the show on Friday and I'll bet any doctor that discusses this with Dr. Ryan will want to tap on our upper detector to see if it flakes."

Norman Prescott said, "Right now nobody can guarantee 24 hours of operation." He pointed at Dave, "And you're trying to shift responsibility on me, if it fails at the show."

"That's nonsense," Nichols said, "Sit down, Norman." Nichols turned to Larry Hughes, "How long does it take to swap-out a detector?"

Vic answered, "Four hours."

"I want us to take two spare detectors to the show." Dave said.

"Those things weigh 400 pounds each."

"I don't care what they weigh. If one fails during the show, we'll change it that night. All we have to do is keep System-17 running for one week. Can we do that, gentlemen?"

When no one dissented, Dave said, "Meeting's adjourned."

Nate stopped Dave as he was leaving. "I need to speak with you for a minute?"

"Sure, Nate, let's go to my office."

"I'd prefer to talk here, where we won't be disturbed. It's personal."

Dave saw the seriousness on Nate's face, "What wrong?"

Once the room was empty, Nate said, "My mother has cancer and I'm hoping, somehow, she can get treated on our equipment."

"You're sure it's cancer."

"She's already had a mastectomy and it has returned. She needs to be scanned and may need accelerator treatment if it's in her spine like they suspect."

Dave put his hand on Nate's shoulder, "We'll get her the treatment she needs, Nate. There's no way these doctors are going to deny your mother treatment after all the fine work you've done for them and their hospitals. I'll speak with Dr. Ryan and ask him to contact his colleagues at the University of Chicago."

"Great. That's great, Dave. But, I don't have any money-"

"It's not about money this time, Nate."

*　　*　　*

Early one Monday morning, Nate took his mother to the University's cancer treatment center. Dr. Strickland briefed Mrs. LaChae on the procedure that Nate had seen many times. An intern injected the isotope and asked a nurse to take Mrs. Lachae to be prepped.

Assured she wouldn't feel anything from the machines, Mrs. LaChae put her life onto the equipment Nate had fine tuned. She winced in pain as he helped position her onto the hard scanner table. After the scan was completed, they gave her a sedative and Nate left.

Instead of going home, Nate checked into a motel. He disconnected the telephone, showered and then meditated for hours. He visualized his mother's body and imagined what her illness looked like. In his mind's eye, he saw the enflamed muscles and bones. Then, he imagined brushing and vacuuming the peppery-looking cancer from every part of her spine.

After he performed the meditation three times, he got dressed and was about to leave, when he fell on his knees crying and prayed. After a while, he got up and went home to Jeanette and the boys.

* * *

Dr. Strickland called the next day and then said there had been an apparent error developing the film. They would need to re-do the scans.

"What happened to the film?" Nate asked.

"Somehow the exposures weren't set properly; there's no useful information on them."

Determined to keep a positive attitude, Nate returned and assisted his mother through another series of scans. The look Nate gave the technician operating the PhoCon warned him not to screw up.

"Okay, Mrs. LaChae, we're all through taking pictures," Dr. Strickland said. "Once we've examined these films, we'll schedule your treatment as soon as possible. All right?"

"All right, doctor." Mrs. LaChae said weakly.

The doctor told Nate, "We'll be sending copies of these films to Dr. Ryan right away. He is your mother's primary physician, isn't he?" Dr. Strickland asked.

"Yes, he's in charge."

* * *

"Try not to worry so much, Nate," Doctor Ryan said, "I've personally supervised the correlation of the PhoCon scans and the accelerator targeting. The president's mother couldn't get better treatment. Come on now, you checked the equipment yourself."

"I know doctor." Nate sat in the leather chair with his head in his hands. "It's just so different when the patient is my own mother."

Dr. Ryan opened his desk drawer. "Here Nate, take one of these."

Nate washed the pill down with water, "Thanks. I'm sorry, doctor-"

"There's no need for an apology. We all have mothers. You were lucky Dave Nichols called me. Most of the other spinal specialist are in Alaska

154

at an international conference. The only reason I didn't go is because my wife is expecting any day now and there may be complications."

"Why do you think so?"

Dr. Ryan rubbed his stethoscope between his fingers, "Because she lost babies in her last two pregnancies."

"Oh, I'm sorry doctor."

"You see, Nate, we both need to be strong these next few days."

"I'll pray for your wife when I pray for my mother, doctor."

"Thank you, Nate. Prayers do help."

Two hours later, the Varian VX7800 linear accelerator began firing a high-energy particle beam at Mrs. LaChae's spine. As the beam rotated around her body, its energy was automatically adjusted so as not to destroy healthy tissue. Only the cancer cells in her spine received a lethal dose. Nate and Dr. Ryan stood in the control room, watching the accelerator's progress. Minutes passed like hours.

Nate went to the back of the room, got on his knees and prayed.

Please God, let this procedure be successful and don't let Motherdear die. I love her so much and want to tell her again. And thank you God for letting me choose the paths that allowed me to be able to get her this treatment. I know this is no accident or coincidence. You have guided me many, many times and I thank you. Just please guide my mother back so she can enjoy life for a while longer. That's all I ask. And I pray for all these things in Jesus name. Amen.

When the treatment was finished, Dr. Ryan told Nate he would meet him in the waiting room as soon as he reviewed the reports.

Relieved, Nate went to the men's room and was sick to his stomach. It wasn't until he saw the fruit in the waiting room that he realized he hadn't eaten all day. He sat staring at the TV, remembering his mother strapped to the accelerator table. He stood when he saw Dr. Ryan coming.

"All the preliminary sign are good, Nate. She didn't move and you know the beam's accuracy was within zero point two-seven percent on all axes."

"Thank you doctor" Nate shook the doctor's hand vigorously, "Thank you very much. When will we know for sure?"

"Her body needs time to recover before we take any scans."

"Of course. But, when?"

"Let's give it one week, Nate. She'll be conscious in a day or so. Have a little more patience, okay?"

"Yes," Nate swallowed, "I will."

Before he let the doctor's hand go, Nate said, "Good luck with your wife."

"I'll tell her that you're praying for her."

*   *   *

After seeing Nate in his despair at work, Denise made a phone call. "Hello?" she said, "Is this Shelia McKnight?"

"Yes, this is Shelia."

"My name is Denise and please excuse me for calling you at work. I'm the secretary here at Serian and I'm calling about Nate LaChae. I've taken messages from you. I need to talk to you woman to woman. Can we do that?"

"I'm game, go ahead."

"I don't have time to explain everything right now, but you need to know that I care about Nate very much.

"Why are you telling me this, Denise?"

"Because his mother had a cancer operation a few days ago and he's been, kinda, out of it ever since."

"What makes you think-"

"Listen to me, Shelia. Please. I know you and Nate are very close. Never mind how I know, I just know. And what I'm trying to tell you is that he needs you now. He's really in the dumps. I've never seen him like this before."

There was silence on the phone line.

"Shelia? Are you there?"

"Yes, I'm here … you listened in on our phone calls didn't you?"

"That's not important now, is it?"

"No." Sheila said, "Are you in-. Never mind, that doesn't matter either. Thank you for calling me, Denise."

"Don't tell Nate, okay?"

"This will be our little secret, girl."

Sheila called Nate immediately.

"Hello, Captain."

"Hi, Sheila."

"I'm gonna be in your neck of the woods today. Think we can get together for lunch or something?"

"Sheila, that's very nice of you, but my mother is sick and I-"

"Yes, I heard, Nate. That's why I'm buying lunch, so come on."

"Okay. What time?"

"I'll see you around twelve. Alright?

It was 12:15 when Sheila arrived. Denise, who was covering for the receptionist, paged Nate to the lobby.

Nate saw Sheila standing by the large glass window in a beige wraparound v-neck dress. The bright sunlight behind her caused a silhouette effect. She was wearing a wide brimmed hat that made her look like a fashion model.

"Wow! You look great," Nate said.

As they headed for the door Denise looked up from the fresh roses on the desk in front of her and reminded Nate about the staff meeting at 2:30. "It was nice meeting you, Sheila."

Twenty minutes later, they were in the pool at the Holiday Inn. Nate wasn't surprised that Sheila had brought swimming trunks for him. They laughed at each other when they discovered neither of them could swim.

Soon they were in the room and didn't bother to dry off. Sheila ran across the beds as Nate chased her. When he caught her they rolled on the sheets and devoured each other in passion, once again.

Afterward, Shelia said, "We could be like this all the time, if we were married."

This caught Nate totally by surprise. After knowing her for years, he thought their relationship was set. The only time the word marriage had come up before was once when he asked her why she'd married Delbert. She'd told him Del had proposed while they were on a beach in the Virgin Islands and it had seemed like a good idea at the time.

"Well?"

"Sheila, I'm not ready to get married. And besides you're already married." he said, trying to buy time to think.

He didn't want to hurt Sheila. He cared for her as a friend and lover; he had told her so several times. But he never tried to make it sound romantic.

"Don't get me wrong," Nate continued, "There's just a lot of things I'm trying to do right now. That's where my mind is at."

Sheila didn't react. She said, "I understand. Now is not a good time."

He looked her in the eyes and said, "No, it's not, Sheila."

She dropped him back at work at 2:35 and gave him a quick peck on the mouth.

He paused long enough to ask, "You alright?"

She smiled and then said, "Yes, I'm fine. Go on to your meeting."

Refreshed, he rushed into the building. They were all waiting for him, in the conference room; it was his two-year anniversary with the company.

Phil Hertz came to Nate afterward.

"Hey, buddy, let me buy you a drink on the way home?"

Buoyed by Sheila's visit and the party, Nate said, "Sure Phil, why not."

The barmaid was a friend of Phil's and kept refilling their glasses for free. Driving home that night, Nate fell asleep at the wheel and coasted to a stop on the Eisenhower Expressway at 3am. He was arrested, for the first in his life, for driving under the influence. They released him the next morning and he had to attend drunk driving class before his license was returned.

*   *   *

Trouble kept brewing between Nate and Jeanette. The Saturday after Nate brought his mother from the hospital, he heard an announcement while he was at his office. It was the security officer, "Nate LaChae, your wife is on her way in."

Why didn't they put the call through?, he wondered.

Suddenly, there Jeanette was – shouting.

"You son-of-a-bitch!" She swung at him and he dodged.

"What are you doing?" Nate grabbed at her arms.

"You didn't come home or call last night. I didn't know where you were. You had me and the boys worried and then you come calling me from here this morning."

"I was at my sister's place. Remember she lives here now? I took my mother there from the hospital. All you had to do was call over there."

Jeanette tried to wrestle loose.

"You're suppose to get your ass home after work."

"I'm not SUPPOSE to do anything. How did you get past the security guard?"

"I took a cab and I told the security guard I had something for your sorry ass and I do." When she reached into her purse, Nate took off running. He hid in one of the offices, under a desk.

"NO-o-o! Come on out Mr. Smarty," Jeanette called out and it echoed through the empty offices.

"Bring your ass on out here. Yeah, I got something for you."

This shit is surreal. Nate thought, *Maybe she has a gun. Where's security when you need them?*

He waited until he heard her footsteps receding in the hallway. It wasn't over yet. When he got outside, he saw her inside their car.

She has the spare keys ...

He started toward her and she raced the engine.

What? Is she going to try and run me over?

He stopped and folded his arms, daring her.

Jeanette gunned the engine and, at the last minute, Nate saw she wasn't going to stop. He leaped out of the way as she sped past. She spun the car around and stopped like a bull in a ring.

Nate imagined a bull dragging a hoof in the dirt before charging. The plant door was an uncomfortable distance away; he decided to walk back to it.

Jeanette came full speed again. Nate jumped behind a lamppost that had a concrete base and Jeanette hit it head on! The car spun around, narrowly missing Nate and hot coolant spilled out of the engine.

Jeanette was unconscious.

The security team came running out.

"Call an ambulance!" Nate shouted, "Call an ambulance!"

*   *   *

They lost the baby and, weeks after her recovery, Jeanette became even more impossible to deal with. They had perfunctory sex that didn't rekindle any feeling between them.

Ironically, their car was repossessed while it was at the body shop. They sent the boys to be with Jeanette's mother, in Des Moines, for a while.

One evening Nate was sitting alone, watching TV, with his arm on the back of the couch. He noticed movement out of the corner of his eye. He turned and saw his thumb involuntarily jumping; he stared in amazement. He thought about the blood he had seen in his stool after arguing with Jeanette.

This shit is starting to kill me, he thought.

The last straw came when Nate came home one Friday, tired and hungry.

"What's for dinner?"

"The same thing as yesterday." Jeanette barked.

"Aw, I don't want any leftovers tonight. I-"

Jeanette slammed a plate down in front of him and then said, "You're gonna eat this and you better like it!"

Nate turned stone cold and sat still for five seconds.

"Fuck all this shit!" He picked up the plate of food and threw it against the wall.

Jeanette cringed and backed away.

Nate got up, went into the bedroom and packed his bags. He finished and came to the living room. Jeanette was sitting on the couch, eyes full of tears.

"Where are you going?"

"I'm leaving."

"I can see that, Nate. What about the boys?"

"I'm already labeled as the kind of guy who abandons his family."

"And now you're going to make it true?"

He picked up his bags, opened the door and stepped outside.

Jeanette called to him, "I think I'm pregnant again."

He paused for a moment, then closed the door.

*   *   *

Nate went to a motel. He called Jeanette's mother's house and Dennis answered the phone.

"Heard, you two had a little spat."

"It's more than a spat, Dennis. We're through. I called to tell your mother that I'll be sending money for Jeanette and the boys."

"Sounds final, man."

"I've tried Dennis, I really have. But Jeanette wants to argue all the time. I can't live like that man."

"At least it's not as bad as it was with her husband."

"What do you mean?"

Dennis proceeded to tell Nate how Jeanette and her husband used to fight so much that the police had nick-named them the Honey Badgers.

"I had to come over with my gun a couple of times." Dennis said.

"Why didn't you tell me about all this beforehand?"

Dennis hesitated, "Well-l-l, she is my sister, and it seemed like you two were going to hit it off."

"Man, I can't stand the arguing. Will you tell the boys I love them."

"Here, you tell them. They're right here. I'll put them both on the extensions."

Nate told Derrick and Dikeba he was going away for a long while. He told them to be good boys and take care of their mom.

"Will you send us our allowances?" Dikeba asked.

"Yes, I will. But it's gonna be every month instead of every week."

*   *   *

Phil Hertz jogged to catch up with Nate in the hallway at Searian.

"Hey, Nate, wait up. Did you hear what happen down at St. Luke's hospital this morning?"

"No, what?"

"The lead screw failed on one of the PhoCon scanners and it came down on a kid's head."

"Oh, No. Did it kill him?"

"Don't know yet. It was sure to have cracked his skull."

"That's horrible." Nate hit his palm with his fist, "I told them and sent memos that the guys in the field should have been checking for filings or shredding from the lead screws. They've been in the field for years."

"What about Dave Nichols?"

Phil shook his head, "They gave him a leave of absence, pending an investigation. Larry Hughes is taking his place for now. I hope you documented your warnings. They're gonna want to find fault somewhere."

"Well, it won't be with me. I'm tech support and I haven't been on that project for months."

"Just be careful, Nate. I heard the legal people are on their way to seal all the PhoCon maintenance records. The shit is surely gonna hit the fan."

"I'm not worried. But, it's a damn shame some kid had to get hurt."

"They should have listened to you, man." Phil said.

"Yeah, it's too late now."

That evening Nate called Dave Nichols, "Hey Dave, What's going on with that PhoCon mess?"

"They finally found a way to get at me."

"What? They can't blame you for what happened."

"They're going to try." Dave said, " But, I don't care, Nate. I hedged my bets. I've had my own company going for a while now. It's called Nova Medical. We've got backers, offices, and employees. I want you to come join us. The PhoCon project isn't going anywhere now."

Nate scratched his head and thought for a moment. "I'll be honest with you, Dave. For me to work for you I'd want to have the same salary I'm getting now, a company car and some help getting a decent apartment."

It surprised Nate when Dave answered, "You got it."

"I'm serious, Dave."

"So am I; when can you join us?"

Having regained his composure, Nate said, "I'd have to give my notice at Searian. Then I could be there in three weeks."

"That's fine with me. It'll give me time to get things together on my end. I've already told my partners about you. We're going to make a lot of money together, Nate. Let's talk again real soon."

"Right."

Inwardly, Nate wasn't sure Dave would meet all his requirements, so he called Paul Riley to see if any computer jobs were available.

"Hey, Nate. Where are you? What's your number? I'll call you right back."

Twenty minutes later Paul told Nate, "I've got something you'll love, it's in California. There's a company that's looking for a Field Service Engineer who knows electronics, optics and computers."

"Do they give a car?"

"I don't know. They've had this opening for a while now. Do you want me to set up an interview?"

"Yeah. Set it up. I'll check them out."

*　　　*　　　*

Nate flew out to California for an interview at MicroStep Company and was surprised when they made him an offer two days after he returned to Chicago. He called and declined their offer, stating that he was going into business with a friend. They told him they'd keep his application on file for six months, in case he changed his mind.

It was Friday. Nate put on a suit and headed downtown. Soon he was sipping a bourbon and soda while watching the sunset from Sibryis Lounge, on the 96th floor of the John Hancock building.

This is like a game of chess, he thought, *and I've just castled.*

A familiar voice interrupted his thoughts, "Hello, Captain. May I join you?"

*　　　*　　　*

Dave Nichols had successfully turned PhoCon into a viable product. But, the litigation that followed the accident, at St. Lukes, doomed the project. Searian opted to push sales of their newer LFOV systems. Shortly thereafter, an out of court settlement was reached; the exact amount was undisclosed. Dave resigned and went full-time with his Nova Medical Company.

Nate was the last member to join the Nova team. He thanked Dave for the job and then said, "I told you I wouldn't forget what you did for my mother."

Dave lived up to his promises. Nate was given a leased company car and assistance getting an apartment in Shaummburg, Illinois. Dave made it clear that he intended to "use" the apartment sometime.

Nate's title was Technical Director, but his duties included installing nuclear camera parts throughout the Midwest. It was simple enough, except for lifting the heavy lead collimators.

Nate met Dave's wife and five-year old daughter when they had him over for dinner. All Dave's conversation was about how much money they were going to make. He spoke of having the necessary business contacts to accomplish his goals.

After reconnecting with Sheila, parties at Nate's apartment took on the atmosphere of semi-orgies. There'd be the party and, when the "outsiders" left, there'd be THE PARTY. Neighbors called the police once to complain about Nate playing his conga drum late at night.

One day, Dave asked Nate to go to Chicago's south side and pick up a consultant for a meeting. "Her name is Lena Wilkenson and she does not drive."

"What time?" Nate looked at his watch.

"Our meeting is for 6 o'clock. I thought afterward we'd have dinner or something. My brother is in town and he'll be here too."

"You know it IS Friday, Dave."

"Yeah, Nate. I know, and I wouldn't ask you if it wasn't important. Ms. Wilkenson has contacts that can help us. That's why I want you to pick her up and bring her out here."

"Okay, what's her address?"

The traffic wasn't heavy on the ride downtown. The slight overcast gave the city a gray background. He knew the lights of downtown would burn through the gloom once it got dark.

Arriving early, Nate knocked on the door and was pleasantly surprised when Ms. Wilkenson answered.

"Hello, I'm Nate LaChae. Dave Nichols sent me to bring you to the office."

"You're a little early." she smiled and then said in a calm voice "I just have to get a few things together and I'll be ready to go. Please come in."

The house was comfortably furnished, with abstract pictures on the walls and several large plants. Nate took a seat while Ms Wilkenson disappeared into another room. She returned stuffing papers into her huge purse. She was completely different from what he'd expected. She was dressed immaculately, with a gold pin on her lapel. Her hair looked like she'd just stepped out of Jet Magazine. Nate thought, *Why can't I find a woman like this.* Suddenly, he wasn't in a rush to get back to the office.

As they headed out of the door Nate said, "You know, traffic at this time on Friday will be terrible. If we go now we'll be sitting on the Eisenhower Expressway. We could stop downtown and have a cocktail. There's a bar up in the John Hancock building where you can see the whole city."

"You're probably right about the traffic," she said, "Okay, I'm with you."

He held the car door open and she pirouetted in.

On the way downtown, their conversation was lighthearted as they entered each other's comfort zone. Nate got a parking space close to the John Hancock building and they were soon zooming up to the Sybris lounge. He was disappointed when they couldn't get seating near one of the picture windows.

Lena said, "This is nice right here. I can see everything." After ordering drinks, Nate excused himself and went to make a call. He didn't want the evening to develop with just Lena, himself, Dave and Dave's brother. He called Sheila just as she was leaving her office and invited her to join them for the evening.

"Sure, Captain. Stay where you are; I'll be right up."

"Hey, remember Ms. Wilkenson is coming out there for a business meeting. Be cool, okay?"

By the time Sheila arrived Lena had her shoes off and her feet tucked under her on the sofa. She was explaining Gibran's teachings to Nate.

Nate stood and then said, "Sheila, meet Lena Wilkenson. Lena this is Sheila McKnight. She's coming out to the office with us."

They greeted each other with a smile. Nate's anticipation grew as it always did when Sheila was involved. Lena continued where she had left off.

"I was just explaining to Nate how colors can effect the way we feel and our health in general."

"I think it has a lot to do with your belief system too." Nate added.

"I believe there's something to it." Sheila said. "In that book, Psycho-Cybernetics, they talk about how you can use your mind to get whatever you want."

"Yes, that's one of the popular books." Lena said with authority. "Many of the ideas in that book are based on Gerald Sheffield's theories. They've been around for a long time."

"I like the way Psycho-Cybernetics pulled together so many ideas and techniques." Nate interjected, "Our beliefs have a lot to do with it too."

Nate enjoyed the two fascinating women in front of him. After another round of drinks he declared, "We better get going. I think the traffic may have died down by now."

They all admired the night skyline one last time and Nate picked up the check. When they reached the car, Nate stepped ahead and unlocked the passenger-side door and was surprised when both ladies laughed. They looked at each other and then said, "We were waiting to see if he was going to unlock our door first." He smiled and opened the passenger door with exaggerated flare.

Nate delivered Ms. Wilkenson to Dave Nichols's office and introduced Sheila. He and Dave quickly made plans for drinks and dinner later.

"Maybe your brother, Sheila and I should go now and meet you two later."

"Good idea." Dave reached for his wallet. "Here's some money for pizza and stuff."

Sheila was casually perusing Nate's office. "So, this is where you do your thing?"

He looked at her and raised one eyebrow.

She smiled, "You know what I mean."

Before he could respond, Dave's brother strolled in. He looked Sheila up and down and then said, "Where we gonna eat?"

"We're gonna head over to the Brass Rail", Nate said, "The others will join us there."

By the time Lena and Dave arrived the second bottle of Chardonnay was being opened and the music was jamming. A huge pizza was delivered to their table.

As time went by, the energy of the group diminished and Dave said he was going to have to leave. He pulled Nate aside he said, "I have one more favor to ask of you."

"What's that?"

"Are you going to be taking Sheila back downtown?"

"Yeah."

"Would you please drop Lena back home? Its way out of the way for me you know."

"Okay, Dave. No problem."

"Did you guys have a good time?"

"Oh yeah, man. This reminded me of when we were over in Amsterdam for the Medical show. Remember?"

"Can't ever forget it."

After Dave's and his brother's farewells, Nate found himself sitting in the lounge, by the fireplace, between Sheila and Lena. They were silent, as the music and the mood mellowed. Grover Washington Jr. was playing and an air of anticipation hung over them. Nate sensed it was his move. But, what move to make? He knew what Sheila wanted, but he didn't know Lena well enough to read her. The wrong words or actions might blow Dave's business deal. Nate smiled as he thought, the right move could give the company a business partner.

Lena broke the silence with, "You want to share that thought with us?"

"I was hoping I won't have to take a breathalyzer test tonight," he lied.

"You sure that's all you were thinking?" Sheila pressed him.

"Yeah", Nate said, "And we better get going … if you ladies are ready?"

Lena and Sheila started for the ladies room at the same time, then laughed.

Nate mentally wiped his brow; I need some coffee.

The drive back downtown was strange. The chit-chat between the ladies died down and a most peculiar thing started happening. Nate believed he could hear Lena's thoughts. At first he thought he was imagining it. But, whenever he'd glance at her in the mirror, she'd nod or give him a knowing smile. *INCREDIBLE!* he almost blurted out.

The telepathy stopped as they approached Chicago's Loop.

"You want me to drop you off first, Sheila?" Nate asked.

"No. I better make sure you don't fall asleep or something. I'll ride with you."

Damn!, he thought.

They listened to the radio for the rest of the ride. Nate was still awed by the silent communication he and Lena had shared. He felt he couldn't simply let her go.

When they pulled up in front of her house Lena said, "I want to thank you both for a really enjoyable evening. Tell Dave I'll be waiting to hear from him."

As she was opening her door, Nate jumped out and rushed around to face her. Then, to both their surprise, Nate grabbed her by the shoulders and kissed her. "I'll see you again," he said.

" …OK." Lena gasped.

Nate stood there until she unlocked her door and entered. He got back in the car and glanced at Sheila who said, "That was some goodbye."

"Yeah, it was, wasn't it?" he said nervously.

"I hope it's not love at first sight or something."

Nate was heading back onto the Dan Ryan expressway.

"No Sheila. It was nothing like that."

Sheila thanked him again for letting her into his "other" life. Until that evening their meetings were always for sex. There were occasional dinners or drinks, but always outside the sphere of Nate's business life.

They rode in silence to Sheila's car and she looked at Nate as if to say, 'aren't you going to rush around and open my door and kiss me?'

Instead, she leaned over and they exchanged a simple kiss. They both sensed something was different.

The next day, Nate couldn't get Lena off his mind. He didn't tell Dave about his psychic experience the night before. Nor did he tell him that he had kissed Lena. By evening, his desire to see her became unbearable. He dialed her number.

"Hi, it's me Nate LaChae."

"Oh, hello Nate." Lena said calmly, "How are you?"

"I'm fine, but I want to see you again."

"Oh?" she said, "For business?"

"No, not for business. Do you think we can get together this evening for dinner or a drink or something?"

"I'm afraid not this evening. I've got a poetry reading to go to."

"A poetry reading? My mother writes poetry. Would you like some company?"

"Nate, I was about to walk out the door. Can you call me tomorrow?"

"Sure. But, where's the poetry reading at?"

"It's down at South Shore Park. I have an invitation."

"Okay, I'll catch you later."

Nate drove to South Shore Park, but couldn't find the building where Lena might have been. He came home disappointed and wondered if she had told the truth.

Two nights later, they had their first of many dinners at Chances Are, in Hyde Park. Nate did a Johnny Manthis imitation of the song: Changes Are.

The following Wednesday, Lena kept her promise and cooked a cherry chicken dinner for him, at his place. Nate bought champagne, tablecloth and candles for the occasion.

Lena spent that night … and many more.

*   *   *

One afternoon, at the office, Nate saw a birthday card on Dave's desk.

"Is it your birthday?"

"Yeah. The card's from Sally-Ann. She's a good secretary and a sweet person, very straight too."

"Hey man, let me buy you a drink."

"Don't mind if you do, Nate. Let me finish up his memo."

They went to a Mexican cantina on the edge of the shopping mall. Dave had Tequila while Nate drank Dos Equis. Unusually talkative, Dave told everything about an affair he had had.

"Dave, I've been meaning to tell you about Lena and me." Nate said, "We have a serious thing going on."

"You? And Lena Wilkenson?"

"Yeah, I guess it's one of those things."

Dave pointed his finger at Nate, "Don't you mess up my deal."

"I wouldn't do that, Dave. It's totally separate from the business."

"I hope so." Dave stared at Nate, "You're serious aren't you?"

"Yeah, we're in love."

"Brother, you better hope you haven't bitten off more than you can chew."

"What do you mean by that?"

"Nobody has been able to get next to her. And I mean nobody."

Nate lifted his beer and then said, "Good!"

"Love is a wonderful thing, Nate."

"How long have you and your wife been married?"

"Twelve years. But, I'm not talking about that kind of love."

Nate ordered another beer. "What other kind of love is there, Dave?"

"Did your father tell you he loved you?"

Nate looked puzzled, "I didn't grow up around my dad. I got to know him after I was twenty-seven years old."

"Whenever." Dave slurred the words, "Did he tell you he loved you?"

"Well, yeah. I remember him saying it. Why are you asking me that?"

Dave looked with red eyes and then said, "My father told me I was the worst thing that happened to him in his life."

"When did he say that?"

"Today." Dave looked down at his glass as if he was going to cry.

"Aw, man. You shouldn't let that bother you. After all, you're a college graduate, you have your own company, a home and a family that loves you. Hell man, you even got me working for you. Come on."

"A person's father is suppose to love his family."

"Not all fathers are the same Dave." Nate sobered, "From what I've seen, you're a good father to your kids. That's what counts. Trust me, I know."

"Do you know, Nate?" Dave was drunk now, "Do you really know?"

"Come on, man, let's get you home. Waitress … check please."

Nate took Dave's car and left his own at the shopping mall.

During the ride, Dave kept muttering about his financial backers, " …they're the only ones that really like me. That's why they put up all that money."

"Sure, Dave. They believe in you."

"Do you believe in me, Nate?"

"Sure, Dave. Sure."

Nate stopped believing in Dave when he learned Nova Medical was selling refurbished equipment as new. It wouldn't have mattered so much to Nate, had it not been medical equipment. Dave was surprised when Nate told him he felt uncomfortable about the equipment being sold as new.

"Look Nate," Dave closed the office door, "If you're not comfortable with the way I do business, you should get out. And you can forget about owing me for helping your mother. I don't need anybody that's not fully committed."

"I guess we understand each other then." Nate said, "Sorry, it turned out this way, Dave."

*   *   *

Nate called MicroStep and asked if the Field Service position was still open. It was, and they sent two airline tickets.

Nate met Lena for dinner in Hyde Park and told her he was leaving Dave's business. "I've been offered a job in California."

Lena sat quietly, playing with the straw in her drink. She looked over the lit candle at him, "So, I guess I won't be seeing you for quite a while?"

"You can see me every day if you choose to."

"What do you mean by that?"

Nate removed two airline tickets from his jacket pocket. When Lena didn't move, Nate reached for her hand and then said, "Come with me."

After a moment, she put her other hand on his and then said, "Okay, Nate LaChae, I'll go on this adventure with you."

MicroStep

Their Chicago-to-San Francisco flight arrived late. By the time Nate and Lena got their bags it was 9:00 pm. They hopped into their rental car and headed south toward Mountain View.

Looking at the lights of homes in the hills, Lena said, "It's so beautiful, like diamonds on a black quilt." Nate smiled and put his arm around her.

"Wait until you see those hills in the daytime." He drove on, describing places they would be visiting soon. Lena snuggled closer and stared, wide-eyed, through her round glasses.

This time it's going to be better, Nate thought, *I've got the right woman, the right attitude, and a working product.*

The Tropicana motel didn't have room service, so they called for Chinese food and was promised it in a half-hour. "We'll have just enough time … ," Nate said smiling at Lena as she dried herself after showering. At that moment, the building shook and the room tilted forward. All the furniture shifted toward the windows. Lena fell on Nate and he fell backward against the window so hard that it cracked. A heavy chair had them pinned.

"Holy shit!" Nate yelled as he struggled to remove the chair, while still holding on to Lena.

"What was that?" Lena asked, "Was it an earthquake?"

"I don't think so. It sounded like a car crash."

"Then why is the room tilted like this?"

"I don't know, Lena. Just hang on for a minute …"

He turned and looked out the window. The tail of a red Stingray was sticking out from the room beneath them.

"Look", he said, "somebody drove their car right into the motel."

"Well, I hope that's not the way they deliver Chinese food." Lena said, laughing nervously.

"Come on, get dressed; we're getting out of here."

The managers, Eli and Ruth Saab, talked them out of leaving the motel by changing their room and giving them one night free.

By the time they did leave the Tropicana Nate and Lena were friends with Eli and Ruth. They were given a set of sheets, blankets, and pillows and promised to stay in touch. Nate tried to convince them that he could improve their computer programs, but Eli said the owners, an older retired couple, weren't interested.

With money they had saved, Nate and Lena rented a two-bedroom apartment in Sunnyvale and bought a bed, folding table, and chairs.

"I have to have a room where I can work", Nate explained to Lena.

"AND", she said, pulling him to the small patio out back,

"I have to have a garden where I can work."

"Deal." he said.

They covered their bedroom window with newspaper, that first night and it all fell off before morning.

$$* \qquad * \qquad *$$

Monday morning, at MicroStep, Perry Penvenne said, "That's the fifty-cent tour, Nate. I've shown you the Stepper and you've met the inventor. Do you have any more questions?"

Looking at the huge, almost empty, room, Nate said, "How many people work here?"

Perry smiled and wrinkled one eyebrow, "You'll be number twenty. Like I said, we're just starting up."

Perry was twenty-eight years old, average build, had dark fluffy hair and prominent cow-dips. There was a nervous intensity about him and he often spoke with exaggerated seriousness.

They returned to Leo DeBos' desk, which sat in the middle of the almost empty building. Looking at Leo, Nate couldn't help thinking of the actor Lee J. Cobb. He had a cigar in his mouth and looked scruffy with his long thinning gray hair. He growled at everyone instead of speaking to them.

"Okay, be here tomorrow morning and work with Perry."

"What about the company car." Nate asked hesitantly.

"Yes, yes," Leo waved his hand, "You'll get everything that's in our ad for Field Service Engineer."

"Thank you, sir." Nate extended his hand and, after a few seconds, Leo looked up and shook it firmly; he looked Nate in the eyes and then said, "You'll have thirty days to prove yourself young man."

Nate turned to Perry, "What time tomorrow?"

"I'll be here when you get here," Perry replied.

Nate walked out feeling as if he was in a dream. *Wait until Lena hears about this!*

*   *   *

Nate and Perry bonded right away. When Perry wasn't talking about The Trilateral Commission or the illegalities of taxes, they talked about science and Star Trek.

At Berkeley Perry had been brilliant in science and math. When Martin Lee invented the Stepper and formed MicroStep, the first person he hired was Perry. His title was Lead Technician and he was the one that made Martin's theoretical hardware work.

Seeing that everything needed organizing, Nate started drawing mind maps like those used to organize his computer programs. He found it easier to keep notes in that graphic form.

Martin Lee decided it was time to give a class for the new employees and the Mobius Business Systems (MBS) contract liaison, Art Chavez. There were only five students and Perry was repeatedly pulled away to do other chores.

Martin gave an overview of the Stepper machine, then began explaining its theoretical background. "To do alignment of different layers, my brother, Peter, came up with a novel idea which we've patented … wait a minute; I'll let him describe it to you." Martin called to his younger brother, "Peter."

Peter walked slowly across the empty room. He was skinny and shorter than Martin's six-foot frame. "What?"

"Will you explain the optics to these guys?"

Peter looked down at the floor for a moment, turned to the whiteboard and started drawing and writing equations. He didn't face his audience when he started speaking in a low monotone. "Consider what happens when a beam of light enters the main objective." He pointed to his drawing, "This prism splits the beam in two and ... " Peter's descriptions continued for over a half-hour.

At one point, Nate leaned over to Perry and whispered, "It's probably FM."

Perry shook his head as if he understood. But, a moment later, he leaned toward Nate and asked, "What's FM?"

"Fuckin' Magic" Nate whispered.

Perry had to cover his mouth to keep from laughing out loud.

For the first time Peter looked toward his audience. "Someone have a question?" he asked.

"No. Sorry." Perry responded, "Please go on."

At break time, Art Chavez told Nate, "I've always admired guys, like Martin and his brother, that dream up new ideas."

"Yeah, me too." Nate said, "I have a patent pending myself. It's for a photoelectric tracking system that I built."

Art looked doubtful.

Martin Lee said, "Okay, let's gather around the machine ... without your coffee, please." Art walked away while Nate was still describing his project.

Peter asked, "Do any of you know about Cassigrain optics?"

"Isn't that a kind of curvature for a lens?"

"That's close," Peter said.

Nate spoke up, "It's a method for folding optical paths so that telescopes don't have to be so long."

"Exactly." Peter pointed to Nate, "And that's what we use in the stepper."

Nate didn't notice Art Chavez frowning at him.

The rest of the morning passed with Perry and Nate taking turns answering most of Peter and Martin's quizzes.

After lunch, Martin asked Nate to make copies of assembly drawings for MBS.

"Can't I make them after class?" Nate asked.

"Art needs to take them back with him today."

The next day, Nate was told to skip class again and finish assembling a part that Perry had been working on.

At lunchtime, Perry confided to him, "I don't know what you said to Art, but he doesn't want you in this class."

"What do you mean? Why not?"

"I don't know, Nate. But, MBS is our only customer and Martin has to go along with Art's wishes. Maybe you should talk to Leo."

Nate did and Leo said, "Art is insisting on having someone with Wafer Fab experience do the field service work. Don't worry about it."

Nate stood quietly for a few moments, not knowing what to think or say.

Leo took the cigar out of his mouth, "Perry says you're a good organizer. Can you take care of documenting the project?"

Nate hesitated, "Yes, I can do that."

"Good. See if you can get things together around here, Nate.

Reassured, Nate replied, "Okay, Leo."

*   *   *

At home, Nate's focus was back and he worked on his Photodisk projector again. The only original parts he had were 16mm sports films. He started designing and ordered parts from Edmund Optics and American Science Center.

All I have to do is demonstrate the Photodisk projector to the right people, Nate thought, *and I'll be 'over'*. Weeks later, he had a rudimentary Photodisk projector working, made mostly from Haltek surplus parts. *It's working again; even got rid of the jitter between picture frames.* Nate thought, *Thank goodness for Radio Shack's new TRS-80 computer; programming the photo sequences is much easier now.*

Nate sat and stared, his eyes darting back and forth. In his mind, he was modifying parts from his kludged projector into a sleek design that would fit into a professional-looking cabinet. With his mind's eye, he saw parts floating in the air and coming together. He saw the type connections that would be needed, the gauges of wire, the colors of paint to use, the lettering on the front, the placement of switches and displays. When something didn't fit, he'd backup and reverse everything, in his mind, until it was right.

He was still juggling parts in his mind when Lena came to the door. "Nate, you want rice or potatoes with your steak?"

"Huh?" he turned towards her in a daze.

"I asked, do you want rice or potatoes with your steak?"

Nate's mind spun like a top; *What was the right answer? Which would work better with dinner? Which had the right balance of nutrients?* He wanted to say, "How the hell would I know?" but cleared his head and made a choice instead, "Rice, Honey; Rice will be nice."

Satisfied, Lena disappeared into the kitchen.

Nate turned back around and all the parts he had been balancing together in his mind were gone. It was as though they had fallen into a heap on the floor. He started all over again, this time he drew, on paper, what came to his mind. He tore up page after page a dozen times before he was satisfied.

Nate saw a flyer, at Computer Literacy bookstore, about an Inventor's Exhibition to be held at the Marriott Hotel. The California Inventor's Council (CIC) sponsored the event and there was a contact phone number for anyone interested in exhibiting.

Three weeks later, Nate was one of many exhibitors at the Marriott hotel. The exhibits extended out of four rooms and lined two of the hotel's long hallways. Bob Truax had his huge rocket, built from NASA surplus, poised outside in front of the hotel entrance.

Nate had his Photodisk projector set up in one of the hallways. He explained its operation to curious passer-bys.

One cowpoke-looking old man asked Nate, "You mean YOU made this all by yourself?"

"I sure did." Nate said. As the man turned away, Nate heard him say, "You're just too damn smart."

Nate didn't try to figure that one out.

An older Black man, in a suit and tie, came over smiling and asked, "Is this your invention?"

Disappointed that none of the officials from CIC had seen his exhibit yet, Nate answered, impatiently, "Yes. It's like a slide projector and movie projector combined."

"Really?" the kind gentleman said, "Would you explain it to me?"

Nate softened and explained how it worked. He ended with, "I can't show you any pictures because I don't have power in this corner."

The man turned and walked to the hotel concierge counter. They spoke briefly, then he returned and then said, "They'll get some power over to you. Do you need a screen?"

Surprised, Nate said, "I, ah ... , No. I can project on this wall behind the table. Thank you sir. Are you with the hotel staff?"

The man smiled and then said, "No. I'm Paul Brown. I'm the president of the CIC."

"Oh", Nate stumbled over his words, "I'm pleased to meet you, sir. I'm Nate LaChae"

"You should come to some of our meetings at the Sunnyvale patent library, Nate. We discuss topics relating to inventing and there are several inventors that attend regularly."

Without thinking Nate asked, "Are you an inventor, Mr. Brown?"

Paul Brown smiled as he gave Nate a business card, "Yes, I've invented a few things. I've got some of them on exhibit at booths 103 and 104."

Nate glanced at the business card and his eyes bulged as he remembered walking past booths 103 and 104. There were more than a dozen items on display there. One of which was the Whizzer spinning top. Almost every American boy born after 1952 played with a Whizzer.

Can this man in front of me be ...?

Paul Brown smiled and nodded acknowledgement.

"Oh, Mr. Brown. I'm very pleased to meet you sir. I didn't realize ..."

"That's quite all right, Nate. I've enjoyed meeting you, and I hope to see you at some of our meetings. I think you'll find them helpful."

"I'll be there, Mr. Brown, for sure. Thank you again."

At the CIC meetings, Nate met aspiring and successful inventors. He learned that Paul was one of the founders of CIC and he held more patents than any other member. Mattel Toy Company had sold more than sixteen million of his Whizzers.

Nate met Gabriel Morris at one of the CIC meetings. Gabriel (Gabe) was a computer programmer who liked building his own computers. Gabe was younger than Nate and usually kept to himself at the meetings. He hesitated when he spoke, as if his words were being carefully processed before being released. Only after he learned of Nate's deep interest in computers did he open up. They went off into a corner that evening and talked about computers for the rest of the meeting. Their backgrounds paralleled each other and both frequented the local technical 'hot spots' for parts and books.

Gabe worked part-time consulting for San Francisco businesses. Although he didn't boast about it, his part-time work supported half his household expenses. His wife Sarah, a schoolteacher, supplied the other half.

Nate and Gabe liked discussing 'ultimate' computer projects - the fastest, the biggest, and the best. They compared notes about things they had heard or read and vowed, one day, to make a contribution of their own.

At one of the CIC meetings, Paul Brown brought a magazine article for Nate. It described how graphic arts companies needed faster slide projectors. Nate was delighted to have found another use for his projector. He stepped up his development activities and, following Paul's advice, applied for a patent.

Nate called Concorde Graphics in Cupertino and told them he had a solution to one of their problems. The secretary put him through to the graphic arts production manager, Mr. Gilbert. He listened, was interested, and scheduled a date for Nate to demo the Photodisk projector.

Nate took two days off work from MicroStep to prepare for the demo and programmed the Photodisk for optimum performance. The images of the football players were programmed in various sequences and patterns. He planned to explain how the images could be graphic designs of his customer's choosing. He had Lena critique his presentation, insisted she play devil's advocate, and challenge him with tough questions.

At 3:30 he was ready. Lena decided not to go, "This is your thing Nate. I'd just be in the way."

He packed everything into his company car and headed for Concorde Graphics.

When Nate rolled his cart up to the receptionist desk, she seemed reluctant to call Mr. Gilbert.

"There's a Nate LaChae in the lobby for you."

Soon a man came through the door, looked at Nate, and looked around as if expecting someone else. He said nothing as he approached.

Nate smiled, extended his hand and then said, "Mr. Gilbert? I'm Nate LaChae … I'm here to demo my projector."

"Oh, yes", Mr. Gilbert frowned and glanced at Nate's cart, "Come this way."

They went to a conference room and Mr. Gilbert said, "You can set up over there", pointing to one end of the table. He excused himself and Nate started preparing the Photodisk system. Soon Mr. Gilbert, and a young man and woman, both in jeans, came in. He introduced them and then said they were members of his graphics arts staff.

"We can only give you a half hour" he said curtly.

"A half hour will be fine", Nate replied and handed out a data sheet.

"From what I read in a magazine article, it's my understanding that your slide projectors are too slow for some of the work that you do. The sheet I gave you lists the specifications for my Photodisk system. I'm going to show you pictures of football plays and you'll see how much faster and more versatile this projector is."

Nate went through his presentation, aware of the constant frown on Mr. Gilbert's face. The projector performed flawlessly and Nate saw that the young couple was impressed. One asked if the projector was patented and Nate said it was pending; the other asked how they would get their art onto one of the Photodisks.

"I'll build another machine, similar to this one", Nate said, "It will be a camera and take pictures of your art work. The pictures can be transferred to a sheet of film that becomes a Photodisk."

Mr. Gilbert looked at his watch and then said, "Is that it then?"

"Ah, yes", Nate was puzzled, "that's all I wanted to show you."

"Thank you for coming, we'll let you know if we're interested." Mr. Gilbert got up, "Jonathan, will you show him out?"

"Sure, dad", Jonathan quickly put two fingers to his mouth.

Nate was packing everything up when Jonathan came over and then said, "I think this is really cool. Did it take long to build?"

"Not really." Nate said, continuing to pack his equipment.

The young woman came over and then said, "I'm sorry, Mr. LaChae. dad isn't very liberal, if you know what I mean."

Nate rolled his cart toward the door and then said, "I didn't think liberalism had anything to do with projection systems."

On the drive home, Nate detoured toward the bay. He sat in the car and stared at the lights reflecting from homes in the hills, thinking. *It didn't matter that the projector worked and was a solution to their problem. I wasn't asking him to believe in anything. I showed him it worked. That guy didn't even ask about the price; all he saw was that I was black. What fucking difference would that make if he were turning out more work than his competition?*

I'll never understand this stupid fucking shit.

He didn't want to go home and face Lena; he knew she would have encouraging things to say and he didn't want to hear it. He had failed and he kept wondering what he could have done differently; how he could win next time.

No answers came immediately.

*   *   *

A week later, the telephone rang as Lena returned from grocery shopping with Ruth Saab.

"Hang on a minute Ruth." Lena rushed to the phone.

"Hello, Mother, how are you?"

"I'm fine", Bertha said, "But, Marilyn is not."

"What's wrong?" Lena asked.

"She's running with the wrong crowd and not taking proper care of Brandon. I'm tired of worrying about her every night. So, I bought tickets to California for both of them."

"You should have asked me first, Mother. I don't live alone you know."

Ruth signaled she was leaving and Lena waved at her.

"Don't tell me what I should or should not do with YOUR daughter and grandbaby." Bertha said, "If Nate don't want them there, maybe you need to get yourself another man."

"I didn't say anything about Nate not wanting them here, Mother. It's just that we have plans and he's trying to get his kids to come and visit. We only have two bedrooms; it can get crowded real quick."

"You better think, girl", Lena's mother said, "whether you want your home full of his kids or yours."

"Mother, it's not about his or mine. It's not fair for me to spring surprises like this on him. I'm not working, you know."

"What? Can't he support you?"

"He's already supporting me, Mother. But, we're still trying to get on our feet."

"I bought Marilyn a ticket that's probably gonna save her life. If you can't appreciate that 'cause you're so in love with that man, then heaven help you. Anyway, she's on her way and she needs you. I'm too old to chase after her like you should have been doing."

"Mother, you know I love Marilyn and Brandon. I wish you wouldn't ..." Lena caught herself, "Look, we'll do all we can, but Marilyn's got to grow up at some point."

"You be careful, Honey, with him talking to his ex-wife, you hear me?"

"Yes, Mother. I'm not worried about our relationship."

"Well, you ought to be. I been married to Chester for twenty-three years and he still tries to put his son ahead of you sometimes."

"Yes, yes, mother; you've told me before."

Bertha hung up without saying good-bye.

Lena lit a cigarette and sat at the dinning room table. She looked through the glass patio doors at her little tomato garden and sighed. Glancing at her watch, she realized Nate would be home from his CIC meeting soon and she didn't want him hungry when she sprang the news. She got up and started unpacking her groceries.

CIC's secretary, who worked at the Sunnyvale Patent library, always had helpful information, particularly that night. Nate could hardly wait to get home and tell Lena.

As soon as he came in, he said, "I've got it, Honey!" He picked her up and swung her around.

"Got what?" she asked.

"The secretary, at the Patent Library, showed me a book called 'A Whack on the Side of the Head'. It's written by the head of Satari, and you know what they make."

Lena's head was spinning when she answered, "What?"

Nate put his hands to his temples and then said, "Lena, why did I invent the Photodisk in the first place?"

"You said it was for games."

"Exactly. And Satari is one of the biggest game companies, and they're right here in Silicon Valley."

"I thought you decided to go after different markets."

"Well, yeah. Only, now there's a change in the plan. I'm going to put the projector into an arcade-game cabinet and sell it that way. Companies like Satari will already understand that there's a need for something like it."

"Sounds good." Lena said.

He headed to the bathroom, "I'm glad I have the extra bedroom to work in." When he returned, he noticed the table was set for dinner.

Nate said, "So, how was your day?"

"Oh," Lena filled their wine glasses, "Not as exciting as yours. Just another change of plans."

Nate rubbed his stomach, "Let's eat."

"I want to bless the table first." Lena said as they held hands across the table. "Heavenly Father, bless this food and bless our home, that we may share it with those we love. Amen."

"Amen." Nate started gobbling his food down. He saw Lena staring and then said, "Sorry, I haven't had anything since breakfast." Between mouthfuls he said, "So, who are we going to be sharing our home with?"

Lena poured more wine and then said, "My mother called today. She wants Marilyn and Brandon to spend some time with us." Before

Nate could respond, Lena blurted out, "She already bought airline tickets for them."

"Cool." he said, "When do they want to come?"

Lena took a deep breath, smiled and then said, "Now."

"Now?"

"Now."

Nate laughed so hard he started coughing; Lena came around and patted his back.

"I wasn't joking, Nate."

"I know it. You just looked so serious; like you thought I was going to be angry or something."

"Well, Mother sprang this on me without warning."

Nate pulled her to him, "Lena, being with you has reminded me what love really is. It includes our families. You're the one that got me to thinking about trying to see my own kids.

If Marilyn and Brandon want to come and visit, we'll just get a folding cot for one of them and the other can sleep on the couch."

"Oh, Nate." She wrapped her arms around his neck and they kissed passionately. Then he asked, "What's for dessert?" Two seconds later, they both started laughing.

$$*\qquad*\qquad*$$

Lena spotted Marilyn carrying Brandon as they came through Gate-29 of San Francisco International. His little neck seemed too small to balance his head. Marilyn was taller than Nate had expected. Otherwise, he would have recognized her by her gumdrop nose, and round eyes. Her chestnut hair was cut in a boyish bob. They hugged and Marilyn quickly pulled away, without smiling. Lena took Brandon and kissed him. When she tried to give him to Nate, he pulled back and stared.

Nate said, "I see, I'm going to have to work at being your friend."

"That was one long cold flight." Marilyn said, "Some of us complained about the air conditioning but they didn't do nothing about it." She held her mouth firm and spoke in a monotone. "I'm gonna write a complaint letter."

"Come on," Nate said, "We'll get your bags and head to someplace warm."

Nate drove from the airport to The Cliff House in San Francisco. Marilyn hardly spoke during the ride and when she did it was in short dry statements. She held her mouth firm and spoke in sullen monotones.

They arrived at The Cliff House in time to get seats by the window. Marilyn all but ignored the view of the sun sinking into the Pacific Ocean. Brandon played with crayons as their drinks and hor d'oeuvres were served.

A television newscaster was speaking about the breakup of a Hollywood couple and Marilyn said, "Men are no good."

Nate sipped his drink, smiled, and then said, "You mean all of us?"

Lena responded, "Marilyn why are you saying-"

Nate touched Lena's arm. "No. Wait, Lena. I want to hear Marilyn's reason."

"Because they're not; that's why." She turned, leaned on the table, and replied coldly. "You're all the same, aren't you?"

"You shouldn't talk to Nate like that, Marilyn", Lena said.

"Why not? I'm just telling the truth." She faced the window again.

Lena said, "Maybe we should just go, Nate"

"I want to finish my Irish Coffee first."

"I'm going to the ladies room." Lena stood. "Will you come with me, Marilyn?"

"No," she lit a cigarette.

Lena stared at her daughter, then left. Nate sipped his drink and looked at the profile of his new twenty-three year old stepdaughter. Her smooth caramel skin didn't match her butch haircut or her compact body. Nate suspected her projected toughness was just a front.

"Your mother loves you, you know."

"How would you know? There's a whole lot you don't know about her."

"Marilyn, I know I love your mother and we're going to be together."

"Oh yeah? Wait 'till you find out she's not always so sweet and loving. I bet she didn't tell you how she left me down at Indiana."

"She told me you were in college there."

"Yeah, and one day MY MOTHER got up and went back to Chicago, without saying anything to me."

"She must have had a good reason, Marilyn."

"What good reason?" Marilyn tilted her head and glared at him.

Nate decided to leave that alone. He couldn't think of anything else to say before Lena returned.

Lena remained standing and announced, "I'm going to take the baby to the car. Give me the keys, if you're not ready to leave."

"Okay, we can go." Nate motioned for the waiter.

Marilyn got up, without looking at either of them, and headed for the exit. Lena followed her out while Nate waited for the check and thought, *Boy, oh boy, that's one angry young woman. Well, nobody said this was going to be easy. I thought the scenic drive up Hwy 680 and Skyline Drive would mellow her out. Now, look at this check. I'm glad I didn't buy dinner today.*

They rode back to the house in silence. Brandon was asleep. As they approached, Nate asked, "Anybody want anything from the store?"

Marilyn said, "I need some cigarettes."

Both women went into the store and Nate saw them arguing at the cashier's counter. They rode in silence to the apartment.

Once they were home Nate laid Brandon on the master bed. Marilyn went into the second bedroom and closed the door. She carried a bag containing beer, chips, and cigarettes. They heard her talking on the phone. Soon the smell of pot drifted under the door.

Lena made some tea and sat on the couch with Nate. They turned the TV on, to have some sound in the room.

"She seems mad about you leaving her or something."

"Oh, she told you about that?" Lena said.

"She mentioned it, when you went to the bathroom."

"That was years ago when she was at Indiana State College, and she never forgave me. That's not what she's so angry about, but I'll tell you about it sometime."

"So, what does that have to do with all men are no good?"

Lena sat her cup down and then said, "The baby's father doesn't want to have anything to do with her or Brandon."

Before Nate could respond, Marilyn came out of the room and announced, "Grandma is on the phone, she wants to talk to you."

Lena went into the bedroom and closed the door.

Marilyn went into the bathroom and Nate heard her vomiting.

Except for Brandon's antics, glumness settled on the apartment for the rest of the week. Nate was glad to escape to work. Marilyn stayed in the bedroom most of the time and ate her meals there. Lena cared for Brandon and asked Nate not to say anything that might upset Marilyn.

He told Lena, "I feel awkward, when I go in there to work on the Photodisk. She either gets up and leaves or just lays on the cot with her back to me."

Lena said, "I'm trying to work through it with her, when you're at work."

One evening, Marilyn came out of the room and announced, "I'm going back to Chicago on Friday. Grandma is on the phone, she wants to talk to you."

Lena went into the bedroom and closed the door.

Marilyn walked onto the patio and smoked a cigarette.

Minutes later, Lena came to Nate with tears in her eyes. "Marilyn doesn't want to stay, Nate. Mother wants us to keep the baby until Marilyn gets herself together. She says he won't be safe there in Chicago. She wants to speak with you."

Nate went to the phone. "Hello, Mother."

"Hello, Nate. I wanted to make sure it was okay with you about Brandon staying there for a while … until Marilyn gets on her feet."

"Yes, sure. I don't have any problem with that. We'll be glad to keep him for a while."

"Good," Bertha said, "Now you and Lena have a son."

I already have sons, Nate thought. *Besides, we've been having unprotected sex for months without conceiving; I don't want to bring anybody else into the world. Still, having Brandon with us will make Lena happy and keep her from getting bored while I work on my projects. Once Marilyn gets herself together everything can get back to normal.*

Saturday morning, Marilyn called a taxi instead of allowing Nate or Lena drive her to the airport.

"I have money that Grandma sent me."

"That's a waste of money." Lena said.

"It's not your money."

Lena held Brandon and watched as the taxi drove off.

Nate put his arm around them and they went inside.

"Hey, let's drive up to Palo Alto for some banana pancakes"

"I'm really not hungry, Nate."

"Come on, we can take Brandon for a ride in the mountains."

*   *   *

Nate and Perry were at the deli when Perry described Leo DeBos' background. He had been The Start-Up Man for General Signal for fifteen years.

"He takes companies from the ground up to an established business entity." Perry said, "Then he moves on."

"And he likes you, Nate," Perry said, "You can't have better job security than that."

"I like him too," Nate admitted, "now that I got used to his ways."

As they returned from the deli, Perry asked, "What are those diagrams you're always drawing?"

"They're called concept charts. That's the way I keep notes."

*   *   *

Nate was glad to have his mother visiting, but he dreaded the inevitable discussion; it came on the third day. Lena and Brandon were gone shopping with Ruth.

Mrs. LaChae put her magazine down and then said, "You know, you should communicate with your kids, Nate. They need to hear from you."

"Whatever is going on between you and Eva should be separate from your having a relationship with your kids."

"Motherdear, I've told you, the judge ordered me to stay away from them. And I have no visitation rights." He got up and walked to the glass patio door. "All because Eva's mother wanted more money out of me for her little Day-Care business."

"Darling, you should have had a lawyer with you in court. That's all water under the bridge now."

Nate turned, with tears in his eyes, "I didn't get a lawyer because I wasn't guilty of anything, Motherdear. Everybody always says a person is innocent until they're proven guilty. Eva stood there and told the judge she couldn't remember the last time I had given money for the kids." Nate pounded his fist into his open palm as he said, "Right ... in front ... of my face. I couldn't believe it. I can't understand how she could do that after all those years together. Her mother must have told her to do it; she was there, you know, outside the courtroom."

"Nate, you can still communicate with the kids."

"Yeah, and as soon as I do everybody will know where I am, won't they? The bill collectors and the courts are still looking for me, you know?"

"Yes, darling, but maybe your wife would feel differently if you-"

"My wife!" he laughed, "I don't have a wife, Motherdear. Don't you get it, she is my enemy!"

"She's still legally your wife."

Nate paced the room. "Why do we have to have this argument, over and over again?"

"We're not arguing; we're talking about your family."

"That's not MY family. It's Eva's family. You've never been close with them anyway. Why are you taking their side now?"

"The only side I'm taking is the side of the kids."

"You used to take my side."

"I still do darling; your kids are a part of you. Don't you feel that?"

"No, Motherdear, I DON'T ... not any more."

"I don't believe that and you shouldn't even say it."

"Motherdear", Nate sat on the couch facing her, "if I go back there, something bad is going to happen. I'm not going to accept visiting my own kids. We're suppose to visit animals in the zoo. And I'm definitely not going to pay for some other … *guy* to sit up in my home. Please, believe me, Motherdear, it's best that I stay away from Eva and her family."

"Nate", she put her hand on his, "do you know the reason I came out here."

He looked down at the floor and then said, "Yes."

"I don't have long and I wanted to see you happy again."

"But, I am happy, Motherdear, here with Lena and Brandon."

"I know you think you're happy, but I know you, better than you know yourself."

It always disarmed him when his mother said that. It was as though she could read his mind, as if nothing was private.

He pulled away and walked to the patio door again.

"I did everything you taught me when it came to my family. I worked hard and always took care of them. I stuck by Eva when we had the tragedy; I stayed strong and kept everything together. I can't follow your rules any more, Motherdear. They don't work any more and I have my own rules now. If you just look around you'll see I'm not such a bad person. We have a lot of real love right here in this house. You may not believe it but Lena has helped to heal my soul."

"Nate, I'm asking you to do this one last thing for me. Get in touch with your kids. I've talked with them and they're wondering what happened to you. Darnell is just like you and he's very angry just like you are."

"Motherdear, it's not fair for you to ask me like this. You know I love you and I'd do anything for you …"

She didn't reply.

Nate choked up and struggled to get the words out. "Okay, I will get in touch with them. I promise."

As if on cue, Lena and Ruth returned from their shopping. Brandon came running in, "Look granddad … I got a airplane.

He threw the balsa wood glider across the room, almost hitting Nate in the face.

"Not in the house, Brandon!" Lena scolded.

Nate caught the airplane and then said, "ALRIGHT! Come on little man, let's go flying."

The two of them headed through the doorway and were gone.

"I've got to go cook for Eli." Ruth said, "Nice meeting you Miss LaChae. Hope to see you again before you leave."

"Same here." JimmieMae said.

Lena stopped unpacking the bags and came into the living room. "Did you two talk?"

JimmieMae looked up from her magazine and then said, "Yes."

"Well?"

"He promised to contact them."

"Thank goodness." Lena said, "Every time I brought the subject up, he turned cold. So, even though I knew it was eating at him, I finally just left it alone. Your son needs a lot of healing."

JimmieMae took her glasses off and asked, "Do you believe you can heal him?"

"I know he has to heal himself, and I love him enough to help him through this if he lets me."

"They'll want to come and see him."

"That's fine with me, I expected that."

"You're a good woman, Lena." JimmieMae put her magazine down, "Now, would you mind telling me why you had me thinking you were a witch when I first came here?"

Lena looked as serious as she could and then said, "Because I am."

*   *   *

At Santa Cruz beach, JimmieMae enjoyed sticking her feet into the Pacific Ocean. She enjoyed it much more than Nate's driving up and down the hills in San Francisco. The more she begged him to stop, the more Nate teased her with another steep hill. Lena knew it was payback and she frowned at him.

They enjoyed dinner at the Fuk-Luk Chinese restaurant. Nate kept saying, "I've never been very lucky anyway ..." His mother and Lena shook their heads and laughed at him. Poor Brandon tried his best to eat with chopsticks, and flipped a shrimp onto Nate's plate. That brought on another round of laughter.

When Nate took his mother to the airport, he reminded her about the free drinks in First-class. She laughed as she remembered her earlier flight. Her glass of OJ and champagne kept getting refilled when she wasn't looking; she had arrived quite inebriated.

Now, when Nate hugged her, she seemed fragile. They said, "I love you" at the same time and she walked onto the airplane.

Lena drove them home and told Brandon he could open the gift Motherdear left for him. When they saw what it was, they assumed it was a message to Brandon.

Nate thought the message was 'Make some noise!'

Lena said the message was 'drive 'em crazy!'

Brandon did his best to prove them both correct, with his new drum.

*   *   *

"Martin Lee saw the notes I've been taking", Nate said to Lena, "and he asked me to put together a formal class. He wants me to teach it too, but I'm not ready. I don't understand the Stepper well enough yet."

Lena curled her feet up on the couch, "So what are you going to do?"

"I'm going to have to go to Level ... I mean I'll meditate on it."

Lena's asked, "What is this going to Level all about? I've heard you say that before."

Nate rubbed the sockets of his eyes with the back of his forefingers. "It's a technique, a way of meditating, that's all."

She hugged him, "Tell me about it."

"I will, even though you might not believe me."

"Try me."

"Just be patient", he said, "and you'll see."

"When?"

"Next week, actually. Jose Silva is giving a class downtown and I've signed us up for it."

*   *   *

Nate gave his best sales pitch to a manager and two engineers at Satari Gaming Company. The Photodisk system performed well, showing his football plays. He said he had a patent pending and finished his presentation with, "You can see the realism this system offers; players get to see real photos instead of cartoon characters."

There was silence around the room. After a few glances at each other, one of the engineers said, "Thank you for that demo. Can we see inside the cabinet now?" The manager said, "No. I think it may be in both our interest that you don't open your cabinet yet, Mr. LaChae."

Everyone looked at him expectantly.

"You see, we've been developing a similar idea and, like you, our patent is pending. For that reason, it would be best that neither of us see the inner workings of our machines. This may very well be an example of simultaneous inventions."

Nate suspected Satari might be using filmstrips, the way Del Adams had suggested. So, he asked, "Can you change the sequencing of your photos?"

"Let's just say we have several sequences available." The manager said, "Really, Mr. LaChae, unless you are willing to sign our disclosure agreement, I'm afraid we can't discuss this any further.

"May I see the disclosure agreement?"

The document was worded so that he would be forbidden from using anything he saw at Satari. Nate understood signing such a document could void any claims he might make for a similar invention. *If we go to court against each other*, Nate thought, *they'll have their corporate lawyers and money behind them while I'll have almost nothing.*

Nate said, "I can't sign this."

"The form is standard practice for companies in the Bay Area."

"Even so, I'm not going to sign it."

"In that case, we won't be able to do business with you, Mr. LaChae."

Afterward, Nate drove the U-Haul, with his tall gaming cabinet in back, over by the Bay and drank several cans of beer. The next day he rented a storage space and put all his Photodisk equipment inside. The only thing left in the second bedroom was his computer, a bookcase and the cot that Brandon slept on.

He told Lena, "I'm not going to work on the Photodisk any more. Video disks are going to make it obsolete real soon anyway."

Lena knew Nate was discouraged about his project, but resisted questioning him after he said, "It's time we focus more on our families. Why don't you call Marilyn and see if she wants to come back out here."

She did, and a changed Marilyn arrived a week later. Their reunion was warm and Marilyn seemed like a different person altogether. Brandon was elated.

*   *   *

Nate decided it was time to keep the promise he made his mother. He went to a public phone and dialed his estranged wife's number. They hadn't spoken to each other in four years. And it had never been with civility.

"Hello, Eva, this is Nate."

There was a pause, "Hello, Nate. How are you?"

"I'm fine. I'm calling for two reasons. First of all I wanted to get in touch with the children and secondly I wanted to see if you're ready to get a divorce."

"Your mother told me to expect a call from you, Nate. The kids and I are doing fine."

"I was going to ask."

"I'm sure you were." She waited for him to respond. When he didn't she said, "As a matter of fact, I was going to try and contact you for a divorce. And it would be a good thing for you to be in contact with the kids. But, I have to warn you they have changed over the past years; they may not respond the way you expect."

"I don't expect anything. I'm open to whatever. And I want you to know I'll start sending Savings Bonds again, if you give me your address."

"That would be nice, but I prefer for you to send the bonds to your mother; I'll get them from her. I won't ask for anything from you in the divorce; you send whatever you feel is right."

"What grounds?"

"Will you agree to irreconcilable differences?"

"That sounds about right to me. One more thing …"

"And what's that, Nate?"

"I want to invite the kids to come out and visit. Not all at the same time of course and only if they want to come. I'll pay."

"I have no objections if they want to come."

"Good." He breathed a sigh of relief. *That went well so far*, he thought, *now for the kids*. "Can I speak to them now?"

"They're not here. It's their cousin's birthday and they're all at Aunt Louise's house. You remember her?"

Disappointed about the kids not being there, he said, "No, I don't. When can I call back and speak with them?"

"It will be late when they come in."

Eva continued, "You want to give me your number and I'll tell them to call you back."

"No. I'll call back tomorrow before noon."

Phone calls, letters, and pictures were exchanged and before long Nate was meeting his oldest son, Darnell, at San Jose airport.

Except for Darnell height of six-three, and his muscular build, he was a copy of Nate. Darnell smiled, hugged Lena and Brandon then, hesitantly, shook Nate's hand.

Marilyn stepped forward and then said, "What about your new sister?"

"Okay", Darnell said and gave her a hug too.

He turned toward a nearby stewardess and then said, "Anybody else?"

Pleased that his son had a sense of humor, Nate said, "No more surprises."

They took the long route from the airport, while Nate and Lena described landscapes as they passed.

"All I see are trees." Darnell said, looking from side to side.

"And that's all you're gonna see", Marilyn was quick to add, "I hope they don't take us through the mountains again."

Their offspring's laughter gave Nate and Lena hope that Darnell might help mellow-out Marilyn. Brandon fell asleep between them.

Lena prepared Cherry Chicken for dinner and Nate asked everyone
to hold hands as he blessed the food:

"Heavenly father, please bless this food
and bless this house and everyone in it.
We ask that you help us share your love
which has brought us together.
And teach us to have patience
and understanding with one another.
All these things we ask in Jesus name.
Amen."

That first night, they played cards until late. Marilyn and Darnell
played as partners and took turns 'dissing' Nate and Lena about their
scores. Marilyn surprised everyone when she offered to let Darnell have
the second bedroom and she would sleep on the couch. But, Brandon
complained and Darnell explained that he preferred sleeping on the
floor anyway.

Nate finished his workweek and took everyone on a tour of the
Bay Area. Once in Oakland, at Jack London Square, the women took
Brandon and went shopping. Nate and Darnell walked onto a long pier
and looked out at the Golden Gate Bridge and Coit Tower. Alcatraz
Island was surrounded by sailboats that dotted the water. The cool
breeze felt good on their faces.

"You know, I always felt guilty about you leaving." Darnell said.

"Why would you feel guilty?"

"Because, I thought I was the reason you left."

Nate looked at him and saw that he was serious. Before Nate could
speak, Darnell continued. "And when you came back and got Malcolm
and Charlene, I was sure you were mad with me and maybe Kelly
too."

"No, no, no," Nate shook his head; "I just picked two of you because
a friend of mine had said she'd baby-sit, but she only agreed to take
two of you. I didn't have favorites or anything like that. Malcolm and
Charlene were at the house when I came, so I took them, that's all. I
was coming back for you and Kelly."

Darnell stared at his dad and then said nothing.

"Motherdear was the one who told me you all should not be separated." Nate said, "So, when I finally realized I didn't know anyone willing to keep all of you, I brought Malcolm and Charlene back."

"But, why didn't you ask me who I wanted to be with?"

Nate continued looking out over the water. "Darnell, that was the main part of the problem. You were all too young for me to explain what was going on. I didn't want it to be happening at all."

Darnell looked out at the water. After a long silence he said, "I used to write on the walls of that long tunnel by grandma's house, where all the graffiti is; I must have wrote your name and mine a hundred times hoping that you might see it. Grandma and them said I was obsessed, but I just remembered my father and all the good times we had had."

Another long silence passed without them looking at each other.

When Nate felt tears well up, he said sternly, "We have to move on; we can't go back to those times."

Darnell looked at his father. "Why not?"

"Because, I found out a long time ago, wishing won't make it so."

They heard Brandon calling; he was running their way with a shiny toy in his hand.

*   *   *

Nate solved the problem of organizing training classes at MicroStep by videotaping the inventors speaking to the first groups of students. Afterward, the tapes were used for training other students. After a time, Nate understood the Stepper and memorized the videos as well. He enjoyed the process of teaching and accepted the humility of not knowing all the answers.

He was given the additional task of turning his notes into Maintenance and Operator's manuals. For that, three consulting writers were hired and Nate did the editing. Getting the information typeset and published on cleanroom paper proved to be costly and troublesome.

Meanwhile, Martin Lee started working from home. Leo DeBos was absent most of the time too. By default, Nate became MicroStep's information-central. His days were long, usually without lunch, and he wasn't sleeping well either.

The company had more than a hundred employees now, each of which had been taught by Nate. Many of them were competing for supervisory positions. At meetings, the group supervisors had started finger-pointing when things went wrong.

On one of his many trips to Fry's Electronics store, Nate saw a computer chess program named Sargon. He almost didn't buy it because of its small memory size and cheap price.

To his surprise, it played a strong game and beat him. Using his TRS-80 computer, Nate disassembled the Sargon chess program, trying to answer his burning question: 'How can such a small program be so smart at playing chess?' He became obsessed with finding the answer.

He bought books on Artificial Intelligence (AI) and became convinced that computer programs could get smarter by themselves. When BYTE magazine ran a series of articles that included AI programs coded in BASIC, Nate began writing an AI program of his own.

His enthusiasm infected Gabriel and soon they were attending seminars on AI at Stanford University, and discussing different approaches to AI.

"You know what this means, Gabe?"

"That computers are going to be able to think?"

"Exactly." Nate said, "This is going to put a lot of people out of work."

"Not necessarily. They'll have to change jobs, that's all."

"I don't know ..." Nate said pensively, "I wonder about the morality of this type of programming. One report, from DARPA, said AI could be as important as The Manhattan Project was."

Gabriel pointed at Nate and grinned, "You're trying to decide if you're going to jump into it, aren't you?"

Nate didn't answer. Instead he said, "I read a book, by Ralph DeLorean, where he presented the question, 'What should a moral man do in an immoral world?' and I never forgot it."

"We know what he did, don't we?" Gabriel drank from his Coca-Cola, "He made a lot of money. Besides, the programmers that do AI, use special processors and languages. That probably means AI programs can't fit in a TRS-80 computer."

"I've already started writing some AI programs on my TRS-80 and running separate modules." Nate said, "I did modular programming before, with my projector; it's not all that difficult."

"But it's so tedious and you can't run an entire program at once."

"Look Gabe, all I know is that that chess program is smart enough to beat me and it runs on my TRS-80. I'm going to use the same techniques they used. Only, instead of figuring out the best chess move, my program will figure out the best move to fix equipment."

"Sometimes you oversimplify things, Nate."

"No, the big guys over-complicate things. Come on, Gabe, we both know it's all ones and zeros inside the computer. All those higher languages are only shortcuts to the tedious programming you mentioned."

"That's not completely true. There are things that are unique to each programming language. For example in Fortran ..."

"Yeah, yeah, yeah. And THEY say it can't be done ... until somebody does it." Nate said, turning in his chair.

Gabriel held his palms up, "Hey, buddy, I'm on your side. I just believe a project should be examined from all sides before jumping in head-over-heels."

Nate put his hand on Gabriel's shoulder and exhaled, "Gabe, I'm sorry, man. I get so much negativity from the guys at work ... not that you're being negative. Actually Gabe, I admire you for analyzing a problem to a point where you can write good code on your first pass. When I program, I throw away code like sheets of toilet paper; a lot of times I start all over again."

"I have to tell you, Nate, you have two things in common with Thomas Edison – persistence and determination. It was obvious to all of us at CIC, when you talked about the years you spent working on your engine. I'm sure you'll get your AI program running."

"Don't you want to work on it too?"

"I'm very interested, but I've started a new contract and it's taking up all my time; I had to buy another computer for it."

"Really? What did you get?"

"Come on, I'll show you."

They talked techno-babble until Nate almost missed the last train home from San Francisco. Nate made plans during his ride home,

First, I'll substitute facts for chess pieces.
Second, I'll program ways to search through those facts.
Third, I'll create a way to input problem-symptoms.
Then the program will decide the best 'move'.
After that, I'll …

Nate's epiphany came when he realized he could load all the segments of his TRS-80 program into MicroStep's main computer and test his full program. To his chagrin, his program needed more disk storage space than was allotted to him. So, when the IT manager, Nikolas Oberlin, refused to grant Nate any more space, Nate decided it was time to do a little hacking.

For the next few weeks, his coworkers complained about having to log into their terminals two times. Within days, Nate had pilfered the storage space he needed from his coworkers.

When Oberlin discovered Nate's violations, he went directly to Leo and complained. Leo paged Nate to his newly built office. "What's this I hear about you breaking passwords?" Leo rocked back in his chair. Oberlin was standing near by, with his arms folded across his chest. His blond hair partially covering deep-set eyes.

"It was just a fun thing to do." Nate said, "There was no harm done."

Leo looked at Nikolas then back at Nate, "We don't look too kindly on these kinds of activities. You're not supposed to go into anyone else's accounts or files. You are not to do any more of this sort of thing, do you understand?"

"Yes, Leo, sure."

Nate wanted to ask permission to get his hidden files out of the other accounts, but thought he had better not. Oberlin marched, triumphantly, past Nate without saying a word.

As Nate turned to leave, Leo said, "Wait a minute, Nate."

"Yes, sir?"

Oberlin stopped at the door, but Leo's stare indicated he wanted to speak privately with Nate. So, Nikolas exited and closed the door quietly.

"I was told you have a passion for computers and this little episode has convinced me." Leo got up, walked around his desk, and sat on the corner of it. "Nate, I need to learn about computers … at least enough to understand the buzz words they throw around at meetings and I want to know how to run programs by myself. Will you teach me?"

"Sure, Leo. But Nikolas knows more about MicroStep's programs than I do."

"That little … ", Leo took a breath, "Nikolas is too impatient. I need someone who can explain things simply and Perry says you're good at that."

"Yeah, I break things down for my own understanding." Nate thought for a moment, then asked, "When would I teach you?"

"On some Saturday mornings?" Leo said, "I'll pay you, of course."

"If you buy lunch, that will be enough pay for me."

"Good." Leo patted him on the shoulder, and returned to his desk.

Following Gabriel's and Paul Brown's advice, Nate filed for a copyright of his AI program, which he named Expert-1.

*   *   *

Nate accepted Paul Brown's invitation for the family to come for lunch on Sunday. Lena and Nate always enjoyed the scenic drive up Hwy-680. It brought joy to his heart when Brandon pointed at some cumulous clouds and exclaimed, "LOOK! Alligators."

Lena said, "Yes Brandon, we see them."

Marilyn rolled her eyes at Darnell.

Nate weaved his way up the hills and pulled into Paul Brown's driveway. The eucalyptus smell was strong. They came up the walkway and Paul's wife, Louise, opened the door, "You brought everybody this time." The onset of Parkinson's disease gave her slight tremors as she hugged each of them. The former school principal still possessed her engaging smile and bright eyes.

"Where's Paul?" Nate asked.

"He's somewhere back there in his workshop. Go ahead. I've got to check on the peach cobbler."

Lena followed Louise toward the kitchen. Brandon ran toward the back, stopped in the doorway and started walking backward.

"OH, WOW!"

Paul came through the doorway holding two white plastic tubes in front of himself. Floating above the tubes was a thin piece of Styrofoam shaped like an airplane. The airplane was balanced in mid-air! Paul banked the aircraft around Darnell and Marilyn, and landed it on the cocktail table.

"How did you do that?" Darnell asked.

Brandon grinned and clapped his hands.

"See Mommy. I told you he got neat toys."

"Maybe I better introduce everybody." Nate said.

The group followed Paul into his workshop and watched him show off his inventions. Nate saw the amazement on Darnell and Marilyn's faces.

At lunchtime Louise sat across from Darnell and Marilyn and then said, "You two look like brother and sister."

"They are now." Nate said.

"Mommy is the oldest."

"Not for long, if I know women." Paul added. "And what about you, Darnell?"

He looked at Paul. "I want to know how you think up all that stuff."

"Thinking it up is easy. Making it work is another story."

"That looks like a fun way to get rich."

"Rich is a relative term Darnell. There's always going to be somebody with more money than you. But, my inventions have made it where I don't have to work for anybody any more."

"What kind of education do you need to be an inventor?"

"It's not a matter of education, even though that helps. You need to have imagination and be able to turn you ideas into physical things. And, in today's world, knowing about computers helps. Isn't that right Nate?"

"I hope so." Nate said, "But, Paul you use such simple materials and get your products sold. My inventions use computers and all that, but I haven't sold anything yet."

"That will come in time" Louise said. "Paul had fifty-six patents before he made any real money. You all ready for some cobbler now?"

"Yeah!" Brandon answered first, "I'm ready."

"Are there any Black women inventors?" Marilyn asked.

"Oh yes, darling," Louise said while dipping up the cobbler, "there was Annie Malone and Marjorie Joyner who, separately, made millions when they figured out how to straighten black hair ... they called it Porow."

"I remember my grandmother talked about that." Nate said, "She told me she used to Porow hair for a living in Alabama."

Black women patented folding beds and ironing boards too." Paul said, "Look up Sarah Goode and Sarah Boone in your encyclopedia."

Marilyn put her fork down, "What about in modern times?"

"I'm sure there are." Louise said, "If you research a little."

"We've had women come to CIC meetings with all sorts of ideas for inventions." Paul said to Marilyn, "You should come to the meeting if you're interested. That reminds me Nate, when are you going to give a talk about computers to the CIC members?"

"Soon, Paul." Nate finished chewing, "Maybe at the next meeting."

Paul pointed with his fork; "You two are lucky to have a computer expert in your home. Almost everything is going to have computers in them in the future. If I were starting all over again, I'd learn all I could about them."

"What about you, Lena?" Louise asked.

"Oh, he's taught me some of the basics and I'm signed up to take a class at his job."

"Granddaddy said he's going to teach me about computers too." Brandon added. "Then, I'm gonna make computer games and have lots of money."

"I'm sure you will, Brandon." Paul chuckled.

After lunch they played Ping-Pong and shot pool. Joy and playfulness was always infectious at Paul's house. Their enthusiasm lasted all the way home.

There was one magic moment for Nate, when he was walking home from work one day and saw Darnell and Marilyn playing basketball together. He stopped where they couldn't see him and watched. *It's so wonderful seeing them playing together and happy.* He thought, *That's all*

I've wanted for each of them. Why can't it be like this all the time? That would truly be heaven on earth.

As he walked past, they waved and tried to outdo each other with the basketball. Marilyn was good, but no match for Darnell's height. Nate had expected his tall son to have trophies for basketball, but Darnell preferred swimming and bodybuilding ... mainly because everyone expected him to play basketball.

$$*\qquad*\qquad*$$

In the morning, as Lena was preparing breakfast, Nate had a revelation: *If I can get Marilyn into one of my classes at the job, she'll be fully qualified for a job as a Process Engineer. I can give my personal recommendation for her interviews; she could walk into a job!*

Nate didn't tell Marilyn his plan until after he saw she was serious about his tutoring at home. She seemed like a different person and learned fast.

Then, without asking Leo, Nate signed Marilyn up for his one-week Process Engineering class. He was pleasantly surprised when Marilyn progressed right along with the other students. Nate got to see a different side of her; she was serious and interacted well with the other students.

On the last day of class, Marilyn arrived in a lovely dress, had her hair done and her makeup was perfect – Lena's touch, no doubt. She was beaming as she received her certificate. It warmed Nate's heart when she hugged him and then said, "Thanks, Pops."

At dinner Nate told Marilyn he had called Mrs. Vandermeer, over at ISL Logic and arranged an interview.

"Don't you think she needs time to practice?," Darnell asked.

"Not really. Right now the material is fresh in her mind."

"You know how to work with computers, Mommy?" Brandon asked.

"Yes Brandon, see my certificate."

"Oh, wow!"

Lena brought out two splits of Champagne and Nate poured for everyone – including Brandon.

On the day of Marilyn's interview, Nate called home three times and each time Lena said she hadn't heard anything. Nate had an uneasy feeling when he got home.

"Where's Marilyn?"

"She came in and went back out, with Darnell, to the mall."

"What did she say about the interview?"

"She said it went okay."

"That's it?"

"Don't worry Nate; she's nervous that's all."

"Yeah, you're probably right. I just thought, since I didn't hear from Ms. Vandermeer, something might have gone wrong."

"Stop worrying, Honey."

"I can't help it; I feel like something is not quite right, Lena."

"Here, eat your food and let's play a game of chess."

Nate was asleep when Darnell returned late without Marilyn. When Lena asked about Marilyn, Darnell said, "I wasn't interested in going with her to her friend's house, so I came on home. She seemed okay to me. Why? Is something wrong?"

"No. Did she talk about her interview?"

"Not really. When I asked her about it, she said it went okay."

Nate called Ms. Vandermeer the next day and was told, "We decided Marilyn was not a good match for the position, Nate, I'm sorry." He was stunned and hung up the phone. When he called home Lena told him Marilyn had spoken with Ms. Vandermeer too.

"How's she taking it?"

"She just told me she didn't get the job and left immediately."

"Shit!" Nate exclaimed. "This doesn't make any sense at all."

That evening Nate waited up for Marilyn, who didn't get in until after midnight. He could tell she was high. She went directly to her room and closed the door. Nate knocked and was told to enter. She was sitting on the bed by Brandon, who was asleep. Marilyn lit a cigarette and exhaled slowly as Nate waited in the doorway. His heart sank deeply when he heard her say, "I knew they wasn't gonna give a job like that to somebody like me."

Nate opened his mouth, but no words came.

Lena gently grabbed his arm and tugged at him. "Not now, Nate. Let her be."

He looked from Marilyn to Lena and back again, then went to the bathroom. He felt empty as he remembered how pretty, bright, and happy Marilyn looked at the graduation. Now, she had that hard look again.

Eventually, Lena got the story from Darnell as Marilyn had told him.

"But" Nate frowned, "why would she tell Ms. Vandermeer she can program in Assembly Language? I never taught her any of that."

"I guess she must have thought the programming you taught her, here at home, was Assembly Language."

"No, no, no. I explained the difference to her, right at the beginning and the Process Engineer class was not about that. She should have known that."

"Well, it's done now, Nate and there's nothing we can do to change it."

"I feel like I let her down. You heard what she said the other night."

"Honey, she feels she let you down too. But, nobody let anybody down. It just wasn't meant to be, that's all."

"Isn't she going to try for some other Process Engineer interviews?"

"No, not now, Nate. She wants to do something else."

Lena put her arms around his neck. "You did all that you could, Honey. Just let it be for now."

*   *   *

One month after Leo DeBos left MicroStep, the new General Manager, Willy Raymond, started firing people that didn't fit his idea of a company image. Neither tenure nor reputation mattered. First, there was the older executive secretary with the strong southwestern accent. Then there was Perry's Production Assistant, who was told he didn't have enough education. There was friction with Perry, whose outspoken political views were opposite to Willy's. However, Perry's relationship with Martin Lee secured his position.

Willy Raymond had a big round head with prematurely thinning brown hair that made him look older than his forty years. He liked to wear suspenders and had a habit of staring at people through his horn-rimmed glasses.

Rumor had it that he was chosen to manage MicroStep as a reward for his brilliance as a corporate lawyer. He tried to hide his lack of technical knowledge by having one-on-one meetings with the staff.

It became obvious that his only priority was to please MBS Corporation through their liaison - Art Chavez.

Every Monday, project status luncheons were held in the conference room and each supervisor was required to make a report. Art Chavez invariably found reasons to admonish those in attendance.

"That's got to improve", Art told the electronics supervisor, "we can't have delays."

"We've hired three more people", Harry said, "but they'll need time to get trained."

"What if I give you two extra weeks here on the Gantt chart", Art asked, "Will that work?"

Harry shrugged, "I guess that'll be enough time."

Art continued down his list and asked, "What about documentation of the mechanical stages, Nate?"

"They're all done", Nate replied, "they're being copied right now."

On cue, Nate's new secretary entered and dropped a stack of papers. She was tall, blond, in her forties, and seemed flustered most of the time. What got everyone's attention, however, was her jogging suit, headband, and tall socks. Two men got up to help her collect the fallen papers. She placed them in front of Nate.

"Sorry, I'm late, Nate", she grinned sheepishly, "The copier jammed."

"Thank you, Stephanie, that's fine."

She looked around the table, "Sorry". Then she turned to Nate. "Oh, I almost forgot, your wife wants you to call her right away."

After Stephanie left, Art asked, "Does she always dress like that?"

Nate laughed, "She jogs at lunchtime."

Someone said, "I'd like to see her jog."

Art Chavez droned on, "So, all the procedures are done. Is that right?"

Nate placed his hand on the stack in front of him. "They're right here."

"Okay, then", Art put his pen down, "unless anyone has something else … meeting's adjourned."

Nate hoped the telephone call wasn't about his mother, but it was.

"She's in a coma, Nate", Lena told him over the phone.

"Is she in a hospital?"

"Yes, that's what your sister said. Do you want her number?"

"No. I'm coming home. Lena, pack a bag for me. I'll try to fly out tonight."

*   *   *

By the time he arrived at Presbyterian Hospital in New York City, it was 4:00 am and his brother and sister had left. A nurse directed him to his mother's ward. He entered the room, slid the curtain back, and saw a person sleeping there. He went to the other two occupied beds and then examined the chart on the first bed; it was JimmieMae. Her head was almost bald, her skin looked leathery, even though she was sweating.

Nate leaned forward and kissed her forehead. There was a scent he didn't recognize. He stood for a moment and stared at his Motherdear. An ocean of tears welled up and he knew if he released them now, he would wake everyone. He pulled up a chair and reached in the bedside drawer for a Bible. It was there.

An hour later, a nurse saw him sitting close by the bed weeping and reading softly.

The next days were hazy. Nate's brother Douglas and Sister Claudette shared their love and took turns sitting with their mother whose condition was marginally stable.

Nate spoke, at length, with the doctor.

"There are procedures I can do" the doctor said, "but none of them would improve the quality of your mother's life at this point. So, I don't recommend doing them."

Nate looked into the doctor's eyes, "That's what it's all about, isn't it?

"What?"

"The quality of one's life."

"Yes, it is."

"How long does she have?"

"It could be days, Mr. LaChae."

Nate swallowed, "Thank you, doctor."

The doctor called, after JimmieMae regained consciousness. Despite everyone's concern over MommaMary's heart, it was decided to bring her to the hospital. Nate and Douglas held her elbows as she slowly made her way down the ward. Nate's uncle, Sam, was hanging on to Claudette's arm. They came into the dimly lit room. The lamp on the table illuminated JimmieMae's face and the photo next to her. MommaMary sat and the family nucleus waited silently.

JimmieMae stirred and turned her head toward them. She opened her eyes and looked into her mother's face. No one moved.

"Momma?"

MommaMary took her daughter's hand in hers and said, "Yes, baby. I'm here."

"Oh, Momma. I'm sick."

MommaMary enclosed her daughter's hand in both of hers and patted it.

"Yes, baby. I know and Momma loves you."

"I love you too, Momma."

JimmieMae slowly turned her head, looked at each of them and tried to smile. Her eyes closed for a while and then reopened. "Brother?"

Sam came forward, on the other side of the bed and kissed her on the forehead. Tears streamed down his face. "Hey, Sister." He cried shamelessly as Nate held him.

One by one the children came forward and spoke briefly with her. Then, a nurse came and said visiting time was over. She started the IV and JimmieMae closed her eyes.

As they were leaving, Nate turned back and whispered in his mother's ear, "You have always taught us how to live, now please teach us how to do this. I love you, Motherdear."

He kissed her on her forehead.

*　　　*　　　*

Nate used up his time-off from work and returned to California. No sooner had he arrived home, than Lena told him Aunt Lil had called about his father being in a car accident.

"Oh, no!"

On the phone, Aunt Lil said, "You have to come now, Nate. The doctors don't expect your father to make it."

Lena convinced Nate to lie down for a few minutes while she called Paul Brown and asked for money for round-trip airfare.

He decided to take Darnell with him; partly because of friction that had been building between Darnell and Lena. Nate figured he'd get money for the return trip somehow. He told Lena to call his job and explain.

On the plane, Nate told Darnell, "Now you'll, finally, get to meet your real grandfather."

But that was not to be. Lena's mother met them at the airport with the news that his father had passed away during the night. Nate was devastated and sat in a corner crying while Darnell got their luggage.

At Aunt Lil's house Nate was told his father was returning from Mississippi one night when a car crossed the median and hit him head-on. Nate went and saw the wreck of his father's big Cadillac, the front end demolished from the impact. He turned away from the blood on the seat and windshield.

How could this happen to dad? He was such a strong psychic?

The fact that his father had been to Mississippi, investigating oil found on family land, made Nate suspicious. But no one else shared his conspiracy feelings. Still, it left him with an uneasy feeling.

Everyone was surprised when Nate didn't stay for the funeral. It was getting difficult for him to make clear decisions. He chose to stay at Lena's parent's house, because he intended to ask his father-in-law, Chester, for plane fare home. In the end, Lena's mother, Bertha, had to insist that Chester give Nate airfare home.

Darnell decided to return to New York. Nate was surprised when Darnell hugged him at the airport and then said, "I'm glad I got to know you better. I'm coming back to California one day."

"When?"

"I don't know, but I like it out there."

"You're always welcome." Nate said.

Two days after Nate returned home, his mother passed away. He sent his entire paycheck to his sister, in Arizona, so she could attend the funeral in New York.

Meanwhile, Lena tried to keep him from becoming a zombie. She came to bed, after getting Brandon to sleep, and the two of them lay there, on their backs, in the dark.

"You know, I miss that tall boy of yours"

"Yeah, me too." Nate admitted, "I hope I didn't push him too hard to get a job."

"No, you didn't. He wanted to work; it takes a while; you know how it is when you're looking for work."

"Do you think he'll come back?"

"We'll see."

Four days later, Nate returned to MicroStep and immersed himself in his job. One of his first tasks was to interview a new secretary; Stephanie had been fired by Willy Raymond.

*   *   *

There were many changes at the start of MicroStep's fiscal year - a new classroom was built and a machine, dedicated for training, was promised. Nate and his secretary, Debbie, organized their new offices and prepared for the arrival of the Techline Training consultant Matthew Anderson. He was young and didn't have a strong presence.

In the weeks that followed, he and Nate worked together until the first Tuesday of class. During a coffee break, Nate told Matthew, "These students need to see the machine now!"

"But", Matthew protested, "The lesson plan doesn't call for any hands-on until Wednesday."

"Well then we need to change the lesson plan," Nate said, "because it's not working." He headed for the production area with Matthew protesting along the way.

"Now look, Nate, I'm the facilitator, and you're supposed to take my advice."

"Matthew, your job is to give advice. I'm responsible for getting the information into these student's heads. I'm not going to argue with you, when I know I'm right."

Matthew stopped and threw his hands up.

Nate's pace didn't slacken. He entered the production area and approached his buddy, "Hey, Perry, I need a favor ..."

*   *   *

After a string of difficulties, Nate brought the new Maintenance Manual to Willy's office.

Willy thumbed through it and then said, "It's late."

When Nate tried to explain, Willy repeated, "It's late." Then he added, "And tell your publisher friend not to park his Jaguar in the employee spots any more."

Nate gritted his teeth, "He's not my friend", then he left Willy's office.

Louis Marbury was the first trainer Nate hired. A young black man who reminded Nate of himself. He had experience as a Field Service Engineer, but his training skills proved to be severely lacking – even after working in the Production area for two weeks.

Nate took him aside, after stepping in to assist with a class. "Listen, Louis, if you want, we can stay late sometime and go over this stuff."

"I'll get it, Nate"; Louis answered nervously, "No matter what you saw in there today, I'll get it."

"Louis, there have been complaints. This is your second class ... "

"I know, I know, Nate."

"I told you", Nate said, "They're never going to say 'Those two black guys sure do give an *average* class.' We've got to have our shit together. Do you understand?"

Louis got louder, "I said, I'll get it!"

"Alright, but tell me if you need any help, okay?"

"Yeah. Yeah", Louis grabbed his attaché case and left.

A few minutes later, Perry Penvenne was leaving and he saw Nate's office lights on; the door was open. He leaned in and then said, "Hey, you look like you're studying a chess move."

Nate looked up. "Oh, hey there, Perry. How's it going?"

"I'm okay. What about you?"

"I can't seem to get through to Louis."

"You know, there's been talk about his classes."

"Yeah. I know." Nate's attention drifted off.

I can't understand why the brother won't open up with me. This is our chance to show what we can do. Our people are always complaining that THE MAN won't give us a chance. Now here we have a chance and Louis can't see it.

"Nate." Perry shook him. "You okay?"

"Yeah, just tired I guess."

"You need a ride home?"

"No, thanks Perry. I'm okay … really."

"See you tomorrow then."

The next morning, it was chilly in the building as Debbie hung up her phone and peeked around the cubicle wall at Nate.

"Willy's back and he wants to see you right away."

"Okay, thanks Debbie."

Nate wanted to ask her about Willy's tone, but he doubted Debbie would give him a useful answer. For all her efficiency, she was a very plain and unemotional person – at least toward him. Nate logged off his terminal, grabbed several folders, and headed toward the front office.

I sure hope Willy got the corporate board to approve our new budget, he thought.

Papers were strewn all over Willy's big oak desk. His sleeves were rolled up and his red suspenders seemed to radiate heat. He was shuffling through the papers and didn't look up. Before Nate could speak, Willy said, "I want you to fire Louis."

Nate sat and then said, "I see you've heard about his class."

"Yes. I heard it would have been a disaster, if you hadn't stepped in." Willy looked at Nate. "How long have you known Louis couldn't hack it?"

Nate shifted in his chair, "It's not that he can't handle it. I think he just needs more time to-"

"Times up, Nate." Willy strummed his fingers on the desk as he said, "if you don't want to fire him, I will."

"Listen Willy, the guy's a good technician. He proved that, when he worked in the production area. Why not transfer him to the Field Service department? They need all the help they can get."

Willy leaned back and grabbed his suspenders, as if preparing to give a summation in court, "You're still willing to stick your neck out for him?"

"It's not that. I'm thinking about the company. We've spent all this time training the guy; why not use him where he can do some good."

Willy stared at Nate, smiled, and then said, "All right; I'll think about what to do with Louis. Meanwhile, I want you to bring back that other guy you almost hired. Patrick ... what's his name? He had experience as a trainer didn't he?"

"Yes, he did," Nate responded slowly, "I'll see if he's still available."

"This time, I want to interview him." Willy lightened up, "we're going to be hiring a lot more people soon, and every one of them will need training."

"You got the budget approved?" Nate asked.

"Yeah, I got it alright, every penny. From now on, everybody around here has got to perform or they won't be around very long. And I mean everybody; you understand that Nate?"

"Of course, I understand," Nate replied, wondering why he was being threatened.

"Good. Now let's talk about your plans for expanding the training department."

After the meeting with Willy, Nate was exhilarated and exhausted. Everything he'd asked for was approved – except a dedicated Stepper for training. He wasn't excited about the prospect of hiring Patrick. But, under the circumstances, he knew he had better accept Willy's choice. Willy had Sally Palmer transfer Louis to the Field Service department before Nate had a chance to explain anything to him. Louis took the news very hard and thought Nate had betrayed him. He avoided Nate for weeks. Eventually, he learned the truth and came to Nate's office.

"I've been wrong about you, Nate and I just wanted to apologize. I heard you saved me from getting fired. When I thought you had got me demoted, I wanted to do some really bad things to you. Now, I know the truth and I just want to say I'm sorry, man." He looked downward.

"I knew you were angry" Nate said, "but you didn't let me explain anything. I appreciate you coming to me and telling me how you felt. I wish you the best of luck, man. If I can help in any way, let me know." Louis didn't look in Nate's eyes as they shook hands.

*   *   *

Meanwhile, Willy hired Patrick Smalls after a closed-door interview that didn't include Nate.

Once Patrick was trained, he and Nate taught classes every week. Their tag-team approach worked well and the students critiqued the classes favorably. It seemed odd to Nate that he and Patrick facilitated classes well together, but remained distant at other times.

Maybe it's because he's gay, Nate thought, *what the hell; as long as the work gets done.*

But, try as he may, Nate couldn't shake an uneasy feeling he had about Patrick. He told Lena about it one night.

"Maybe he sees you as a threat," she said.

"Not that again!" Nate laughed, "You think everybody sees me as a threat. I'm his boss for goodness sake."

"Yeah, and there's still an opening for Training Manager, isn't there?" she responded.

"I don't think that's it, Lena." Nate sipped his drink. "Patrick always has an attitude when I ask him to do something. He's worse than

Debbie was when she started. I hope it smoothes out soon like it did with Debbie."

"And you said he's always talking with Debbie about things they don't want you to hear?" Lena asked,

"That's probably that old boss versus worker attitude; you know - us against them."

"I think you need to put him in his place. Some people will keep challenging you if you don't."

"That's the point, Lena. Patrick doesn't challenge me directly. He just comes up with impractical ideas and doesn't like it when I tell him why they won't work at MicroStep. Like today, he suggested building a small mock-up, of the Stepper, until we get a real one for training. He said, the students would see how the parts come together – like Lego blocks. And when I tried explaining the cost and time to do such a project, he just walked away."

"Well, whatever. You still need to straighten the situation out before he gets too bold."

"I'll handle it," Nate said, "I can't figure out what he wants."

Lena smiled, put her arms around Nate, and whispered, "You better hope he doesn't want what I want right now."

They made sure Brandon was asleep and then they lit up.

*   *   *

The following morning, Nate was in Sally Palmer's office being told, "Debbie is being promoted. So, you'll need to look for another secretary." Also, I've decided to hire a full time technical writer and I want you to discontinue using all those consultants."

Surprised, Nate said, "Shouldn't we, at least, try to hire one of them, since they know so much about the Stepper?"

"No. I've already hired someone that I worked with before."

"I see," Nate said, "Are there any other changes you want to tell me about?"

"As a matter of fact there is one more. Willy will explain it." With that, she closed one folder, opened another and ignored Nate.

When Nate arrived at Willy's office, Perry Penvenne was exiting. They acknowledged each other, in the doorway, as Nate was beckoned to enter.

"Good morning, Nate. How's everything going?"

Surprised at Willy's jovial attitude, Nate replied, "Full of surprises so far."

"I've got another one for you. I'm promoting you to Training Manager effective today."

Nate didn't know what to say. He saw that Willy was waiting for a reply.

"Thanks, Willy. Thanks a lot."

"You'll have to give up the company car. There will be an increase in salary and you will be an exempt employee from now on. And don't worry; your take home pay will not be any less. We've made sure of that."

"I'll continue to give it my best shot, Willy."

Then Willy said, somberly, "There's something else we need to discuss."

"What's that?"

Willy sat back and grabbed his suspenders and asked, "What's going on with you and Patrick. We need to keep him happy."

"Willy, I treat him the same as I treat everyone else. What's his complaint exactly?"

"I'm not going to get into specifics, Nate. Just remember we need him."

"Some of his suggestions aren't practical, and I've told him-"

Willy cut Nate off, "You're a manager now, and part of your responsibility is to manage people. A lot of things around here will be changing; we'll all be facing new challenges. And don't expect everyone that's here today to be here next quarter." With that, Willy handed Nate a folder. "Here's a copy of the revised Training budget. You'll see there's allocations for equipment, more trainers, and management courses for yourself. Sally has a copy. The two of you should go over it sometime this week."

Nate examined the equipment figures, "Does this mean I'll get a machine dedicated for training?"

"Our production quotas don't allow for that right now."

"Willy, won't that always be the case?"

"You'll get your machine, just not right now."

Nate turned to leave, and then turned back. "Are you aware that Sally wants me to get rid of all my tech writers and she's already hired a newspaper reporter friend of hers to write our manuals?"

"We're spending too much on consultants; I told her to hire a writer." Willy looked at his watch, "I've got to prepare for a meeting. Are you onboard with what we've discussed or not?"

"Yeah, Willy, I'm onboard."

*   *   *

Willy's next complaint came weeks later. Too many high-priority customers weren't getting into Nate's classes. Consequently, Nate wrote a computer program that automatically made student selections based on Willy Raymond's own criteria. When Nate described it to Willy, his only comment was, "Good."

Meanwhile, the issue of not having a dedicated training machine was growing. Nate began exploring computer simulation programs as a training aid. *After all*, he reasoned, *the astronauts used simulators and they're able to land on the moon – on their first try.*

He realized there were two problems: the cost of buying simulation software and the time it would take to write simulations.

Maybe I can hire Gabe, he thought. When he suggested it, at a CIC meeting, Gabriel said his time was limited due to consulting contracts. However, he had a suggestion about getting a training machine. "Why don't you get the other managers to sign a petition stating that you need a dedicated machine? You said it would be to everybody's benefit … right?"

"Yeah … that might work, Gabe. Thanks."

Willy relented and scheduled a machine for the training department. Three weeks later it was rolled into the small room, which had been built for it many months before.

The new writer was competent, but lacked technical understanding. Nate assigned her to go through one of the standard training sessions, which she completed. Her usefulness quadrupled afterward and Nate checked-off another item on his to-do list.

Debbie went to another department and Nate hired Isabella. She proved to be a good typist and very loyal. It wasn't long before she was telling Nate about things Patrick was saying and doing to undermine him. Still, Nate was determined not to be pulled into feuding with someone who was probably neurotic. He remembered Willy saying, " ...handling people is now part of your job." Nate decided to rely on The Golden Rule and *do unto others as you would have them do unto you.* And that might have worked, except Patrick wasn't playing by the same rule.

Nate hired two new trainers. The first had been the principal of a school and the second had computer programming experience. Nate was counting on their maturity and experience to curb Patrick's antics.

However, things came to a head one Monday when Willy called Nate to his office. "What's this I hear about you having your people come in on a Saturday without your being here?"

"I had tickets to take my family out of town, Willy, and I gave instructions to my team on how to assemble some manuals for the new class. That's all."

"Are you kidding me?" Willy leaned forward, "You don't ask staff to come in on a weekend and not show up yourself. Sally says this shows you're not ready to be a manager."

"Willy, all they had to do was insert updated sheets and punch holes. I felt they didn't need supervision for that."

"Sally says this isn't the first time you've left them on their own. You were out sick one day, too."

"Yes, I was," Nate shot back, "and I told them to call me if they needed me."

Willy threw his pen onto the desk, "That's not acceptable. They need you here every time they're here."

Nate waited and then said, "Listen, why don't we go over to the deli and get a couple of sandwiches and talk."

"No. We'll talk right here. And you're missing the point. You're not being effective as a manager. Sally has written you up three times in the past two weeks."

"Written me up? What for?"

Willy opened a folder and threw copies of Sally's documents across the desk.

"I didn't know anything about these accusations," Nate said.

"Do you deny that they happen? Are they true or not?"

"I can explain-"

Willy's intercom buzzed. His secretary said, "Mr. Harriman is on the line for you."

"I'll take it." Willy said, "We'll have to finish this later, Nate."

Drained, Nate went directly to the H.R. office to examine his personnel folder. There he found more memos, from Sally, complaining about him. It was the first time he knew about some of the incidents, others he remembered and had dismissed. He never thought she would write him up about things that seemed so trivial. But, the wording didn't sound trivial at all.

On his way back to his office, Nate was stopped by Frank Thomas, the purchasing agent. He was packing boxes with papers from his desk drawers.

"Watch your back, man."

"What do you mean?" Nate asked.

"They just fired me." Frank admitted, " …Hell, they been getting their own kickbacks for all those word-processing stations. Nate, they're searching through all their paperwork for anything they can get on you. Watch your back, man." Willy walked by and Frank turned back to packing his things.

"Thanks, Frank." Nate said, "Good luck to you, man."

The last straw came later that day when one of the production workers told Nate what he overheard at a pizza parlor on Saturday. Art Chavez had been drinking with four other guys and running off with his mouth. After he heard what Art had been saying, Nate knew it was time to go on the offensive.

That night, Nate told Lena he had decided to go to a lawyer.

"It's about time and I hate to say I told you so. Have you said anything to Patrick?"

"I told him his actions were starting to affect how I feed my family and it had to stop."

"What did he say?"

"He asked me if I was threatening him."

"And what did you say?"

"I told him he could take it any way he wants. But it has to stop. He stomped out of the room. I suppose he went and told Sally or Willie."

Lena kissed Nate on the cheek, "You did the right thing, Honey. You have to defend yourself."

"And now, I know why Willy told me to just mind my own business when I told him we were wasting money buying all those word-processing stations. I thought he didn't understand that our HP computer could do all the word-processing using cheap terminals."

Lena massaged the back of Nate's shoulders; his muscles were tight as ropes. Neither of them slept well that night.

*   *   *

It was a cool, San Francisco evening, when Nate and Lena arrived at the lawyer's office.

"May I ask what your relationship to Paul Brown is?" the lawyer said.

"We attend inventor's meeting together and he's a friend of mine."

"Normally, I don't take cases like yours, but Paul asked this as a favor. Why don't you tell me exactly what's going on."

The lawyer took notes as he listened to Nate's story, then he said, "Mr. LaChae, they're setting you up to be fired."

"Yeah, I've figured that much out."

"And this guy," the lawyer glanced at his notes, "Patrick, is their main pawn."

The lawyer asked if Nate was the only one being mistreated and Nate told him several others had mentioned filing lawsuits.

"Well? What can we do?" Nate asked.

"Not much, I'm afraid. You've described a company full of disgruntled employees. We can't say you're been discriminated against, because you haven't been treated differently from the others. Unless you're ready to spend a lot of money with no guarantee of winning in court, the best I can do for you is to send a letter and maybe it will scare them into behaving fairly towards you."

"That's it?" Nate asked.

The lawyer held his open palms upward, "I wish I could do more. But, it would have to be a class action suit including all the disgruntled employees. Do you think you can get them to sign a petition?"

"No," Nate admitted, "Not really."

The lawyer tried to reassure Nate, "Sometimes, sending a legal document can change things."

"I hope so." Nate said.

*   *   *

On Thursday, Nate was summoned to Willy's office. Willy tossed the lawyer's letter on his desk and leaned back in his chair. He put his thumbs behind his red suspenders, stared through his horn-rimmed glasses, and then said, "Is this supposed to be some sort of a threat?"

Nate stood with his hands on his hips, "No, but it's something I felt was necessary. After Sally Palmer wrote me up again, I checked my personnel folder and saw all the new stuff in there from the past month. And the other day when I tried to talk with you about it, you said you had to believe what your managers tell you. You wouldn't even take time out and go to lunch with me, so we could talk off-line like we used to. That's when I went to a lawyer."

Willy rubbed the back of his neck. "This company has got too big for me to keep up with everything that's going on. I have to depend on the managers to keep me informed."

"But, Willy, how can you believe I would start screwing up now when I've become a manager? There's been nothing negative in my personnel record since I started here three years ago. And now, in thirty days, I've been written up and put on probation … for doing the same job I've been doing since before you came here."

"Don't you think you're being unreasonable?" Willy said, "Sally had just cause each time she wrote you up."

"No! I'm not being unreasonable." Nate pointed at Willy, "I know about Art Chavez' comments the other night. He said you two were going to find a way to get me 'out' of the company; and I have witnesses who will swear to it."

Willy squinted, put his palms on his desk, and leaned toward Nate. "You want to play hardball with me, Nate?"

Nate took a deep breath and then said, "I'm not trying to play any games with you or anybody else around here. I just want to do my job so I can take care of my family. And when I see anyone trying to take that away from me I will defend myself."

"I'm still the president of this company and I'm not going to listen to any more of this." Willy stormed out of his office and down the hall.

Nate called after him, "Now, who's being unreasonable?"

Willy turned the corner and was gone. His secretary and others were in the hallway staring at Nate.

I'm going to wait for Willy to return and get everything out in the open - today! Besides, he didn't deny what Art Chavez said.

Minutes later, Nate saw Willy coming up the hallway, huffing. He didn't seem surprised that Nate was still there. He sat behind his desk without a word, pushed his glasses up, and leafed through a folder that Nate recognized. Willy scanned the documents and, without looking up, said, "I'm going to let the new H.R. manager, Robert Weston, handle this. I'll schedule a meeting with you, Robert, and Sally for tomorrow morning."

Nate said nothing.

Willy gathered the papers together, closed the folder and sat back in his chair. He studied Nate for a moment, and then said slowly, "And, for the record, I don't know anything about what Art Chavez may have said. I'm surprised you would believe anything so asinine."

"With all that's been going on lately, Willy, it didn't seem asinine to me."

"In any case", Willy shifted in his chair, "I brought Robert Weston onboard because of his expertise in H.R. matters. He's neutral and will work to get these issues resolved. Can you accept that?"

Nate gave it a moment's thought, then said, "Yes, I'll meet with him tomorrow" and he left.

After dinner that night Lena told Brandon to finish his homework in his room. She told him granddad might not tell him a story that night. She joined Nate in the living room on the sofa.

Nate stared at the muted television, sipping herbal tea and then said, "I ignored all those warnings my co-workers gave me about Patrick.

They said his complaints to Sally and his behavior were classic for someone who wanted to take my job.

I thought my only enemy was Art Chavez. I never felt good about him since that time he had me removed from the first training session. Then, there were all those times he smiled in my face and always wanted to shake my hand when we met. He didn't shake anybody else's hand." Nate shook his head dejectedly.

"Now you know Willy's been behind it too," Lena said.

"Winning these battles is not what I want, Lena, but I see I can't ignore them any more." *Why is all this happening?* He wondered, *what does it really mean?*

*   *   *

It was late when Art Chavez returned from San Jose. Willy had left three messages. Art was deciding if it was too late to return the call, when the phone rang; it was Willy.

"What the hell did you say the other night at the pizza house, Art?"

"What are you talking about?"

"You idiot! I received a letter today from some lawyer that Nate LaChae went to. And before I could get Nate to back off, he told me your stupid ass had told people we were going to get rid of him!"

"Willy, take it easy. That was just talk after a few beers and-"

"Take it easy! Is that what you just said?" Willy barked. "Nate told me to my face he has witnesses that would swear, in court, about what you said. How god damn easy do you think I took that?"

"Listen, Willy I know you're upset and it was a mistake. I said it like a joke. I didn't think-"

"No you asshole you didn't think." Willy lowered his voice, "You didn't think about what a lawsuit from him would mean right now? You didn't think about the contract negotiations going on with MBS did you? We have to show compliance with government rules and regulations now. For Christ sake Art, why do you think I haven't simply fired the bastard?"

"Okay, okay," Art said, "What do we do now?"

"I'll tell you what YOU are going to do." Willy spoke deliberately, "You are going to get your ass in here tomorrow morning for a meeting with Robert Weston, Sally and Nate. And you are going to give a convincing apology. You got that?"

"Yes, Willy. I'm sorry I messed up."

Willy ignored Art's words, "Weston is good at smoothing things over. You had better hope he can get Nate to cancel this lawyer business. Otherwise, you can forget about any further payments to your account. You got that?"

"I understand, Willy. I'll make good."

Willy hung up and poured another scotch.

*   *   *

Robert Weston's office wasn't at the front of the building where Willy and the VPs were. He had an office near the break room where he'd have more opportunity to interact with the workers. It was important that they feel comfortable with him. His good looks and toothy mile helped.

Born in Seattle, he and his brother attended St. Edwards's seminary. After graduation, he chose to work as an industrial psychologist. He quickly built a reputation for settling union disputes. Corporate sent him to MicroStep in the position of Human Resources Manager.

Tuesday morning Art Chavez came to Weston's office and gave a brief, almost tearful, apology to Nate. When Nate refused to shake his hand, Art left. For the next half-hour Weston refereed Sally's accusations and Nate's rebuttals about his performance as a manager.

Finally, Sally asked, "What do you really want, Nate?"

Robert Weston echoed the question, "Yes, what do you want to do?"

No one had asked him that before; a sudden calm came over Nate. He surprised himself, when he changed his tone and then said, "What I want is to set up a computer program that will help this company move forward."

The three of them were silent. Then Robert Weston said, "What computer program are you talking about?"

"It's called an Expert System. It's a database that uses artificial intelligence to answer questions. It can store the knowledge our experts have and make it available to everyone."

Sally stared in disbelief.

Robert Weston said, "And, you know how to set up such a program?"

Nate resisted the urge to say, "I've already started," and then said instead, "Yes, I do."

On Friday, Willy allowed Nate to give a presentation about Expert Systems to the department heads. Nate spoke about how every department could benefit. Neither Willy nor the IT manager attended. However, the assistant, Alan Klein, enthusiastically confirmed technical references and information in Nate's presentation.

Willy drew up a contract that provided for a 90-day development period, after which an evaluation would decide whether to set up the program permanently. There would be weekly goals and checkpoints. Failure to meet any of the goals would void the contract; it was alrtight.

Willy presented his summation to Nate, "You understand you'll have consultant status while doing this. I'm not going to pay you as an employee and a consultant."

"Yes, I understand", Nate signed the contract and slid it toward Willy.

"And the software program," Willy smiled and wiggled his pen between two fingers, "will belong to the company afterward."

Nate said, "Ah ... No, I never agreed to that. Besides, I have a copyright on it."

"What? You never said the software was copyrighted."

"Well, it is. I copyrighted it before I joined MicroStep."

Willy struggled to keep control. This was not what he had planned.

In the end, Willy signed the contract and everyone thought they had won. Sally gave responsibility for Training to Patrick Smalls; Art Chavez celebrated what he called a partial victory; Robert Weston felt he had proven himself and Nate went off to fulfill his contractual obligations.

*   *   *

Nate felt out of character the first time he entered the plant as a consultant. He headed for the Quality Assurance(QA) department where the manager, Johan Koening, greeted him. They got right down to business.

The six-man QA team gathered in the cafeteria for Nate's briefing. They thank Nate for the doughnuts and, as they got their coffee, one of them asked, "Does this mean we won't get one of those big lunches like you used to give your classes?"

Nate laughed, "Those lunches were on MicroStep; these doughnuts are out of my own pocket. But, I'll tell you what, when this project is over we'll have lunch at the Decathlon Club, how's that?"

Nate knew that would get their approval. The Decathlon club's three-story atrium and indoor/outdoor pool was part of the reason it was the premier sports and dinning club in Silicon Valley. International events were held there annually.

Nate spoke to the group. "Let me start by saying the whole idea of this project is to make your jobs more efficient by putting Stepper information in the main computer system where it will be available to everyone. I've promised Johan that I won't slow you down or get in your way."

As Nate handed an outline to the participants, he remembered training each of them.

"Johan has already reviewed this schedule; let's go over the assignments together. You can see from the outline there will be three stages. First, I'll meet with each of you to get an understanding of what information you need to do your jobs and what information is generated by your work. Afterward, I'll input that information into SIMON ... that's the name of the program ... and make it available to everyone in the group; and in the last stage, everyone will be able to input information on their own."

Nate patiently answered all of their questions. He wasn't sure if their lack of enthusiasm was because they didn't understand or because it was just too early in the morning. However, he sensed he had gained the one thing he needed most – their trust.

For the next two weeks Nate interviewed each of the QA workers and flowcharted the information they used. He knew the information they needed came from the production group. When he approached Perry Penvenne, his old friend surprised him.

Perry handed him a diskette and then said, "Here's what you want."

"And just how do you know what I want?"

"I've heard how you've been squeezing the brains of the QA guys and I've been expecting you."

Nate smiled and said, "Oh, Really?"

Perry continued, "You'll find all the final assembly data on those disks. Only our vendor's data is missing. It's still on paper. I can give you hard copies."

"Hey man, this is great, Perry; thanks a lot."

Perry looked down at his fingernails, "You know ... I've never been to the Decathlon Club ..."

"You're in!" Nate said without hesitation. Then he frowned and then said, "Just you. Not your whole crew."

Perry pretended to be disappointed.

"Catch you later."

Nate looked at his watch; he was early for his Project Status meeting with Robert Weston. He went to the break room and saw Isabella getting coffee. She told him Willy was gone - he had been fired.

"You're kidding, right?"

"Go look at his office for yourself" she said.

Arriving at Willy's office, Nate found an empty room. He wondered if Willy was allowed to keep his corporate gift - a Morant sports car.

Perry walked up beside Nate. "I heard Corporate found out he used a $1,000,000 "gift" from Omron Company to doctor the books. That's how we got the Most Profitable Division award. He was also getting kickbacks for each of the word processing stations we bought."

"Yeah, I heard about the word processing stations."

Willy Raymond's prophetic words echoed in Nate's mind, '*Some of us might not be here next quarter*'.

Nate walked pass the main conference room and saw Sally Palmer speaking to a crowd. Martin Lee and Art Chavez were also standing at the front of the room. Seeing Nate at the door, Nikolas Oberlin reached over and closed it. Nate grabbed the doorknob, then remembered he was no longer an employee and let it go. He turned and started back down the hall, wondering what Willy's dismissal would mean for his project.

They have to honor the contract that Willy, so carefully, prepared and signed, Nate thought. *When I meet every stipulation and deliverable, the contract binds MicroStep to adopt my Simon project permanently. All I have to do is make sure it works.*

Nate looked at his watch; it was time for his meeting with Robert Weston.

The meeting went smoothly and followed its usual script. Weston read off each contract deliverable and Nate responded with documents, diskettes and/or a discussion of its successful completion. The meetings were polite, but Nate always felt Weston wasn't sincere in his congratulations. It seemed odd to Nate that a man who was suppose to be an ordained minister would give such a pretense.

The project progressed to the point where Nate needed a printing terminal in the QA area. He went to Nikolas Oberlin's office.

"There's no money for your terminals in my budget," Oberlin kept typing and didn't take his eyes off his computer screen.

"Listen, Nikolas," Nate crossed his fingers to enhance his ESP, "I don't know why you're not supporting the Simon project, especially since you and Alan are probably the only ones who understand what it could mean for the company. But, that doesn't matter now. Willy signed my contract and it says terminals will be provided."

"I don't care what's in your contract!" Oberlin spate, "I didn't sign it, Willy did and now he's gone."

"You and I both know," Nate said calmly, "the company is still obligated."

Oberlin stopped typing and turned toward Nate. He stared menacingly with his piercing eyes. "You people think you can shove your agendas down our throats, don't you?"

Nate put his palms up, "Oberlin, this is not a personal thing-"

"Oh, yes it is!" Oberlin voice was stern, "Who the hell do you think you're fooling with all this talk about AI? At Carnige-Mellon, it took us two years to get an Expert System running and we had all the resources. You can't possibly accomplish even half the goals in that contract using HP-Basic. That's why I'm not wasting my time with your silly project."

"I'm not here to argue with you Nikolas. If you won't order the terminals, I'll go over your head."

"You do that, Nate and see how far you get."

As he left, Nate started to slam the door, but didn't.

Yeah, sure, guys like Nikolas believe it can't be done, Nate thought. *They always think things can't be done without the latest, expensive, specialized equipment – which only they have access to. It's the same attitude those Stuyvesant High School guys had when I competed with them at the school science fairs. But, my rockets flew as well as theirs and my Simon project is going to work too! Oberlin is just pissed-off because he didn't think of it himself, that's all. I'd better run check-sums and keep backups, in case he decides to sabotage the project. In fact, I better run my SNATCH program too, so I can get administrative access to the computer if I need to.*

Heading for the front offices, Nate suddenly realized he didn't know who had inherited Willy's job. He went to Sally Palmer's office and knocked on her door.

He heard her say, "Come in."

Sally sat at her round conference table with the service manager, the finance officer, and Art Chavez. There were stacks of papers on the table.

"Hello, Nate. What can I do for you?"

"I was wondering who took Willy's place."

Art Chavez said, "No one yet" and glanced at the finance officer.

"For now, the three of us will be running things." Sally said, "Is there some problem?"

Nate explained his need for printing terminals, and Oberlin's unwillingness to provide them. Sally responded with, "Let me see about getting some terminals for you. Can you check back with me in the morning?"

"Sure," Nate said, "tomorrow will be fine."

Sally surprised Nate with her friendliness; "How's your project coming along?"

"So far, so good. I'm at the point where the workers will start interacting directly with SIMON."

"Yes, of course," Sally said, "Now we need to get back to work. will you excuse us, Nate?"

"Sure, thanks."

Nate headed for the door and when he grabbed the doorknob, Art Chavez said, "You still on schedule?"

Nate turned, "Still on schedule, Art. There's nothing to worry about."

Art smiled, "Oh, I'm not worried, Nate, not in the least."

Nate closed the door and wondered what other affects Willy's leaving might have on his project.

*   *   *

The next morning, Nate arrived in the QA area as Alan Klein was finishing setting up a video terminal.

"Morning, Nate. I was asked to tell you that this terminal is only temporary. A printing terminal will be delivered later this week." He rubbed his hands anxiously, "I hope that will be okay with you."

"Yeah," Nate said, "there won't be anything to print for a day or so anyway. Oh … I'll need to load new program tapes onto the mainframe."

"Give them to me," Alan said sheepishly, "I'll load them for you."

Nate hesitated for a moment, and then remembered he had backup tapes.

"Be sure to set the program for my access only."

"Okay, Nate," Alan extended his hand, "and good luck." Then he said, "I'll help you as much as I'm allowed to."

Nate sensed Alan's sincerity and then said, "Thanks."

An hour later the updates to the Simon program were loaded into the HP-mainframe and Nate began a session:

Simon:	Password?
Nate:	********
Simon:	Mode?
Nate:	Request.
Simon:	Request Mode.

Nate: List facts.
Simon: Database is empty.
Nate: Who created you?
Simon: Copyrighted by Nate LaChae, 1982
Nate: Import datafile - IQ100.
Simon: Importing …
Simon: IQ100 imported successfully.
Nate: Count all.
Simon: 1437 Facts. 96 Rules. 14 Procedures. 2 T/S sessions.
Nate: Thank you.
Simon: Session ending. Duration: 7.36 mins.

Time went by rapidly and Nate extended his interviewing to the optical department, where he met his first, staunch resistance. It didn't come from John, the senior engineer. It came from Jimmy - the youngest employee in the company.

"I don't understand your reluctance, Jimmy."

"I have nothing against your program, Nate. But, you want me to put what I know into that program where everybody can call up the information."

"What's wrong with that?"

"It took me two years to learn about all this stuff," he waved his arm around, "and I'm not willing to give away my knowledge."

"I can understand what you're saying, but you will still have job security."

"I'm not so sure about that."

John had been listening from the other side of the lab. He came over carrying a thick data book. "Here, Nate, what you need is the ability to get this information into your program."

"Yeah, it's all there." Jimmy added, "All you need is a scanner."

"That would be nice," Nate said, "except information has to be input in a special format and right now the only way to do that is to type it."

"In that case, just input the glossary," John opened to the back of the book.

After a moment's thought, Nate asked, "Would you guys be willing to go through and highlight the relevant terms in the glossary?"

John and Jimmy looked at each other. Then Jimmy said, "I wouldn't mind doing that."

"In the next two weeks?" Nate asked.

"Yes, yes, we'll do it in two weeks." John scowled, "Now will you get out of here, so we can get back to work?"

Weeks passed, and Nate demonstrated automatic transfer of QA data from the Stepper to the mainframe computer. Hundreds of Stepper facts and information were loaded into Simon. Additionally, the QA personnel were trained to enter information on their own. Two printing terminals, dedicated to Simon, were set up around the plant.

Robert Weston became supportive and even suggested Nate hang posters encouraging employees to use the terminals. The poster's slogan was:

NONE OF US IS AS SMART AS ALL OF US.

*   *   *

Despite detractors at the top, Nate continued to meet every contractual milestone on schedule. All the technical experts were interviewed and their information transcribed into SIMON. It now had 3562 facts and 537 rules for using those facts. The program had grown beyond the levels Nate and Gabriel had experimented with.

Nate called his buddy, "Hey Gabe, you won't believe how much info SIMON has now."

"How's the search routines performing?"

Nate smiled at Gabriel's reference to his contribution to the SIMON project.

"They must be operating very well; there's been no searching errors."

"So ... " Gabriel paused, "are you going to use meta-level routines?"

"I haven't decided. That stuff can be unpredictable you know."

"You should decide soon", Gabriel said, "while Simon's database is small enough for you to trace what it's doing."

As soon as Nate hung up, he decided he would make a duplicate program, SIMON-2, and turn on the meta-level routines - just to see what happens. It would run in background mode and he would have the only access. All new information would go to both programs. Meanwhile, SIMON-2 would be, for all practical purposes - thinking!

Friday's meeting with Robert Weston went well. Once again, Weston complimented Nate on meeting all the contract goals on time.

"There's just two more weeks to go."

"I like to think there's just two more weeks before the real beginning." Nate replied.

"You've come a long way, haven't you? Do you have any other business prospects lined up?"

"Actually, no. This one contract has kept me so busy; I haven't had time to consider others."

One of the secretaries knocked as both men were signing their weekly audit sheet.

"Excuse me, Nate you're wanted in the main conference room."

Surprised, Nate said, "I'll be right there."

All the main players were in the conference room and some Nate didn't know. *Probably from Corporate,* he thought. There was standing room only. The Process Engineering manager, Ron Voisen, was at the front of the room. With his beard and rotund frame, he looked more like a rocket scientist that a marketing VP. As usual, his tie was open and he was sweating.

"Ah, here's Nate now ..." Ron waved Nate forward, "Please, come up here, Nate."

Nikolas Oberlin was grinning and Nate realized he had never seen him smile before. There was a printing terminal at the front of the room.

"Maybe you can help us out, Nate. We're having trouble running your SIMON program."

The room quieted down. Nate glanced at Nikolas who tilted his head upward slightly. Nate typed command after command and couldn't find SIMON anywhere in the computer. He stepped back and then said, "It must have gotten erased somehow."

Ron Voisen asked, "Didn't you make a backup copy?"

"Of course I did." Nate spat, "it's gone too."

"It's useless to us for now." Nikolas said, "I'll have last week's backup copy reloaded later."

Embarrassed, Nate asked, "What information were you trying to get?"

Ron Voisen put his hand on Nate's shoulder and then said, "We wanted to see if your program could help us solve a major problem that's come up."

"There is another copy." Nate said triumphantly. "It's running in background mode."

"Are you sure it's not erased too?" Ron asked.

"It can't be erased in background mode" Nate turned toward Nikolas Oberlin, "can it?" Without waiting for an answer, Nate activated SIMON-2. He turned to the assemblage, "I have to tell you, this version of SIMON is different from the one most of you have seen. This program creates some of its data automatically. So, there might be references to words that only make sense to Simon."

"Yes, okay, Nate. We have disks from all twelve customers' sites. They are all failing Scan Test and we haven't been able to determine why. Will you input the disks and ask SIMON to troubleshoot the problem?"

"Sure", Nate complied and fed each disk's information to SIMON-2. Then, he typed ANALYZE and mentally crossed his fingers.

The room was silent.

"How long will this take?" someone asked.

"I'm not sure", was the only answer Nate could give.

Ron Voisen announced, "This is a good time for us to take a break."

Perry Penvenne approached Nate. "Looks like this will be an acid test for SIMON, huh?"

"Yeah", Nate responded, "I hope we can understand its answer."

"Hey, I've been wanting to tell you, Nate, we're using Simon every day in my group. I think you've done a terrific job."

"Thanks Perry." then in a low voice, "I've surprised myself on this project."

"I'm going for some coffee." Perry said, "Good luck."

Nate answered questions from some of the attendees, while part of his mind wondered what SIMON-2 was thinking.

As the group reconvened, Simon's printer started typing. It seemed to get louder with each printed line. People crowded around; Nate fed the paper up and tore it off. Everyone waited …

"It says", Nate announced, "Theta-stage vibrations can cause Scan Test to fail during the processing cycle."

Everyone started talking at once and Nate passed the printout around. It read:

T/S Case 0015
Diagnosis:
Theta-stage instability >> Scan test failure >> Step: processing cycle.
Reasoning:
15Feb-09:30 User:JHadley taught: Theta-Stage has stepper motors.
30Mar -14:53
User:TDuncan taught: Vibration can cause Scan test to fail.
05Apr-03:57 NewFact: M701 4325 A968
05Apr-03:57 NewRule: A968 4325 ZQ34
05Apr-03:58 AutoDeduced: All stepper motors have vibration.
12Apr-03:58 NewRule: A969 4325 ZQ34
12Apr-03:58 NewRule: A967 4325 ZQ35
12Apr-05:03 NewRule: A967 4326 ZQ34
27Apr-16:01 AutoDeduced: stepper motors can cause instability.
Confidence level: 92.36%
Processing time: 00:22:34

The consensus among the engineers was that Simon's diagnosis was probably correct.

Ron Voisen congratulated Nate and then said, "We'll test this in the factory immediately. Thank you, Nate."

Two weeks passed after Nate successfully completed the Simon pilot project and there was no word from MicroStep. Sally Palmer became the acting president. She kept dodging Nate and not returning his phone calls. Nate couldn't reach Robert Weston either.

What do I do now? Nate wondered.

*   *   *

Brandon opened the door as Nate was inserting his key.

"Hey, little man," Nate gave him a hug, "where's Lena?"

Looking sad, Brandon said, "Grandma is in her room. I think she's crying."

"Crying?,"

Nate opened the bedroom door, "Wait here, Brandon."

Lena was sitting, staring out of the window, and weeping. Nate squatted beside her, "What's wrong, Honey? What is it?"

"My cousin, Billy-Ray, called at lunchtime ... my father had a heart attack and died."

Tears welled up in Nate's eyes. He held Lena gently by her shoulders and then said, "I'm so sorry, Honey."

Her tears flowed freely now, "I just spoke to him on Saturday."

"I know, baby. I know."

"He told me that he would always love me and to be happy" Lena said between sobs, "I think he knew something was going to happen."

"Maybe he did" Nate rubbed Lena's back and her head.

She continued, "Something told me to go down there last month, around the time of my birthday. I should have gone."

They turned and saw Brandon in the doorway. Nate waved him in and the three of them hugged.

"Grandma's dad has died, Brandon."

"Was he very sick?" Brandon asked.

"Yes, darling," Lena picked Brandon up, "but he's not suffering any more."

"When do you want to go down there?" Nate asked.

"As soon as I can. I'll ask Ruth and Eli to watch Brandon until school is out in three weeks. After that, he can go live with Mother. I know that you can't leave right now."

Nate tried to pull away in anguish, but she pulled him back.

"You've worked too hard to let anything stop you now, Nate. Not even this."

"MicroStep should have already signed."

"I'll be alright." Lena said, "You do what you have to do."

He thought for a moment, "I'll join you in one week. They're gonna have to tell me something!"

However, Nate didn't get any resolution from MicroStep that week. He joined Lena anyway for her father's funeral. Afterward, they decided he would return first and secure their critical financial position. They began to realize he might have to look for a job if MicroStep continued to balk.

*   *   *

When Nate returned to the Bay area, he found a lawyer that gave an hour of free consultation. He was told he had grounds for a lawsuit, but that it would take time and be costly because of a loophole Willy had included in the contract.

He was told, "It could cost up to $20,000."

"Can't I use legal-aid, since I don't have any money?"

The lawyer raised his eyebrows and then said, "I'm afraid not Mr. LaChae. These things are not handled by legal-aid services."

Nate looked from side to side at the floor.

The lawyer added, "I can send MicroStep a letter showing that you've contacted me and that might get some movement out of them. But, frankly, it's not going to make them sign the long-term contract you're seeking."

Hesitantly, Nate said, "No, that bluff probably won't work."

"Have you approached any other businesses with your product?"

"No. MicroStep took up all my time." Nate said, "Besides, I was so sure they would sign a new contract ..."

"Mr. LaChae, it sounds like you have a viable product. I suggest you approach other companies. You'll still have seven years to litigate this case."

Nate called a meeting with Gabriel and they drew up plans for selling Simon to other companies. Gabriel got a copy of the Simon software and was tasked with reviewing the code.

Nate hurriedly, got business cards and stationary printed. He used part of his savings to get a business phone service at a company that provided temporary office services for businesses.

Time and money ran out quickly. Responding to an eviction notice, Nate moved all his furniture into storage except a few personal pieces that were in the garage: picture of his kids and family, the last Gamma engine he and Bill Davis had built in Chicago, and clothes. He asked his neighbor to watch over the things in the garage, while he went to rent a car. When he returned, he found the police and the landlord at the house. He drove past slowly and saw that the garage was empty.

Paul Brown rescued Nate with a loan of $500 that paid for a motel until he found another job. Lena and Brandon went to Chicago and lived with her mother for a while.

*   *   *

Weeks later, Nate saw his former secretary, Isabella in a grocery store and she told him MicroStep was still using his program.

"That can't be!" Nate responded, "They have no right to use it now."

"I'm telling you, Nate, it's true."

Nate hopped on a bus and went to MicroStep immediately. His badge still worked. The busy workers hardly noticed him and didn't seem surprised at his presence. He went to a corner of the plant and logged onto a terminal.

He typed 'Run Simon' and began a session.
Simon: Password?
Nate: ********
Simon: Mode?

Nate's anger rose. Those dirty, bastards! He looked around and saw no one paying attention to him. Turning back to the screen, he realized

Simon was in protected mode and would not allow any changes or deletions. Still he tried.

Nate:	Exit
Simon:	Command denied. You do not have authorization.
Nate:	End
Simon:	Session ending. Duration: 2 mins. 15 sec.

Nate frowned at the terminal as if to intimidate it. He sat back, put his fingers together, and took a deep breath. He closed his eyes and waited ...

It occurred to him that, if he could produce a System Error, the program would stop immediately, and he would have full access. He'd have to ask a question that would make Simon generate a System Error. Gabriel's searching routine would allowed Simon to cycle 500 times, attempting to answer a question, before it would produce a system error. That could take hours.

But Simon's troubleshooting section wasn't as robust.

Simon:	Mode?
Nate:	T-shoot.
Simon:	Enter symptoms.

Nate, carefully, entered a scenario that told Simon a certain action would cause a problem and then he entered information that the same scenario was the solution to the problem. The wording had to be precisely deceptive.

Nate:	Start T/S.
Simon:	... ...

... ...
... ...
... ...System error 3037 at FF37

Ready>

Nate typed the administrator's code, that he had acquired using his SNATCH program, and was immediately granted full access to MicroStep's mainframe computer. A wicked smile crossed his face.

He typed a command to globally erase every copy of Simon and all its associated files. The computer asked for confirmation, which he gave. He knew backup copies still existed, in a cabinet somewhere. But, he couldn't do anything about that right now.

For a moment, he considered entering a time-bomb program that would erase all the files at a future date.

He left the building and immediately called the lawyer in San Leandro, instructing him to send a strongly worded warning letter about copyright laws and penalties.

Shirotronics

The Shirotronics Field Service Manager, Darryl Wilson, finished his prep talk about professional attire with, "Anyone not following these rules will have to face the consequences." As he headed toward his office, he heard one of the twelve seated Field Service Engineers (FSEs) mumble something.

Darryl turned slowly, came back and asked, "What did you say, Delgado?"

The FSEs stopped watching the live pre-launch broadcast of the Space Shuttle and turned toward Darryl.

Ricardo Delgado kept smiling. "I said, we'd have to go a few rounds with you, in your office."

"What do you mean by that?"

The smile on Rich's face froze. "You know; I heard you use to be a boxer and all …"

Darryl stared at him, "So, you're a comedian too?"

Rich shifted in his chair, "I just made a joke, that's all."

Darryl slowly shook his head up and down then walked into his office. Rich raised his eyebrows and looked around at the other FSEs.

"LaChae," Darryl called out, "wanna come in here?"

Rich made a gesture with his fists as Nate passed by.

"Close the door." Darryl said, "Have a seat." He remained standing and seemed to fill up the room to its ceiling. Even when he was relaxed, in a suit, Darryl had an intensity about him that kept most people on guard. Searching through the stack of papers on his desk, he said, "See what I have to put up with out there?"

Nate assumed the question was rhetorical. "That's just Rich. He's a good worker."

"Yeah, well he needs to show more respect here in the office. The Japanese don't understand that kind of humor. They might think he was mocking what I had said."

"I hadn't thought about them."

"You better think about them all the time, Nate; you're a supervisor and this is their company."

Darryl started reading through documents as he spoke.

"So, how's things working out between you and Hisimishi?"

Nate relaxed and remembered his Hiroshi Electronics Company (HEC) customer contact.

"He's a hard man to please, I can tell you that. He and I have our morning meetings and they go pretty well. It's the weekly meetings, where everyone speaks Japanese, that I don't like."

"That's why I assigned Yamaguchi up there with you. Doesn't he translate?"

"Yeah, I bring him to those meetings and he occasionally translates something that requires my input."

"You can ask questions, you know."

"I do, Darryl. But, sometimes they'll give Yamaguchi a very long answer and he'll turn to me and just say 'Yes' or 'No'."

"And they laugh too, don't they?"

"Yeah, sometimes they do."

Darryl stopped reading and looked at Nate, "Hisimishi has complained that you don't follow cleanroom protocols."

Nate turned in his chair and shook his head. "That's because sometimes I do what I've seen him doing. He doesn't follow all the rules either."

"I believe you." Darryl said, "But, HEC is his site and he's always finding something about our service to complain about. Remember, you're only in charge of our people and equipment up there. Hisimishi wants us to jump through hoops, like Shirotronics does for HEC in Japan; but, that's not going to happen as long as I'm Field Service Manager. We'll give him the same level of service we give all our other customers."

"I understand that." Nate said.

"How's that tall kid, Andrews?"

"Lance Andrews tries to be macho all the time." Nate said. "He's not the problem, Clarence is."

Darryl chuckled and sat down. "And what's that little brother doing now?"

"Darryl, I don't want Clarence up there with us. He's lazy and won't even come in on time. I've taken him aside and tried to talk to him, but it's a waste of time."

"I sent him to you because I thought you might help him get his act together."

"Well, I can't. I've tried, but Clarence doesn't want to work. He could jeopardize our whole operation because the other guys are watching. If I let him get away with anything, they'll think its favoritism. Besides, I need real workers not ... Clarence."

"Okay, okay, I'll bring him back down here, starting Monday. There's something else we need to discuss."

Darryl answered his phone, gave a few short answers and then said, "Yes ... he's right here ... I'll ask him." He cupped his hand over the phone and then said, "It's HR, they want to know if you know Art Chavez. He's applying for a job with us."

Nate felt his stomach churn. "Yeah, I know him."

"What kind of recommendation can you give about him?"

"Darryl," Nate said, "I have a rule that when I don't have anything good to say about someone, I don't say anything at all."

"It's like that, huh?"

"Definitely."

Darryl studied Nate's face for a moment then spoke into the phone. "Mr. LaChae says he didn't work closely with Chavez." He hung up, glanced at some paperwork and then said, "You might be amused when you hear your next assignment."

"What's that?"

"We want you to go down to Texas Devices, in Lubbock, for six weeks. We're cycling all you supervisors through there, until we hire a permanent supervisor for that area. Dave Coleman is down there right now."

"Why did you say I might be amused?"

Darryl leaned forward, with his arms on the desk.

245

"We're sending you down there to compete against your former employer for a 35 million dollar contract."

Nate sat, unblinking as Darryl continued.

"We're going head-to-head against MicroStep. Three of our machines are set up across the aisle from three of MicroStep's for evaluation. At the end of the evaluation, one set of machines will be moved out and Texas Devices will purchase twelve more machines from the contract winner."

"No shit?" Nate said.

Darryl laughed, "No shit."

Nate touched his mouth with his fist. "When do you want me to go?"

"In three weeks."

"Darryl, I promise you, I will give it my very best."

"I believe you will."

They stood and they shook hands firmly.

Nate's exuberance was interrupted by sounds coming from outside the office. Darryl opened the door just in time to see a replay of the Challenger space shuttle exploding shortly after take-off.

Nate went outside and started walking through the sparse business district. He was thinking about how badly he'd wanted to be an astronaut. *That could have, and would have, been me instead of Ronald McNair. All that training, effort, and technology ... and there was nothing they could do to save themselves. Oh God, they have been blown to bits.* His tears flowed in a deluge as he walked.

*   *   *

It wasn't until Nate's pager went off, that he became aware of his surroundings. He had walked more than three miles from the office. He called the office and heard Rich's voice.

"Where did you go?" Rich asked, "It's five-twenty; our carpool buddies are ready to go."

"I'll be there in ten minutes."

"Where are you?"

"I'm nearby." Nate hung up and started looking for a taxi.

Halfway through their ride home, the carpoolers made their routine stop for coffee. Afterward, Nate was glad their conversation, finally, shifted from the shuttle's explosion.

"Hey, Nate", Rich called out from the back seat, "I heard you sold a troubleshooting program."

"Yeah, why do you ask?"

"'Cause they're looking for something like that at my wife's job. She said they're trying to computerize their repair records."

Nate perked up. "Where does she work?"

"Up at Hybrid Precision (HP), in Sacramento."

Nate looked in the rearview mirror and then said, "Ask her to get me the name and number of who to contact up there, okay?"

"Yeah, man; I'll get it for you."

"I'm serious."

"I know you are, Nate. Chill-out."

*   *   *

Both Nate's daughters, whom he hadn't seen in years, lived in New York. He was quite pleased when they accepted his invitation to come and visit. The oldest, Charlene, stayed for only one week, after she realized she was pregnant. The other, Kelly, decided to stay and got a job at a department store. In the evenings, Nate would meet her at the bus stop and they'd walk home talking about her workday.

Kelly's uneasiness about her father lessened as she got to know him better. He wasn't what she'd expected, nor did he behave as her mother said he would. At least not until he took one of the photos Charlene sent to Kelly.

It started when Nate accidentally opened Kelly's letter and saw several photos of Charlene showing her protruding stomach. When Nate gave the letter to Kelly he said, "I saw LaChae on it and accidentally opened it. Sorry."

A little while later, Nate was sitting in the living room reading. Lena was sitting across the room, sewing.

Kelly came and stood over Nate, "Where's my other photo?"

Nate smiled, "I, ... ah, kept one."

"I didn't say you could have it, so will you give it to me?"

"I want this one. It reminds me of when your mother was pregnant for the first time."

"I don't care about that. It's mine and you shouldn't have taken it."

Lena continued sewing, without looking up. Nate returned his attention to his book. "You have all the others, so go on now and forget about it."

"Now look, you're not my far-" Kelly caught herself repeating a remark she'd said to her stepfather, "Well ... I mean ... you are my father, but that's my picture and I don't want to have to take it."

Lena's sewing quickened, but she didn't look up.

Nate put the book down and then said, "Young lady, you need to go to your room."

"No."

Before Kelly knew it, Nate got up and grabbed her from behind in a bear hug. His grip was like a vice. He picked up his tall daughter and headed down the hall.

"What are you doing?" Kelly yelled.

"I'm going to cool us off!"

Kelly twisted and tried to free herself. Nate carried her into the bedroom and headed toward the shower.

"Put me down! What are you going to do?" Kelly yelled.

They were in front of the walk-in shower now. Kelly leaned back and propped her feet on either side of the narrow shower doorway. For a while, they went back and forth. Each time Nate tried to push her into the shower, she'd straighten her legs and push back. Exhausted, he finally let her go.

Kelly went crying to her room and slammed the door.

Nate returned to the living room where Lena was still sewing. She shook her head at him, but said nothing. She remembered Nate giving her a cold shower once years before. After a while, Nate knocked on Kelly's door and didn't get a response. He opened it slowly and went to Kelly. He sat on the side of the bed and then said, "I'm sorry, Kelly. I wasn't going to hurt you. Here's your picture."

"I don't want your apology or the picture now."

He left it laying on the nightstand.

It was days before things returned to their normal, peaceful state. Kelly and Nate even had a Soul-Train-style dance competition one evening. Lena said it was a draw.

*   *   *

Monday morning, Nate's flight was bound for Lubbock, Texas. He stared out of the window and closed his eyes as the airplane started its takeoff roll. He was asleep before getting airborne. For the next six weeks, he was going to supervise a group of FSEs he had never met. As the plane started circling for landing, Nate decided he'd play this one as if it were a military campaign.

Shortly after Nate arrived at the hotel, Dave Coleman phoned. He was the supervisor Nate was relieving; Nate accepted his invitation to dinner in the hotel. Dave was a pudgy, balding man, in his mid-forties. Even though Dave's manner was friendly, Nate sensed that he was the authoritarian type.

Dave explained how the situation at Texas Devices could go to either Shirotronics or MicroStep. He gave his assessment of each of the Field Service Engineers (FSE) and Nate learned that each one was competent. Nevertheless, Texas Devices was dissatisfied with the performance of the machines and the men.

Next morning, Dave arranged a breakfast meeting so Nate could meet the FSEs. There they were: Ephrem Nunez, who had a habit of looking away when an answer didn't suit his taste, Gordon Cooper, a big Texan with a drawl right out of a cowboy movie, Michael Malt, who sat quietly most of the time, and their Japanese expert, Tanaka, who reminded one of a Cheshire cat when he smiled.

After introductions and placing their breakfast orders, Nate went into what was to become known as his 'General Patton' routine.

"Men, I am not here to boss you guys around. I understand that each of you know more about the Steppers than I do. From what I've heard, the customer has been giving you a hard time even though you've been doing your jobs. I'm here to help you get the rest of the machines installed and to keep the customer off your backs. To do that I'll need all of you to work with me and show me what's been working and what hasn't.

We're competing with MicroStep here in Lubbock and there will be only one winner. I know our Shirotronics Steppers are better machines than MicroStep's because I used to work for them. I also believe each of you are experts at what you do or you wouldn't be here. So, let's prove that we're better than those guys by working together and winning this contract. Are there any questions?"

There were none.

In the days that followed, Nate did his General Patton routine every morning and was pleasantly surprised as the FSEs responded to it. Nate found that the conflicts with the customer were primarily communication problems and he put procedures in place that resolved them. He told the FSEs one major problem was the customer's perceptions of them. He asked them not to come in late. If they were going to be late, they were to call-in, but not show up until lunchtime. He even convinced them to wear ties for the next few weeks.

Gordon Cooper and Ephrem Nunez, separately, described their conflict. It was about who had the better idea for fixing certain reoccurring technical problems. Nate saw that both men were correct in different ways. He developed objective tests, which resolved that issue.

Tanaka opened up one day and admitted, in his poor English, "Nate, San, sometimes, I not do what other supervisors say because they young man. But, you older man. I do what you say. You real supervisor."

Only, straight-laced, Michael Malt was withdrawn. He had hurt his back in the Army carrying a radio that was much too heavy. The fact that he was a Mormon didn't concern Nate.

At the hotel, in the evenings, Nate worked on his software project and hoped for a chance to demo it to HP in Sacramento. Once he got things under control at Texas Devices, he used his spare time programming in his cubicle. Michael Malt was the only one who asked Nate why he was spending so much time on his laptop. Nate responded with, "I'm working on a project for Darryl."

One afternoon, Nate was surprised by a voice from his past. "Well, if it isn't Nate LaChae." Sally Palmer said, and extended her hand. Nate turned and unconsciously wiped his hand on his pants before shaking Sally's hand. "I heard that you were down here. How's everything going?"

"Not too bad." Nate replied unenthusiastically.

Sally smiled and then said, "I can't honestly wish you luck in this particular situation …"

"I can understand that." Nate said as he turned back to his paperwork.

Sally took the hint and continued down the hall with her entourage.

By the time Darryl Wilson came, for his monthly meeting with Texas Devices, things were going well with the FSEs, the equipment and the customer.

Ephrem, Tanaka and Nate were working late one evening; Tanaka was explaining an optical principle, in his broken English. He drew a circle with a radius in it and started speaking, "Hauke will-" Ephrem's and Nate's outburst of laughter made Tanaka stop.

"What wrong?" Tanaka asked, "Why you laugh?"

Both Ephrem and Nate found it hard to stop laughing long enough to explain. Finally, they wiped their eyes and explained that honkey was an offensive term to some people. Tanaka insisted that it is the correct Japanese pronunciation for the radius of a circle, "Hauke … I not know English translation word."

"Yes, we understand that. But a white American might get offended." They explained. Finally, Tanaka seemed to understand. Nate was thankful it had only come up in an isolated room.

The next morning as Nate was doing his 'General Patton' routine, Tanaka sat next to Michael Malt. Tanaka was grinning.

Nate was saying, " …so men, what we have to do is …" and " …I know you can do it." Then, he overheard Tanaka saying to Michael Malt, "I-i-i know something about you-u-u." Michael shushed him and concentrated on what Nate was saying. Tanaka repeated it, "I … know … something … about … you."

Annoyed, Michael Malt said in a low voice, that Nate barely heard, "What? What do you know about me?"

That's when Tanaka said, with his biggest grin, "You Honkey."

Michael snapped around and then said, "What did you say?"

Tanaka grinned and repeated, "Oh yes … you Honkey. Last night Ephrem and Nate tell me … you Honkey."

Not everybody heard it, but Nate did. For a second, he froze in mid-sentence, but had to continue. The cold stare Michael Malt gave him told him everything he didn't want to know.

Later, Nate tried to explain to Michael Malt what had happened, but Michael made it clear he wasn't buying the explanation. Nate was disappointed and wondered if he could count on Malt's continued support.

Nate searched for Tanaka that day, but couldn't find him anywhere; he didn't respond when Nate paged him either.

After three weeks, Lena came to Lubbock, and shared their Friday ritual of eating barbecue ribs and drinking tall Colorado Bulldogs.

During Nate's sixth week, Darryl Wilson came down for the customer meeting. Mr. Hammond of Texas Devices said how pleased he was with the Shirotronics machines and the excellent service. He said his recommendation would be for Shirotronics to get the contract. The meeting almost went sour when Darryl mentioned that a new Shirotronics supervisor would soon be hired for the site.

"I thought Nate LaChae was staying." Mr. Hammond said.

"No", Darryl said, "he's returning to his own territory in Sacramento."

"Well, you'd better make damn sure his replacement follows the example Nate has set." Hammond said.

That week the Shirotronics team had their ribs and Colorado bulldogs a day early because Nate and his wife were flying home Friday morning. Everyone celebrated and told 'war stories' about the past few weeks. Many things, that could have turned into problems, had been averted. Everyone had concentrated on winning and that's what they had done. For Nate LaChae, it was sweet revenge.

*   *   *

Back in Sacramento, Rich Delgado gave Nate the phone number of the manager of HP's Repair Depot, Mark Spellman. Tell him you're a friend of Juanita's husband." Rich said, "He's expecting your call."

"Thanks, Rich, I won't forget this."

"Does that mean I get to sit on your board of directors?"

"Maybe not all that. But, it means you get some stock when the time comes."

"I'll take it. Good luck, Nate."

Nate phoned Mr. Spellman the next day. "I believe I have a computer program that can help you with your repairs, sir."

"So I've heard. When can you come in and show it to us?"

"What I'd like to do first is get a better understanding of your needs. That way, we can put together a demo specifically tailored for you."

"You have a company?"

Nate hesitated, "Yes. We had a contract with MicroStep, down in Silicon Valley. And now we're looking for other opportunities."

"Okay, let me switch you to my secretary; she'll schedule a meeting."

"Great. I look forward to meeting you, Sir."

Lena shared Nate's excitement as he came in, kissed her and swung her around in a circle. She looked over Nate's shoulder at Kelly and then said, "The meeting went well."

Kelly stared in amazement.

"You bet it did!" Nate exclaimed, "They're setting up another meeting where we'll discuss their specific needs. I told them I have a company."

Lena stepped back, "You going to contact Gabriel?"

"Definitely."

"Will somebody tell me what the excitement is about?" Kelly asked.

Nate grabbed Kelly and hugged her too. "It looks like your dad may be going into business again."

"Don't say *may be going*," Lena chided, "say you *are going* into business again."

"Are you talking about your Simon program?" Kelly asked.

Nate reached for a cold beer, "Yep."

"I thought you sold that to the MicroStep Company."

"No, Kelly, I have a copyright and that means I own the program. I'm never going to sell it; I'll just lease it. Now, if you ladies will excuse me," Nate exaggerated, "I've got to call my business partner."

"Gabe, I've got a HP meeting scheduled to discuss Simon."

"That's good news and it's perfect timing. I'll be finishing a contract soon for the Board of Education. What's the plan?"

"The plan is, essentially, the same as it was at MicroStep. Except, this time we'll lock-in the contract. No more wishy-washy."

"Sounds great. How are you going to divide the project up."

"Fifty-fifty this time, Gabe. I'm not going to be wishy-washy either."

"That's fine Nate, but I was asking how we're going to divide up the work."

"I'll have a better idea about that after the meeting."

"Okay, I'll wait for your call."

"This is it, Gabe."

"I hope so, Nate."

*   *   *

The meeting wasn't what Nate had expected. It included other software companies. Representatives from Simbolics, Oracal, Boreland, and even Macrosoft were in attendance. Somewhat intimidated, Nate wished he had brought Gabriel along.

Mr. Spellman let his underlings describe the troubles they were having searching through technical documentation while trying to repair HP equipment. Their Sacramento repair depot handled equipment from all the other branch offices. It was an ideal setting for implementing an Expert System.

"I've prepared these packets for each of you," Mr. Spellman said as he passed out folders, "it describes one of our toughest problems and gives references to the documents we use to solve it. I'd like each of you to submit your solution within two weeks. Is that agreeable?"

"What will the next step be?" someone asked.

"We'll evaluate the solutions and choose which of you will get the technical manuals. You can then input the information into your databases, after which we'd like to see a live demo."

The representative from Macrosoft asked, "Am I to understand this site will be the only customer for the program?"

"That's correct. Our European depot has their own software project."

The Macrosoft rep closed his folder and sat back in his chair.

"If there are no other questions," Spellman said, "I'll see you gentlemen in two weeks."

Gabriel spent several nights in Sacramento, at Nate's house. They went over HP's requirements and tested the Simon program with a variety of modifications. Some were for speed, some for size of files, and some were for display features.

"Gosh, Nate, I didn't think we'd be up against Simbolics and Macrosoft."

"We're working from the same basic theories that they are, Gabe. It all comes from Minsky's and Feigenbaum's work. And please don't get started; we've debated LISP language versus BASIC language a hundred times."

Gabe laughed and then said, "I know – it's all ones and zeros inside the CPU. But, you have to admit, we can't compete with LISP processor speeds."

"Speed isn't important in HP's application. They need smart answers, not number crunching."

"Are you going to use Simon's meta-level?"

"I'm counting on it to get us over."

"The concept is no secret." Gabriel reminded.

"But it'll be our secret that Simon's using it." Nate replied.

"Nate, I'm with you either way, but there's an inherent danger in letting the program generate information that we may not be able to interpret. Sure it seems to work, but Simon can't even explain some of the information it generates now."

"I'm thinking about putting a level above the meta-level, where Simon *can* explain how he generates meta-facts."

"Will we have time to incorporate that into our proposal."

"I don't know, Gabe; I don't know. Let's just move ahead with what we have, okay? Now, look here on page five of HP's requirements ..."

They continued late into the night.

At the next HP meeting, Macrosoft had dropped out; they were only interested in products intended for millions of customers. Simbolics and Oracal were eliminated because their software required purchasing expensive LISP processing machines that Spellman had no budget for. That left, only, Boreland and LaChae Associates competing. Their proposed solutions were almost identical. Each relied on meta-level artificial intelligence strategies.

Boreland was eliminated in two steps. First, Gabriel explained the difficulties of using Boreland's Fortran for symbolic manipulation of text. Secondly, Nate reminded Mr. Spellman that the Simon program was already compatible with HP's computer systems.

With the competition out of the way, Nate and Gabriel went through months of frustration with HP. Every successful demo resulted in a request for another demo with more features.

After Nate gave a demo to HP's artificial intelligence group, Spellman said, "If you can prevent the program from getting into an infinite loop, we'll be ready to show it to our VP."

"Mr. Spellman, that kind of loop occurs because of your troubleshooting tree."

"We understand that, Nate, but the program has to know when to stop."

Acquiescing Nate said, "We'll work on it" and he got up to leave.

"I think you should know," Spellman said, "budgeting for the next fiscal year ends in six weeks."

"I understand."

Nate used a telephone in HP's lobby. "Gabe? Simon must be able to detect when it's searching through an infinite-loop."

"Oh, is that all? I thought they might want Simon to reprogram itself or something."

"I'm serious. Spellman said our next meeting will be with one of their VPs."

"Okay, I'll work on it."

"This is the last step, Gabe, we're almost there."

"What about the trappings of a company? A VP will want to see that?"

"Leave that to me." Nate said, "You just create a loop-checker, okay?"

"When do we need it?"

"Four weeks - max."

*　　　*　　　*

Meanwhile, at the Shirotronics office the next morning, Darryl told Nate, "Art Chavez is now in charge of Technical Support."

"Art? Tech Support Manager?" Nate said, "You've got to be kidding."

"We asked you about him." Darryl said, "His resume says he's been doing tech support for years. Is that not true?"

Nate thought for a moment, "I guess you can call it that."

"All right then, let's move on to other things. We'll be shipping the last three Steppers up to Sacramento next week. I need you to get your people ready and coordinate the installations." Darryl handed Nate a large brown envelope, "Oh, and see that Hisimishi gets these new facilities specs."

As Nate took the large envelope and got up to leave, Darryl said, "That was a fine job you did in Lubbock",

"Thanks." Nate smiled, "It was my pleasure."

*　　　*　　　*

Nate was at the Friday HEC meeting where he sat like a ghost at the table until Yamaguchi, occasionally, translated a question to him. Nate noticed his replies didn't require any translation. Still, he recorded everything that he understood in his logbook.

At the end of the meeting on 17 April, Nate stopped Hisimishi at the door and handed him the large brown envelope. As usual, Hisimishi was in a hurry and asked, "What is this?"

"It's from Mr. Wilson."

Hisimishi tucked it under his arm, "I'll look at it later."

Nate remained at the table and updated his logbook.

The following Monday, Nate was relieved to know the three Steppers were being shipped by the same trucking company that had made previous deliveries. Everyone was experienced and knew what to do.

Tuesday, the first Stepper arrived. They kept it in the truck until a path from the loading dock to the cleanroom was lined with cardboard.

The forklift operator complained that the openings in the pallet, under the Stepper, were spaced closer than ever before. Nevertheless, he expertly removed the one and half ton instrument from the truck and positioned it three feet over the loading dock. The aluminum bag covering was removed before the Stepper was lowered onto its wheels. Nate oversaw every phase of the work and Hisimishi took pictures.

Nate's team rolled the Stepper onto the freight elevator. They stripped away a plastic bag and saw the shiny instrument, wrapped in a second bag. On the third floor, they rolled the Stepper to the doorway of the cleanroom and stripped away its final shroud.

Lance and Benjamin, in their cleanroom bunny-suits, continued moving the SSR to it's final resting place. The balance of the day was spent securing the delicate instrument and wiping-down it's outer casing.

Wednesday was a repeat of Tuesday in every way.

Thursday was windy and a light mist was falling. Everyone had their jackets on and things were proceeding as normal. The Stepper was on the forklift, three feet above the loading dock. The workers were stripping the aluminum bag away, when someone yelled,

"STOP PUSHING!"

"LOOK OUT!"

The Stepper slid off the forklift and crunched onto its side with a sickening thud.

"OH SHIT!" Nate exclaimed.

Everybody started yelling back and forth.

"WHAT THE HELL HAPPENED?"

"WHO WAS PUSHING?"

"NOBODY PUSHED! IT WASN'T BALANCED?"

"GODDAMN IT!"

Hisimishi rushed around snapping pictures of the Stepper and everyone present.

Nate phoned Darryl Wilson.

*   *   *

Shirotronics Deputy Director, Mr. Yoshida, gave orders for the dropped Stepper not to be moved until he arrived. Darryl Wilson told Nate he would not be coming up to HEC.

"I've got a bigger problem here. Handle things as best you can and report to me. Be sure to keep Yoshida informed of everything."

Bigger problem? Nate thought, *How can Darryl believe any problem is bigger than this? What's he thinking? I can't believe he's setting me up to take the blame for this.*

There was no coherent communication between the trucking manager and Mr. Yoshida. Nate struggled to keep from smiling as the trucking manager told Yoshida, "Looks to me like this here corner can be welded back in place and that box over there is only dented a little."

Mr. Yoshida made a sucking sound through his teeth, "You don't understand. This is a delicate instrument. It's accuracy is measured in microns. It is junk now."

"Aw, come off it. You expect me to believe the rest of this machine can't be salvaged and reused?"

"What I am telling you is the cost of rebuilding would be greater than the cost of a new one." Yoshida turned to Nate, "Mr. LaChae, did you sign for this one?"

"No sir. We don't sign until after all the covering is removed and we do a visual inspection."

Mr. Yoshida took out a gold cigarette case and calmly spoke to the trucking manager, "Your company is responsible for shipment and delivery. The Stepper is not delivered until we sign for it."

The trucking manager said, "Now, you wait one damn minute!" When he saw Yoshida's smile, he said, "I'll let our lawyers sort this all out."

Mr. Yoshida blew a stream of smoke into the air and then said nothing.

Minor problems continued to occur with the installation of the two Steppers. Then Lance and Benjamin discovered some of the connections wouldn't mate properly. It was HEC's responsibility to use drawings provided by Shirotronics to ensure a perfect fit. When Nate approached

Hisimishi he was told, "I will only speak with Mr. Yoshida about this matter."

Yamaguchi told Nate, "He thinks everything is your fault."

"How can he think that?" Nate asked, "He was right there. We all know the Stepper was off-balanced. The wind and the wet aluminum bag made it slide off the forklift."

"Yes, but if he can not put it on you, he will have to take the blame."

"That's just great." Nate sneered, "I'll call Darryl."

"Darryl Wilson is gone." Yamaguchi said.

"What do you mean, gone?"

"He has been fired."

"Fired? Darryl? I don't believe you."

"It is true, Nate San."

"Why? It was an accident. He couldn't have prevented it."

Yamaguchi stood still, looking at Nate.

"What?" Nate asked, "Is there more?"

"They want you to come to the office tomorrow."

"Why didn't they page me or something? Am I gonna be fired too?"

"I don't know, Nate San. I was only told to give you the message."

"Great." Nate sat and shook his head, "That's just great."

*   *   *

Nate finished telling Brandon his bedtime story and came into the living room. Lena was burning incense and had a log in the fireplace.

"Care for a game of chess?"

"Chess?" Nate stopped, "what makes you ask that? We haven't played for quite a while."

"I can see something is troubling you. Thought you might want to take your mind off whatever it is." She held out a glass of wine, "Here."

He sat on the couch next to her and sipped the wine. She cuddled and asked, "You want to talk about it?"

Nate said, "Something is about to happen."

"I've been sensing that."

Nate turned to her and asked, "Do you trust me, Lena?"

"In most ways?"

Nate smiled, "I mean do you think I know what I'm doing with the Simon project?"

"I've believed in you all this time; why are you asking me now?"

"Because, I'm ninety-nine percent sure, we're going to get the HP contract and I want to quit Shirotronics and get my bonus check now." Before she could respond, he added, "There's a lot going on right now at Shirotronics and all I know for sure is that Darryl is gone – fired."

"Have you spoken with him?"

"Only once, on the phone and he asked me to send him my logbook. I think he's going to sue Shirotronics."

"So, do you think they might fire you too?"

"They might. But, it won't matter after I get my bonus. I'll have enough start-up money for the HP contract."

"All right!" Lena clinched her fists, "That's the Nate LaChae I love to hear talking."

"Yeah, but they might not give me my bonus."

"You're entitled to it, aren't you?"

"That doesn't mean anything. They can do whatever they want. You know that."

"So, what are you going to do?" She waited while Nate emptied his glass.

"I've got a Plan-B." he raised one eyebrow.

Without asking for any details, Lena lifted her glass and then said, "Here's to Plan-B."

*   *   *

Nate finished his morning shower and stared into the mirror.

It can't be a coincidence that everything is happening at the same time. The final HP demo in two weeks and now all this at Shirotronics. I've got to get the money for starting-up the HP contract. I can't let anything stop me this time. HP will expect to be dealing with a bona fide company, and that's what I'll present to them. I promised Lena and Gabe. Kelly and Brandon need to see me succeed too.

He leaned forward and wiped the condensation from the mirror. This is one of those moments when the right decision can win the whole war. I've got to do it!

The ride to the Bay area seemed longer than usual. Before going to the office, Nate stopped off at San Francisco International airport and initiated Plan-B.

Darryl's secretary greeted him and then said, "Art Chavez is expecting you."

It seemed profane for Art to be sitting so comfortably behind Darryl's desk. He was typing on the terminal and didn't see Nate come in.

"They said I was to report here this morning."

Art stood, "Ah yes, Nate", he extended his hand.

Nate shook his hand, thinking, *Why do they always want to shake your hand before they try to screw you?*

"Sit down. We have some things to talk about."

Nate sat without comment.

"We're asking everyone to sign a new confidentiality agreement."

"Oh?"

"Is that all you have to say, 'Oh?'"

"What else can I say, until I've seen the agreement?"

"Aren't you curious as to why we made this decision?"

"To tell you the truth, Art, no I'm not."

"Well then, if you'll just read and sign this document, I have your bonus check here." Art placed an envelope in front of Nate, sat back and crossed his arms.

Nate read the document. It stated that he would not take any legal action against Shirotronics or assist anyone else in such actions. Near the end of the document, Nate saw a line that read, "I, further, understand failure to sign this agreement disqualifies me for discretionary bonuses."

Nate stared coldly at Art and then said, "I'm not going to sign this. And I've already qualified my bonus."

"Nate", Art said with great exaggeration, "that's not the way we see it."

There was a period of silence between them. Then Nate stood and placed his company car keys and company credit cards on the desk.

"What are you doing?"

"I'm quitting, Art, effective right now."

From that moment on, he ignored Art's words. Nate walked outside and felt the weight of servitude lifted as he hailed a taxi to the airport. There he got in the rental car he had reserved an hour earlier and examined the round-trip airline tickets he'd bought. He checked the destinations one more time: Phoenix, Chicago and Little Rock.

When he phoned Lena, she asked, "How did it go?"

"We're going with Plan-B." he said.

*   *   *

Darryl Wilson met Nate at Phoenix Harbor airport. They went to breakfast and discussed recent events at Shirotronics. It was as Nate suspected, Shirotronics fired Darryl, partly because of the Stepper accident at HEC.

"Hisimishi had a long list of complaints", Darryl said, "and he tried to blame you and me for the dropped SSR."

"But, we did everything right. I told them, it was the combination of the rain, wind, and forklift prongs being too close together. Hisimishi was right there, he saw what happened."

"Yeah, I know. They loss their case against the Trucking Company because of the way the pallet was built." Darryl said, "It made the Stepper unbalanced as it was lifted. They were lucky one hadn't fallen before."

"Are you going to sue them?"

"I've already started; my lawyer says I have a strong case. He says international companies can't stand bad publicity regarding their American employees. But, they'll drag it out.

"Damn. Sorry to hear about your troubles, Darryl."

"Don't be concerned about me; I'm going to be alright. Tell me about your new venture."

Nate related the progress he'd made with HP and the upcoming demo. He showed Darryl documents from the MicroStep contract as examples of how the contract's payments might flow.

"So, you see," Nate said, "all I need is enough money to establish an office and run for a month or two. After that, HP will be paying the bills."

Darryl read through the documents, "You've really planned this out, haven't you?"

"I believe I've covered all the bases."

Darryl closed the folder and placed his hands on it palms down.

"I tried to tell you, before you came all the way down here; my money is tied up right now. Shirotronics is counter-suing me and, even though I'm going to win, I have to pay legal fees up-front. Otherwise, I'd be glad to help you with this. Do you have any other prospects lined up?"

"I can understand your position, Darryl. And I do have other people that I'm going to ask to invest with me."

Nate thanked Darryl for listening and then said he was on his way to Chicago to talk with his father-in-law next.

"I wish you luck", Darryl said, "I think this is going to go over."

Nate was on the 3:45 PM United airlines flight to Chicago.

*   *   *

After visiting Chicago and Little Rock, Nate returned home and told Lena his story.

"Mother should have been there" Lena said.

"Well, she wasn't. It was unbelievable, Lena. I showed Chester my papers and explained everything and he actually understood. I mean he turned it around and then said things like, 'This is what more of our young men should be doing.' and 'These are the kinds of projects that need to be supported'. Then when I asked him if he was going to give me the money, he puffed on his pipe and calmly said, 'No.'"

"You know what that was all about?"

"No, what?"

"He thought you still owed him money."

"But, I paid him back."

"He's old and forgetful." Lena said, "Mother told me Chester had that much cash right there in the house; he's just like that. She said he would have given it to his son immediately. He even made comments about photos of our house and the pool."

"What does that have to do with anything?"

"He said our pool looked bigger than the one his son has."

"So what? You're his daughter."

"Daughter-in-law."

"Oh hell, now we're competing with Chester's son?"

"Let that go, Nate. Tell me about your trip to Little Rock. What happened with the Granville brothers?"

"I arrived late and didn't recognize Billy-Ray, but he remembered me. He had his son with him. They asked about you and how we liked living in California. His wife cooked a big dinner and everyone was friendlier than I remember them being at your father's funeral."

"Was Johnny there?"

"No, he came over later. He seemed real serious."

"That's him. We tell him, all the time, to smile a little."

"Well anyway, after dinner they offered me a cigar and some corn liquor. They watched me take a sip and seemed pleased when I didn't cough. But, I've got to admit, that shit was stronger than anything I've ever drank in my life."

"I hope you guys didn't get drunk before you showed them the plans"

Nate laughed, "No, but I knew the liquor was going to kick-in soon. So, I showed them my paperwork and we talked a little about programming and the computer business in general. Johnny knew more than Billy-Ray did. In fact, he said he had bought some Macrosoft stock once."

"Did they ask a lot of questions?"

"Not really. They wanted to know how long it would be before they'd see some profits in their bank account and I told them three months. That's when they excused themselves and went into another room. When they returned, Billy-Ray had his checkbook with him." Nate pulled out a check and handed it to Lena.

"Lena, when they gave me this check and we shook hands, I told them that it was a great day when black men helped each other like that. I told them I wouldn't let them down.

I'll never forget what Johnny said then. He said, "You have a dream, like Doctor King only different, and now we're part of it."

"How did you reply to that?"

"I said, 'Amen' and swallowed down the rest of my corn liquor."

"I never doubted you could do it; I'm proud of you, Nate."

Nate held her close and then said, "I still have to get the contract."

"You will, Honey." Lena whispered, "We've come too far not too."

*   *   *

Nate and Gabriel sat in Marty Spellman's office, waiting for Mr. Viceroy, the VP of Equipment Maintenance. They both wore suits and ties, Gabriel's was gray while Nate's was navy pin-striped.

"He's spoken with people that were at your last demo." Spellman said.

Just then, Mr. Viceroy entered the room with a briefcase. He was a big barrel-chested man with a rock-like face and hooked nose.

He smiled and greeted them in a deep voice, "Good morning, gentlemen."

After introductions, Spellman reviewed his department's needs and explained how the infinite-loop problem had not been solved to date.

"We've developed a solution." Nate said, "Can I show you now?"

"Please do." Mr. Viceroy said.

Nate gave Spellman a tape that he loaded onto the minicomputer. The familiar SIMON logo came up and Nate entered a password. He rolled his chair back from the terminal and turned to Spellman. "Now, if you will enter some symptoms that usually cause an infinite loop."

Spellman was about to comply, when Mr. Viceroy said, "Here, enter these symptoms". He took a tape from his briefcase and gave it to Spellman.

"Keep in mind," Nate said, "it may be several minutes before any loop is created."

"Meanwhile," Mr. Viceroy's said, "tell me how you came up with a solution."

"I'll let Gabe describe it; he came up with it."

Gabriel moved to the edge of his seat and squinted as he spoke. "Imagine someone walking through caves in the dark. All they have is a torch and a loaf of bread."

Mr. Viceroy glanced at Spellman and back at Gabriel.

"To determine whether he or she is in a loop, they drop pieces of bread along their path. Then, it becomes a simple matter of seeing if they cross a path with bread on it. If they do, they put a second breadcrumb down. They continue walking, following the crumbs, only this time they count their steps. If they returned to the spot where there are two crumbs they remember the number of steps it took and continue again. If they take the same number of steps and return to the two bread crumbs again, they can be reasonably sure they're walking in a loop."

As Gabriel finished, the computer terminal beeped. Mr. Viceroy came and leaned over the computer screen. He read everything carefully then turned and stared at Nate and Gabriel. "Well, done, gentlemen", he said, and returned to his seat.

Spellman examined the screen too. "It works. The program detected an 87-step loop. It might have taken my guys hours to figure this out."

"Very impressive." Mr. Viceroy said as he turned toward Gabriel, "Looks like your bread crumbs got counted."

There was a knock on the door and a secretary entered, "Coffee anyone?"

"Yes, please." Spellman said, "Regular everyone?"

"I'll have mine black." Mr. Viceroy said.

By the time the coffee arrived, Nate had reviewed the history of the project, noting each of the demos they had given. He described their plans for implementing Simon and future development plans. He ended with costs charts and a sample contract.

Mr. Viceroy said, "Would you gentlemen mind giving me and Mr. LaChae a private moment?"

Gabriel and Spellman left the room.

This is it, Nate thought, *He's going to take the contract!*

"Mr. LaChae, my people told me how you guys have worked hard responding to our demo requests. My programmer's said this infinite-loop thing was unsolvable in our context and it seems you've proven them wrong.

But, I have to tell you, we're not prepared to sign your contract as it is. It may be possible, however, for us to do some sort of joint venture in the future."

Nate spoke deliberately, "Mr. Viceroy, we did spend months meeting every condition and demo request HP asked for. We were told that this would be the last meeting before a decision would be made. All our plans are based on the contract as it stands and we haven't considered any joint venture ideas."

"I understand how you feel. But, that is the best I can offer you." Then he added, "Take some time and discuss it with your partner. Then get back to me. Okay? Here's my card."

"I'll do that sir, but I already know Gabriel feels the same as I do about this."

"Have you approached any other companies with your program?"

"No, all our efforts have been toward getting this contract."

"Again, I congratulate you and your partner on what you've accomplished. There's no doubt, you can be successful with this."

He got up, opened the door and summoned the others. There were polite farewells as Nate and Gabriel left.

*   *   *

Back at the house, Lena tried to cheer them up. "You can still sell your Expert-1 program by mail-order, like you planned."

"Yeah, right. Do you want to work with me on that, Gabe?"

"No. Expert-1 has always been your thing, Nate."

Lena brought sandwiches, "Come on you guys and eat something."

"I'm going to head home." Gabriel said.

"It's late. You're welcome to spend the night."

"Thanks, Sarah is expecting me to come home. I'll be there by ten."

"Hey, Gabe, man, I'm sorry, I thought it was in the bag."

"We all did, Nate. I think they don't want to spend money for something they're paying their own programmers to develop."

"They could have said that months ago."

Lena said, "Then they wouldn't have gotten all the information you guys gave them."

"What the hell's a joint venture anyway?" Nate said.

Lena and Gabriel knew the question was rhetorical and didn't answer.

*   *   *

Nate telephoned the Granville brothers, in Arkansas, gave them the news, and told them money would still be made by selling Expert-1 via mail-order. He spent two-thirds of their money running an advertisement in a magazine devoted to Radio-Shack's TRS-80 computer users. The ad ran for two months and the orders, which barely paid the rent, dwindled to a trickle in five months. All sales were cut-off when Nate's business mailbox contract couldn't be renewed and his mail was not forwarded.

Nate sent info packets to MBS and other companies that he believed had a need for Expert System programs. To his surprise, MBS responded with a request for a demo in Seattle, Washington. Nate had to reschedule and postpone the demo twice, while he tried to get the money to go to MBS. When he couldn't get airfare, he cancelled his offer.

*   *   *

Nate waited too long to start looking for another job and applied for unemployment insurance. Two months after the unemployment checks started coming, they stopped. They discovered Nate had a business license and demanded he repay the unemployment money he'd received.

He couldn't understand Lena's reluctance to look for work. She was taking courses at the local college and then said she didn't want to lose her credits.

Nate began drinking heavily and walking the streets of Sacramento during the day. When Lena found out he had had a sexual encounter with one of their neighbors, it strained their relationship to its limits.

Nate's brother, Douglas, invited him to come to New York City for a while and then said he'd send a ticket. Nate asked him to send two tickets.

"What for? You bringing some woman with you?" Douglas asked.

"No, of course not. My daughter, Kelly, is here; it's for her. I want her to be able to get back home after I tell her I'm leaving."

Before Nate could explain his plans, Lena opened his mail and saw two tickets. She showed them to Kelly and put them back into the envelope.

Nate arrived in no shape to explain anything to either of them. Kelly thought he was sending her home and Lena thought he was going to run away with the neighbor. He failed to convince either of them differently.

When he was ready to leave, he put his keys on the kitchen table along with one of the airline tickets and a note in an envelope. It said, "I need some time alone."

New York City

The flight to LaGuardia arrived two hours late and the passengers waited another twenty minutes before disembarking. At the gate, Nate peered over the other passengers and saw his brother waiting. Douglas looked older than Nate expected.

"Hey, Doug, is that you?"

"Yeah, it's me."

They hugged and Nate said, "I almost didn't recognize you. What's it like without any hair?"

"Nobody fucks with me any more, I can tell you that."

"But you're the police, I thought that gun got you lots of respect."

"Shi-i-it, anybody can get a gun. To get respect you have to look like you're ready to kick some ass. Otherwise, these young bloods will try you."

Nate laughed, "I'll keep that in mind. But, I'm not shaving my head."

At the baggage claim, Douglas grabbed Nate's suitcase and then said, "Come on, the subway is this way."

"I thought you have a car?"

"I do, but I don't trust it to come all the way to the airport and back."

Nate matched Douglas' fast pace.

They stood for most of the ride to the Bronx and often had to shout over the subway's noise to hear each other. Nate watched the New Yorkers as they entered and exited the train. It was all familiar to him, except for the newer fashions. He felt good to be home and wondered how long it would take to get back into the swing of things.

They took a cab from the Bronx subway station to Douglas' woman's house. During the ride, Douglas described the living arrangements. "You'll be sharing the second floor apartment with me and Liller and you'll have your own bedroom. Her sister lives downstairs."

"Her sister?"

"Her *much* older sister."

"And?," Nate scrunched-up his shoulders, "I'm your older brother."

"That's not the kind of *older* I mean." Douglas laughed, "You'll see."

It was early afternoon and the neighborhood park was empty as the cab drove pass. The closely built brownstones on Ely Avenue were identical. Each was iron-gated and three stories tall with a stoop leading to the second floor. Garbage cans were kept covered in the front yards. The house was clean and comfortable. A pot of something that smelled good was simmering on the stove. Douglas dumped Nate's bag on a tall bed in one room.

A raspy woman's voice came through the bedroom door, "Is that you Douglas?"

"Yeah, come on out here and meet my brother."

A dark, big-boned woman, wearing glasses, came out and then said, "Hello, Nate. Welcome back to New York. I'm Liller."

"Thank you, Liller. It's good to be back.

"Y'all ready to eat something?"

"Yeah, we're ready." Douglas said.

Soon, Nate was enjoying collard greens, potatoes, and ham. He turned to Liller and asked, "So, you and Douglas planning on getting married?"

Liller put her fork down, "Married? What for?"

"I just thought-"

"Your brother is too irresponsible for me to even think about marrying him."

"I don't want to marry your ass either." Douglas said, "So there."

Liller rubbed Douglas's baldhead, "But, I love him."

Douglas turned to Nate, "What are your plans?"

"I'll only be here a couple of weeks."

"You gonna write that Numbers program for me?"

"Doug, I've told you, lotto-numbers are random. No program in the world can predict random numbers – that's why they're random."

"I just want a program to tell me what numbers came out the most on a certain day, that's all."

Liller asked Nate, "What about your wife?"

"I think me and Lena might be through."

"You don't sound so sure."

"A lot happened between us in the past year and most of it wasn't good."

"That's life." Douglas said, "Shit's always gonna be happening."

"We'll see." Nate got up and went to the bathroom.

Liller and Douglas looked at each other with raised eyebrows.

When Nate returned to the table, he said, "Now, please let me read some of Motherdear's poems. Claudette said you have most of them."

"Come on", Douglas said, "They're down in the basement."

Douglas opened a small trunk and started pulling out stacks of papers wrapped in huge rubber bands. "No, not that", he said as he put some aside. "Here," Douglas handed a batch to Nate, "I got these during training."

Nate examined the certificates for marksmanship, hand-to-hand combat, and paramedic responder procedures. "This is great, Doug. You should put these up on your wall or in a notebook."

"I started to, but Liller don't want any holes in the walls."

"Well then, put them in a loose-leaf notebook, inside some of those acetate sheet protectors; that's what I did with the ones I had."

"Yeah, I will one day." Douglas said, then he handed Nate a large brown envelope. "Here, most of Motherdear's stuff is in here. I'll be back in a minute." Douglas went up stairs.

Nate opened the envelope and removed original handwritten documents. He handled them as if they were delicate ancient scrolls. Besides some photographs, that his sister had, these writings were all that was left of their mother.

He recognized most of the pieces and saw some she had written late in her life. His eyes started to tear when he saw *A Sonnet to my Son*. She had written it before he was one year old. Nate tilted his head back as if to contain his tears.

Douglas returned with two beers and saw the redness in Nate's eyes. "Here man. I cried too."

Nate looked at his brother and then said, "You know, these papers tell what she was really all about. Look at this one *Definitions of Love.* And this one here, *You Cannot be my Master.* I'll bet she was talking about our fathers."

"Yeah, she was one tough, romantic lady."

"Not really so tough, I think."

"Oh yeah, well let me tell you about the time she chased me down the street."

Douglas tuned the radio to a jazz station and they exchanged stories about their mother. After a while, Douglas said, "Come on, I've got the chess board set up."

Their chess battles lasted the rest of the evening.

*   *   *

It was Monday morning and Nate headed to his old neighborhoods. In the rush hour crowd at the Gun Hill Road subway station, Nate felt a comfort he had missed for years. Everybody, all around him on the subway platform, was black. All the various expressions of blackness were present and he was one of them. He was surprised at how much he had missed being part of the herd.

He spent his day retracing his life from Harlem's 125th street to Mount Morris Park and on to 115th street. The building across the street from his earliest memories was still standing. His family had left his dog Spot there when they moved to an apartment that didn't allow pets. *Wonder why we moved around so much,* he thought.

Nate continued on to Central Park and retraced steps where he used to ride his tricycle while his mother sat on a blanket, writing poetry. She taught him not to go too far and to come back and check on her often. He retraced his steps climbing over the rocks - choosing the same paths he had chosen forty years before.

He got back on the subway to Brooklyn and visited the Marcy Projects. He went on to Hancock Street where he had met Henry. Where he and Eva had met, conceived their first child, and were married.

Halsey Park was across the street from where his mother lived during her last years when she was bedridden with cancer.

He walked to St. Marks Avenue, to the house Beatrice had lived in, with her mother. The names on the mailboxes were different now. He was tempted to ring the bell anyway, but didn't.

At 841 Eastern Parkway, Nate stared up at the windows where his grandmother and uncle lived for thirty years. He missed everyone terribly. Nothing was the same without the people.

It was getting late and he wasn't ready to contact Henry yet. So, Nate squeezed onto the evening rush-hour subway traffic and returned to the Bronx.

During the ride, he kept thinking. *Got to get my mind active and creative. I could probably get Douglas to buy some neural-network software if I told him it could be used for his lotto-numbers project. Nah ... that won't be fair to him, there's no underlying pattern to the numbers game.* Nate laughed, *... Unless it's a pattern of how the bookies choose what numbers are going to come out. And the only way to figure that out would be psychically – the way those guys at Stanford did their stock market predictions.*

Maybe I should check out the local SMC group meetings.

Nate found and attended a Silva Mind Control meeting in Long Island that weekend. They were all beginners, except the instructor, and still awed from the basic classes. There was little interest in Nate's suggestion to repeat some of the Stanford precognition experiments. A woman named Illyana said she'd like to try it. But, Nate got turned off by how eagerly she gave him her phone number.

Someone made reference to "the late Krishnamurti".

"Why did you say 'the late'?" Nate asked guardedly.

"Didn't you hear? He passed away in 1986?"

Nate was grief-stricken. He stared, unhearing, and became tearful.

"Are you all right?" Illya asked.

Nate looked at her pleadingly, "No, I'm not ... right now."

"Why don't we all go to Level" the host said, "and share our feelings with Nate?"

The host played Sufi music as the group formed a circle and held hands. Nate was between the host and Illyana. They closed their eyes, took a deep breath, and shared their mental state called Level-1. In a few moments, Nate felt as though he was bathed in warm white light. He allowed the tears to run down his face.

When the exercise was finished, Nate thanked them and left.

*　　*　　*

Days later, Nate was having coffee, across the street from the Empire State building when someone in the bustling crowd outside stopped and blocked his view. Nate looked up and saw his old friend Jeff Cohen; he motioned for him to come inside.

Nate rose and they shook hands. "Hey, Jeff."

"I thought the resemblance was too striking for it not to be you, Nate. What you doing here."

"I'm just visiting." Nate said, "I'm staying with your favorite camping partner."

"Oh, God." Jeff sat and rubbed his fingers through his hair, "How is your little brother?"

"He's fine. He's a cop now."

"Let me get a cup of Joe." Jeff headed for the serving counter.

Once they got their small talk done, Nate asked, "What ever happened about that stolen car?"

"Nate, I wanted to explain that to you but you didn't respond to messages I left.

"I didn't want the police to know we knew each other."

"I can understand that." Jeff said.

Nate sipped his coffee as Jeff continued.

"I didn't realize what Karl and Byron were up to. A guy I know told me they could get cars - and quick. That's how we brought you one. They volunteered to drive it to Chicago, so I came along for the ride."

"But, why did they steal it back from me?"

"Nate, I learned later, that was their game. They had only one car that they used over and over."

"So, what happened to them?"

276

"I heard Karl got arrested for armed robbery and Byron left town."

Nate studied Jeff's face and decided he was lying. Despite the hardship the incident had caused, he smiled at Jeff and then said, "How's your son doing?"

"Healthy, I guess. We don't communicate often."

"Oh no, not you too." Nate put his cup down. "I thought you kept him with you after you and Wanda broke up."

"I did. He lived with me and my present wife and daughter until he was seventeen."

"Didn't you do all the father-son stuff with him?"

"Yeah, we did the Boy Scouts, went fishing, and even took flying lessons together. None of that seemed to matter when he got older."

"Damn", Nate shook his head, "I thought if you did all that kind of stuff with your kid, it would automatically make things work out later. Now you sound like your relationship, with your son, is similar to mine. And I didn't get the chance to do hardly anything."

"These modern kids have their own values, Nate." Jeff turned sideways in his chair, "They believe whatever they want, the old formulas don't work any more."

Their conversation trail off and they exchanged phone numbers before Jeff left. Nate gave him a phony number.

* * *

Meanwhile, on the thirtieth floor of the old Walsh building in Manhattan a security officer dialed a special number. Miriam Streisand accepted the call. Moments later, she informed Colonel Abrams, "Nate LaChae has turned up in New York City, sir."

"Good work, Miriam." Colonel Abrams said. "What's he doing?"

"He was observed talking with Jeff Cohen, in a coffee shop on Thirty-Fourth Street."

"How serendipitous. Are we tailing him?"

"Yes, sir. Our people are waiting for instructions."

"I want regular updates of LaChae's activities."

"Shall I communicate this new information to Taggart?"

"No. Let the F.B.I. do their own homework." Colonel Abrams said.

"Yes, sir."

Miriam quietly closed the door as she left the Senior Massad agent's office.

*   *   *

Douglas sipped his coffee and then said, "You know I'm still thinking about my numbers project."

Nate finished his bacon and eggs as Liller was leaving.

She stopped at the door and then said, "That's all he thinks about since you got here, Nate." She pointed toward the stove, "Be sure to turn them greens off before you leave."

"Have a good day, Liller." Nate said.

"What about a TRS-80 Model-II?" Douglas asked.

"What about it?"

"Could you do the numbers program on it?"

Nate rolled his eyes at the ceiling. "Doug, any computer can crunch numbers. But, it would take a very long time for some of them to run a program like the one you want."

Douglas poured more coffee. "Think about what it would mean? We'd have enough money to do whatever we want." Douglas spoke softly, "You could finish your Gamma engine."

"Douglas. Douglas!" Nate grabbed his brother's arm, "You have got to get it through your head that, even if we find patterns in the past, it won't mean they will be the same in the future."

Douglas looked his brother in the eyes, "And you've got to get it through your head that I KNOW patterns repeat every year. I've seen it too many times."

*   *   *

Friday, Nate lay on his back, reading Krishnamurti when Douglas came in.

"Hey Nate, you want to hang out tonight? Shirley got us tickets to a big dance down in Harlem."

278

"Yeah, I want to, but I don't have any money."

"I told you not to worry about money; I've got you covered."

Nate opened the closet door, "So-o-o, which one of your suits can I wear?"

" Any one, except the grey one; that's me tonight."

By the time their taxi blew its horn, Nate stopped his brother and pointed to their images in the mirror. "Now, THIS is what I call a big brother. Man, you were so tiny the first time I saw you. Everybody had told me my new brother was coming from the hospital with Motherdear. All I could say when I saw you was, 'Is THAT my brother?' I wish Motherdear could see us now."

"Nate, we're past the little-brother big-brother stage now."

"I know. I'm just glad we're here. Let's go party!"

They slapped their hands together in a high-five.

The Castle Club, on 125th Street, was downstairs in an office building. They could hear soulful music from the street. The crowd inside was in one huge, smoke-filled, room with a bar at one end and a DJ and dance floor in the middle. People sat at long folding tables that weren't covered. The room was bathed in blue lighting.

Douglas lit a cigarette and made his way toward the bar. Nate followed. Several people acknowledged Douglas as he passed. He stopped and tried to introduce Nate, but the music was too loud for him to be heard. Nate smiled and waved anyway.

"We're not going to find a seat in here." Nate said.

"Don't worry about that, I see Shirley, come on."

Douglas walked right through the crowded dance floor, drink in one hand and cigarette handing out of his mouth; while Nate detoured around.

At the table, Douglas introduced Shirley and others in her party, who all nodded toward Nate. Shirley had saved a chair, but Douglas remained standing on the edge of the dance floor, surveying the crowd.

Shirley looked at Nate and pointed to the chair; he took it. "I hear you've been away for a long time", she shouted over the music.

"Yeah, and it's good to be back."

Shirley laughed and then said, "I guess, I should say you've been out of town. Saying you've been away sounds like ... "

"I was thinking the same thing." Nate laughed.

Douglas glanced at Nate and Shirley then back to the dance floor.

Nate tapped Shirley on the shoulder and pointed at her plate. She motioned toward the end of the room where Nate saw a long line of people.

"I'm gonna get something," Nate shouted, "you want anything else?"

Shirley shook her head from side to side and smiled.

Douglas remained at the edge of the dance floor with his back to them.

As the party continued, Nate noticed the people sitting near him looked hard. He tried to define what it was. One guy had scraped knuckles. Two other people had old cut marks and he'd seen one guy with a cut mark that went all the way around the back of his neck. Nate thought he was imagining it, but it was real.

That's what I've missed by not being here – the danger. he thought, *We party so hard, because we live so hard. Shit, I have my blackjack in the back of my pants right now and I'll bet Doug brought his snubnose-38. I used to think everywhere was like this. But, now I know better.*

I remember there was always one fight at these big dances. Just one. Sure hope the one for tonight has already passed. Nate smiled and headed for the bar.

*   *   *

Douglas gave Nate the keys to his '72 Buick. It ran, but needed work. It had recently passed its New York State inspection – thanks to repairs secretly made by Massad intelligence agents, unbeknown to Doug or Nate. The agents were concerned that their tracking transmitter might fall out due to vibration; it was held in place by magnets.

Nate was happy because the entire city was now accessible. He headed to Brooklyn and his old friend Henry. Arriving at the apartment, he knocked on the door and heard Henry say gruffly, "Who is it."

"Brother Rat."

"Who?"

"Brother Rat", Nate repeated. He heard several locks turn and a chain scrape the door, then it opened.

"Nate! Hey, Man!" They enthusiastically exchanged the Black Power handshake and Henry pulled him in. "I'll be damn!"

"Where's Margie?," Nate asked.

"She's at work. She won't be in until later." Henry stepped back and then said, "Why didn't you tell me you were coming? I could have put something together for you."

"Hey, man, you don't have to do all that."

"How long you staying?"

"I'm not sure. Maybe just a few weeks, maybe longer."

"Well, sit on down. I'll send one of my boys out to get us a taste." Henry call out, "Leroy, come here!"

Henry's second son, came out of one of the back rooms. He was short and had a big Afro. "How you doing, Uncle Nate."

"Just fine, Leroy. I wouldn't have recognized you. What have you been into?"

"You should ask him who he's been into." Henry said, "He's making babies faster than we did, Nate."

"That's not true, Pops. Why you telling Nate that. Only two of those kids are mine."

"Yeah, right", Henry said and pulled out a twenty dollar bill. "Go get us some bourbon - Walker's Deluxe, right Nate?"

"Oh, yeah."

By the time Margie arrived, they were drunk and watching a Charles Bronson video.

Margie hugged Nate and then said, "I see you two haven't changed a bit."

They roared with laughter.

*　　　*　　　*

During their trips together, Nate, Doug, and Henry stopped in Queens, at a park where they used to play handball. Douglas and Henry quickly beat the pair that had been on the court. As a new pair of challengers took their place, Henry, who played barefoot, called to Nate.

"Come on in Nate, the ground's too hot for me."

Nate and Douglas began a marathon that lasted all afternoon. And even though they beat all comers, the crowd, behind the fence, cheered for the local champions.

"Ronnie and Mookie will beat 'em!" they yelled. And it looked like they might, when the score got tied at twenty-all.

Wham! Nate served the ball high and hard. Ronnie ran way back, and with a big sweep of his arm, sliced the ball hard and low. Douglas was right at the wall when the ball hit. He robbed his opponent of a "killer" point by lightly tapping the ball and letting it roll out.

"Point game", he said as sweat poured off him.

Nate served cross-court and immediately moved to the rear. He had correctly anticipated his opponent's return shot. The ball came to him high and fast. It would have hit Douglas in the face if he hadn't ducked. Nate returned the ball cross-court to the spot where he had served from. Mookie had good position and played the ball fairly. He and Douglas volleyed so many times the crowd cheered.

Nate yelled from the backcourt, "Mine!" and Douglas let the ball pass.

It bounced …

Both opponents expected a low "killer" and rushed to the wall. Instead, Nate hit the ball high and hard. Mookie jumped and missed; Ronnie chased the ball all the way to the rear fence.

Nate and Douglas called out in unison, "Next!"

It started raining hard as Nate, Douglas and Henry ran to the car, laughing all the way.

*   *   *

When Douglas showed up with an old Radio Shack computer, Nate got started programming the numbers project. The work went fast since he had already thought the project through. He created an input screen for the user to specify what dates to be analyzed. The program, then, sorted all the numbers that came out during the time period and displayed the frequency of their occurrence.

For weeks, two of Douglas' girlfriends had been recording lotto numbers onto diskettes. So, Nate and Douglas tested the program with the data they had. The results convinced Douglas that the program could not make predictions; his disappointment was obvious.

"Nate, what would it take for a program to make predictions? And don't say it's impossible; they do it with the weather every day."

Nate laughed, "Okay, there are neural-network programs that can find patterns and make predictions. But their results are only a probability – not a certainty."

Douglas's eyes bulged behind his glasses. "How much is the cheapest one of those programs?"

"There's one called BrainMaker that sells for $200", Nate said "But it might take weeks to run it on that old Radio Shack computer."

Douglas put his hand on Nate's shoulder, "You just tell me what you need and I'll find a way to get it."

Nate wrote the name of the software company, and then said, "And the fastest PC you can get."

Douglas put his coat on and was almost outside the doorway. He turned around and asked, "What are we gonna call this project?"

Instantly, Nate said, "The Onyx Project".

"Why Onyx?"

"Because Krishnamurti said everything comes from the blackness."

Douglas frowned, "Whatever" then he headed down the stairs.

Three days later a brand new computer was sitting in the kitchen when Nate came in.

"I ordered the software you wanted" Douglas said.

Nate transferred the TRS-80 programs to the new computer and stayed up all night programming.

*   *   *

Nate was lying across his bed reading one evening when he heard Liller coughing and moaning. At first, he thought she was crying; afterward he heard her praying. He knocked on her door and asked, "Are you all right?"

He couldn't understand her reply because of her coughing and wheezing.

"Do you want some water or something?"

"No, thank you", she said, "I'll be all right."

Moments later, he heard her again. He hesitated, wondering what Douglas might think if he came home drunk; then he knocked on the door again. "Liller, can I come in?"

"Yes."

She was lying on her back, sweating.

"What's wrong?"

"I'm sorry, Nate. I get like this sometimes." She wheezed, "It will pass."

Nate hesitated again, then said, "I can help you, if you let me."

"What do you mean?"

"Just relax and let me pass my hands over your body. I don't need to touch you or anything."

Liller lay still and closed her eyes as Nate went into his meditative state, leaned over her, and slowly passed his hands from her head to her feet. He repeated it several times and then cupped his hands near the top of her head and kept them close to her scalp. He whispered a mantra and told her she could say it, or think it, whenever she needed to.

Nate stood up and brushed his hands together as if they were dusty.

Liller was staring, "What did you do? I feel fine."

"It's not me, Liller. I'm just a channel that this healing energy passes through. Everybody can use it if they learn how. We don't need to discuss this ever again, okay?"

"Thank you, Nate. Thank you."

"You're welcome. I'm glad you feel better."

He returned to his room and continued reading about the coming Harmonic Convergence.

*   *   *

At a critical point in their evening chess game Douglas asked, "Have you seen any of your kids since you've been back?"

"No", Nate moved a pawn forward, "I don't even know where they are."

Douglas moved his bishop on a rank, preparing to attack. He finished his beer, got up for another and then said, "Malcolm used to call, but I haven't heard from him since he gave me a sob story about how bad his mother and his woman treated him."

"Un-huh", Nate concentrated on the chessboard.

"I knew he was full of shit," Douglas continued, "because I used that same story when I was his age. I told him it didn't work for me and it wasn't going to work for him either."

Nate castled on his queen's side and then said, "Check".

"If he calls here again, you want me to tell him you're here?"

"Yeah, sure, get his number. I do want to see him."

Malcolm called on Wednesday and Liller gave the phone to Douglas.

"Somebody here wants to speak with you, Malcolm." He gave the phone to Nate.

"Mr. LaChae?"

"Yeah. Who's this?"

Nate remembered his own dad's response to that question, when he visited New York during Nate's adolescence.

"My Name is LaChae, too."

"Hey man!" Malcolm said, "When did you get here?"

"A little while ago. Douglas said you might be calling."

"I want to see you man. How long will you be here?"

"Just a few weeks. Where are you going to be this evening?"

"I'm over here in Brooklyn. I don't have train fare to come up there to the Bronx."

"That's all right. I have a car. I'll come to you."

Nate hardly recognized his second son as he pulled up to the corner of Fulton Street and Nostrand Avenue. Malcolm was big; he had on a pea coat and a seaman's cap. He reminded Nate of his grandfather. His eyes were deep set now, but he still had his shy smile.

Malcolm hopped into the car and Nate greeted him with a hug. Surprised, Malcolm returned the hug.

"Hey man. I was thinking about you the other day; wondering what my father was doing."

Nate pulled out into the traffic and then said, "What kind of food do you like?"

"I like all kinds of food, but some foods don't like me. I have a lactose condition. I've been wondering if I got it from my mother or you."

"Not from me. I eat almost everything – except *escargot*."

"What's that?"

"Snails."

Malcom grimaced, "Me neither!"

They laughed and ended up eating Kentucky Fried Chicken. Malcolm hadn't communicated with his siblings for months.

Almost immediately, Malcolm started repeating the story he had told Douglas.

" ... then I got kicked off of welfare, because my woman said I didn't live there with her and that made my food stamps stop because I had no address ..."

Nate looked at his son and saw the sadness in his tired eyes. He listened and began formulating a plan.

Meanwhile, Malcolm continued, " ...so, when I didn't get that job because ... "

Nate had heard enough, "Listen, Malcolm, I have some friends that live near here who might be able to help you-"

"I been to them agencies and all that-"

"No, I'm not talking about an agency. I'm talking about some people I've known since before you were born. They know the streets and the hood. Margie worked down at the welfare office so she knows the system and she probably still has some contacts there too. Just give me a couple of days and I'll get back with you."

"You not gonna disappear again without telling anybody, are you?"

"No, Malcolm, I promise."

"Yeah."

After getting their approval for his plan, Nate brought Malcolm to Henry and Margie's apartment. Margie cooked black-eyed peas and cornbread for dinner.

Margie explained how Malcolm could get on welfare and get food stamps. Then she said, "Now, you understand, I'm doing this because you're Nate's son. You've got to do your part or I'm through with you."

Henry belched at the table and then said, "Yeah, I remember I didn't do my part one night and she said she was through with me."

"Be serious fool." Margie said, "We're talking about his life."

"Shit, I am serious. This is my life too. Malcolm is old enough to know what time it is." Henry turned to Malcolm, "You better be glad you got a father that cares about you. I never even knew my father or my mother. Now, as long as you respect yourself and my house, you are welcome here. But, I'll tell you the same thing I tell my kids, start some shit and out you go."

Malcolm shook his head in agreement.

"Malcolm", Nate said, "Henry and Margie have agreed for you to stay here for six weeks only."

"Because, that's how long it will take for you to get your cards" Margie said, "and get registered for an apartment."

Henry's son, Leroy, came rushing in and was introduced to Malcolm.

"He's gonna be staying with us for a while." Henry said.

Leroy and Malcolm looked at each other and neither seem impressed, pleased, or displeased.

"Cool", Leroy said impatiently, "Later, Malcolm." He went into the bedroom for a moment and then left the apartment.

"So, what do you think, Malcolm?" Nate asked.

Malcolm chewed his food and wiped his mouth with the napkin.

"I'm happy that you all are going to help me. I felt like I had nowhere to turn."

"Well, you do now." Nate said as he pat his son on the back.

It was cold outside when they left Henry's house. They walked toward the subway.

"So, how's your car?" Malcolm asked.

"It's not running well. That's why I didn't try driving it today."

Nate notice Malcolm's coat had no pockets and asked, "Where's your gloves?"

"I don't have any."

They arrived at the station where they would go separate ways and Nate gave his leather gloves to Malcolm. They hugged and Nate said, "Malcolm, take care of your self. Don't let the world get to you"

"I think everything is going to be all right now."

Nate bought two tokens and gave Malcolm two twenty dollar bills.

"See ya later."

"Yeah."

*   *   *

Douglas took Nate on a tour of after-hours spots. Craps, card games, video games, dominos, it was all going on. Nate got drunk and almost fell off a barstool at one point. "How come nobody's dancing?" he asked.

"Cause this ain't no damn disco" a big man next to him said.

Nate grabbed the man's arm, "It don't have to be a damn disco to dance?"

As the man grabbed Nate's hand, Douglas stepped in and shook his head from side to side.

"He's my brother, man."

The man didn't let go of Nate's hand until Douglas opened his jacket just enough to expose his service revolver.

The man let Nate go. "You need to tell your brother to be cool."

"Come on, Nate. I think it's time to go."

"Aw, Doug, I didn't finish my drink yet."

"I'll buy you another one."

Outside, the cool air hit their faces and Nate looked around.

"Oh, wow! You know where we are?"

Douglas looked for a cab, "Where, Nate?"

"This is 115th street. This is the first place I remember living at when I was a little boy. I had my third birthday here."

Douglas tugged at Nate's arm, "Come on, we need some coffee."

Soon, they were in a taxi, on their way home.

The coffee cleared Nate's head enough for him to think … Maybe Doug will hit it big and I'll have enough money to do something – get my own clothes and an apartment. They'll do a credit check though … I would have to use my middle name and get another driver's license.

Crossing 125th street, Nate thought about his kids. *Best that I stay away from Eva. There's nothing I can say or do right now anyway. I don't want them to see me like this.*

Wish I could find Beatrice. But, what good would that do? Only, mess up her family life or something. Better to let her be happy where she is. I have nothing to offer her right now.

I'm not going to worry about all that tonight.

Nate fell asleep in the taxi. Douglas took the coffee cup out of his brother's hand and stared at the man he used to idolize.

*   *   *

It was almost noon when Liller woke Nate.

"Are you going to get up at all today?"

"Yeah, thanks for waking me. Where's Douglas?"

"He's in the living room." Liller said, "Not as young as you used to be, are you?"

"You got that right." Nate groaned through his headache. I don't even remember how I got home." He still had all his clothes on, except his shoes.

"Coffee is still hot", Liller said, "I'm not fixing any lunch."

Nate got up and put his robe on. He greeted his brother and then noticed Liller and Douglas were too quiet.

"What's wrong with you two?" Nate said groggily.

"Your brother, that's what's wrong."

Nate poured coffee, "What do you mean?"

"He almost got us killed this morning."

"Aw, woman" Douglas said, "Jimmie wasn't gonna do shit."

"Will you tell me what you two are talking about?"

"Just some bullshit" Douglas said, "It was nothing."

Liller pointed at Douglas, "You! You better watch your back from now on. Jimmie Sparks don't play. He's got people that do his dirt for him, you know."

"I'm gonna ask one more time … ", Nate began.

"I went with Douglas to collect some winnings today. And when Jimmie Sparks said he heard about you programming a computer, then he said some bad things about you."

"Yeah, he said some things alright." Douglas shifted in his seat, "That's when I told his punk ass to back off."

"What did Jimmie say, Doug?"

"He said some of his people didn't like how often I was winning."

"So, what does that have to do with me?"

Douglas stood up, "Nate, that son-of-a-bitch said you were too damn smart and that your brain might need an adjustment."

"Doug, I told you something like this would happen if you used that program too much."

"I've been spreading my bets around; nobody had to make any big payouts."

Liller walked over to the window, "Doug, you need to listen to your brother."

"And you need to stay out of my business!" Douglas retorted.

"Me!" Liller turned and looked at Douglas, "You're the one that told Jimmie, you would fuck him up if he ever touched your brother. I don't know what were you thinking?"

Douglas frowned at Liller and stood up slowly.

"Take it easy, will you?," Nate stepped into the middle of the room, "Both of you, sit down … Please."

"I'm not gonna sit here and be insulted in my own fuckin' house." Douglas said.

"This ain't your house, Douglas", Liller said.

Nate gripped Douglas's arm. "Come on Doug, let's go for a ride."

Douglas pulled free of Nate's grip. "Yeah, let's get the hell out of here."

Outside, Douglas said, "I'm going to Shirley's house, you coming?"

"No, you go ahead", Nate said, "I'm going over to Henry's."

*   *   *

Douglas didn't return to Lillier's place until four pm the next day. All smiles and smelling like liquor, he threw car keys on the table and announced, "Who wants to go for a ride?"

Nate picked up the keys, "Pontiac."

"It's only two years old and I paid for it - cash." Douglas said proudly. "Come on, let's go."

Nate held out his hand, "What about my cut?"

"Hey, man, I had to use all the winnings to get the car and-"

"What about my third?"

"Take it easy, Nate. Listen to me. You can keep the other car."

"I hope you're kidding."

"He's probably not kidding, Nate", Liller walked out of the room.

"Come on, Nate, don't be like that, we won and you can share my ride."

"No, man. That wasn't our deal."

Douglas raised his voice, "What did you expect? I was the one who put up all the money. And what about those times when I loss? You didn't lose one third of that money with me."

"That's just bullshit and you know it! I'll tell you what I expected." Nate got in Douglas's face, "I expected you to keep your word like I kept mine when I wrote the program for you."

Liller came in and stepped between them, "You two stop it, you hear?"

Douglas stared at Nate. He knew he could whip his older brother, but remembered promising their mother he would never fight with Nate. "The money is gone and that's it. Now, you can borrow the car whenever I'm not using it or you can just stay out of my face."

Nate shook his head, "I should have expected something like this." He went and grabbed his coat and left.

The old Buick stopped running two days later. Nate had it towed to a garage where the mechanic asked, "When's the last time you had any service done? I gotta tell you, this car needs a lot of work."

"Yeah, I suspected that. How much will it cost to get it running again?"

Nate and the garage owner haggled for a while, and finally settled on a price.

"It'll take three days to get the parts in."

"Okay, just do it as quick as you can."

Nate took the subway to Brooklyn.

*　　　*　　　*

As evening turned into night, Nate and Henry sat in the back yard drinking Colt-45.

"How's your mother doing?" Henry asked.

"She and my father passed away, in the same month, a few years ago."

Henry cocked his head and then said, "Now, you're an orphan like me."

Their eyes met and for the first time, Nate understood how Henry had felt all his life – without parents.

"Yeah", he said, "I guess I am."

A peaceful silence descended between them as they drank their beer. It was the silence of old friends, who didn't have to speak to communicate.

Henry shook his head and then said, "It's just not right, Douglas having you live down there in the basement."

"Liller asked me to move down there 'cause she don't want me and Douglas arguing any more. It's alright with me; I have my privacy."

"Yeah but, when I think of all you've done for your brother when he was small … "

"Henry, don't sweat it. I'll be out of here soon anyway."

"It's still not right."

Nate changed the subject, "I've always wanted to ask you something."

Henry waited.

"How come you didn't show up when Sonny and I rented that studio to record you playing the drums?"

Henry sipped his beer and thought before he said, "For the same reason I didn't come to your wedding."

"I've wondered about that too. What was it? Did I say something wrong?"

"No, Nate, it wasn't you."

"What then? I wanted you to be best man, remember?"

"I couldn't stand Sonny. He was as two-faced as they come."

"But, he was one of the Cervaza Kings."

"No, not really. We had rules and principles in the CKs that Sonny didn't care about."

"Why didn't you say something then?"

Henry turned to Nate, "Because you seemed to be so happy."

"But, I would have been even happier if you had told me-"

"No. You wouldn't. If I had told you how many times I saw Sonny over at Eva's house, you wouldn't have believed me." Henry continued, "That's why I didn't want to have anything to do with him."

"Even if you thought I wouldn't believe you, why didn't you tell me anyway?"

Henry stared at Nate and then said, "Because I'm your friend."

After a while, Henry said, "You know, I believe we should start up the CKs again. Not for us, for our kids and other young black men They need something like that now. I watch them in the streets and they don't have any kind of rules or respect for anything."

"I know what you mean, Henry, but the time for the CKs has passed. Maybe if we had started with our boys years ago ... "

"No, man. It's not too late, now that you are back here; even if we have to start with our grandsons."

"Henry", Nate turned to him, "I may not be staying."

"Why not? Where you gonna go this time?"

"I don't know for sure. But, I can just feel it."

"You going back to your woman?"

"I don't know. Maybe."

Henry laughed, "Can I tell you something, man?"

"What?"

"You always running to some woman or from a woman; you know that?"

Nate laughed, "Yeah, I guess it does look that way, but there's more to it than that." Nate finished his beer. "I've learned a lot of things,

Henry, a lot of other things. Maybe, I just haven't learned how to pick the right woman."

They didn't speak for a few moments, then Henry said, "I always thought Beatrice was the right woman for you."

"That's what my father said too. But, that's all history now. Beatrice is married. And so am I, for that matter."

It started raining and they headed back into the house.

"Don't tell me the rain brought you two back so early." Margie asked, grinning.

"My car's in the shop." Nate said.

"Ah-huh." Margie said it like it was retribution for their partying.

Henry put an Italian Western movie into the video player and soon he was asleep on the couch and Nate was asleep in a sofa chair. They both snored loudly. Margie came into the room and shook her head from side to side.

*   *   *

On the second day of the Harmonic Convergence, Nate was lying across his bed when Liller yelled down the stairs "There's a phone call for you, Nate. It's long distance."

He came up from the basement, "Hello, this is Nate."

There was a pause, and then Lena said, "Hello, Nate. How've you been?" She waited for his reply.

"I'm okay. What about you and Brandon?"

"We're okay. You know about the Harmonic Convergence?"

"Of course."

"And what do you think about it?"

Nate laughed, "Well, here we are talking to each other …"

"And?"

"And, I guess it means something."

"You have to guess?"

Nate paused, "Not really. We both know everything that happens has a meaning."

There was a long silence.

"What's Brandon been up to?"

"He's doing well in school and keeps asking when you're coming home."

"Do you want me to come back?"

"I love you, Nate. Of course, I want you to come home."

"I love you too, Lena. I've been doing some serious thinking lately.

"Me too. I've got a job now and a two bedroom apartment."

"Lena, all I have is an old car that I might be able to drive back there in."

"That would be good. You know how Sacramento public transportation is."

"Let me get things together on this end and ... what's your number?"

She gave him her number. "When do you think you'll be ready?"

"In a few days; a week at the most", he said.

"Okay. I won't tell Brandon until you're on your way."

"I understand. That's cool. I'll tell him myself when I'm sure about the date."

"The Harmonic Convergence must be working."

"I knew you were going to say that."

"Well? Isn't this an example of moving toward the light?"

"Yes, Lena, it must be."

*   *   *

When Nate went to get his car, he was told, "There's no way you gonna make it to California in that car." He decided to sell the car and ran a classified ad, in the *New York Daily News*. Liller insisted he not give out her phone number, so he only gave the address. There were no responses for a week. One day Liller handed him a letter.

"Guess somebody finally saw your ad."

"It's about time."

He looked at the return address. It was from a Mrs. Headley and the address was Elmhurst Hospital. Nate laid the letter aside and ate dinner. When he opened the letter, he saw it was from Beatrice.

This is too much of a coincidence, he thought, *and there's no mention of the car. How could she have got gotten my address? ... Aunt Lil?*

The next morning, when he called the number, he recognized Beatrice's Bajan accent immediately. Her voice sounded the same as twenty years earlier. She was cheerful and invited Nate to lunch near her job at the hospital.

He waited, in his car, by the hospital's construction site entrance. Suddenly, there she was. Dark and lovely strolling toward him. He got out of the car and resisted running to her.

They smiled as the distance between them closed.

"Hi", she said.

"Hi. How are you? You look the same."

"So do you; maybe a little taller than I remembered."

Nate came around and opened the car door for her.

"Where to?"

She directed him to a small buffet. It was nearly two-thirty and there were only a few people still eating. Before he knew it, Nate was relaxed and casually talking with Beatrice as if they had never been apart. He felt more comfortable talking with her than with anyone. Her laughter and West Indian accent were the same as he remembered. Neither of them mentioned their breakup or their current marriages. He wanted to kiss her.

"So, are you going back to California?" Beatrice asked.

"Yeah, I'm going to try to do the right thing."

Beatrice opened her purse and started searching. "Do you have a pen?"

"No, I'm afraid not."

Is she actually going to give me her number? he wondered.

"There's a little gathering, on Friday, at a friend's house. If you'd like to come, it'll be nice and I think you'll enjoy yourself. Here's the address. Things will be getting started around seven."

"Thank you Bea but, I don't know if I can make it because I'm leaving Saturday."

They finished lunch and he drove her back to her job. He got out of the car as she was leaving.

"It sure was nice seeing you again, Bea."

"I enjoyed you too."

She put one hand on his cheek and kissed the other cheek. She turned and strolled away, hips moving to her own unique rhythm. She disappeared into the entrance, Nate put both hands on the steering wheel and sat … remembering. He was in the same position, fifteen minutes later, when a security officer told him to move from the No-Parking zone.

All the way back to the Bronx, he replayed their luncheon and wondered.

Why now, after all this time.

Why couldn't I find her before?

We're always missing each other one way or another.

What does it mean?

She's married and so am I – still.

If I go to that party on Friday …

No. I can't go.

… she did give me that kiss on the cheek.

No. I mustn't go. Lena and Brandon are waiting for me at home.

Beatrice is married and she has a daughter too.

I don't want to spoil anything. I should leave things alone. But, it felt so good and natural, sitting and talking with her.

And she did give me that little kiss …

I better get my ass home before I make a whole lot of people unhappy again.

*　　　　*　　　　*

Friday night Nate was at Henry's house. They were sitting on the couch, listening to oldies. Henry poured another drink for himself and motioned to see if Nate wanted more.

"Yeah, go for it, Brother Rat," Nate said. "So, there's been no word from Malcolm?"

"Man, your son hasn't called, stopped by or nothing," Henry replied, "I asked my kids if they seen him and they said no."

"Shit. I don't know what's wrong with him."

"Let him hit bottom and he'll straighten up, Nate. Some kids are just like that. Leroy got his act together after he saw there was nothing for him in the streets. Now he got a job and he's taking classes at night."

"Well, we can't help them if they won't help themselves."

"You got that right." Henry said.

They paused and listened to the music for a while.

"You sure you don't want to try and get Beatrice back?"

"Man, that's a dream. I've got to deal with reality."

"What is reality, Nate?"

A that moment the DJ, on the radio, played the old Latin tune: Cervaza.

"OH SHIT!" Nate and Henry exclaimed simultaneously. They got up and danced the cha-cha, side by side, the same as they had done twenty-three years earlier when they named their social club The Cervaza Kings.

As the evening went on, they used cans for bongos, sung doo-wops and reminisced about the times of their lives.

Finally, Nate said, "Hey man, I got to get going."

"Margie's gonna be mad if you leave without telling her goodbye."

"I know Henry, but I got to go, man."

They walked to the door. Nate paused, and then they did something they had never done before. They hugged.

"Later man."

"Later."

*   *   *

When Nate was packed and ready to leave New York, he said to Liller, "I need you to put the chain-lock on the door so Douglas doesn't see what I'm about to do on the computer."

"What are you going to do?"

"Save his life, I hope."

Liller looked puzzled as she locked the door, "But, what if he comes soon."

"I'll be finished before he gets here."

"He's not going to like it if you change the numbers program?"

"Just trust me, Liller."

"Okay, I do."

Nate installed a virus into the Onyx program.

*   *   *

When the taxi horn blared Nate said, "I guess Doug is not going to make it."

Liller put her coffee down, "That's your brother. Did you really expect him to be here on time? He'll make you miss your plane, if you let him."

"I want to thank you again, Liller, for everything. You have been very kind to me and I won't forget it."

"Hey, you're like family, Nate."

They stood up, hugged and then Nate said, "Here, I want you to have these"; he gave her his car keys and registration.

"Nate. You know I don't like to drive."

"Yeah, but you can sell it or something."

"Well, I guess it'll have to be 'or something', huh?"

Liller started to cry, "I'm being silly. Thank you for what you did when I was sick."

They heard the taxi's horn again.

"Take care of my brother."

Nate grabbed his bag and rushed down the stairs.

*   *   *

United flight 453 started its take-off roll at exactly 8:06 pm. Nate was sitting in a window seat with his eyes closed. He was asleep before they reached cruising altitude. Somewhere over Pennsylvania, he awoke, stared out of the window and smiled.

Kyle Measurement Systems - US

To get the cheaper airfare, Nate flew to Oakland and took a two-hour bus ride to Sacramento. He saw Lena and Brandon before the bus pulled into its berth. Brandon was taller and Lena seemed smaller. Nate didn't recognize the woman with them.

"HEY GRANDDAD!" Brandon jumped into Nate's arms.

"Hello, Brandon. Hey, Baby." Lena kissed him on the cheek and the three of them hugged for a while.

"Well, are you going to introduce me, or what?"

Lena let go, stepped back and then said, "Oh, sorry. This is Trudy."

"So, this is the Nate I've heard so much about. Lena talks about you all the time at work." Turning to Lena, she said, "You didn't tell me how handsome he was."

Nate shook her hand and then said "Hello, Trudy. I hope what you heard was all good."

Trudy laughed, "Most of it, anyway."

"Granddaddy, I can skateboard real good now, come on I'll show you."

"You can't skateboard here, Brandon," Lena chided, "Besides, Nate has to get his bags and Trudy is parked in a no-parking zone."

"I hope you don't have many bags" Trudy said, "We're in a Volkswagen Rabbit."

"No, just one. We'll be alright."

It was dark when they arrived at the apartment. Nate put his bag inside and, as he had promised, came back outside to watch Brandon skateboard. The board was thin and Brandon had to work to keep his balance, but he managed to showoff anyway. The adults clapped and cheered as he did his acrobatics.

"Alright now," Lena said, "it's getting late."

"Yeah and I've got to get going." Trudy said, "Nice meeting you, Nate. Take care of our girl."

Back inside, Nate realized there was no furniture downstairs in the living room, only a folding table and chairs. Besides two beds and dressers in the bedrooms upstairs, there were only cardboard boxes of clothes. Brandon turned the television on.

"What happened to all the furniture?" Nate asked.

"I sold the living room set and some other stuff to get in here."

"I guess we're really starting all over again."

"Yes we are, aren't we?" she waited for him to take her into his arms. When he did, they both felt a chill and embraced for a long time.

"I love you, Lena. I'm sorry I had to leave."

"I know and I love you too. And Brandon loves you very much."

"I'll try to make it up to both of you."

"Let's just move on with our lives. What's past is past."

Brandon insisted that Nate tell him a bedtime story. Of course, he wanted to hear one about Nate and Henry – back in the days. Nate stretched the story until Brandon fell asleep.

When Nate finished showering, he came to the bedroom where Lena had incense and candles burning. She offered him a joint. "This was a gift from Trudy."

They embraced and Nate said, "Do you want it tonight?"

Lena buried her head in his chest and then said softly, "Not really." An old, familiar thrill went through them and they clung to each other most of the night.

*   *   *

Nate got a part-time job, repairing McIntosh computers. He kept sending out resumes in hopes of getting something permanent.

Two months later, he flew to Silicon Valley for several interviews. One was with Kyle Measurement Systems (KMS) in Sunnyvale. They were looking for a technician to work on a new computerized microscope. The starting salary was more than twice what he was making.

The offer letter came one week later; it directed him to report to the main KMS plant in three weeks. It included a cashier's check for moving, meals and a hotel while they looked for a permanent residence.

"ALL RIGHT!" Nate shouted and hugged Lena and Brandon. They bounced around together. Then Nate and Brandon danced around like Indians on the warpath.

Lena read the letter and then said, "Here comes our next adventure."

*   *   *

As soon as they got settled into a Sunnyvale townhouse complex, the LaChae's discovered they had troublesome neighbors.

"That Black couple, named Ross, that lives downstairs have a problem." Lena told Nate, "They've both told me the white people in this complex are racist, but everyone treats me just fine. Meanwhile, everytime I look around, the Ross' are yelling and screaming at someone's kids. I saw the wife … I forgot her name … grab one kid by his collar the other day and she shook him."

"Let's stay away from them."

"Don't worry, I plan to."

Nate turned to Brandon, "Come on little man, it's time to go to the bank. You ready for your allowance?"

Brandon ran to Nate and gave him a hug. Larkspur barked as if he wanted a hug too. Nate loved Brandon, but wasn't enthused over their new dog. They crossed the street and Brandon was off into the park on his skateboard, Larkspur chasing and barking.

"Meet me at the corner by the bank", Nate shouted.

Just because me and Lena have lousy saving habits, doesn't mean Brandon has to be the same way, Nate thought, *we can make him better than us, if we just try. After all, it just boils down to habits anyway. I hope Lena can see that.*

Approaching the bank, Nate asked Brandon,

"Do you remember what to do?"

"I know, Granddad, I know."

Nate stood back and watched as Brandon waited in line; he had to tiptoe to reach the teller's counter.

"I want a receipt, please", he announced.

"Why certainly, Mr. Allen."

He read his receipt and counted his change, then came over to Nate.

"Everything is okay, Granddad, I checked. Can I go play now?"

"Yeah, sure", Nate took the bankbook, "stay nearby because we're going for some ice cream when your grandmother comes downstairs."

Nate watched Brandon hop on his skateboard and take off into the park. Nate reminisced about his own grandfather giving him money to buy comic books and the two of them reading together.

I wasn't a good father, he thought, *but I KNOW how to be a granddad; I had an excellent role model for that.*

Lena came downstairs and they headed to the ice-cream parlor. They watched Brandon doing Ollies and Kick-flips as they walked along. After a while Brandon announced, "You know what, Grandduddy? I have big balls", and he continued skateboarding.

Nate stopped walking as his mind refused to accept what he thought he had heard.

"Brandon, what did you say?"

"I said" Brandon repeated, "I HAVE BIG BALLS!"

Nate's face and mind went blank. He looked toward Lena for understanding, but couldn't see her face; she was looking away. For seconds the neurons in Nate's brain centers stopped firing. Stupefied, Nate thought, *you DO have big balls, telling me something like that!*

Lena managed to hold her laughter long enough for Brandon to pick up his skateboard and point to the logo on the wheels, "See, Granddad? Big Balls." It was the brand name of the wheels.

They laughed all the way to and from the ice-cream parlor. Lena told Nate how Brandon had gotten her with that one earlier in the day.

"Nate" Lena said, "You should have seen your face."

"You really got me that time", Nate said as he got Brandon into a playful headlock.

*   *   *

Nate knew things were going to be all right, at Kyle Measurement Systems, as soon as the Project manager, Peter Eastlund , showed him the lab. Peter was a small Austrian man with a beak nose and receding temples. Nate looked around and saw an array of familiar test equipment. In the center of the room sat the unfinished emission microscope (Emmi). All its cabinet doors were wide open, as if it were being overhauled. The development team surrounded it, each doing their own thing.

Everyone was intent on bringing the machine to life. Aron Balsam, the mechanical engineer, was on his back, with his head and arms into the front of the cabinet; he was calling out instructions to Mr. Lam, who was around back, making adjustments while looking at a meter. The chief software engineer, Eliezer Rosenberg stared, intently, at his monitor analyzing code. His programmer assistant, Gary Chin, was playing his computer keyboard like a concert pianist; lines of code scrolled up the screen. Nate felt comfortably at home, as if returning after a long journey.

"Come on", Peter said, "I'll introduce you."

Nate made friends with the manufacturing team when he helped build the first three production models of Emmi. The machines were built by a competent, multi-ethnic team. They answered Nate's many questions with pride and confidence. He felt good working with a start-up team again.

Peter had the team set up an Emmi in the new demo room and began inviting potential customers to bring their samples for testing. Nate sat-in during the demos, learned how to answer questions and run test without damaging the samples. Soon, Nate took over responsibility for doing the demos.

One difficulty he repeatedly encountered was software changes. Eliezer made last-minute changes and had Gary Chin install them without informing Nate. When Nate complained, Peter told him to put a lock on the door.

The company's patent rights didn't extend internationally and a competitor, Hamamatsu, started selling their own emission microscope in Japan. To counter this market threat KMS hired a new Japanese salesman/technician, Mr. Matsiyama, in the city of Kyoto.

When Matsiyama came to the plant, he was teamed up with Nate for training. They quickly became friends, especially after Nate told him he knew how to play Shoghi. Little Matsiyama was a flamboyant individual who went all over the plant asking questions, giving suggestions and arguing when he disagreed with the way something was being done. On Fridays, he joined the team for pizza and beer. He asked where a Karaoke bar was and no one knew.

The annual Semicon convention was held in Los Angeles that year and Emmi was displayed to the world for the first time. Peter, Horst, Eliezer, Nate, and Matsiyama went to L.A. to support KMS's exhibit.

After the third day of the show, Matsiyama approached Nate. "Nate-San, I want to ask you for a favor please. Will you take me to Sunset Strip and Beverly Hills Hotel?"

"Sure. But, I don't know if they will let us into the hotel if we are not guests."

"We go and see, Okay?"

"Okay, but first let's have dinner."

"Oh no, Nate-San. You and I have dinner at Beverly Hills Hotel." Matsiyama smiled, "KMS will pay."

Nate weaved his way through traffic on Sunset Boulevard, while Matsiyama took pictures of everything.

"We will make lots of money with Emmi." Matsiyama said, "Many companies in Asia want Emmi."

"Good. I hope we can beat Hamamatsu."

"Do not worry, Nate-San. I have many contacts. As long as Emmi perform good, I can make deals better than Hamamatsu. You will see."

Nate glanced at the man sitting beside him and remembered they were comrades in arms. Matsiyama was on the front line, selling an American machine to Asians who had a choice to buy from an Asian company. Nate realized he and the production team at KMS were supplying Matsiyama with the weapon and ammo to win their war. Nate silently vowed to give Matsiyama all the support he could.

When he called Lena that night, she said she had good news and bad news; she wouldn't elaborate.

Lena met him at the airport and during their ride home he asked, "You gonna tell me the news now?"

"The good news is I got a job doing graphic arts for a newspaper in Cupertino."

Nate smiled, "That's great. Now what's the bad news?"

"First, you have to promise you will stay calm."

"Aw, come on, Lena. Just don't say you had a run-in with our black neighbors."

Lena stared at Nate through her round glasses and shook her head up and down.

"So?" Nate said, "What happened?"

"We don't need any more trouble from them. But, I know Brandon is going to tell you everything anyway."

"Tell me what, Lena?"

"Moses came upstairs and was banging on our door. He-"

"WHAT?" Nate exclaimed, "Banging on our door?"

"Yeah. He said Brandon beat up his son."

Nate turned and looked out of the window of the limo and tears of rage came to his eyes.

"We're not going to be living like that", he said, "I'll take care of Mr. Ross."

Lena wrapped her arm around Nate's, "Honey, we don't need to take on their troubles."

"Don't worry", Nate patted her hand, "we're not."

As the limo driver pulled up, Moses was in the parking lot, with the hood of his van open. Nate instructed the driver to go around to the other side of the building. The driver unloaded Nate's bag as Brandon came running.

"Hi, Granddad, come and watch me shooting marbles."

"In a few minutes, Brandon. Let me take my bags upstairs first and then I've got to take care of some business."

"Did you tell him, Grandma?"

"Yes, he knows what happened."

"I was scared, Granddad. But, Grandma said for me not to be."

"That's right, Brandon. You should never have to be scared. You wait for me, right here. Okay?"

Lena trailed along as Nate grabbed his bags and climbed the stairs to their apartment. He took off his suit coat and tie and went to the kitchen. He put a butcher knife inside the back of his pants, pulled his shirt out, and tightened his belt. He turned and checked himself in the bathroom mirror.

Thought I had left this kind of shit in New York! Just when everything is going all right with my life, I have to deal with some idiot like Moses. Nate grabbed the bathroom doorknob and hesitated. *Wish I had a blackjack or something; I don't want to have to stick him. But, even if I have go to jail, he's got to understand he can't be scaring my family.*

Nate asked Lena, "Why didn't you tell me on the phone?"

"You were out of town" Lena pleaded, "and I didn't want it to interfere with your work."

"Lena, it's not my work! It's their work and it's never more important than you and Brandon. I go to work just to-"

Lena interrupted, "I know, I honey, I know. We were all right"

"Yeah. That son-of-a-bitch is going to stop his shit right now! Where's Brandon?"

"He's outside playing. Please calm down, Nate."

"I am calm" he turned to her, "Lena, I want you to stay upstairs. Okay?"

She tried to hug him, "Be careful with Brandon down there."

He kept her from putting her arms around him and possibly feeling the knife. "Brandon will be fine. You just stay in the house. Okay?"

"Alright, Nate, I won't come out."

Nate found Brandon still playing marbles.

"Hey, Granddad."

"I want you to come with me for a minute, Brandon."

"Aw, I wanted to finish-"

"Now, Brandon! This can't wait."

They went around front, to the carport, where Moses was working under the hood of his old van. Nate instructed Brandon to wait within hearing distance, then he walked over to the van.

Moses came from under the hood with a wrench in his hand, "Hey, man. I was coming to talk to you."

Nate put his hands on his hips - under his shirt, "Well, I'm right here, right now."

Moses stammered, "Listen, man, I was upset about some kids hitting little Moses and I thought Brandon was one of them. But, it was all a mistake and-"

Nate's patience was almost gone, "Ross, you need to listen to me", Nate interrupted, "I had a son once who was beat to death by an adult when he was only a year and a half old and-"

Moses started to interrupt, "Now wait a minute … "

With his last ounce of restraint, Nate said, "Listen to me, Ross" and he started over. "I had a son who was beaten to death by an adult when he was only a year and a half old and I'm not going to let anything like that ever happen again. I'm telling you man-to-man, if you have any problems with my family you take it up with me. Don't you ever scare my wife or my grandson again. Do you understand me?"

"Look man, I-"

"Do - you - understand - me?" Nate said through clenched teeth.

Moses looked off to his left into the distance; the wrench was still in his right hand.

Slowly, Nate grasped the knife under his shirt. He calculated it would take three motions for Moses to turn his head back around and swing the wrench. He knew he could stick Moses before the wrench could reach him.

Moses faced Nate again with tears in his eyes. "Yes, I understand." He glanced over at Brandon and then stared at the ground.

Nate didn't move until Moses returned to working under the hood of his van.

Brandon and Nate walked back to the marbles game. Suddenly, Brandon hugged Nate saying "I love you, Granddad."

"I love you too, Brandon, very much." He started to leave the boys.

"Hey, Granddad" Brandon called after him, "you want to break the pack?"

Nate turned "You got a big shooter marble I can use?"

"Yeah! Right here." Brandon held up the blue sphere.

"Okay, I'll show you boys how to really bust up the pack."

Two weeks later, someone set the Ross' van ablaze in the carport. The entire building had to be evacuated. The guilty party was never found and the Ross' moved away soon afterward.

*   *   *

Peter Eastlund's return from Europe was welcomed at KMS. Tensions between Nate and Eliezer had not abated. The new Plant Manager, Danny Marks, decided to sit in on the debriefing.

"The story from Europe is what we expected", Peter said, "All the players have heard about Emmi. And there is a window of opportunity for us, if we can get it to them during their next capital spending cycles. Everywhere I went they were curious about how we intend to calibrate Emmi since it's so sensitive. Therefore, that has to be one of our top priorities. Additionally, there's a big concern about whether support will come from the US and where their local field engineers will be trained."

Each of the engineers responded to Peter's report and commented on the problems in their own area. Danny Marks was tapping his pen on his writing pad and flipping it over. He looked at his watch, put his pen down and then said, "All right, I've heard enough. What we need are more people. Agreed?"

No one disagreed and within a few weeks, a production supervisor, another field service engineer, and two technicians were hired to work on the Emmi project. Peter was back in Europe doing demos and trying to drum up business.

The new Production Supervisor Oscar Carlisle was a tall roly-poly fellow who smiled a lot and leaned his head sideways as he spoke. Even though he was from Ohio, his drawl led people to think he was from Texas.

When Nate told him an Emmi was available to start his training. Oscar responded with, "Okay, Sambo, let's hop to it."

He said it in such a casual manner, Nate was stunned for a moment. Then he shouted, "HEY MAN! I DON'T PLAY THAT SHIT!"

Oscar looked surprised, "What?"

"You know what!"

"Aw, I didn't mean nothing …"

"Yeah, well don't ever say anything like that to me again. Understand?"

Several coworkers were staring over their cubicles at Nate and Oscar.

Aron came over and asked Nate, "What happened?"

Nate ignored Aron and challenged Oscar again, "Do you understand?"

"Yeah. Okay, I understand."

"Come on", Aron smiled and put his hand on Nate's shoulder, "let's get a cup of coffee".

Nate looked at him, took a deep breath, and then said, "Yeah, I could use a cup." They walked off, leaving Oscar under the scrutiny of half a dozen of his co-workers.

When Nate returned, Oscar was reading one of the Emmi manuals. Neither spoke of their previous exchange and Oscar followed Nate to the production area. In less than two weeks, Oscar proved himself technically competent and assumed his role as production supervisor.

*   *   *

The EMMI marketing and sales director, Horst Kruger, looked across his desk and asked Nate, "Are we ready for these guys from Sandia?"

"We're all set; I ran a test, this morning."

Horst laughed, "I hope you locked the door afterward."

"Oh, yes! I had to tell Gary there won't be any last minute software changes today."

"I'm glad you did, I can't overstress how important today's demo is. These scientists, that are coming, are with the US nuclear agency. If we get a machine into their lab, we'll be guaranteed other military sales."

"I understand, Horst. Don't worry, Emmi and I will do our best."

"I know you will." Horst stood, signaling the meeting was over.

Three scientists arrived and were exactly what Nate expected. Having mastered Emmi's operations, Nate was still thankful Eliezer was present to discuss its theory and answer questions. That allowed Nate to finesse Emmi's controls and give one of his best demos.

"That was excellent!" The scientists were jubilant at the conclusion of the testing.

Horst came into the room and changed the discussion to where he was taking them to dinner. Nate exited and was halfway down the hall when Eliezer caught up to him and then said, "That went very well. For a moment there I thought their sample was going to pop."

"Yeah, I know." Nate continued walking, "I didn't want our chances for a sale to go pop too."

Eliezer didn't share Nate's humor, instead he said, "My new software could have compensated for that surge we saw. Why didn't you let Gary install it this morning?"

Nate stopped and turned to Eliezer. "Look Eliezer, every time I get things ready for a demo you guys come in and change the software and I don't have enough time to learn what affects the changes have." Eliezer took his glasses off and put his hands on his hips. Nate continued, "Sometimes, if there's bugs, in the software, the whole demo can go bad."

Eliezer narrowed his eyes and pointed at Nate as he spoke, "That wasn't your call to make. Peter is the project manager, not you."

"I know that. But, Peter is not here and, when Horst told me how important this demo was, I wasn't willing to take any chances. Besides, you said yourself everything went well. That was our goal, wasn't it?"

Eliezer ignored the question, "I want a key to that room."

"The room is open now. You'll have to get a key from Peter."

Nate saw Eliezer's jaw muscles moving, but neither of them spoke. One of the secretaries came down the hall and walked between them before they moved off in their separate directions.

*   *   *

Six weeks later, Nate was on an airplane, landing in Albuquerque. He stared out of the window as the plane bobbed over the Sandia mountains.

After getting a rental car, he went straight to the military base instead of checking into his hotel. There wasn't much to see as he approached the fenced-in guard booth, just sparse sandy land, mountains, and odd shaped antennas in the distance. As he waited in line, behind another car, Nate read the a nearby sign, "AUTHORIZED TO USE DEADLY FORCE."

He presented several pieces of identification, was photographed, fingerprinted, and given a yellow badge. A soldier, in combat fatigues, directed him to park his car and took him in a jeep. There were no buildings in sight and neither of them spoke during the drive.

The facility revealed itself as the jeep came around a bend; everything was in a huge crater. Nate's first thought was: *it looks like a crater on the moon or a crater made from an atomic* ... , he cut the thought off. *It can't be a nuclear crater, there would be radiation.* He thought, *It must have been made with conventional explosives.*

The jeep pulled up to a two story brick building. The modern lobby contrasted strongly with the landscape they had just crossed. A pretty receptionist directed him to sign-in and gave him a radiation badge. Soon, a lanky fellow, who wore old jeans and a plaid shirt, greeted him. His hair wasn't combed and he spoke with a southwestern accent. Nate guessed he was about thirty-five years old. The driver handed him a clipboard to sign and left without a word.

"You're a little early, aren't you?"

"I wanted to be sure I could find the place." Nate said.

"I see," he looked Nate up and down, "Well, Jerry Soden isn't available right now. I'll take you up to the lab; all your boxes are in the hall up there. You gonna work today, in those clothes?"

"Is there some place where I can change?" Nate asked.

"Yeah, I'll show you." He looked at Nate again and then said, "I didn't think you'd want to work in them shoes. How'd you get such a mirror shine?"

Nate didn't know how to respond, "I ah ... , they're new."

"Johnson and Murphy?"

"Yeah, they are."

"Last time I saw a shine like that," he continued to stare, "I was in the military, stationed outside Atlanta."

Nate wondered where the conversation was heading, so he didn't respond. Instead, he did a quick inventory of the crates. His mind raced,

Who is this guy? And what's the big deal about my shoes? Hope he's not going to start some shit – way out here in Albuquerque.

By the time Jerry Soden showed up Nate had the Emmi out of its crate, powered up and running a diagnostic test.

"Glad to see you again, Nate."

"Same here, Mr. Soden."

"I see you met Rip already?" Soden asked. Rip formally acknowledged Nate and they shook hands.

"How long before Emmi will be ready?"

"I'll need about thirty more minutes."

"Okay," Jerry Soden looked at his watch; I'll be back by then. Rip, watch over his shoulder and learn what you can."

"You bet," Rip said.

That afternoon Nate ran through his standard demo routine and learned that Rip would be the Emmi operator. Nate trained Rip on the intricacies of the machine. Rip's questions reflected his concerns, "What type fuses and light bulbs will I be needing? What are the routine maintenance procedures that I'll need to follow?"

At four-thirty Jerry Soden returned, "Sorry, I couldn't get back sooner. You going to be here tomorrow?"

"Sure, I'll be here until the weekend."

"Good, I have some chips I'd want to test. You ready to run this machine, Rip?"

Rip scratched the back of his head and then folded his arms across his chest, "I can dam sure run that test sample of his. I've seen a bunch of different ways to do that."

Everyone laughed.

"I guess we can power Emmi down for tonight then." Nate said, "And can you tell me where's a good place to eat?"

Jerry Soden told him of several steak houses and a Mexican restaurant at the edge of town. Then Rip added, "For the best beer in town and the prettiest waitresses you need to go over to The Wrangler's Club. They have live music there Thursdays, Fridays, and Saturdays. They'll be playing the Blues tonight. They got a fella that plays guitar like Chuck Berry. You ought to come on down there."

"I might do that" Nate lied, "after I check back at the hotel."

That evening, Nate rode the tram to the top of Sandia Peak and had dinner at the restaurant up there.

The next day went smoothly, with Nate demonstrating how to finesse Emmi for it's best performance. Jerry Soden brought a metal box with a combination lock on it.

"Nate, I'd like for you to see if Emmi can show us what's wrong with this chip". He put on rubber gloves, opened the box, and took out an unusual looking computer chip. "It's one of a kind, so I'd prefer that you test it, instead of one of us. Here - wear these gloves when you handle it. And please keep in mind, any current above 20 milliamps will destroy it."

For almost an hour Nate tried to get a reading from the mysterious computer chip. Jerry Soden encouraged him to take all the time he needed. Rip kept suggesting things to try. Finally, Nate knew what he had to do - tactfully. He turned and then said, "I don't mean to be rude, but why don't you guys go and get a cup of coffee."

"Too many cooks in the kitchen." Jerry Soden smiled, "Want us to bring a coffee for you?"

"Yes, please. I just need a few minutes ..."

As soon as they were gone, Nate put three fingers together and closed his eyes.

They returned as Nate was closing Emmi's cabinet door.

"Anything?" Jerry asked.

"We didn't know if you wanted cream and sugar", Rip added, "so we brought some."

Nate made up a believable story. "I checked the optics and connections to the chip."

"You didn't touch it?" Jerry Soden asked.

"No. I used the gloves."

"It's not radioactive." Jerry said, "It's extremely sensitive to the sodium on our skin."

Nate opened his coffee and added two sugars then put the lid back on the Styrofoam cup. He powered-up Emmi's camera and asked Jerry Soden, "Are all the wire layers in that chip made of the same material?"

Jerry pushed his glasses up on his nose, "Actually, they're not. There are some gold layers. Why do you ask?"

"I'll show you."

Examining the video image of the chip, Nate positioned Emmi's camera to the area where he had visualized a crack. Then he announced, "There's a defect right below those wires."

"How do you know?" Rip asked, "I can't see anything."

Jerry Soden was quietly staring at the screen.

Taking a sip of his coffee Nate said, "Watch this." Using the joystick, he slowly moved Emmi's camera from side to side. Each time he did, there was a small flash beneath the visible wires.

"Bright field?" Jerry Soden said and sat back in his seat.

"Exactly" Nate responded.

"What's bright field?" Rip asked.

"Think of it as indirect light that doesn't take a straight path to the camera."

"What you're saying is there's a fault in that chip somewhere down below those wires? How'd you find that?"

Looking very serious, Nate said, "I could tell you, but then I'd have to shoot you." After a three-second pause, everyone started laughing. Nate almost spilled his coffee.

When Nate was ready to leave, Rip said, "You wanna see some nukes?"

"Are you serious?"

"Oh yeah, I'm dead serious. Building-23 is a museum, its on your way out. We got some ass-kickers in there. You can take a look; it's free. Just ask the MP to stop there."

As he got out of the jeep, Nate read the sign outside the small white, one story, building "Nuclear Weapons Museum." No other cars were parked in the lot. The heat from the sunlight made the building appear to shimmer. Opening the heavy metal door, he felt a cold damp breeze hit his face. At first, it seemed so dark he thought the power was off; then he realized he still had his sunglasses on. But, even when he took them off, the room was dimly lit. There were recessed spotlights that shined on the placards near each bomb. He stood there and looked at the long round cylinders of mega-death, three along the walls to his left and three to his right.

The room was like a dungeon with sleeping monsters. Some of the bombs were painted black and two weren't painted at all. There was no lettering or pictures of pin-up girls on them either. The plate in front of the first one said, "Fat Boy" and Nate realized he was looking at a replica of the device that destroyed Hiroshima. Nate thought of Matsiyama and the other Japanese he'd worked with at Shirotronics. Sadness swelled up in his heart as he wondered if any relatives of his ex-coworkers were consumed in the fireball. Next was "Little Boy". The placard gave a description of the bombs equivalent power in TNT.

When Nate read the placard behind the third bomb, a replica of a thermonuclear hydrogen bomb, he was too depressed to continue.

I don't want to be helping them make these things! He thought. *I mustn't! This is beyond evil ... it's ... it's ... ;* he couldn't find a word that could define what the room represented on a spiritual level.

He walked slowly to the door and had to push very hard to exit. What he'd seen, and the hot air, made Nate want to be sick. He rushed to the jeep and got a bottle of water from the cooler in back. He poured water in his hands and wiped them over his face. He wanted to wake up, but couldn't; It was all too real. He saw the MP, standing in the shade, smoking and staring at him.

"You ready to go?"

"Yeah", Nate said, "I've seen enough."

Driving back to the motel, Nate kept thinking of Matsiyama and how they had become friends over time. *I would never nuke Matsiyama and his family and his city.* He thought, *but, my country did.* Nate anguished at the thought of being with the people that caused such horror and suffering.

*   *   *

Soon, after Nate returned home, Gabriel extended an invitation for dinner. The wives had never hit it off, so Nate wasn't surprised when Lena bowed out. *Good,* he thought, *Gabe and I can talk about computers as long as we want. Sara always leaves us alone.*

Nate rang Gabriel's doorbell at exactly 7:30 pm. He knew Gabriel would notice his punctuality. They greeted warmly and Sarah called to him from the kitchen, "Hello, Nate, I'm finishing dinner. Gabe, why don't you take Nate into the living room until I finish the Farfel."

They walked pass Gabriel's computer room and Nate asked, "You still running that old PDP-11?"

"Not very often these days. Come on I'll show you the new system that I built from scratch."

In minutes, the two of them were deep into techno-babble about motherboards, CPUs, clock speeds, caching, interleaving, and multitasking. Gabriel had just finished powering the system up when Sarah called them to dinner.

Sarah sat two plates on the table, "I'm not having anything". She left the room for a moment, then returned and then said, "I'm going over to Mary's for a while." She placed a business card by Gabriel's plate. Gabriel put it in his shirt pocket without looking at it.

"Do you want the car keys?"

"No. I'll walk. You can pick me up later."

"Would you like something to drink, Nate?"

Expecting wine, Nate said, "Yeah, sure."

Gabriel poured seltzer and raised his glass, "L'Chaim"

They talked briefly about Paul Brown, and the CIC inventor's group. Then Gabriel asked, "What about your gyroscopic engine? Have you been working on it any more?"

"Gabe, I think about it sometimes and I even write notes, but if I ever work on it again, it will be just to prove to myself why it works."

"Why didn't you talk about it more at the inventor's meetings. You already disclosed it when you applied for a patent and published your report in 1970."

"Because that's the kind of thing people aren't going to believe until you fly one over their head or something. I'll get back to it someday, but not now."

Gabriel glanced at his watch and then said, "Oh, before I forget", he pulled the card from his shirt pocket, "this if from a friend of Sarah's father. He's an entrepreneur and he's looking for really innovative ideas. You should give him a call."

"Hey, thanks Gabe." Nate read the card. "Mr. Abrams, huh? Have you met him?"

"Not really. My little programming projects aren't innovative enough."

"I wouldn't say that." Nate countered and lifted his glass in the air, "You did come up with The Loop Checker."

"Yeah, I did, didn't I?"

"You know", Nate continued, "I still think you should have published that.

"Maybe." Gabriel looked at his watch and then said, "I better go get Sarah."

The evening ended on that note.

Nate made an appointment with Mr. Abrams' secretary and met him in an office in Palo Alto. Nondescript would have been an understatement. Mr. Abrams sat behind a plain metal desk, with his back to a window. Even in a double-breasted gray suit, the old man was obviously military. His short gray hair and sun-tanned skin made him appear younger than his 71 years. He rose quickly and gave Nate a strong handshake. Nate sat in one of the two straight-back metal chairs in the room. The only other piece of furniture was a filing cabinet. There were no pictures on the wall.

"I'm pleased to meet you, Mr. LaChae. Would you care for some water?" He took a paper cup and reached for the metal pitcher at the corner of the desk; it was covered with condensation.

"No, thank you."

Mr. Abrams filled one cup, but didn't drink. Sitting quite erect, he placed his fingertips on the edge of the desk and then said, "I understand you've applied for some patents."

"Yes, years ago I built an optical tracking system that used a novel scanning method and more recently I got a copyright for some software I developed."

"I see." Mr. Abrams sipped the water without taking his eyes off Nate. "What about inertial propulsion, Mr. LaChae?"

"Ah, yes, I've experimented with gyroscopes and got a patent pending in 1970. I wanted to build a helicopter, but only got as far as building an engine that propelled a toy car."

It startled Nate when Mr. Abrams quickly reached inside his suit and then said, "Do you mind if I smoke?"

"Not at all." Nate said, thankful the man wasn't reaching for a Beretta.

"So, have you continued working on your helicopter?"

"No, not for quite a while. Most of my work now is with computer software."

"Yes ... software ... ," Mr. Abrams took a long drag on his cigarette, "much easier to work with than hardware." He put the half-finished cigarette out while still looking at Nate. He leaned forward, with his elbows on the desk, and crossed his fingers together on the desk.

"What would you need to make your helicopter fly?"

Nate wasn't prepared for that question. It felt as if everything had stopped - waiting for his reply. He didn't know what it would take or how long. Still, he had to reply. "I don't know. I'd have to develop a proposal."

"Mr. LaChae, the investors I represent are interested in novel propulsion systems as well as other defense related technology. We have substantial resources." He sat back, looked at his watch, and then said, "Please contact me if you decide to resume development of your helicopter. You have my card."

"Yes, I will." Nate lied.

They stood, shook hands and Nate left.

That night Nate told Lena about the meeting and how his Gamma engine was intended for traveling to the stars. He told her how Wehrner Von Braun had said he aimed at the stars. But, Von Braun's V2 rockets rained death and destruction on England during WW2.

"I don't ever want to help any military power kill other people." Nate said nodding, "Never."

Lena kissed him on the forehead and they slept.

*   *   *

Marcus Ryan came to KMS like a whirlwind. His Scandinavian accent and blond flop-hair made him the spitting image of David McCallum from the old TV show 'The Man From U.N.C.L.E'. He was finishing his interview with Nate.

"Nate, I'm promoting you to supervisor of Emmi's Field Service. From what I've heard, it's been long overdue and you deserve it.

"Peter has told me how he depends on you and I will be depending on you also. My background is not technical, so I'll need good people like yourself. Danny Marks spoke highly of you also. I want you to tell me about anything you see going wrong. The Emmi project has high visibility at the corporate level right now."

"I will do my best."

"Good." Marcus said, "We're going to be adding to our staff too. If you know of any competent technical people, please refer them to personnel."

Marcus went on to describe his plans for expanding the project and emphasized there would be opportunities for advancement for all. Nate left the office impressed and inspired; he felt like saluting Marcus Ryan.

Marcus didn't hire Perry Penvenne, even after Nate's strong recommendation. Nate knew Perry was smart, and technically competent from their days working together at MicroStep Corp.

Nate was equally surprised when Louis Marbury was interviewed for a Quality Control job. After the dismal performance Louis gave at MicroStep, there was no way Nate was going to recommend him to be a supervisor.

When Nate questioned Marcus about Louis' qualifications for the QC job, Marcus said, "I knew he wasn't qualified; I wanted to see what you would decide."

Disturbed by Marcus' implication, Nate asked, "And why didn't you hire Perry Penvenne, he would have been perfect for the job?"

"He didn't have any fire in his eyes ... not motivated enough for me."

Nate stared at Marcus and then said, "I think that was a mistake." Then he left the office.

Mr. Lam, from the production group, came into Nate's cubicle with a bag. He interrupted the conversation and grabbed Nate's hand with both of his. He kissed Nate's hand and then said, "Thank you. Thank you. Thank you."

Embarrassed, Nate withdrew his hand. "What are you talking about, Lam?"

Mr. Lam bowed twice and then said, "I got a big raise because of you. You are a good man, Nate. I will not forget."

Slowly Nate realized Lam's was reacting to his recent performance review. "Oh, that," Nate said, "I only told the truth. You have been very helpful to me and my group. Without your help, it would have taken us forever to fix some of the problems we've had out in the field. You're welcome, Lam."

"My wife made this for you," Lam opened the bag and gave Nate a Mooncake."

Aron eyed the cake, "You gonna cut that now?"

"Sure. Why not?"

The three of them headed for the coffee break room.

Word came back from Japan that an Emmi arrived badly damaged. The microscope-camera section had broken loose from its support and bounced around like a pendulum during its 5,000 mile flight.

Marcus called a meeting. Matsiyama was on the speakerphone yelling, "I tell you, camera was not tied down properly for shipment."

Oscar jumped up, "That's a goddamn lie!," he was livid, "That machine was okay when it left here ..."

Marcus picked up the phone and spoke calmly to Matsiyama; "We'll see what we can do about sending another machine to you. -Yes, right away ... I know how important this sale is. I'll get back to you in an hour."

Oscar was pacing in place, with his hands on his head, "I knew that little Jap would try to get me. He probably sabotaged that machine, I'll bet that's what happened."

Nate snapped a look at Marcus to see his reaction to the racial slur. Marcus showed no emotion as Oscar continued his ranting. "I knew Matsiyama was going to do something. He was always trying to tell us what to do when he was here."

Peter Eastlund spoke, "Matsiyama is rightfully sensitive to the needs of his customers. The Japanese do things differently. He wanted to be sure-"

"What the hell do you expect", Oscar cut in, "when I have Vietnamese and Mexicans working for me."

Nate had had enough; he stood up, abruptly, in the tiny office and grabbed the doorknob.

"What the-," Oscar flinched as if he thought Nate was coming at him.

Nate turned to Marcus and then said, "I'm leaving."

"Hold on Nate." Marcus said, "Let's all calm down. We'll take a short break. Oscar will you stay for a moment."

When the meeting reconvened, Oscar was absent and Marcus polled everyone with one question. "What could have caused the cantilever to break loose?"

Peter Eastlund answered first, "We have shipped nine other machines to Europe and Asia without any damage to the cantilever."

It was unanimous, the cantilever hadn't been secured properly before shipment. Nate was the last to leave the meeting. His and Marcus' eyes met for a moment, then Marcus looked away.

Oscar kept his job, but his true character had been exposed.

An Emmi, intended for Germany, was unpacked, rechecked and sent to Matsiyama. It arrived safely and the sale was closed. In fact, the customer ordered Emmis for each of their four production facilities.

As soon as Nate got home Lena said, "You should call this number right away" and handed him a note. He was annoyed, but he heard the urgency in her voice.

"Who is this from?" he asked.

"They said for you to call as soon as you got in." Lena said coyly.

Shit! He dialed the local number. It can't be business because it's after 5 PM.

A man's voice answered. Nate looked at Lena. She was obviously expecting some reaction from him.

"Hello. This is Nate LaChae, I was told to call this number."

There was a pause. "Hello?" Nate repeated.

"Hello, Mr. LaChae. This is Mr. LaChae."

"Darnell!" Nate exclaimed at hearing his oldest son's voice, "Where are you?"

"I live ten miles away from you."

Darnell and his wife Carol were living at the Coast Guard base, in Alameda, for three years. He had given up trying to find his father. Carol simply looked in her local phone book and started calling LaChaes in the Bay area. When she spoke to Lena, they introduced themselves and promised to let their husbands surprise each other. It was a joyful telephone reunion and Nate was invited to dinner that night. Lena bowed out saying, "No, Nate. It's late, you go ahead. You two need time together. I'll come with you next time."

"Fine", Nate bolted out the door and drove up to Alameda. During the drive, he realized how pleased he was that Darnell was friendly. After all the time they'd been apart, he thought Darnell would have been resentful. *How many years has it been?* he wondered, *What will we say?*

Carol greeted her father-in-law at the door and they hugged as Nate looked past her to his six-foot-three, smiling, son.

"Hey, there, Mr. LaChae!"

As they hugged, Nate buried his head in Darnell's chest – he held back his tears. They stood there for a time.

"Where's Lena?" Carol asked.

"She said it was so late and she would come next time."

The two-story apartment was furnished in contemporary style.

Similar to my own place, Nate thought, *right down to the Stanton chess set on the coffee table.*

"You want something to drink before dinner?"

"Yeah, I'll have some wine if you have it."

Carol laughed; "See, I told you your father might want something other than beer."

Darnell prepared a delicious dinner. He and Carol told Nate how they met at the Coast Guard academy and became inseparable. Coincidentally, Carol was born in a North Carolina town neighboring Bethel, where Darnell's mother was born.

It amazed Nate to see how his little boy, who had gotten so big, had the same mannerisms as before.

"There's a surprise upstairs," Darnell said, as he tried to look serious. "Go ahead, you'll understand."

Nate didn't know what *or whom* to expect. They smiled at him as he, slowly, went up stairs. At the top, he looked into a well kept bedroom. As he poked his head in, he heard Darnell say, "The other room ... open the door."

Nate opened the door and immediately saw a model rocket. It was nearly three feet tall, finished in red and white and on a launch stand that had exhaust burn marks. Nate leaped into the air and yelled, "YES! OH, YES-S-S!." He turned around and saw Darnell and Carol, in the doorway, smiling. Nate grabbed his son by both arms and then said, "You didn't forget!"

They hugged again, Darnell said, "No, I never forgot. And I go shooting too. I have a 9-millimeter pistol and a 30-odd-6 rifle. I had always said I would have the guns you and your buddy Jeff had when you used to go hunting. I don't hunt though, I target shoot."

In the weeks that followed, Nate and Darnell got together often. They launched rockets with Brandon in San Francisco Bay. Brandon was especially happy that his rocket was as big as Darnell's. Both rockets scraped the clouds before their parachutes opened. Nate recalled lines from one of his mother's poems titled Cloud Burster: ... *I burst a cloud of ignorance and found understanding, I burst a cloud of fear and found love, I burst a cloud of rain and found heaven's rainbow.*

When summer came, Brandon went to Chicago to visit his mother and great-grandmother. Nate drove Lena, Carol and Darnell to Los Angeles to visit his cousin Myheir and her daughters. She took them to their cousin Danny's boathouse in Marina Del Rey.

Danny always managed to live inexplicably well without breaking the law. His newest venture was a couple of limousines that he rented out on weekends. That weekend, the family traveled in luxury and saw the sights. Darnell chose to go to Disneyland with his young cousin Kim. After nine hours with the energetic twelve-year-old, he promised himself never to volunteer for anything like that again.

One evening, before they left L.A, Myheir and Nate were walking to the store and she said, "Jeanette has been calling me."

Nate had grown too close to Myheir to give the flippant response he thought of. So, he said, "What does she want?"

"She keeps asking when you are going to come see your son."

Nate was always uncomfortable talking about his failed relationships. However, talking to Myheir was like talking to his conscious. She never pressured him or took sides. But, he knew she was for him, even if she didn't always approve of his behavior. They had bonded, long before, in the way that loving blood relatives do. The honesty and candidness between them was genuine. She waited for his answer as they continued their walk.

"I think I better stick to building a relationship with one son at a time," he pleaded.

"You should see him, Nate, before he's all grown up like Darnell."

"I know, and I will, but not right now. Jeanette can be so volatile and I don't want to deal with her right now."

"Okay, I only wanted to mention it to you."

"And I'm glad you did, Cuz. Aunt Lil always gets around to asking me about Daniel. She also mentions Beatrice. I wish she could see that I can't go back and change the past. I'm trying to make good with the present."

"She loves you, Nate and she thinks she knows what's in your heart, that's all."

"Yeah, and she's probably right, but I've got to go on from where I am."

They returned in time to meet one of Danny's musician friends who had sets of conga drums in his van. Before long, everyone was dancing on the boat to the beats of Nate and Danny's friend. Danny made a few phone calls, put Mongo Santana on, and The Party really began.

Nate *played* the conga drums to the slow tempos and *beat* the drums to the faster tempos. He sweat and beat the drums until his hands were sore; then he beat the drums some more. Everyone enjoyed the music. What they didn't understand was that he was beating out his past.

*   *   *

Weeks later, Nate drove through the scenic mountains along Highway-17. Lena folded the cover back on Nate's coffee cup and handed it to him. Brandon was sleeping, on the backseat, with his head propped up on a blanket.

Lena sipped her latte and then said "I'm glad you decided to take the day off from your project Nate. You've been working so hard lately and I miss our long drives together."

Nate glanced at her and smiled, "Me too, Lena. I don't ever want us to stop taking our drives. It's the one time I feel we are free of everything. All the bills, the job and my projects too." Moments before, he had been thinking of how to get the Emmi calibration-standard to work.

Lena stared out the window and munched on grapes she'd bought at the Farmer's Market. "I had a strange dream last night."

Nate kept his eyes on the road, "What kind of strange dream?"

"Well, we were living in a different place. It seemed like we were in another country."

"Oh yeah, what country?"

"I don't remember, but the people spoke a kind of English there and they were friendly."

"What makes you think it was another country? It might have been another state."

"No, the shops and stores were different and ..." she sat upright, "you were having trouble steering the car."

"Was it out of control or something?"

"No, not really. It was more like you were trying to start in third gear. Lena smiled and looked at him, "That wasn't the strangest part though."

"No?" Nate chuckled.

Lena hesitated, "Maybe we were on another planet, because there was something that would fly over, very fast and high up."

"Was it an airplane?"

"I don't think so."

Nate smiled, "A bird?"

"No." Exasperated, Lena said, "It was a flying saucer, okay?"

"Okay ... a flying saucer, huh." Nate didn't laugh. "Was Brandon with us?

"Yes, we were taking him to school and he was about the same size he is now. I'm telling you, it was one of the most vivid dreams I've ever had, everything was so real ... even the flying saucer."

Nate put the car into low gear as they started their descent toward Santa Cruz.

"Maybe you saw an alternate reality or something, you know like Jane Roberts talks about in her books."

Hesitantly, Lena said, "What do you think about us living somewhere else?"

"I always like to travel."

"No really, I mean *living* in another country."

Nate couldn't resist, "a country with UFO's flying overhead?"

"Come on, Nate, I'm serious."

"Where do you have in mind?"

"England might be nice."

"So, that's what you've been getting at."

"Well, the dream got me started and England is the closest thing to it."

"That would take some heavy programming."

"Yeah I know, but we can do it if we put our minds to it."

Nate pulled into a parking space at the beach; "You're serious aren't you?"

Lena stared at him through her glasses that made her eyes appear bigger than they really were. "Yes, I am, I've got a feeling we're going places."

∗   ∗   ∗

Nine days later, Peter Eastlund told Nate that the head of International Operations, Barry Rapozo, wanted to talk with him about Emmi's European introduction. Even with all his and, Lena's programming, Nate could hardly believe what he felt was about to happen.

At lunchtime, Nate sat across the table from a man who looked and spoke exactly like Walter Cronkite. "You're probably wondering why I ask you here?" he said, while chewing.

Nate resisted the urge that said, "*No, I know exactly why you've asked me here.*"

"Yes, Mr. Rapozo, Peter didn't give me any details."

Barry Rapozo explained how the company was ready to introduce Emmi in Europe and they needed an expert to be available on a daily basis.

"Someone has to be responsible for demos," he tapped his forefinger on the table "installations, training, and tech support." He asked, "Are you the man for that job?"

Nate straightened up and then said, "Yes I am, Mr. Rapozo. I believe you've probably seen my resume and personnel records, so you know I've done training and tech support before. I get along well with people and enjoy field service work. And I imagine you've spoken with Peter about me also, so I'll be frank with you. I believe I am the right man, in the right place, at the right time."

Barry chuckled, "You come on strong, Nate. I like that. How old are you?"

"I'm forty-five."

Barry looked up from his soup, "You look younger." Then he added, "Why don't you call me Barry. I think you may be the right man for the job too, Nate. What about your family; you know we'll want you to live over there for a while?"

"No problem Mr. Ra ... Barry. There's just my wife and grandson. Our families are not here in California anyway." Nate thought quickly and asked, "Would we get to visit back here in the States?"

"Of course, Nate. There will be meetings at the factory that you'll attend a couple of times a year, just like Matsiyama does. Your business trips back here will be on company expenses. You'll have to pay your family's airfare out of pocket."

The server poured more coffee and Barry Rapozo asked, "Do you have any more questions?"

Nate asked, "What about salary?"

"I was waiting to see if you'd ask. Money has to be important to you for this job Nate because part of your pay will be commissions on each Emmi sold. As far as salary, we're going to give you what amounts to a lateral transfer with your same salary in British pounds. It will be worth more, with the exchange rate,.."

Barry Rapozo motioned for the waiter then reached into his attaché case and gave Nate a manila envelope. "Read through all this carefully and, if it's agreeable to you, sign and return the forms to my office."

They stood and as they shook hands Barry Rapozo said, "Nate, remember you can call me, direct, at any time."

"I'll remember that, Barry."

* * *

A month later, at lunchtime, Aron Balsam asked Nate to accompany him to the break room. Once there, he said, "We were about to start your party without you."

"Anybody that didn't get champagne", Peter teased as he poured sparkling apple cider into a paper cup and handed it to Nate.

"If we were over seas", Peter said, "this would be real champagne in the office."

"I'll keep that in mind", Nate said.

Everyone was there: Lam, Eliezer, Horst, Gary Chin, the production team, and Marcus Ryan. One of the secretaries cut the melting ice-cream cake and passed it around.

"So, how does your wife feel about moving over there?" someone asked.

"She's very excited", Nate answered, "about seeing the castles."

"Maybe there's been a misunderstanding", the secretary said, "You're booked into Kensington Palace *hotel*; it's not a castle." That brought another round of laughter.

Photos were taken and Peter presented Nate with a leather attaché case. "That's from the manufacturing team."

As Nate was thanking everyone, Marcus grabbed a box from under the table.

"This will help you keep track of all the customers' details." It was a laptop computer.

Peter took a small packet from his jacket pocket and then said, "This is from Matsiyama. He said to tell you it brought him luck."

Nate opened it and found an old Japanese coin. It had the face of a warrior on it.

"Tell him I hope it brings me as much luck as it did for him." He squeezed it in his hand.

Horst raised his cup and then said, "We won't need luck, we're sending you."

"Here, here!," everyone chimed in.

Marcus spoke, in a serious tone, "Nate, we expect that you will do as well in Europe, as Matsiyama has done in Asia."

"Or better!" Horst called out and others voiced agreement.

Nate was moved, "Thank you all, really, and I promise you, I'll give it my best shot."

Shortly after the group broke up, Nate walked out to the main lobby thinking, *everything is ready. I got my final check, plus a check for moving costs and a credit card for expenses until we get settled-in. The movers have already packed our stuff. We'll be there in time for Brandon to start school and-*

"Nate" the receptionist called to him, "this just came for you."

She handed him a Fed-Ex envelope. The return address looked like a legal form. His heart dropped. *What now?* He opened it and found a statement from his 401K and a check for $6,734.18. He jumped into the air and let out a holler, "Yaa-hoo!"

The young receptionist was startled as he rushed toward the tall counter that separated them. "Look at this! It's six grand; I wasn't expecting this! Holy shit!," he caught himself, "I mean, Holy cow."

Sharing his joy, the secretary said, "No, for six grand, you said it right the first time."

On the way home, Nate decided not to tell Lena about the extra money right away. He bought $15,000 worth of US Savings bonds to keep as a reserve. It was more money than he had ever had and it strengthened his resolve to be successful in his new assignment.

Three days later Lena, Brandon and Nate were on British Airways flight-54 headed to London.

Kyle Measurement
Systems - UK

After arriving at Heathrow airport and going through Customs and Immigrations they took a taxi to the Kensington Palace hotel.

Brandon begged to go to the park across the street and skateboard. Nate and Lena took pity on him, after the long flight.

"You stay where we can see you when we come back downstairs. You hear?"

"Okay, Grandma."

They checked in and had their first challenge when Lena called Nate to the bathroom.

"What's that for?" she pointed to a second toilet bowl that had four spigots pointing upward.

They stared at it and guessed at its purpose.

"Maybe they explain it in the hotel guidebook."

"Well, I'm not going to sit on it until I know what it does." Lena said, "At least the shower looks normal. I'm going to freshen up."

"I'll join you as soon as I call my office and let them know we're here."

Nate came into the shower before Lena finished lathering up.

"That was quick."

"Dick Keating wasn't there. I'll have to call back."

They embraced as the hot water cascaded over them.

Nate sat, wrapped in a terry cloth robe that had a silver "K" emblem, and called his office again. Maggie, the secretary, put him on hold. He cupped the phone and asked Lena, "Will you iron a shirt for me?"

Lena stopped doing her makeup and glared at him.

"What?" Nate asked Lena, as Dick Keating started speaking on the phone.

"Hello, Mr. Keating. I was just checking to see when you want me to report to work. Yes ... I see ... No, we haven't yet ... Oh, that will be fine with me ... Okay, I'll see you then, sir."

Nate noticed Lena had set up the ironing board and plugged in the iron, but she wasn't ironing anything. She was looking out of the window.

"Can you see Brandon?"

"Yeah." She said dejectedly.

"What's wrong?" he asked.

"I'm disappointed that you asked me to press a shirt."

"Disappointed? What are you talking about?"

"I didn't come all the way over here to be your maid."

"I don't know where all this is coming from." Nate said, "All I asked you to do was press a shirt for me so we can get going. What's the difference between pressing a shirt for me back home or over here?"

"I don't feel like pressing shirts now."

Nate got up and walked over to her.

"You know what? I don't know why you're acting like I'm being unfair to you or something. But, I want to tell you something, Lena. You've always been talking about those classy, power people you associated with – Jessie Jackson and Harold Washington and all them. Well, they didn't bring you all the way over here – I did. I'm the one that loves you and tries to show it all the time. If you-

"Oh, Nate." Lena embraced him, "Everything was so romantic."

"Well, damn, Baby, I didn't mean anything. I just wanted a shirt."

"I know. I know, Honey." They kissed, "I feel like I'm in a movie."

Nate laughed, "Me too. Only now we're not sitting in the audience, we're on the screen."

Lena began pressing the shirt while Nate shaved.

"It's 7:00am back home." Nate shouted from the bathroom, "You tired?"

"Nope."

"Let's get out of here then." Nate said, "We can unpack later."

He put the shirt on, and grabbed his camera while Lena grabbed their travel guidebook. They left the key downstairs, at the front desk, and emerged facing Kensington Park. Red, double-decker, buses cruised past in both directions. Taxis that seemed to be from the Roaring 1920's rushed past.

"I didn't expect the streets to be this crowded, did you?"

"Not really." Nate said, "Come on, let's get Brandon."

They found a Tube station and headed downtown.

Emerging from Westminster Station, they looked up and were awed as Big Ben struck four o'clock. High overhead they saw a supersonic Concorde go zipping by. Nate looked at Lena's arched eyebrows and laughed, " ...a flying saucer, huh?"

*   *   *

The next morning, Dick Keating gave Nate the keys to a 1984 Saab and told him they'd talk more when he returned from a trip. Nate thanked him and went to the front desk where Lena and Brandon were talking with Maggie.

"All set then?" Maggie asked.

"Yes, and thank you for making all the arrangements for us."

"It wasn't a bother. Ring me if you need anything else; here's my home number ... in case something comes up after 5pm."

"Thanks again, Maggie."

Once they were in the Saab, Lena stared mischievously as Nate turned the ignition key with his left hand. Brandon leaned forward and asked, "You know how to drive this kind of car Granddad?"

"You just sit back and buckle up little man and we'll find out."

With that, Nate eased off the clutch, the car lurched forward and the engine cut off. Lena turned her head to avoid laughing in his face.

"Hold on." Nate said, "I got this."

"Yeah, right." Brandon said softly.

During those first few days, Lena kept reminding Nate to drive on the left side of the road. They found navigating the roundabouts particularly challenging. For a while, they didn't dare try driving into London; they took The Tubes instead.

Eating out became an adventure too. Especially kidney pie, black pudding and whip cream that wasn't sweet. Nate remembered Barry Rapozo saying it would take six months to get acclimated.

They rented one of the houses Maggie had scouted for them and soon were settled in. Nate wondered why Lena insisted on a house with four bedrooms. She had said, "We need two extra rooms so we can both have a room to work in." Nate agreed since all the rooms were small and the house was affordable. The garage was so narrow that it only allowed them access to one side of the car.

In a foul-up, two separate phone lines were installed. The LaChae's were told they could use one for free. Nate suspected his old friends at the F.B.I. were still interested in him, but he didn't tell Lena. It amused him to think of getting free phone calls; *Thanks to Ernest*, he thought.

When Saturday came, Nate said, "You know what, Honey? Let's use this deck of tourist cards to decide where we go on weekends."

"Okay", Lena spread the deck out, "you pick one and I'll pick one." That set a pattern that they followed for the next three years.

*   *   *

Dick Keating was a tall imposing person with dark bushy hair and a beard. He showed Nate around the office and introduced him to everyone. They were friendly and expressed how they were looking forward to working with him. He returned their greetings and felt like his adventure was unfolding. His association with the staff developed slowly because he spent most weekdays in other countries demonstrating EMMI and training the local service engineers.

Maggie, the pixyish secretary that everyone shared, spoke with a strong Cockney accent. Every time he returned from a trip, he had to get used to her again,. The only way he could tell when she was joking was by the wide clown's smile she gave.

Nate found he couldn't rely on Maggie to always send the correct information or parts; he didn't know if it was a failure of communication or what. He felt his only recourse was having Lena go to the office and straighten things out when he was traveling. That made for a strained relationship between Lena and Maggie.

Dick Keating's surly British humor could be heard often, especially when referencing his US counterparts. He and his wife Helen had no children and at their annual December party, they gave away Christmas trees grown on their land. Helen's hobby was raising sheep, each of which she had named. At one party Lena got so comfortable drinking champagne that she asked Helen, "Tell me how the heck can you tell all those sheep apart?"

Helen answered politely and in detail.

At the end of the party, Nate shook Dick's hand. Then, to everyone's surprise, he gave Helen a bear hug.

Later he explained to Lena, "I just felt good and wanted to show it."

*   *   *

Dick Keating told Nate, "You'll earn a 2,500 pound bonus for each Emmi that's sold throughout the UK and Europe. How does that sound to you?"

"Sounds great." Nate replied.

"Splendid.

Now about your demo at Inmos today. I've asked Danny to go with you and Duncan. He has a toolbox and he knows where to buy parts if the need arises; there's no Radio Shack in Wales."

"Yes, I've been told." Nate said.

Dick Keating pushed the button on his intercom, "Maggie, have you any word yet about the arrival of the Emmi?"

"Yes. The truck arrived this morning; Emmi is sitting on Inmos' dock."

"Excellent." Dick Keating rose and extended his hand, "Good luck."

Duncan Barlow drove west for more than an hour to get to Inmos Corporation. Nate got to hear Duncan expound the superiority of Rugby over American football. Danny tried to defend football and Nate refused to be goaded into the debate, even when Duncan switched the topic to basketball. Instead, Nate opened the Emmi Maintenance Manual and read.

Arriving at Inmos Corporation, Nate was pleased to see one of the engineers that had visited California for a demo. They were ushered to the shipping dock, where Nate and Danny began opening crates. Three hours later, Nate turned the key to activate Emmi and the $250,000 microscope came to life. Ian Michelson, an Inmos engineer, suggested they take a lunch break before beginning their testing.

During lunch, Michelson explained their product yield was down by 15% and they hoped EMMI would locate the source of the problem.

"Normally, we run at 87% yield." he said, "So, we have lots of defective samples for you to test."

"I'll get started right away", Nate said. He was thankful for multiple samples. It meant he didn't have to be too concerned with blowing one of them up. Nate began the testing and quickly went through seventeen samples before he pointed to the computer monitor and then said, "There! That's where a defect is on many of the samples."

"Print a hardcopy, please." Michelson said, "I'll have that sample sliced and scanned on the SEM immediately."

"What are your transputer chips used for?" Nate asked.

"They're parallel processors that can be grouped together to form supercomputers."

"For government use only?"

"No. Actually, some universities allowed students and lay-people to use the supercomputers during off-peak times.

Nate made a mental note to investigate Transputers further and to buy an evaluation kit.

Just a few of these chips, programmed properly, could easily outperform any PC, he realized. *And, scaled up, they could be programmed to do almost anything.*

The SEM operator returned. "Eureka!" he said, "The defect is at the epsilon site of the seventh layer."

"You're certain?" Michelson asked.

"There's no doubt, Ian. Here, see for yourself."

Michelson looked at the SEM photograph and then said, "Hummmn. Congratulations, Nate. Your machine has lived up to its reputation."

Michael's boss insisted on purchasing the demo Emmi.

Duncan got on the phone to Dick Keating and Nate heard him saying, " ...He says they can't afford to wait for another Emmi to be shipped from the states. ... Yes, I told him that. ... No. He said he only wants this one and may buy another one before year's end. ... I know. I tried to explain that to him, but he's adamant. ... Right ... Right, I'll tell him. Goodbye."

Duncan turned to Nate and Danny, "We're going to sell it to them."

Nate realized he had just earned his first bonus. *That was easy,* he thought.

*   ᴀ   ᴴᴵ

Marcus' statement reverberated in Nate's mind, "You'll have new and different responsibilities now." He felt as if the curtain had opened on a new scene in his life and the audience had settled down to see what he would do next. It was no longer simply a matter of fixing machines. Now he had to do all the planning and demos for the KMS salesmen to sell Emmis.

Marcus is in Switzerland and he expects me to put a plan together. I need to build a database of prospects somehow. Nate headed for the coffee machine. Mira, the accountant, looked up as he passed her office. He smiled at her and continued on pass Duncan Barlow's office.

"Getting settled in, are you?" Maggie said as she rushed pass him in the hallway.

"Yes, I am." Nate got his coffee and went to Duncan's office. "Excuse me, Duncan, do you have a minute?"

"A minute, is about all I can spare right now. I've got an appointment in half an hour. What can I do for you?"

"I need to get a list of UK prospects so I can start putting a plan together."

Duncan shuffled through his briefcase, "That's an easy one. Every company that has a wafer fab is a potential customer."

"Yes, I understand that, but I need their addresses and phone numbers."

"I'll go over my contacts list with you when I get back. For now you might want to look at this issue of *Semiconductor International*." Duncan handed Nate a copy of the magazine. "At the end of the year, they prepare a proper list of the top 100 companies in the industry."

Nate took the magazine. "Thanks." Back at his desk, he thumbed through the annual listing. A few pages further on, he found an advertisement for an industry report; it cost $600. In his old job, Nate was accustomed to submitting request for anything he needed and then waiting for approval.

I bet Marcus wouldn't approve a request for this. But, if I go ahead and get it …

Nate ordered the report and bought a database program as well.

In the days that followed, Duncan seemed minimally interested in helping Nate. He and Dick Keating were constantly having closed-door meetings where they were overheard discussing boats and fishing.

By the time Marcus Ryan visited the UK office, Nate's database of prospects was up and running.

"This is excellent, Nate." Marcus said as he turned to Dick Keating, "Have you seen this?"

"No, can't say that I have." Dick replied as he leaned forward.

"I could use something like this for my other products. How did you gather all this information so quickly?"

"I bought it", Nate said smiling, "You haven't signed my latest expense report, have you, Marcus?"

"Not yet. But, this was money well spent. Look here Dick, he even has each company's budget for defect analysis equipment."

Nate was surprised that no one asked how much money he had spent.

*   *   *

At International Computing Machines Corporation (ICM), in Evry, France, Mr. Cassell, who spoke very little English, told Nate, "We can not use Emmi this way. We need the long focal lens."

"I understand", Nate said, "And I will see that you get the lens as soon as possible."

"When?"

"I will call to the US today and give you an answer tomorrow."

Nate could see Mr. Cassell wasn't pleased.

Why did they ship the Emmi without the long focal lens? Nate thought, *That's what makes Emmi unique. They should have, at least, told me. I've got to get that lens here ASAP.*

Nate called the California plant that evening and was told there was only one long focal lens in stock. They promised to ship it immediately; it would take days to clear customs.

The following week, when Nate called the plant, he was told the lens still hadn't been shipped.

What the hell is going on?

Nate spoke with his buddy, Mr. Lam, and was told the long focal lens had been shipped to Matsiyama in Japan. Peter Eastlund assured Nate another long focal lens would be sent within days. Nate asked for the shipping info to be faxed to the UK office.

Monday afternoon, Nate called his UK office from Charles DeGaulle airport; Maggie said no fax had arrived for him. How could he face Mr. Cassell again after all the promises and assurances he had given him.

He called the French salesman, Jean-Marie, who said, "I'm not surprised; the Americans don't see us as a priority."

Nate recalled attending weekly meetings, in the US, where international topics were placed at the bottom of the agenda. Now he was on the receiving end of that attitude.

He rented a car and tried to decide what to do as he drove on route-A6 toward ICM at Evry.

Faced with disappointing Mr. Cassell, Nate told him,

"I think you should tell your boss to complain to Kyle Measurement Systems."

Mr. Cassell stared at Nate for a moment. "Tell my boss? That will be trouble for you, no?"

"Not really." Nate replied, "It will make more pressure on KMS. Maybe we can get the lens here sooner."

"You are sure?"

"I think it might work."

Mr. Cassell rubbed his chin, frowned, and then said, "Wee."

The next morning Maggie called Nate about a fax she received from Barry Rapozo's office. It gave the time and shipping information for a long focus lens that was in transit.

Four days later Nate installed the lens and Mr. Cassell ran his first critical test on Emmi. He was quite pleased with the results. In the days that followed, Mr. Cassell's testing continued and Nate worked to tweak Emmi to its full capabilities. At times, he made changes that went beyond the standard configuration.

When Eliezer Rosenberg heard of Nate's software modifications, he hit the ceiling. Nate argued, over the phone, that the modifications simply avoided showing duplicate information on Emmi's two screens. But, Eliezer told management that software control would be loss if changes were allowed in the field. Subsequently, Nate was ordered to restore the software to its original form.

Jean-Marie had warned Nate that Mr. Cassell could be a hard person to deal with. However, Nate found Mr. Cassell to be a serious, dedicated engineer – like himself. In spite of their language differences, they developed a friendly working relationship. And Nate expected nothing more, until one day Mr. Cassell said, "My wife and I would like you to have dinner with us."

"I'd be delighted. When?"

"Is Wednesday be okay for you?"

"Yes, Wednesday is fine. Thank you very much."

Following Mr. Cassell's map, Nate had no trouble finding the house. Mrs. Cassell and her two boys spoke no English at all. The house was small by American standards, but it was comfortable and had a warm feel to it.

While they waited for dinner, Mr. Cassell explained to the boys who Nate was. The older boy understood and bowed as he shook Nate's hand. The younger, who was only six, was having trouble pronouncing Nate's name. Suddenly, he bolted upright and pointed toward Nate. Excitedly, he ask his father something and Mr. Cassell responded with laughter. The boy rushed over and shook Nate's hand vigorously. Mr. Cassell explained to Nate that his name was the same as one of the boy's favorite comic book heroes.

Mrs. Cassell served a Chateau La Gaffeliere wine and dinner began. Nate was conscious of their staring at him as he looked at the red meat.

Mrs. Cassell spoke to Nate in French; Mr. Cassell translated.

"She wants to know if you want more cooking of the meat?"

"Yes, please", Nate smiled politely, "until there's no red."

When Mrs. Cassell returned with the meat, Nate did his best to enjoy the half-cooked beef.

Nate asked about a photo of mountain climbers that he saw on the wall.

Mr. Cassell cleared his throat, "It was many years ago, in the French Alps."

"Is that you?"

"Yes, I was a climber."

"I was a climber too", Nate said, "I climbed in the Catskills Mountains and Mount Washington. But, I did not need ropes."

"Ah, yes. I know of this mountain, the wind is very strong there."

"That's right." Nate said, " But, not when I was there or I would be flying like your son's hero."

Mr. Cassell laughed, then translated for his wife and sons who laughed also.

"Nate, have you been to Fountain Bleu?"

"No. What's there?"

"It is the place where you will find many French climbers practicing."

"I'd like to go there; where is it?"

"South. I will show you on the map." Mr. Cassell said, "Ah, but first we must have dessert."

Mrs. Cassell served rum-raisin truffles as the two mountain climbers shared stories of their exploits.

After some espresso, Nate headed back to the Novotel hotel with thoughts of going to Fountain Bleu as soon as he could.

*   *   *

One day Brandon's school soccer team played Duncan's son's team. Everyone from the office came to see the game. Danny Junior, also played on Brandon's team.

Duncan could be heard, above the crowd, cheering for his son Shawn and shouting at the referees.

Nate and Lena did their share of shouting too as, time after time, Brandon charged the net. After having points taken away for being "off-sides", Brandon started passing the ball more.

One man leaned toward Nate and then said, "Brilliant. The way your son avoids the spikers."

"That's my grandson." Nate said excitedly, "There he goes again!"

At the end of the day, Brandon and Danny's team won by three points. Duncan declined to go with the others for pizza and took his son home.

That night, at bedtime, Nate told Brandon, "You made me very proud today. The way you charged down the line and jumped over the boys who tried to tackle you. One day you can tell your grandson that story."

"I could have scored more points, Granddad, but they kept telling me to pass the ball."

"That's all right, it's a team sport. You were magnificent today, Brandon." Nate gave him a hug. "Good night."

*   *   *

Nate came home after another trip and then said, "It's hard for me to believe Brandon stays down there fishing all day long."

"Well, go see for yourself." Lena said.

"Boys say whatever they think you want to hear."

"I know, but not in this case." Lena said, "He simply loves fishing. He even took his lunch box."

"Well, I'm going down there." Nate got up, and headed outside. The sun felt good on his face as he strolled toward the pond. He waved at his neighbors. *I hope Brandon is not getting into anything. Those twins he plays with are always getting into trouble. At least I know he's a good swimmer. That was so wonderful, watching him learn to swim in our pool in Sacramento. That first time, before he jumped into the water and asked me if I was going to catch him. He trusted me completely. He's a great little guy. I don't want him to be doing something he shouldn't be doing.*

At the base of the hill, Nate followed a path through the bushes to the edge of the water. He saw two people fishing on the other side and several lines in the water on his side. But, the bushes blocked his view. He backed up and followed a trail around the pond. There were several enclaves, each with a solitary young fisherman. He found Brandon sitting patiently at the third enclave.

"Catch anything?"

"Oh, hi, Granddad. Look what I got." Brandon lifted a line from his pail. It had several fish on it.

"Wow. That's great."

"I caught a bigger one", Brandon said, "but he got away."

"Yeah, the big ones do that sometime."

Nate sat on a rock.

"You want a soda Granddad?" Brandon reached into the cooler he was sitting on.

"Sure."

They sat quietly for a time. Brandon had everything organized around him. One line was propped on rocks and he gently played he other line. Nate felt ashamed for having suspected Brandon of any mischief. He felt like an intruder; this was Brandon's place.

Nate looked at his watch and then said, "Well, I'm going back up to the house. Dinner will be ready soon."

"Okay Granddad." Brandon was busy baiting another hook.

At dinnertime, Lena told Nate, "I made friends with a sister from The States the other day."

"Really." Nate continued eating.

"Yeah, she's a real *sister* too. From Atlanta and she's been over here for two years. She doesn't plan on ever moving back."

"What does she do?"

Lena took a sip of wine. "Nothing. Mercedes spends her time shopping and going to shows."

"Must be nice to be rich" Nate said, "How did Mercedes get that way?"

"She has a gentleman friend."

"You mean she's a kept woman, don't you?"

"You don't have to say it that way. She happens to be in love with a married man."

"Sounds like she's in love with a rich married man."

"She is." Lena said, "You'll like her, Nate. She knows where all the good clubs are. She's got tickets for Hugh Masekela's show at Ronny Scott's."

"Hugh is going to be at Ronny Scott's?"

"In three weeks.," Lena said, "Mercedes is treating us."

Nate stopped eating and then said, "In that case, your friend is my friend."

"I thought so." Lena said, "I invited her out to dinner with us this Saturday, I hope you don't mind".

"Sure, that will make us even."

Saturday, they stopped at Mercedes before going to dinner. She was in a white chiffon robe. After introductions, she poured champagne for everyone. Nate didn't show his annoyance that she wasn't ready to go.

"Girl", Mercedes said, as she sat in front of a propped up mirror adjusting her wig, "I missed Hugh last time he was in town because Sheldon couldn't get away that night. But, he made it up to me with this." She extended her finger for Lena to see the huge ring.

"See that's something I wouldn't expect from a black man."

Nate shifted uneasily in the cushy chair and sipped his drink.

"That's one of the main reasons I like Sheldon. He'll do anything to please me." Mercedes puffed on her Virginia Slims cigarette. "I got some smoke", she said, "You want some?"

"No, I don't think so." Nate said for both of them.

"It's the good shuff." Mercedes coaxed.

"This champagne is enough for me", Lena said.

"Girl, I got to tell you about this dream I had last night." The women went into the bedroom and closed the door. When they emerged, Mercedes had on a red leather suit and said, "Okay, we're ready, Sugar."

This broad is starting to get on my nerves, Nate thought. He did his best to be polite throughout dinner and the rest of the evening.

*　　　*　　　*

Back at home, the phone rang in the middle of the night. Nate was surprised to hear his brother's voice.

"Hey, Doug, what's up?"

Douglas said solemnly, "You better sit down for this."

"What? Is it our uncle?"

"No, man. It's Henry, he's dead. Margie found him laying in the bed."

Nate was stunned. "You're kidding right?"

"No, here ... Margie wants to speak to you."

Margie came on the phone. Nate couldn't imagine her not having that permanent smile on her face.

"Henry had been sick for weeks." Margie said, "I kept telling him to go back to the hospital, but every time he went they couldn't find what was wrong., and he said he wasn't going for any more tests. He said he was tired of being sick."

"So, what happened?"

"I came home and he had the door locked. So, when I knocked and he didn't answer, I got Leroy to bust in and that's when we found him."

"You saying he committed suicide?"

"No. I don't think so. The police came and they said they would do an autopsy to find out what happened." Margie broke down sobbing.

Douglas came back on the phone,

"I'm sorry, Nate; I really am."

Nate's mind raced searching for a reason, a culprit, fate, destiny – anything! He wanted to scream. He hung-up and told Lena, "I'm going for a walk."

"You all right? You want me to come with you?"

"I just need to walk. I'll be back."

It was midday and the sun was unusually bright. Nate walked slowly to the Thames River. He found a closed restaurant that had patio tables. Some fellas were over in a corner, drinking beer at one of the tables. Nate choose a table near the river's edge and sat. He stared at the slowly moving water and remembered his buddy.

"If only ...", he began over and over again. Then his mind was quiet.

His serenity was broken by a voice with an Irish accent.

"Hello, mate, are you American?"

"Yes." Nate said without facing him.

"Mind if I ask you a question?"

Nate looked up through teary eyes. "My best buddy died today."

"Sorry, mate. I truly am." The young man backed off, then he said, "Would ya care for a beer?"

Nate sensed compassion and accepted the offer. The other three young men came over and expressed their condolences. They were about to leave when Nate said, "What did you want to ask me?"

"We were trying to decide who was the better fighter, Joe Louis or Muhammad Ali."

Nate drank from the beer. "I think Mohammed Ali is the greatest."

"See", the young man turned to his buddies, "I told ya."

A conversation ensued about how the world needed heroes that make a difference. Nate was, reluctantly, drawn into the conversation as the five of them discussed problems all around the world. They drank beers from a cooler as they solved international problems all around the world. Their success rate was excellent as they discussed country after country.

"Tell us, mate, why your Civil Rights Movement didn't solve all the racial problems in America?"

Nate patiently described the unexplainable to the uninitiated. Then he asked, "What about Ireland? How can you even tell who is Catholic and who is Protestant?"

"Aye, you can tell one of them from one of us easy enough", one said.

Then, for the first time, their conversation turned into an argument among the Irishmen. They had four, passionately different, opinions about the conflict in their own country. Nate wished he hadn't asked the question; they seemed to be on the verge of fighting. Nate started laughing; he laughed so hard, the others stopped arguing and started laughing too. That reminded Nate of Henry all over again; Henry would get people laughing simply by how hard he was laughing.

"Why are you laughing?" one of the Irishmen asked while coughing and laughing.

Nate wiped his eyes and then said, "You know, we solved all the world's problems; we had solutions for everybody else's problems. And then when it got to your homeland, look how much you disagree."

"That is the problem isn't it?," one said, "we can only agree when its not important to us."

"Yeah, you're right; as long as it's not personal."

The Irishmen shook Nate's hand and invited him to visit Ireland. They gave him their addresses and phone numbers. "You'll be welcome in our homeland; we have no racism there." We admire American black people.

Yeah, As long as I'm either Catholic or Protestant, Nate thought.

After they left, Nate felt some of his grief lifted.

He walked home wondering, *Why don't they know what Henry died from? It's like when Frank Jr. died all over again.*

*   *   *

That was the weekend Mercedes had tickets to hear Hugh Mastekela at Ronnie Scott's jazz club.

"Come on, Nate", Lena said, "it will do you good to get out more."

"All right, but if Mercedes starts in with her black man/white man shit ... "

"It's not going to be like that. Let's just go and enjoy the show."

Nate did enjoyed the show, as did everyone else. Mastekela did the old favorites and had the audience all singing in African lyrics.

After the show, they walked toward Piccadilly Circus. They heard drums. Nate's mind went back to Henry and his gloom returned. As they came to the corner, they saw the source of the thunderous rhythm. A crowd had gathered around a group of black men, presumably from many lands, who sat in a circle playing congas and African drums. The sound was intense and reverberated off the buildings in the open square.

Nate ushered the ladies into a restaurant near the drummers. Once there, they went upstairs, ordered drinks and stood by the window. Nate loosened his tie and opened his collar; he had no interest in conversing. He watched the drummers playing and noticed they, occasionally, changed seats.

"I'm going down there."

"What for?," Mercedes asked, "We can see better up here."

Nate was gone. He went and stood at the front of the crowd. His eyes met the eyes of the drummers as different ones took the lead. He saw the fire he'd seen in Henry's eyes sometimes. There was a lull in the playing. One drummer stood and offered a drum to Nate; the others maintained a rhythmic beat.

Nate took off his sports jacket and sat on it. He rolled up his sleeves. Someone in the crowd whispered something to their companion. Lena and Mercedes pushed to the front of the crowd.

A base drummer started a deep rhythmic beat.

Two other base drummers intensified it.

Nate closed his eyes as the circle of drummers joined in the rhythm.

A tenor drum began a cadence.

Nate's hands erupted on the drums … stopped, then rolled a beat.

He repeated it once more, then he made the drum speak …

It shouted and screamed the love he had for Henry.

It roared in anger and killed all hatred with love.

It blasted away ignorance with compassion.

Nate's hands tore at the drum, now.

The crescendo increased and the crowd swayed to the beats.

Nate was dripping sweat.

A challenge came from a drummer sitting opposite Nate in the circle. He stood with a drum held under his arm and played it with a curved stick. The tone changed as he squeezed the drum. He made the drum talk and then stopped playing, looking at Nate.

Nate made his drum echo the rhythm he'd just heard.

A percussion battle ensued, with the other players providing background.

Nate and his challenger alternated, playing fiercely.

It was a clash of percussive methods.

It was Malcolm-X versus Martin.

It was Booker T. arguing with DuBois.

It was Lumumba challenging Mobutu.

It was the dichotomy of the African Diaspora.

Every drum spoke and each was heard – as one.

Nate and his challenger took turns leading the crescendo.

Back and forth, everyone was caught up in the rhythm.

The drummers gave a long powerful roll and suddenly everything stopped.

The crowd exploded in applauds; some whistled, others cheered.

Nate got up and waved to the other drummers. His challenger rose, put his hands together in the sign of Namaste and bowed. Nate responded in kind.

Lena gave Nate her handkerchief and he wiped the sweat and tears from his face. Some of the crowd complimented him and patted him on the back.

"Can we go now?," Mercedes asked sourly.

Nate looked at her, then at Lena who pleaded with her eyes.

He smiled and then said calmly, "Yes, we can go *now*."

*   *   *

The following Monday Nate found himself unpacking at the Colleoni hotel in Agrate, Italy. The phone rang, he picked it up and heard, in a strong Italian accent, "Hallo. Nate LaChae?"

"Yes", he replied hoping for no more complications after all the time he'd spent at the airport and the car rental agency.

"This is Mario Messina, I am suppose to meet you here, for the installation. The people at the front desk told me you had checked in."

"Yes, I just got in. I'm still unpacking. Why don't we meet in about an hour and have dinner?"

"That will be fine." Mario agreed "I'll meet you in the lobby. I'll have on a brown leather jacket."

They hung up and Nate wondered what sort of guy Mario Messina might be. The FSEs he'd met in France and Germany were friendly enough. They were eager to learn about Emmi and Nate's laptop computer.

After unpacking Nate checked the power outlets and the phone to see if he'd be able to use his modem from the hotel. Everything seemed okay. He checked the time and saw that he could give Lena a quick call before dinner. She told him all was well at home. Brandon scored two goals in the school soccer game. Lena told him about her experiences buying groceries and driving on British roads. Nate reminded her to deposit his check and he promised to call the next day. They ended their phone calls with "Namaste".

Nate showered and put on his black slacks, turtleneck sweater and herringbone sport jacket. He grabbed his attaché case and headed downstairs. The lobby wasn't crowded and it was easy to spot Mario coming toward him. Mario was 10-15 years younger than Nate. His features reminded one of Arnold Schwarzenegger. While he wasn't as muscular, he was obviously in good shape. He had a big smile. They said each other's name simultaneously, laughed and shook hands.

"Have you been here long?," Nate asked.

"I flew in this morning from Rome and I had lunch here at the hotel."

"How's the food here?"

"It was very good at lunchtime", Mario said, "And since it is getting late, I suggest we try dinner here. I don't know about other restaurants here in Agrate."

"Good idea." Nate replied, as they moved toward the dining room. "I've got some installation papers and other stuff I want to show you."

The waiter took them to a table just off the center of the dinning room. Nate couldn't help noticing how the waiters in France, England and Germany never seated him in the rear corner. He remembered, in the US he could expect to be hid away in a back corner of dining rooms more often than not.

"Hey, Mario, can you help me with the menu? I always have to ask the waiter."

Mario said, "Sure, I'll try. But, my English is not so good. What kind of food do you like?"

"I think your English is very good. Anything but pork."

"Which aperitif do you like?"

Nate felt comfortable enough to ask, "What's an aperitif?"

Mario patiently began the first of several explanations of proper Italian dinning.

They drank their aperitifs and Nate presented paperwork describing their tasks for the next week. They went over a plan for dealing with the facts that Nate spoke no Italian and Mario didn't know anything about Emmi. Nate intentionally got into some of the minute details to test Mario's technical knowledge. Mario responded with comparable jargon, encouraging Nate that things would be okay the next day at SGS Company. The rest of dinner went well as Nate and Mario exchanged stories of their histories and experiences.

They arrived at the SGS plant early the next morning and spent 45 minutes filling out the security forms. They were escorted to the Failure Analysis Laboratory. Nate saw the EMMI system, and got a feeling of comfort that he was back in familiar territory.

He enjoyed being 'The Expert'. He especially liked the respect and friendliness he'd experienced in Europe. He felt everything was as it should be at work. He was relieved when he found almost everyone he dealt with spoke English. The only second language Nate had studied was Spanish and KMS didn't expect to have any Emmi sales in Spain.

After introductions Mr. Bellantani, who spoke very little English, excused himself from Nate and spoke Italian, rapidly, to Mario who translated.

"He wants to know how long it will take to set up the machine so he can have some samples prepared." Mario explained.

"Tell him, if we have no problems, it should take two days. We should be able to run his samples on Thursday."

Mr. Bellantani seemed pleased when he heard Mario's translation.

Urgency forced Nate to interrupt and have Mario ask where the men's room was. They directed him down the hall and gave him a key attached to a wooden slab. Once inside the men's room, he rushed to a stall. What he saw made him wonder why they hadn't taped the door closed. There was no commode. Instead, there was a porcelain-like toilet seat built into the floor. It was only two inches high. There were indentations for where to put your feet.

Surely, this one is being worked on or something, Nate thought.

But the two adjacent stalls were identical. As he looked around for some normal stalls, a man came in and looked quizzically at him.

"Do you speak English?" Nate pleaded.

"No. No English." the man shook his head.

At that point, Nate no longer cared about figuring out anything. He realized Mario was too far away to help so, he jumped into one of the stalls and dropped his pants. With seconds to spare, he squatted and with one hand jutting straight back to the wall behind him and one hand on the door in front, he went!

"This is ridiculous." he wanted to shout. *How the hell can people balance themselves like this and not shit all over their clothes? Nobody back home will believe this,* he thought, *and at a high-tech semiconductor fab too!*

By mid-week, they were doing live tests of SGS samples. The translation teamwork was going very smooth too. Mario's intelligence came through as he chose words that relayed more than the simple translation. He'd explain to Nate why Mr. Bellantani was asking certain questions. Likewise, some brief statements Nate made were translated into paragraphs of Italian. Thursday evening Nate reported to the home office that the machine was running well and the customer was happy.

Nate and Mario fell into a routine of having "one evening drink", on the patio, at the hotel. Their "one drink" always lasted for hours as they emptied a bottle of wine and discussed life in Italy and the US. Their friendship grew as they exchanged stories and remarks about the day's work. Each was glad to converse with the other about his homeland.

Mario explained what the Mafia was originally all about and Nate explained the Civil Rights movement. They didn't debate; they exchanged information, usually in comical anecdotes or personal experiences. They found that wanting to give the appearance of being "cool" was universal.

They also concluded every country had someone they discriminated against. The British didn't like the French, The French didn't like the Germans and the Italian didn't like the French or the British. Nate laughed as he realized it was like the children's game of tag; somebody was always 'It'. But, at least in Europe, it wasn't him.

Things went well all week. On Friday, the KMS salesman came and took the whole crew to lunch. They drove, in three cars, to a restaurant in the countryside and sat at a long table, out back under a veranda.

There was the aperitif, the antipasto, the pasta, wine and more wine. It continued for two hours. Nate was admiring his surroundings; it was sunny and the wine had him in a warm mood. A voluptuous waitress came to him as he was thinking, *the boys back home should see me now.*

What the waitress said and what he heard was the same, but didn't have the same translation. Nate turned, slowly, after he heard her offer, "Nooky?" He tried to clear his head and looked around the table to see if Mario or the salesman was playing a joke on him. But, no one was paying any attention to him. He looked at the waitress and then said, "What?"

"NOOKY?" she said, impatiently.

Unbelievable!, he thought, *I had heard you people were friendly, but I had no idea!*

"Yes!" he blurted out. *Whatever it is, I want some.* He thought, *Nobody's going to ever say Nate turned down some nooky in Italy.*

This was so funny to him, he knew if he started laughing he wouldn't be able to translate the humor. So, he just sat there and nearly burst as the waitress served the gnocchi.

The KMS salesman didn't return to SGS with the others. He asked Nate to find out when Mr. Bellantani would permit a demo of his Emmi for professor Giovanelli of the University of Bari. Later that afternoon, Mario made the request and Nate could tell something was wrong by Mr. Bellantani's body language and Mario's expression.

Mario turned to him and then said, "The demo may have to be postponed. I'll explain later." Nate knew Mario well enough not to inquire any further. It was almost five o'clock. They ran one more test for Bellantani, then packed up and headed to the hotel. On the way through the parking lot, Mario explained what had happened.

"When I asked Mr. Bellantani when we might give Dr. Giovanelli a demonstration on his machine, his reply was "NEVER".

Nate recalled the sound of the Italian word spoken by Mr. Bellantani and the deep sound of his voice when he said it. Seconds later, Nate and Mario burst out laughing. Nate decided that would be one problem he'd let the salesman solve.

They went to a restaurant that had live Jazz that night. To their surprise, some of the younger people from the SGS lab were there and invited them to their table. The band was jamming and Nate was surprised at how much the Europeans were into jazz.

Nate knew Mario hadn't really understood his explanations about racism when Mario, who was seated at the opposite end of the table, called out the name of one of the menu selections. "Hey, Nate did you see they serve Nigroni here?" Nate examined the menu and, sure enough, there it was. All Nate could do was shake his head and laugh. He knew Lena would get a good laugh too.

On the morning of his flight home, Nate strained himself loading equipment and luggage into his rental car. The strain was so severe that it hurt him to lift his attaché case or his laptop. An SGS doctor examined him and recommended surgery. Nate opted to go home instead. Mario accompanied him to the airport.

By the time the airplane arrived at Heathrow, Nate had recovered somewhat, but still couldn't lift anything. He made an appointment at a British clinic and declined their recommendation to undergo surgery for a tear they discovered in his digestive tract. Instead, he chose to miss a week from work and took sits-baths, in hopes the tear would mend.

*   *   *

"I've got great news", Lena said, "I found a SMC group. They meet in London, every other Wednesday. I've attended one of their meetings already."

"How was it?"

"It's an interesting group; they're all beginners."

"Any blacks?"

"Oh, it's a very mixed group. There's an African guy, a black barrister, and people from Switzerland and behind the Iron Curtain." Lena went on telling Nate about the mental exercises the group did and the discussions they had. "You should come Nate. You'd enjoy them."

"I will, sometime. Right now, I'm too wrapped up with my job."

"Going to Level with the group could only help."

"I've been going to Level. That's how I healed myself and got home." Nate said, "I'll come to the meeting, but not right now."

*   *   *

Being back in England for a while felt good. At breakfast time Nate asked Brandon, "Have you been going to the bank?"

"Grandma said to wait until you came home."

"Wait? Wait for what?" Nate turned toward Lena, "You mean you haven't been taking Brandon to the bank?"

She was washing dishes, "I thought it would be better if you took him."

"Aw, Lena. Why do you say that? He needs to learn to go regularly. That's why I send the money instead of waiting until I get home. All you have to do is walk with him to the bank, he knows what to do."

"I don't have time to be taking him into town just for that."

"You have time; you just don't care about teaching him this."

Brandon interrupted, "Can I bring my skateboard, Granddad?"

"Yeah, sure."

"You're home now", Lena said, "You go on and take him."

Nate turned to walk away, then turned back.

"Lena, I know you don't feel the way I do about this, but why can't you do it for Brandon's sake?"

Lena stopped doing the dishes, water still dripping from her hands."

"I'm not going to get into another argument with you over this. I take him to the bank sometime when we go into town. He doesn't have to go every week."

Nate shook his head, "You simply don't understand. He needs to get into a regular habit. That's the whole point."

Lena turned away.

"Can we go now, Granddad?"

"Yes, Brandon, let's get out of here."

On the way to the bank, Nate kept thinking, *why can't she see that we can make Brandon better at handling money than we are. Even if she doesn't understand, it seems like she'd help me. Whatever happened to our teamwork. Now that we're over here, we don't seem to have the same agenda or priorities. And she keeps putting off looking for work too. Maybe, I need to go to that SMC group meeting more often, that seems to be her only interest these days.*

*　　*　　*　　*

Nate and Lena decided to cash some of their savings bonds to travel to France. They drove to Portsmouth and took the ferry. The sunny day was chilled by the wind as the boat bobbed on the waters of the English Channel. Nate started describing the D-Day invasion to Lena while Brandon headed for the front of the boat, with the binoculars.

Lena called to him, "Stay back from the railing, you hear me?"

"Now, Honey", Nate said, "By the time we get to Paris it's going to be late and I've got to attend a meeting in the morning. So, what I want to do is drive to Evry tonight and we'll spend the weekend in Paris. Okay?"

"You still want to go to that blue fountain place?"

"Fountain Bleu? Yes, it's south of Evry. We can go there and still spend the weekend in Paris. I promise."

"Alright", Lena said in a warning tone, "you've promised."

Nate drove off the ferry and faced the challenge of driving a British car on French roads. He adapted quickly and felt he had everything under control – until he skidded on wet cobblestones and bumped another car. No damage was done, and they continued on their way.

A while later, Brandon whooped, "I see the Eiffel Tower!"

"Where?" Lena sat up.

"Over there! Aw, it's gone."

Nate kept his eyes on the road, "I don't think you can see it from here, Brandon."

"I saw it, even without the binoculars, when you came up over that hill."

Lena leaned and scanned the distance. "I don't see it."

"There!" Brandon pointed as Nate crested another hill.

Nate gritted his teeth as the pleading began.

"It was right there, Granddad"

"It wouldn't take long to just drive by it", Lena said.

"All right, all right. But, we're not going to get out of the car."

Once Nate left the highway, he was on winding roads and hills. He tried to head in the general direction of the tower. They got closer at times, then they'd find they were driving away from it.

While at a stoplight, Nate rolled his window down and motioned to the driver next to him. The woman, in the passenger seat, rolled her window down.

"Excuse me, can you tell me which way is the Eiffel Tower."

The couple looked at each other and began speaking French to Nate.

"Eiffel - Tower." Nate said slowly and distinctly.

The couple shook their heads and continued to speak French. The light changed and, when the cars behind them started honking, the couple drove off.

"I can't believe it!" Nate said, "Even if they don't speak English. Everybody here must know where the Eiffel Tower is."

"And they were black too." Lena said.

Nate shook his head. "Yeah, but black doesn't mean the same thing over here. What we need to find is an American."

After another half hour and another unsuccessful encounter with a French driver, Nate said, "I've got to get going to Evry. We'll see the Eiffel Tower on the weekend."

The next evening, Lena and Nate had a good laugh when he explained how Mr. Cassell told him French people call it Tur Efel.

The morning meeting went well and closed with commitments by each attendee.

"I will give these specifications to the US this evening." Nate said, "And I'll make sure they understand the requirements."

Mr. Cassell's boss said, "Bon."

Nate, dressed in his suit and tie, joined the other attendees heading for the cafeteria. Mr. Cassell offered to translate the menu for Nate.

"Thank you, but no." Nate said, "I know what I want." He ordered the eggplant and a coke. He noticed a man who had a raw hamburger patty with a raw egg on it.

That's a neat idea. Nate thought. *Wonder why he didn't have the chef cook it? Maybe there's a Hibachi at the dining table and he'll cook it there.*

Moving toward the cashier, Nate watched the man go to a table. The man put salt and pepper on the raw combination, cut it and, to Nate's astonishment, began eating it.

Mr. Cassell noticed the shock on Nate's face and leaned over and then said, "We call it Coq-up au vin."

Nate smiled and shook his head. *I call it disgusting*, he thought.

After lunch, Nate checked out of the Novotel. He and his family headed south to Fountain Bleu. Two hours later, they pulled into the park and Nate wondered why there were no mountains. As Nate finished parking, Brandon exclaimed, "Look Granddad, that man is crawling upside-down on that rock."

"Yeah, I see him."

All the climbers at Fountain Bleu were climbing over and around boulders. Many were dressed in tight-fitting mountaineering outfits with soft rubber boots.

Lena laughed when she saw the expression on Nate's face. "You said Mr. Cassell told you this is where they practice."

"Yeah, but I thought they'd, at least, be up on a mountain."

"This way, if they fall, they won't get hurt." Brandon said.

Nate stared in amazement.

They walked through the park and paused to join others watching four deer feeding. Brandon slowly approached the deer. Nate grabbed Lena's arm as she was about to call to Brandon. Three of the deer sauntered away as Brandon got closer. He stopped, picked some weeds and extended his hand. The fourth deer came toward him, hesitantly. The entire scene seemed frozen in time; no one moved. The deer came to Brandon and ate the weeds from his hand. It looked at Brandon and then at the people watching. It turned and walked away slowly and joined the others. Brandon remained motionless. Then he turned and waived to Lena and Nate who had tears of joy.

Nate remembered a time, many years before, when he called Brandon to see a butterfly and Brandon stomped it. *Now, he has learned to love animals and respect life,* Nate thought.

They spent the next two days in Paris, visiting landmarks, museums, shops and Tur Effel. Lena bought so many items on Champs-Elysees that Nate angrily told her, "You know, we came here to see Paris, not to buy Paris!"

After visiting Pompidou Center, they joined a crowd watching three young men performing pantomime. The three were very skillful and performed in slow motion. The crowd applauded the performance and gave a generous amount of bills and coins.

As the crowd dispersed, the clacking sound of skateboards could be heard. Lena and Nate gave each other a knowing look as Brandon clutched his skateboard and then said, "Come on, let's go over there."

Minutes later Brandon was doing Ollies and Kick-flips with the French boys. A crowd gathered and watched the competition.

"I guess, skateboarders don't need a common language." Nate said.

The boys were trying to jump a ramp, but it was unstable. The first skaters chickened-out. When it was Brandon's turn, he twisted his baseball cap around backward and charged the ramp. He built up speed and went up and over. His skateboard went out from under him and he was flying through the air. He landed on his feet momentarily, but his momentum carried him forward, so he flipped forward and landed on his feet again. The crowd cheered and applauded. The other boys congratulated and high-fived him. Meanwhile, Lena and Nate gave sighs of relief.

At Basilique du Sacre-Coeur, Nate made up for his outburst, about Lena's spending; she sat still, for an hour, while one of the freelance artists painted her portrait. The likeness was striking and Nate was happy to pay for it. Brandon stayed busy skateboarding.

Their visit to Paris ended with an American-style dinner at the Marriot on Champs Elysees.

*   *   *

Nate's flight to Munich arrived late and there was a long delay getting the luggage. It was the first time he wasn't being met by someone from the local KMS office. By the time he rented a car it was midnight. Maggie hadn't been able to book a room in Munich until the following day, so Nate headed northwest, on the Autobahn. He had been told to follow the signs toward Dachauer.

Hope the hotel is not going to be hard to find, Nate thought. *Got to be ready for tomorrow's demo. I better ask for a wakeup call too.*

Lights flashed in his rearview mirror and he, casually, changed lanes to his right.

SWOOSH! A big BMW shot pass in the lane Nate had vacated. The rush of air rocked his car.

Holly shit! That car might have slammed into me.

He became fully alert and changed to the rightmost lane. Exiting at Ludwigsfeld, he followed a mental image of his map and found Schroppenwiesenstrabe. The house numbers increased as he drove on. He passed 84 Auf den Schrederwiesen, made a u-turn, and went back to a twelve-story building that appeared to be vacant. There were construction materials in front and a few cars were parked nearby, but no lights were visible.

He pulled up next to the parked cars and saw 84 above the door.

The hotel must have gone out of business. Now what? Here I am in the middle of the night and nobody's around. This isn't even a city, just some small town. No phones in sight. Shit!

The building's front door was ajar and had a sign on it. Nate poked his head in and pushed on the door. The heavy door opened with a creaking sound that reminded Nate of old Dracula movies. The dim streetlight was the only illumination into what seem to be a large empty room.

"Hello-o-o", Nate called out, "Anybody here?" He repeated it twice and thought he heard an echo.

He was about to go back and try sleeping in the car when his eyes adjusted to the darkness. He saw it was a lobby, seemingly old and dusty. There was a counter on the other side of the room in front of him.

Maybe there's a bell I can ring. This is so weird; I can hardly believe I'm awake.

The darkness closed in as he walked toward the counter. He felt for a bell and found some keys instead. There was a piece of paper attached. Nate walked back to the front door and read the paper by the dim street light.

Herr LaChae; the key had 323 on it.

No way! Nate thought, *Somebody must be playing a joke or something.*

"Hello-o-o. Anybody here?"

To hell with this, I'm not staying in an abandoned building and sleeping here tonight. They're not going to find my body and ask 'What was he thinking?'.

Nate walked outside, looked up at the windows, and didn't see any lights. He returned to his car and sat, looking at the key and the note.

Regaining his composure, Nate's curiosity prompted him to want to see the room. With a burst of bravado, he grabbed his suitcase and went back into the building. The elevator and the stairs were in darkness. He felt his way to the third floor and used the light from his pocket-planner to read numbers on the doors.

One room did have light coming from under the door but he dared not knock.

He found room 323 and his key opened the door. Nate reached in and found a light switch right where it should have been. The lights came on and the room looked like a normal hotel room.

Thank God.

Nate entered and quickly latched the door behind him.

He let out a nervous laugh and started unpacking.

Good thing Lena isn't coming until the weekend.

He left the curtains open in hopes he wouldn't oversleep.

He awoke early the next morning and was surprised to find people in the halls and lobby, going about their business in a normal manner.

The attendant, at the front desk greeted Nate.

"Herr LaChae. Did you sleep well?"

"Yes, thank you." Nate lied. "Why were all the lights off last night?"

"Conservation." The attendant said, "After twenty minutes they automatically turn off. You can activate them by pressing a wall switch."

"What wall switch?" Nate asked.

The attendant came around the counter and showed Nate the switch near the front door. "There are also switches in the elevator and the hallways." The attendant stopped talking and looked at Nate expectantly.

"I see, now." Nate said, "There should be some kind of sign or something telling people that."

"There is, Herr LaChae. It is outside, on the door."

Nate remembered a sign - written in German.

"Will you be having breakfast?"

"No, I'll be checking out." *And I won't be back*, Nate thought.

The staff at the Munich office were amused by Nate's story.

"It's part of the conservation programs", Hannah Rausch said, puffing on a cigarette. Her fair hair and blue eyes didn't betray her acerbic edges; but her rasping tones did. The government wants to regulate everything. That's another reason I eat only natural foods now. They're putting all kinds of additives into everything else. I don't give that crap to my cats at home", she said.

"Ya, and it's going to stay that way until we get different politicians", Siegfried Gerber said with a chuckle. Blond-haired and square-faced, young 'Siggy' was the fast-talking office comedian.

"Look at you." Hannah pushed Siggy, "You eat too much no matter what the food is."

Siggy patted his stomach. "This is from Weiss beer, not food."

"Wilfred and Max drink beer", Hannah retorted, "and they're not big like you."

"Ya, They don't drink enough beer, that's all. And Nate probably drinks that British piss they call beer."

Nate laughed, "They don't keep beer in the office refrigerator at the UK office."

"Ya, ya. They're too, how you say … up tight. I'm telling you, one day governments will try to regulate the water and the air. You'll see."

"Water is already regulated in some places in the US", Nate said.

Maximillian Buhler came into the room and extended his hand. His expensive suit lay perfectly on his athletic build.

"Hello again, Nate", a smile broke through his chiseled features.

"Hello, Max."

"How's life in the U.K.?"

"The weekends are great. That's the only time I get to spend there."

"Maybe KMS does not want you to get bored."

"No chance of that", Nate said, "I've been crossing national borders every week and dealing with different languages, currency, phone systems and power."

Max removed his delicate, thin rimmed, glasses and started cleaning them. "The Bosch engineers will be here within the hour. They are bringing samples for testing, of course."

"Of course", Nate echoed.

"Come" Max motioned toward his office, "We need to talk before they get here."

Both the EMMI and Nate performed well. The only concerns the Bosch engineers had was about Emmi's automation.

"We are accustomed to using manual control with our samples", one said. "Often, we have only one sample and it must not be damaged during testing."

Nate said, "The computer controls all movements very precisely."

"We understand that. However, if we give the computer a mistaken command or if it has a fault, our sample could be damaged. That is not the case with manual controls."

Nate knew it was a comparison to Hamamatsu's machine. He thought it odd that anyone would want less automation – except for the cost savings.

"You must understand", the Bosch engineer said, "Our laws require us to keep paper records and not rely on computers. It's because tapes and disks can get erased."

Max responded in German then switched to English. " ...Emmi can print hard-copies of the data and the images. And, I believe, limits can be set on the movement of the probes. Is that correct, Nate?"

"Yes, it is. Let me show you." Nate typed commands into the keyboard.

It took four hours, to put EMMI through its paces and test the samples the Bosch engineers brought.

"Shall we have dinner?" Max asked.

"We have a flight back tonight at ten."

"That will be no problem", Max said, "I'm flying out tonight myself and there's an excellent restaurant near the airport." Max turned to Nate. "Will you join us?"

"Not way out there near the airport, Max. My hotel is right here in Munich. Thanks anyway."

*   *   *

On Saturday, Nate met Lena at the airport.

"Come on we'll take a taxi to the hotel."

"A taxi?" Lena said, "I thought you rented a car."

"I did. But, I think you'll enjoy riding in one of *these* taxis."

When they got outside, Lena grinned as she saw all the taxis were Mercedes Benz.

They spent the afternoon touring Munich and chose to have dinner at a restaurant near Maren Platz. The server, who spoke no English, tried to understand their request. They motioned that any choice on the menu would be all right, but they didn't want pork. Finally, the server's face lit up and she said, "Oh-h-h", she shook one finger from side to side, "No oink-oink?"

Nate and Lena agreed excitedly, "That's right! No oink-oink."

The server walked away, then came back and asked, "Moo-o-o?" with her open palm facing up.

Delighted, the Americans shook their heads up and down, "Moo-o-o, yes!"

After dinner, they walked around downtown Munich before returning to the hotel and its sauna. They lounged, in their swimsuits, by the huge windows on the third floor and had cocktails.

"Seems like another world, doesn't it?" Nate asked.

"It is another world. It's the one we imagined and programmed for."

"You know, some people live like this all the time, Lena."

"Don't you believe we can too?"

Nate took a sip. "I cashed the last of the savings bonds before I left. We don't want to get into a financial hole."

"When I get a job everything will be all right." Lena said, "Let's just enjoy being here for now."

"And tomorrow … ," Nate said, "the castle, at Neuschwanstein."

They clicked their wine glasses together in a toast.

*   *   *

Nate's sister called and told him his uncle had fallen and was in the hospital; he wasn't expected to recover. When Lena returned from her SMC group meeting she found Nate, in the bedroom, packing a suitcase.

"My uncle may be dying; I have to go see him, Lena."

Lena sat on the bed. "You said we couldn't afford any more trips back to the States."

"I'm getting an advance from the job."

After a moment, Lena asked, "What made you decide to go?"

"When I asked myself 'what would my uncle do if things were reversed and I was dying', it was clear. He would be there for me."

"Shall I call Mother and tell her you'll be staying there?"

"No, I'll stay at Aunt Lil's. But, call your mother anyway. I'll stop by there too." Nate stopped packing and then said, "I don't understand how a fall, in the bathtub, can lead to somebody be terminally ill."

"They must have discovered something when they examined him."

"Yeah, you're probably right." Nate continued packing, "Where's my socks?"

Nate experienced his flight from Heathrow like a dream. He stared out of the window during takeoff and remembered his uncle.

As Spiderman climbing outside the fifth floor window to save him when he was locked in a room filling with hot steam.

Uncle carrying him on his shoulders at the Macy's Christmas parade.

Uncle giving him his allowance every two weeks.

Uncle combing every knot of hair without hurting.

Uncle teaching him to tie a tie.

Uncle letting him borrow clothes to go to church.

Uncle playing the piano.

Uncle spanking him once, much gentler than his Mother or Grandmother would have.

Uncle embarrassing him, playing ball and calling out, "Chunk the ball, Champ! Chunk it!"

Riding together across New York harbor on the Staten Island Ferry.

Always greeting each other with a smile and a hug.

During the in-flight dinner, Nate thought about how he and his uncle drifted apart once. Nate was fourteen when he overheard an argument between his mother and uncle. Afterward Nate approached his uncle and hesitantly told him, "I want you to know, I'm not going to ever let anybody hurt my mother."

His uncle stared at him and then said, "Boy, you better go on."

Nate stood his ground for a moment as their eyes locked, then he backed away.

His mother came to him that night. "Nate, I know you love me and want to protect me and I'm glad you do. But, I want you to understand that me and your uncle have disagreements sometimes and it's not serious. We have done that since we were kids. And no matter what we say or how it might sound, we would never do anything to hurt each other. Do you understand?"

Nate shook his head and wanted to cry. "Ah, huh."

"We apologized to each other already", she said.

"You hurt your uncle's feelings. I think it would be nice if you apologized too, don't you?"

"No. Because then he'll think I didn't mean what I said."

"Will you do it for me?"

"Okay," Nate said uncomfortably. But, I'm not going to take back what I said."

It wasn't until Thanksgiving that Nate and his uncle reaffirmed their friendship and love for each other – with a hug.

*   *   *

Arriving at O'Hare airport, Nate took a taxi to the South Side. He asked the driver to wait while he bought flowers for his Aunt Lil. Her warm welcome was as if he had never left and his room was ready – with his photo by the bed. Nate hugged her and his cousin Frances.

"Sorry, I didn't get any flowers for you too, Fran."

"Oh, you're so sweet, Nate." Frances laughed, "That's all right. You didn't know I was going to be here. You want to eat something?"

"No, I'll eat when I get back. I'm sorry."

"It's alright, baby." Aunt Lil kissed him on the cheek, "I understand. You done traveled all those miles and you want to see your uncle right now."

"I'll be back before long."

"Take your time baby. I'll be here."

"Come on Nate," Fran said, "I'll take you in my old car, if you don't mind riding in it."

"We have to roll the windows down." Frances said as she pulled out of the parking space. The station wagon's rear window was broken out and exhaust fumes reentered the car as they drove along.

"How you been, Cuz?" Fran asked, "Traveling all over the world and everything."

"I've been all right. What about you?"

"Lately, I've been taking it one day at a time. But, I'm making it."

They pulled up in front of the hospital.

"I'm not going upstairs, Nate. I need to make a little run. Tell me what time I should come back for you."

"Give me a couple of hours."

"If you come out before I get back, meet me at that coffee shop across the street."

The receptionist gave Nate directions to room 502. It was midday and the hallway was bustling with nurses and aides. He entered the room and immediately saw his frail uncle laying in a fetal position. Their eyes met and his uncle struggled to focus.

"Champ! Oh, Nate, is that you?"

"Yes, Uncle, it's me."

His uncle's eyes got big and he started shouting, "Watch yourself! Watch yourself! Watch yourself!"

Startled, Nate turned around expecting some danger. His uncle frantically repeated the warning. Saliva was coming from his mouth.

"What?" Nate asked, "What's wrong?

A male nurse came in with a syringe and rolled up Sam's pajama sleeve. "Now, Sam, you calm down and stop yelling like that."

Sam cowered as the nurse's injection quickly took affect.

The nurse turned to Nate, "Are you his son?"

"No, I'm his nephew."

"Oh, you're the one who lives in England?"

"Yes."

"Sam has told everybody about you. He says he and his wife are going there to visit you."

"His wife? He's not married."

"Sure he is. He introduced us to Patricia"

Nate looked at his uncle who closed his eyes full of tears.

"I don't know anything about that."

The nurse pat Nate's uncle on the top of his head and then said, "You rest now, Sam. I'm going to take good care of you."

Nate noticed his uncle flinch at the nurse's touch.

After the nurse left, Nate stood, silently, by the bed. He wiped his uncle's forehead with a facecloth. His uncle turned toward him, opened his eyes and then said softly, "You talk too much."

"What?"

Sam repeated, "You talk too much."

Nate asked softly, "Who is Patricia?"

"She's a friend of your sister's who comes by sometime. I told them Patricia was my wife. You got to have someone close to you, if you want to get out of this place alive."

"Take it easy. I'm here now."

"Yes." Nate's uncle raised his hand and Nate grabbed it. "I'm so glad to see you, Nate."

"I'm glad to see you too. What happened?"

"I knew I was sick for a long time. I just didn't want to go to the doctor. Then I fell-out a time or two. This last time my landlord found me on the floor and he called an ambulance."

"But, what do you have?"

"It's spread all over my body ..."

Nate was silent; words didn't come; the silence grew. He looked at his uncle, balled up under the sheet. He refused to cry. *Got to be strong for him,* he thought.

"Nate, will you do something for me?"

Nate squeezed his uncle's hand and then said, "Yes, sure, anything."

"Will you do what you did to my legs that time? "I can't straighten them out."

"Yes, Uncle." Nate looked around. The only other patient in the room was asleep. The hallway traffic had lessened. Nate walked over and pushed the door almost closed. He came back to the bed, pulled the sheet back and saw his uncle's thin wrinkled legs sticking out of a diaper.

"Just relax." Nate said as he rubbed his hands together. "Close your eyes and think about the last time I did this."

Nate closed his eyes too and passed his hands over his uncle's legs several times. He took a deep breath and repeated the motions several more times. He applied the technique with all the silent passion and love in his heart. When he was finished, he felt weak. He opened his eyes and then said, "There." He covered him with the sheet.

Slowly, his uncle stretched his legs, then drew them up and stretched them again. Tears flowed down the sides of his head and Nate wiped them away.

"Thank you, Nate."

Choked up, Nate said, "I love you Uncle; I'm glad I can help."

An awkward moment of silence passed.

"You must have spent a lot of money coming here all the way from England."

"I'm just paying you back for all those allowances you gave me."

Sam's smile revealed brown teeth. "You still remember that? I had forgotten all about it."

"Oh, I remember it very well."

"A little thing like that?"

"Those allowances meant a whole lot to me. And you know what?"

"What?"

"I always wanted to be like you. I always-"

A female nurse interrupted them, "Okay, Sam it's time for your procedure. Well-l-l, I see you're moving your legs again."

Nate winked at his uncle and he winked back.

"I'll have to ask you to leave now, sir."

Nate grabbed his uncle's hand again, leaned over, and kissed him on the forehead. His sweat smelled like his mother's did when she was in the hospital.

Their eyes met for a time and Sam told his nephew, "You take care of yourself, Champ."

"You too."

Sam said, "The Lord will take care of me now."

As Nate was leaving, he saw the male nurse, that his uncle disliked, talking on the phone. They acknowledged each other with a nod and Nate got an uneasy feeling.

Outside, Nate thought, *the sun shouldn't be shining so bright on such a sad day.* He didn't see Fran's car and she wasn't in the coffee shop yet, so he walked around the block of the Illinois Institute of Technology. It was then that the full realization came over him that he would never see his uncle again. Crying, he circled another block of the campus. When he returned to the coffee shop, Fran was parked outside with the engine running. The car's exhaust was drifting into the shop.

Seeing the redness in his eyes, Fran said, "Wanna go sit by the lake for a while."

"I was going to suggest that."

They parked by Lake Michigan, enjoyed a joint, some beer, the music on WVON and each other's conversation. Whenever they were together, something in their common roots reconnected and always cheered them up. When they got back to Aunt Lil's, they stuffed themselves.

He visited his in-laws the next day and took a late flight home that evening.

Wednesday, of the following week, Sam passed away. They said he died, in his sleep, *of complications.*

*   *   *

Monday morning, Dick Keating called Nate on the intercom, "Would you come to my office for a minute, please?"

Maybe they're going to give me the loan I asked for, Nate thought.

Keating motioned for Nate to close the door and take a seat, "He's here now, Barry."

Nate realized the speakerphone was on.

"Hello, Nate. This is Barry Rapozo. Can you hear me okay?"

"Yes, Barry. How are you?"

"I'm fine. How's your family?"

"My uncle passed away, that's why I went to The States recently. Otherwise, everybody is okay."

"Sorry to hear about your uncle, Nate. I know it can be difficult living so far away from your family."

"Thanks, Barry."

They discussed the importance of selling an Emmi to Dr. Giovanelli at the University of Bari, in Italy.

"Let me know if there's anything you need." Barry said, "And don't let any of the salesmen drag their feet. It's a limited market and we have to capitalize on this narrow window of opportunity while we can."

"I understand." Nate said.

Barry Rapozo closed with, "Remember, Giovanelli must spend all his budget before the end of the year. That way he can get more funding for the next year."

"I'll do my best." Nate replied.

*   *   *

When Nate got home, Lena told him he needed to go to the school to discuss Brandon's fighting.

"Fighting? About what?"

"The class bully kept picking on him." Lena said, "That principal is always asking where you are. I started to tell him it was none of his business where you were. Please, just go talk with him, so I won't have to curse him out."

"How many times have you had to go up to the school?"

"Only, three times", Lena said, "One time they said Brandon was challenging the teachers by asking a lot of questions in class.

"Challenging?" Nate laughed.

"Yeah. Brandon asks 'why', like any American kid would do. Over here, they see that as a challenge. This is the first time Brandon got into a fight."

"Okay, I'll go talk with … "

"Mr. Plummer."

"What kind of a guy is Mr. Plummer?"

Lena tucked her chin in and then said, "Quite British … you'll see."

During his drive to the school, Nate reminisced about his mother coming to school for his disciplinary problems. The dean would describe Nate's transgressions and his mother would smile and say, "Oh, he did?" Then she would glance at him and say, "We'll have to see about that." That was the promise of a whipping when they got home.

Nate didn't want Brandon to feel fear today. Whatever happened, Nate wanted Brandon to know he loved him and everything would be all right.

But, I mustn't condone his actions, if they were wrong, Nate thought.

Nate opened the door to the secretary's office, Brandon was sitting nearby, looking sheepishly at him. The other boy sat on the opposite side of the room. Nate winked his eye at Brandon.

"Mr. LaChae?" the secretary asked. "Mr. Plummer is expecting you. You may go right in."

"Thank you."

Nate entered the office and was startled to see the school principal petting a tall greyhound dog. Even more surprising was how lean and grey the man looked. He didn't get up when Nate entered. Instead, he peered over his half-glasses and then said, "Won't you have a seat? Can I have Meredith get something for you?"

"No, thank you."

"Your wife tells me that you travel a great deal, Mr. LaChae."

"Yes", Nate felt defensive already, "that's true. But, I keep in touch with my family every day."

"Of course.," the principal said, "However, some boys need the daily guidance of a man."

"Let me assure you, Mr. Plummer, my wife is very capable of guiding Brandon and disciplining him whenever she feels it's necessary."

The principal paused and scratched his dog behind the ears. "There have been several incidents between the boys and it has culminated in a brawl in the hallway this morning."

"I wasn't aware of any other incidents." Nate said.

"They were minor in comparison. I have to tell you, Mr. LaChae, fighting is not tolerated here at Chatsworth. Such behavior can be reason for expulsion."

Feeling uncomfortable, Nate said, "Do you mind if I speak with the boys alone for a few minutes?"

Surprised, Mr. Plummer said reluctantly, "Why, no. I guess that would be all right", he stood and ushered the greyhound toward the door. "I'll send them in." The dog gave Nate a forlorn look as he left.

The boys came in and watched Mr. Plummer leave. Nate pulled up two chairs and motioned for the boys to sit.

"Alright, you guys. I know you don't want to be pussies and that's okay. But, you're both going about it the wrong way." Nate leaned forward, "When you fight you get into trouble with the school and your parents and everybody. If you keep doing that, you will end up in jail one day. There is another way to be tough and make everybody like you and be proud of you. And you don't have to like each other to do it."

The boys looked at each other, then back at Nate as he continued.

"Do you think all the players on the Manchester United team like each other? I'm not so sure. I'll bet they have arguments sometimes. But, they don't fight. They play really hard against the other teams.

That's where you can be tough, on the soccer field and you need to do it together. That's right ... together. When you're on a team or in the military, everybody will cheer for you and give you medals when you're tough. You'll be heroes and you'll be showing people that you're smart too. That's the way to do it. Do you both understand what I'm saying?"

The boys looked at each other again, then nodded their heads agreeing.

"Okay, I hope you'll both stay out of trouble from now on."

Nate stood, "I'll ask Principal Plummer to come back in now."

*   *   *

The next weekend, Nate, Lena and Brandon were at Covent Gardens, when a black couple approached them. The man asked, "Are you from Brooklyn?"

Surprised, Nate said, "Yes, I am."

"I thought I recognized you. I'm Andrew, Bob Hartnett's brother. You and my brother used to play chess together."

"Bob's little brother?"

"Yeah, this is my wife and my son is somewhere around here."

"Oh, wow." Nate said, "This is my wife Lena and that's my grandson over there. I sure didn't expect to meet anybody from Bedford-Stuyvesant over here."

"Me neither. What troop are you with?"

Nate went on to explain that he wasn't in the military. Afterward, the six of them went to a pizza parlor for lunch. As they talked about where they'd been, Nate and Lena noticed all the places Andrew and his wife mentioned were American-style places.

"We're always with other military personnel when we go out." Andrew explained.

His wife invited them to come to the base and shop at the PX. They accepted the offer and were astonished at the number of choices of food there. They brought two grocery carts of food home that day.

In the months that followed, they communicated often with the Hartnett's. Andrew's son invited Nate and Brandon to one of his overnight Boy Scouting outings. Nate told a ghost story around the campfire and one of the British fathers came over to him, puffing his pipe and then said, "I dare say, that was one of the scariest stories I've ever heard."

"And I cut it short", Nate said, "when I saw the looks on the boys faces."

"Indeed", the pipe smoker said, with raised eyebrows.

*   *   *

Marcus Ryan called Nate at home on the weekend. "We've located your lost demo machine. Its been sitting on a dock in Milan since the Semicon Europa show."

"I don't understand why", Nate said, "Mario and I packed it ourselves and we made sure the paperwork was in order."

"I'm sure you did." Marcus said, "The Italian officials probably saw the French and German shipping labels on the crates. There's a hatred between those countries that you wouldn't understand, Nate. Anyway, Emmi should be delivered to Giovanelli's place next week. And I want you down there. He says the power converter and other facilities are all in place.

"Okay", Nate said, "I'll be on my way Monday morning."

"Nate, I don't have to remind you of the importance of this sale."

"No, you don't. We'll get it, Marcus, don't worry."

"Good luck. Call me after you meet with him."

*   *   *

After traveling 1,084 miles and changing planes three times, Nate arrived, in Bari, at the "heel" of Italy. When morning came, he found Dr. Giovanelli's lab in a building that looked like a monastery. He was reassured it was the right place when he saw students with armfuls of textbooks. One of them directed him to the doctor's second-floor office.

Nate knocked.

"Pronto", a growly voice said.

Nate entered and saw a middle-aged man with dark hair and a long bloodhound face. He was smoking a pipe and wearing a black turtleneck sweater. When he stood, he was taller than Nate.

"You are here about the microscope?"

"Yes, the EMMI.," they shook hands, "I am Nate LaChae."

"I'm pleased to meet you. The machine is still in its crate on the dock. When you're ready to install it I'll have someone help you move it."

"Dr. Giovanelli, first I'd like to discuss your requirements and expectations."

The professor laughed. "That won't be necessary, I've discussed that with your salesman, Mr. Chaput. I have samples for testing, that will be enough proof for me."

"I see." Nate said. "May I ask if Hamamatsu has demonstrated for you.

"You are inquisitive, Mr. LaChae. Yes, Hamamatsu was here a month ago. They tested the same samples I'll be giving you. Will that present a problem?"

"Not so long as the characteristics of the samples can be measured before and after Emmi's tests ... to establish a reference point."

"Of course; that's a good scientific plan." Giovanelli said, "Now, if you'll excuse me, I must prepare for a class. My students will show you to the dock and the laboratory. If you need anything they will assist you."

"Thank you, sir." Nate felt no warmth coming from the professor.

Nate successfully tested Giovanelli's samples and demonstrated the range of operation that Emmi offered. He asked if Hamamatsu's performance was as good.

"Not quite", the professor said, "But, they have manual control of the probes. With manual controls, I am more confident my samples won't be accidentally damaged."

"I understand your concerns." Nate said, "Let me show you how easy it is to program safety limits into the automatic motion controls."

Patiently, Nate addressed each of the Giovanelli's concerns and some that he hadn't mentioned. Then the doctor said, "I've heard that you tried to develop a calibration standard using a UV-RAM chip."

"Yes, I did try. But, no emissions were detected."

"Did you try reversing the voltage polarity?"

"No, that would probably blow up the chip."

The professor puffed on his extinguished pipe. There was a twinkle in his eye and he smiled.

"Have you tried it?" Nate asked.

"Only once. The current did destroy the chip and I didn't have another. But, Emmi has automatic current limiting, doesn't it."

"Yes!" Nate exclaimed excitedly, "yes, it does."

"If you can get another UV-RAM chip, I propose that we test it on Emmi."

"I can get some from the States. It may take a week or more."

"I'm afraid I don't have two weeks to spare. I must make my decision by next Monday. And frankly, your Emmi is priced too high."

"But … " Nate started to protest.

Dr. Giovanelli raised his hand, "There is a way for both KMS and my research center to be winners. If the price is reduced by, say, thirty percent and assurances made that I will get the calibration chips before anyone else, then I would be inclined to buy from KMS instead of Hamamatsu. They have already quoted a price that is less than 80% of Emmi's price."

"Doctor, I'll have to talk with my sales and marketing people to see what can be done."

Giovanelli headed toward the door, "There's a phone in my office."

Jean-Marie told Nate he couldn't make the decision for such a discount. Nate couldn't get through to Marcus or Dick Keating. He promised Dr. Giovanelli he'd call the US later that night and try to have an answer the next day.

Nate called Barry Rapozo, from the hotel, and explained the situation. Barry told him, "I appreciate your efforts, Nate. And you are doing a remarkable job over there. But, I can't get involved in setting margins for those guys. That's their business. Marcus and Dick will have to sort this out with Henri Zimmerman. That's why we have him - for making deals."

Nate had to put off Dr. Giovanelli for another day while he tried to get a decision from his superiors.

"No! Absolutely not." Marcus told Nate, "We can't give him thirty percent."

"How much are we willing to give then?"

"Giovanelli is trying to play us against Hamamatsu. I've asked Henri Zimmerman to fly down there tomorrow. He'll negotiate a price."

"Marcus, I'm telling you, Giovanelli is ready to buy. He's excited about getting the calibration device I worked on and-"

"That project is dead. You didn't promise him anything, did you?"

"No, Marcus. I didn't promise him anything. Somehow, he knew I had tried to make a calibration device and he thinks he knows what went wrong. He's willing to work with us on it."

"Listen Nate, you are not down there to form joint ventures or agreements for experimental work. Your job is to demo the equipment."

"You told me I had different responsibilities now, Marcus. Responsibilities that include making sure we got the sale. Can't you see that that's what I'm trying to do?"

"I see that. But, you're getting carried away, Nate."

"Marcus, I'm not getting carried away. I'm here and I see what's happening. We can sell an Emmi in the next two days and make a smaller profit or we can lose to Hamamatsu. That's the facts. There's no time for us to play games with this guy."

"I'm well aware of the facts, Nate, and I'm not going to argue this point with you any longer. You let Henri do the negotiating when he gets there. If Giovanelli doesn't accept our offer, I want you to pack up Emmi and ship it back, is that understood?"

"Sure. I understand perfectly." Nate said. *I understand I'm not going to get a bonus this time*, he thought.

The following Monday, Dr. Giovanelli signed a purchase order for Hamamatsu's version of an emission microscope.

*   *   *

Back in England, Nate left the KMS office and headed for the bookstore. He wanted to get his mind off the memo he had accidentally seen. It described the marketing window for Emmi as being closed. He had visited all of the major companies in his database and realized he'd have to start thinking about the next chapter in his career.

Oh well, Nate thought, *time to climb the Monkeybars again.*

At the bookstore, he scanned the science fiction section and found his favorite authors' new books. There was Larry Niven, Orson Scott Card, Poul Anderson, but nothing new from Clarke, LaGuin, Lem or Asimov.

He tried the popular science section and found old friends: Zukov, Sagan, Wolf, and Gleick. Nothing piqued his interest until he saw a book titled, "Beyond 2001: The Laws of Physics Revised" and a name that was vaguely familiar - Sandy Kidd.

That's the guy I read about that got financial support for his gyroscopic engine project.

Nate read the book's flaps, then quickly opened to the center section containing photos that didn't show enough detail. As he read portions of the chapters, Nate's mouth fell open. *This guy is doing the same thing Bill and I did in 1972.*

He could hardly believe his eyes as the chapters presented an identical progression of experiments and discoveries. He found he could predict what was in the next chapter of Kidd's book!

This is incredible. Bill needs to know about this. He needs to know that our work was not all in vain.

Nate could hardly wait to tell Lena.

"When are you going to contact this guy?" Lena asked as she brought Nate's dinner into the bedroom that he used as an office.

"As soon as I can. I'll try contacting the publisher first. Do you realize what this means?"

"Yes, Nate, I knew you and Bill must have been doing something important. And you kept your records and patent application didn't you?"

"Definitely!" Nate replied while frantically searching through Sandy Kidd's book looking for technical details. "He never mentions doing a pendulum test. That's the most critical test of all; it cancels out the effects of gravity."

Lena smiled sympathetically and picked up the dinner he hadn't touched. "I'll put this food in the oven for when you get hungry."

"OK, baby, I'm sorry. This is just so phenomenal."

Lena and Brandon fell asleep watching TV. After midnight she came into the spare bedroom where Nate was still reading. He looked up with a distant stare and then said, "I'm sorry baby. I've got to finish this."

Lena yawned, "I'm going to bed."

By the time he finally went to bed, he knew he wasn't going to the office tomorrow. Emmi wasn't his main priority any more.

After a few inquiries, Nate was speaking with the book's publisher.

"Sandy Kidd is a very private person. However, he will be showing a film of his work at the Space Show at Thistlehouse school on Thursday. You may be able to meet him then."

Nate got the address and thanked the publisher. He'd been careful not to reveal any of the similarity of his own work. The space show was to include launching of model rockets by British students. So, Nate decided to take Brandon along and let him fire the rocket they had brought from the states.

They were on their way to the space show when Brandon asked, "Granddad, is Sandy Kidd's engine faster than yours?"

"I don't think so, Brandon. And it's not a matter of speed with that type engine. It's not like a rocket. If you can takeoff at all, then you can just keep going faster and faster, for a very long time."

"Can your engine take off, Granddad?"

"No, we didn't generate enough lift to take off. But everybody thought it was impossible to generate any lift at all with my kind of engine." Then he added, "Brandon, when we get to the school, don't say anything about my engine okay? I want to tell Mr. Kidd myself."

The signs at the campus directed them to a huge auditorium. Nate told Brandon to leave the rocket in the car until they checked out the place. Arriving at the front desk, Nate recognized Sandy Kidd from a picture in his book; he was talking with some of the students. He was stocky, with a receding hairline. He looked a lot like Gene Hackman. When he glanced Nate's way he gave no sign of recognition or expectancy. Brandon pulled Nate's arm and pointed to a poster describing the time and location of the model rocket launches. As Nate turned and followed Brandon he thought, *I'll listen to Sandy Kidd's presentation first and see his film before I approach him. That way I can see how far he has gotten.*

The poster invited them to a classroom nearby where student's model rockets were displayed.

"Look, Granddad" Brandon laughed, "their rockets are all small".

Nate was surprised that the rockets, built by teenagers, were only 12 to 18 inches in length. They were similar to the most basic kits one could get in The States. Instantly, he realized launching Brandon's four-foot G-powered "monster" rocket would only embarrass the British students. He also realized he needed to convince Brandon to leave their rocket in the car.

The Headmaster directed everyone to the auditorium where Mr. Ron Thomas was introduced. Mr. Thomas described Sandy Kidd and the decision to publish Mr. Kidd's book. He went on about how revolutionary Kidd's engine was and what it would mean to space travel. Then, he introduced Sandy Kidd.

Sandy talked about how Newton's laws said that such an engine could not work and that Newton was wrong. He encouraged the students to experiment and discover new and exciting principles of their own. He showed a black and white film of his earliest work. Nate found it especially interesting to see Kidd's solutions to problems he and Bill had overcome.

Nate was intently focused and saw how Sandy Kidd had taken a different approach to producing the same effect as the Gamma engine. Kidd described how he almost gave up and then decided to use much higher rpms before he succeeded in producing lift. Instead of a pendulum test, he built an elevator system. A counter weight was used that equaled the weight of his engine. The slightest lift generated would unbalance the elevator and cause the engine to rise.

Neat, but the driving electric motor is much too heavy to fly. Nate thought. That was the same problem he and Bill had had.

The brief film was followed by a question and answer period. Nate withheld his questions.

Mr. Thomas came to Nate at the end of the presentation. "Mr. LaChae?"

"Yes, how did you know?"

"I detected your American accent on the tele. Is this your son?"

"This is my grandson, Brandon, he's here for the model rocket launching."

"Right. Come, let me introduce you to Sandy."

"Please to meet you." Sandy Kidd said with a slight smile. Ron tells me that you have done some work with gyroscopes.

"Yes, back in 1963 and then in 1970 I built a toy car that could propel itself up an incline."

Sandy replied with, "I never heard of your work. Are you with a university?"

Nate smiled and then said, "No, nothing like that. I've done all my work on my own. My buddy, who's a machinist, helped make the gyroscopes."

Kidd was slow to respond and then said, "So, you're not with the US government?"

"No", Nate replied, "not at all."

Kidd talked about different groups that had tried to buy him out and his suspicions about governments spying on his work. Nate realized, *this guy is a little paranoid.* To alleviate some of Kidd's fears Nate showed photographs he'd brought and began discussing technical details that only another gyroscopic engine researcher would know.

Nate didn't know if Kidd was convinced or not, but soon they were laughing about mutual experiences they'd gone through with their failures. Nate even related how his Grandmother helped him with his first gyroscope experiments and he showed her hand in a photo from 1961.

Brandon interrupted with, "Granddad, they're getting ready to launch the rockets. When are we going to get ours?"

"You brought a rocket?" Sandy seemed interested and accompanied them to their car. Nate opened the trunk and asked Sandy to excuse him and Brandon for a moment.

"What, Granddad?"

"Brandon, you see how all their rockets are small? These are the best students in all of Britain."

"Yeah, and we can beat them all-" Brandon started.

Nate interrupted with, "That's why I'm going to ask you not to launch or even show our rocket today; we know it can out perform theirs. But, we're Americans and it's easy for us to get bigger and better rocket parts than they can get over here. If we show our rocket, they won't cheer for us. It will only make them feel bad and embarrass them. I'm asking you to pass-up flying today and we'll find a field and launch next weekend."

Seeing the disappointment on Brandon's face Nate said, "We can go ahead and launch if you want to, but it won't be fun like before."

Slowly, Brandon said, "Alright, but you promise we will launch next weekend for sure?"

"Yes, Brandon well find a place and launch for sure."

When they returned to the car, Sandy said, "That's one fine rocket you have there. How high can it go?"

"It went over two thousand feet when we flew it in San Jose." Brandon replied.

"We're not going to fly it today." Nate said and closed the trunk.

Mr. Thomas said, "Master Brandon, shall we go and watch the launchings while Sandy and your grandfather talk?"

"Okay, let's go." Brandon said looking at Nate who nodded his approval and then said, "Were coming."

"Why did you stop working on your engine?" Sandy asked.

Nate paused for a moment, realizing that the Scotsman might not understand. Then he said, "After the pendulum test, we realized that nothing we did was going to convince the powers that be. Their minds are closed to the possibility of somebody like us violating Newton's laws even a little bit. I saw that our experiments could go on and on but nothing would change their opinions. Besides we were getting smaller and smaller improvements and there wasn't enough lift to fly a vehicle. We finally realized that a breakthrough was needed ..."

"A non-mechanical analogue." Sandy interjected.

"Exactly!" confirmed Nate. "Yes, I started thinking along those lines myself. Mechanical gyroscopes are just too heavy, even though they can produce lift."

Both men stopped walking and stared as the supersonic Concorde flew overhead. Then Sandy said, "You can never give up on something like this, you know?"

Nate shook his head in agreement, "I've tried to, several times."

They continued walking to the launching field and watched the rockets fly. Afterward, they exchanged phone numbers before Nate and Brandon left.

The following weekend, Nate kept his word to Brandon and they fired their rocket in an open field near Stonehenge. A patrol car, with two Bobbies, pulled up as Brandon and two friends retrieved the parachuted rocket. Nate approached the patrol car as the officers got out.

"What have we here, then?" one asked.

"The boys fired a rocket."

"Aye, a decent sized one it seems. We got a call from security."

As the men and boys converged on Nate's car, Lena hopped out, smiling. "Hello there, officers. Did you see the boys fly their class project?" The officers didn't notice the surprise on Nate's face.

"No, Mam", one of the officers replied, "can't say that we did."

"Why don't you fire it again, Nate, so they can see?"

"Yea!" the boys cheered.

"Would that be all right, officer?" Nate asked.

They looked at each other and one said, "I'd like to see it fly."

Nate and the boys prepared the rocket and slid it onto the launcher. They did a countdown and Nate touched the ignition wires to his car battery. Swo-o-o-o-sh! The rocket leaped into air and almost touched the clouds.

"Brilliant! That was simply brilliant!" one officer exclaimed.

In spite of the parachute, one of the fins broke on landing. The officers bid them farewell as they headed home. Nate looked at Lena, wiped his brow, and then said "Whew, that was close."

She winked at him.

*   *   *

It wasn't easy finding Bill Davis after all the years. Nate composed a letter and sent it to every Bill Davis in the Chicago phone book; and it worked! When Bill replied, Nate sent him Kidd's book and waited for another reply. Within two weeks, Bill sent a lengthy letter that echoed Nate's feelings. Bill also wrote that he and Etta had broke up and their two daughters were in college. He had remarried and gone to Mexico to build a church.

He had been diagnosed with lung cancer and in a colossal mistake, the wrong lung was removed. Bill ended the letter with, "But don't give up on me yet".

In the weeks that followed, Nate's mind was back in its creative mode. Sandy Kidd was right, he couldn't give up on his engine. He thought about where he and Bill had left off. Nate realized he now had 15 years more technical expertise, faster computers, better mathematical software and cheaper interface hardware. *Everything can be miniaturized too,* he thought as he finished a sketch of a new teststand and titled it Gamma-Max.

He paid different machine shops to build the components and the Gamma-Max teststand came together quickly. Nate became obsessed again. Even, the wobbling of a ceiling fan, in a restaurant, reminded him of gyroscopic principles.

Nate shared his enthusiasm for his project with Sandy Kidd. He called and asked him where to get bearings and gears in England. Sandy was helpful in this way, but always had an excuse that prevented Nate from visiting him - even when Nate's job sent him to Scotland.

*   *   *

Nate and Lena realized they were financially overextended. To make matters worse, Lena couldn't get a work permit and some job ads stated "No one over 35 need apply."

One Monday Nate was summoned to Dick Keating's office. When Nate saw Marcus Ryan, he was sure they were responding to his request for financial assistance.

"Do you know why we've asked you here today?" Dick began.

"Yes, I suppose you've found a way to help me with a loan." Nate responded.

Dick leaned back slowly and looked at Marcus then said, "No, Nate, your job has become redundant. We've been asked to reorganize our operations."

"Well, I guess that's one way to solve my financial situation," Nate said.

Dick added, "We do want to help you, Nate. We're prepared to offer you another job. It's at the plant in Switzerland", Marcus said, "You'd still be reporting to me. Do you think you'd be interested in that?"

"What about a position back in The States?" Nate asked.

Dick responded with, "we can't promise anything in that regard. They're a separate organization. Of course, we will give you an excellent recommendation if you decide to return to the states."

There was a long silence. Nate felt they expected him to say something, so he did. "Let me talk it over with Lena. Can I get back to you tomorrow?"

Dick stood and then said, "Certainly, we can continue this then. But Nate, we need to get this matter settled by Friday."

Nate could imagine continuing his European odyssey in Switzerland. Even though the only overt racist he had met at KMS, Oscar Carlisle, was now at the plant in Switzerland. Nate was more concerned about Lena and Brandon. Brandon could adapt easily. Some of British culture annoyed Lena, even though she always found her own friends. Surely, Switzerland would be even more conservative. So, during the short drive home, Nate decided the best course of action would be to return to the USA. He was surprised at how easily Lena accepted the news.

"All things come to an end one day", she said.

They took their last drive in the British countryside that weekend. They went to Oxford and enjoyed the Medieval Festival. Inevitably, Brandon found skateboarders, Lena found crystals and Nate found hand carved chess sets.

During the drive home, Brandon exclaimed, "Oh, wow! You know what? We have been to all the places on our tourist cards."

"I guess that's a sign that it's time to go home", Lena said.

Brand jumped up in his seat, "Are we going back? Huh?"

"Take it easy Brandon", Nate said, "You'll see."

*   *   *

Nate thought Monday's meeting in Dick Keating's office would go easy when he told them he was considering returning to the US, but it didn't go that way. Marcus pushed a bunch of papers at Nate for his signature and then said, "We want to help you, Nate. According to your contract, we owe you three months salary upon termination."

"I would still like to attend the Semicon Europa meeting next week as planned. All the semiconductor companies will be there. That'll give me a chance to look for employment in the UK and Europe."

Marcus was about to speak when Dick Keating said, "I don't see any problem with that. Sure, we can still send you to Semicon; its already budgeted."

Marcus looked at Dick in disbelief. Surprised, Nate realized, *Marcus is ready to simply write me off.*

No one mentioned the clause in Nate's contract that the company wouldn't pay for his return to the US if he were terminated while abroad. Danny Marks, Dick Keating's counterpart in the US, left the company and one of his last official acts was to send a company check to Nate. It was labeled "moving expenses". Nate was thankful he had friends in high places that had not forgotten him.

Nate changed his mind about going to Semicon as the Gamma-Max teststand neared completion. Things happened fast after that. Andrew Hartnett brought his video camera over and recorded a test run of the new Gamma device. They made a video of the countdown and initiation, but the test was a failure when the gyros didn't come up to speed. Later examination showed the equipment didn't fit together precisely enough.

When they were done, Andrew said, "I feel like I just witnessed something important."

"Almost", Nate said. He knew there wouldn't be enough time to have the teststand parts re-machined before their trip back to the US.

One week before leaving for home, the SMC group partied at Lena and Nate's house. All the regulars were there, except John - who was depressed over his lost portfolio, Gavin – who was running a marathon in Greece, and Tanya – who had stopped attending the meetings. There were tears and hugs and promises to stay in touch – physically and mentally.

Back at the office, Dick Keating took Nate to lunch and the two of them had a couple of Pints at a local pub.

"Have you decided what you'll do when you get back to the States?"

"I've sent my resume to three different departments within KMS. I expect something will develop from that."

"Right.," Dick chewed his food. "You've done an excellent job, Nate. We're all going to miss you."

"Thank you. It's been a pleasure working with all of you. Lena and Brandon have enjoyed being here too."

Dick asked for the check, "Tell them I send my best wishes."

"And to your wife Helen also", Nate said.

*   *   *

The movers were as meticulous as before, wrapping every glass carefully and taping every piece of wooden furniture at their corners.

Nate, Lena and Brandon had dinner, at the Hartnett's, on the military base.

"So, when will you guys be going home?"

"Not for another seven years." Andrew said, "I re-enlisted."

The next day, Andrew drove them to Heathrow airport. The two families gave their farewells and the LaChaes boarded a 747 for home.

A supersonic Concorde roared off the runway ahead of them.

*   *   *

Arriving at JFK was more hectic than ever. Nate remembered working for the Port Authority at JFK, trying to manage baggage for arriving international passengers. Now he was part of the mass of people. Still he felt like kissing the ground because they were home. They went through several checkpoints, collected their luggage and had it checked by customs.

The Customs agents seemed rushed, impersonal and downright impolite at times.

"Notice anything", Lena said, "or is it just me?"

"Oh, I've noticed it already. You can feel it in the way they look at us and treat us."

"Welcome back to America."

The crowd pushed forward. Brandon wore his Chinese dragon jacket and clung to his skateboard.

"You know what else I've noticed, Lena." Nate said, "For the first time in the past three years, I'm seeing people that resemble people in my family."

Macgillan Research

"So, tell me, how does it feel to be back?" Eli puffed on his pipe and shuffled a deck of cards, as they sat in his living room.

Nate sipped his Amaretto, "The short answer is real good."

"Yeah", Lena said, "except for some of the people you meet. I was talking with one woman, in the supermarket, telling her about the grocery stores in England. And she turned to me and then said, 'Now you're back to reality'.

I stopped and told her that was my reality, over there."

Ruth laughed, "I know what you mean, Lena. They're always trying to put us in our place."

"As if the only reality is their reality", Lena said. She cut the cards and Eli started passing them out.

"We noticed a difference as soon as we landed at JFK", Nate said, "little slights and looks. I had got used to not having to deal with that kind of stuff."

Eli laughed and then said, "Yo name is Toby now, boy", reminding Nate of a line from ROOTS, where the slave master tells the African his name is no longer Kunta Kinte.

They all laughed and started playing Bid Whisk.

"Tell them, Eli." Ruth said.

"My God woman, you have no patience at all."

"Tell us what?"

Eli removed his pipe and spoke like a preacher, "I assumed you would be looking for a house or apartment and you'd need transportation." He reached in his pocket and dropped a set of car keys on the table. "So, we rented a car for you, for two weeks."

"Hey man, thanks." Nate shook Eli's hand.

"That was very kind and thoughtful of you guys." Lena said.

"We wanted to do something useful for you."

"I thought about buying a car that's for sale in our hotel's parking lot." Nate said, "But, I'm too suspicious of things like that."

"Yeah, we saw that car the last time we came by."

Ruth got up and checked the roast in the oven.

"We've been waiting for KMS to rehire me, before we do any serious house hunting."

"How's it looking?" Eli asked.

"I've been on three different interviews and I expect, at least, one of them to come through."

"Can't you get back into your old group?"

"No. They've been absorbed into another department."

Lena picked up her cards, "I keep telling him to contact Barry Rapozo. He's the big international boss and he likes Nate."

"I will contact him, Lena. I just don't want to start asking for favors so soon."

"Why wait? You need a job now."

"I can understand Nate's reluctance", Eli said, "You don't want to use up all your favors too soon, especially when you don't know what your future holds.

"Exactly!" Nate said and pointed for Eli to play cards. The men won the game and boasted about it all during dinner.

"How's your daughter?" Ruth asked Lena.

"Marilyn's in Los Angeles now."

At that moment, Brandon burst through the door, with his skateboard under his arm. "Is the food ready yet?"

Weeks went by and, as their money dwindled, the LaChaes decided to get out of the hotel. They were still confident KMS would rehire Nate.

"Remember that one house we looked at in Cupertino?" Lena said, "It was cheaper than staying here in this hotel."

"I know, Lena. But, we don't know where KMS might send me. That house could end up being on the wrong side of town for us."

"The owner said he'd give us a six month lease."

"It was nice", Nate admitted, "with the fireplace and all. I'll give him a call tomorrow."

They signed the six-month lease and the moving company delivered their furniture the following week.

The day Lena registered Brandon for school, she stopped by one of Ross Perot's campaign offices in San Jose. She spent hours there, talking about politics with Mary Cummings.

That afternoon, Nate came home looking dejected. He plopped down on the couch with his suit coat still on.

"Did you get to see Barry Rapozo?" Lena asked.

"Yeah, I did. Let me have some coffee first?"

"I already have the pot on. You want some Amaretto in it?"

"I sure do - I'll pour."

Lena brought the liquor and a mug of coffee three-fourth full. She sat next to him and curled her feet up. "How did it go?"

"I waited an hour at Barry's office and when I stepped out, to go to the men's room, I saw him coming down the hall. Lena, he looked really worried. I've never seen him like that. When I asked what was wrong, he said there is going to be a big layoff and nobody can do any hiring for a while."

"For how long?"

"He didn't say. He said the international layoffs, like mine, were just the start."

"So, what now?"

"What now?" Nate snapped, "I have to find another job, that's what." He saw Lena recoil and he softened his voice, "How has your day been?"

Lena sipped coffee, "I got Brandon registered in school. I had to argue with them not to put him back a grade. I told them English schools were ahead of US schools and he should be skipped ahead one grade. They finally compromised and put him in the grade where he belongs. He's going to have to take a bus every day."

"You look at any job ads?" Nate asked.

"I'm going to do some volunteer work."

"Volunteer for whom?"

"Ross Perot."

"Who's that?"

"Our next president, I hope."

"How much are you going to get for that?"

"I told you, it's volunteer work."

"Lena, you know we spent a lot of money expecting KMS to rehire me. Now that they didn't, we're going to be hurting unless we get real jobs real soon."

"This is something I've got to do, Nate, and it's only part-time.

Disgusted, Nate got up and headed for the bedroom, "We should have waited before renting this darn house."

Lena called after him, "We have to live somewhere."

Weeks went by with Nate applying for jobs and going on interviews. Lena got deeply involved in the Perot campaign. Her part-time involvement became full-time.

Nate continued to criticize her about it. "I'm only saying you need to get a job and help out, that's all."

"I've been looking through the ads and there's nothing."

"Maybe, If you spent more time at the employment office and less time at campaign headquarters-"

"Don't you start on me. Okay"

"I'm not starting on you. I'm trying to show you how tight our money is, that's all."

"Then why do you have to keep sounding like the time I spend at campaign headquarters is hurting us."

"Because I think it is, Lena."

"Now listen Nate, I'm doing what I can to help out and I'm also doing something I feel is important."

Nate started to speak, but Lena said, "Will you let me finish? Whenever you did something you thought was important, I supported you and didn't criticize it. Now, I expect you to support me."

"I do support you, but you're missing the point. We're going to be out of money very soon."

"Then why don't you just take any job for the time being?"

"If it becomes necessary, I will. That doesn't change the fact that you're not working or trying to work?"

"I'm not going to keep debating with you, Nate."

"I could understand it in England", he said, "but you have no excuse over here."

"I don't need any excuse. I know what I'm doing. The future of our country may depend on Ross Perot and I'm not going to shirk from my responsibility. Me and Mary have-"

"Not, her again!" he said, "I don't care about what you and Mary have done down at campaign headquarters. Besides, who takes care of Mary and her daughter?"

"She gets aid. And she said I might start getting a salary when the voting primaries start."

"You know", Nate said, "None of what we're saying is going to matter when our money runs out."

"You're so negative about everything. Why don't you use your SMC techniques?"

"I have been programming for a good outcome. I just feel we have to work toward it; we can't simply wait and see what's going to happen."

They walked away from each other, Lena to the kitchen, Nate to the bedroom and his computer.

Nate's interview with Dennis Lyons, of MacGillan Labs, went so well that he was asked to report for a second interview with the big boss. He was told the hiring decision would be made that Friday.

Thursday evening, Nate asked not to be disturbed. He closed the bedroom door, reviewed the company's brochures and then meditated.

How can I get the job tomorrow? Must assume, the other candidates are equally qualified. We're all going to say how much we want the job and how hard we'll work. It won't matter to the boss man how badly I need the job.

And then there's the fact that I have to supply my own car too. If I file for my back taxes, I should get enough money for a car. It'll probably take a month to get it. I can rent a car until then.

Somehow, I've got to separate myself from the other applicants. Let's see now ... the person they hire will be working up here in San Jose alone ... they use Sigma stepper motors in their products ... I used Sigma stepper motors in my Gamma engine ...

Slowly, Nate formulated a strategy.

It was pouring rain Friday and Nate couldn't afford a taxi. He ran to and from the bus and arrived soaked for the interview. Three other candidates smiled as Nate entered the office dripping wet. He removed his notebook from a plastic garbage bag and took a seat.

To his surprise, the candidate exiting the inner office was Josh Winston, a former co-worker.

"Hey, Nate", Josh said, "I thought you were overseas."

Nate stood, "Hi, Josh, you applying too?"

Jerry Steinman came out behind Josh, "You two know each other?"

"Yeah, we worked together, at KMS, before Nate was sent overseas."

"So, you're Nate LaChae?" Steinman shook Nate's hand.

"Yes sir."

"Josh, I'd like to have another word with you." Steinman said.

The two of them went back into the office and closed the door. Nate was still embarrassed about being soaked; his shoes squished as he walked back to his seat.

Josh came out soon afterward and Mr. Steinman asked Nate in. The other candidates looked at each other smugly.

Once inside, Nate took the initiative. "Mr. Steinman, I've thought long and hard about what you need from the person who gets this job. Each of us candidates are qualified to fix equipment, but you need more than that."

"Oh?" Steinman said with raised eyebrows.

"Yes, sir. The person you hire will be working up here in San Jose alone and you need someone you can depend on; someone mature. You need someone who understands fixing the equipment is only 50% of a Field Service Engineer's job. The other 50% is customer care. You need someone who will keep you informed about everything. Someone who can be creative and think on their feet when novel situations come up. Am I right?"

"So far." Steinman smiled and sat back in his chair.

Nate continued, "Every one of us candidates can fix equipment, but I have the other qualities that you need. I brought this notebook that shows some of the projects I've worked on."

Nate handed over the notebook.

"You'll see that I've worked with Sigma stepper motors like those Macgillan Research uses in your Flying Height Tester. In fact, because of my hobby, I'll still be working with Sigma stepper motors even if I don't get this job."

Steinman examined the notebook, occasionally looking up at Nate. When he finished, he said, "Josh had good things to say about you, Nate. In fact, he probably talked himself out of the job. I'm glad you brought this notebook; none of this is in your resume."

"Yes, I know."

"I like what I've heard and seen." Steinman paused.

Nate waited.

"I want to know why KMS didn't rehire you?"

"They have a big lay-off coming, plus there's a hiring freeze."

"Nate, I owe it to those guys out there to interview them. But, if your references check out, you will be the first one getting an offer."

"Thank you, sir. Thank you very much."

"Now, tell me how would you handle a problem of lost sync pulses." Steinman put his elbows on the desk and rested his chin on his fists as Nate described bipolar phasing of stepper motors.

The offer letter came the following Wednesday. Nate accepted over the phone. Dennis Lyons asked for Nate's license plate number and insurance information. Nate told him that he would be renting a car for a while.

Dennis said, "Didn't you understand a car was a requirement?"

"Yes, and I will buy one as soon as I can."

There was silence on the phone for a while, and then Dennis said, "I'll tell you what, I'll see if I can get the company to pay for your rental car for a while."

"Really? That would be great."

"They may do it because we've been sending someone up there and paying for a hotel and car rental for months now. The company will actually be saving money by hiring you. I'll work on it. But, it will only be for a short time … understood?"

"Yes, I understand." Nate said, "And I really appreciate it."

"Okay, let's talk about getting you down here for some training."

*　　　*　　　*

"They're going to rent a car for me for three months." Nate said.

"See", Lena replied, "I told you things would be all right."

"We're still in a money squeeze for now", Nate said, "I'm going to ask for a travel advance and we can use some of it to pay bills."

Lena put dinner on the table.

"Where's Brandon?" Nate asked.

"I told him to be in here before it got dark. I think you need to have a talk with him."

Nate finished dinner and was about to go searching for Brandon when he came in dirty and smelly.

"Your grandmother told you to be in here before dark. Where were you?"

"I was over at Billy's house with some other boys."

"Where's your skateboard?"

"I left it at Billy's house."

Nate and Lena glanced at each other.

"After you eat your dinner", Nate said, "we're going to have a little talk."

"I didn't do nothing; it's only eight-thirty."

"Just go wash up and come eat your dinner."

Nate scolded Brandon and saw his disinterest.

"Are you listening to me?"

"Yes, Granddad."

Nate finished with, "So, don't be worrying us like this any more. Okay?"

"Yeah."

"Yeah?"

"Yes, you won't have to be worrying about me any more."

"If you do, I'm going to give you more than a talk next time."

"Uh, huh."

At bedtime, Nate told Lena about Brandon's attitude.

"I've noticed it too", she said, "He's changed since we got back."

"He's picking up those American street ways."

"And he'll be a teenager soon."

"All the more reason, we've got to nip that attitude in the bud."

*　　　*　　　*

Nate spent two weeks in Los Angeles, learning MacGillan's Flying Height Testers (FHT) and their Scantron microscope. The FHT measured the gap between a disk drive platter and its read/write head. Scantron was a semi-automatic microscope used to check read/write heads for defects.

Nate took to his job like a fish takes to water; it quickly became routine. He was excited to be working with the advanced stepper motor controllers that MacGillan Research used.

If I can borrow two of these for a while. I can hook them up to my computer and precisely control the stepper motors of my Gamma engine. My Simon program could be modified to automatically vary each parameter. I could find which settings give maximum performance. I could, finally, run the Gamma-Max test that I've dreamed of since the 1970's.

Can't ask for anything more right now though. I've got to be patient.

After completing his training in L.A, Nate quickly established rapport with his five customer accounts in San Jose. Four of them had FHTs and the fifth had a dozen Scantrons.

The Scantrons were all operated by women. It reminded Nate of his days working for Lorrell. Particularly, when one of the women, named Stephanie, kept making eyes at him. Her machine continually needed realignment and Nate suspected it was not by coincidence.

Whenever Nate's got inundated with work, Dennis Lyons would fly up from L.A. and help out. They worked well together and a friendly relationship developed between them. Dinner conversations were usually about Dennis' time in the marines.

*　　　*　　　*

"It's time we filed our back taxes", Nate told Lena, "we can get the money they owed us from before we went overseas."

"I don't know why you waited this long in the first place." Lena replied.

"Me! You mean 'why WE waited so long' don't you?"

"You know what I mean."

"Anyway, it will be enough money to catch up on our credit cards and some of the other bills."

"When do you want to get started?"

"I've already started some of them; we just need to finish them and get them in the mail."

When the I.R.S. reply came, Lena opened the mail. Later, she told Nate, "You're not going to like what we got in the mail today."

It read, 'We have no adoption records or guardianship documents to support your claim for legal custody of Brandon Allen. He is, therefore, not an eligible dependent.'

Subsequently, we have reduced your dependents from three to two, which results in a negative balance for the years in question. We've made corrections and added the interest due. Please sign and return the forms, with your check.

Nate flipped the pages and saw the totals.

"What the hell is this $17,341.32?"

"I called them today.," Lena said, "Even after I explained that we could prove Brandon has been with us for all those years, they said their decision was final."

"Holy shit!," Nate plopped down onto the sofa.

*　　*　　*

Nate had calculated how much money he'd need to buy a car in three months and was saving accordingly. He decided some bills were intentionally not going to get paid.

Lena still wasn't working and didn't have any prospects lined up.

One day, Nate noticed a money order receipt on the floor. It was for money that had been recently sent to Marilyn, in Los Angeles. He decided to confront Lena as soon as she got home.

"What's this?" he pointed to the Western Union receipt.

Lena put her bag of papers down and sat down. "You know what that is."

"Why are you sending money to Marilyn when we are falling behind in our own bills? You know your mother sends her money and she has an apartment down there in L.A. too."

"It wasn't your money, Nate."

"Oh, really? Then where did it come from?"

"I have some money of my own put away. And I don't have to answer to you like some child."

"No, you don't. And I don't have to keep supporting Marilyn while she's down there getting high on money from us."

"You don't know what she's doing." Lena said.

"Oh come on", Nate put his hands on his hips, "She's not working and yet she has an apartment in L.A. and receiving money. What am I suppose to think she's doing, singing in the choir?"

"You don't have to be so sarcastic."

"I don't need you to tell me what I don't have to be." Nate went into the bedroom and slammed the door.

Brandon called and asked if he could stay out late.

"No", Lena said, "I want you to come home now and eat with us."

When Brandon came in, three hours later, Nate was waiting for him.

"I suppose you think you can just ignore us now, huh?"

Brandon knew what was coming and ran behind Lena. Nate came after him with a belt in his hand. Brandon tugged at Lena and tried to stay on the opposite side of her from Nate.

"Hey! Wait a minute", Lena protested as Nate tried to reach around her. Lena fell over on top of Brandon.

Nate was furious, "You gonna make us hurt Lena? Get your ass up!"

"Wait, Granddad! Grandma, help, he's going to hurt me."

Before Lena could get up, Nate pulled Brandon, by the arm, into his bedroom. He proceeded to spank Brandon harshly. Brandon's cries and pleading didn't abate the punishment Nate gave him.

Finally, Lena grabbed Nate's arm and then said, "That's enough. That's enough, Nate; you'll hurt him for real."

Nate was puffing and sweating.

"You're not going to be like Billy and those other little hoodlums. Do you understand? When Lena or I tell you to do something, you just do it; we're not asking you, we're telling you. Do you hear me?"

"Yes. I hear you." Brandon cried and went to his grandmother.

Nate turned and walked out with his head down. "I'm not going to let you grow up to be some kind of lazy drug addict."

Lena petted Brandon as he whimpered.

Interaction between Nate and Lena wasn't warm or friendly after the spanking. Lena told him the welts on Brandon's legs could be grounds for child abuse.

Lena became a district leader with the Ross Perot campaign. And Brandon continued hanging out with Billy and the other boys, but he came in before dinner every night.

Nate focused on his job and saving money for a car. He paid the rent and as many of the other bills as he could. The utility bills fell two months behind.

Everything came to a head when the electric company sent a final notice at the same time that Nate had to return his rental car.

"Are you going to just let the lights be turned off?" Lena asked.

"I'm going to do whatever it takes to buy a car - NOW."

"You're serious, aren't you?"

"You could be helping, you know."

"We've been all through that, Nate."

"Yes, we have, haven't we."

He bought a 1982 Pontiac Grand Prix, the day before the house electricity was turned off.

That night, Nate tossed and turned, as he had many recent nights. He got up, went into the living room and lit the fireplace. He sat, watching the flames, as a pressed-wood block slowly disintegrated.

After a while, he poured a drink. Then he got up, took the portrait of himself and Lena from the mantle and placed it in the fire.

Lena smelled the paint burning and came into the living room. She spoke low, "What's wrong?"

"I want a divorce." Nate said.

"You don't mean that."

"I do mean it, Lena. I want a divorce."

Lena sat in a sofa chair opposite Nate. She stared into the fire.

"I'm not totally surprised", she said.

"Well, I am. I don't want to go on like this any more. We are not going in the same direction any more. And you say the things that's happening are not against me, but I feel the same as if they are."

"Tell me what you really feel, Nate."

"I have told you. There's nothing new. You won't get a job and help with the bills, even now. We were supposed to be taking care of Brandon until Marilyn got on her feet. Well, she has an apartment, money, and living good down there in L.A. now. You and your mother send her money and yet I am the one taking care of her son."

"But, Nate-"

"Just listen. You asked me to tell you how I really feel, so just listen. You all say you want Brandon to be like me, but it doesn't seem to apply to us going to church or him having a bank account. I'm the only one that thinks those things are important. And when I talked about adopting him, you were against that too. Now we owe all that tax money. It's like, you just want Bandon to dress and talk like me, but you're not concerned about him having my values. It makes me feel like I'm being ripped-off."

"Nobody's trying to rip you off, Nate." Lena said.

"No matter what your intentions are, that's how I feel. I have my own kids, you know. If I only wanted to give money and nothing else, I could have done that years ago. That's all the courts would allow me to do anyway."

"Maybe, that's what you need to do then."

Nate looked at her as she got up to leave the room.

She turned back and then said, "You had no right burning that portrait, it belonged to both of us. This is why I put money aside. I didn't expect us to stay together." She went on into the bedroom.

"I did." Nate said as he stared into the fireplace.

*   *   *

After sending Brandon to live with his grandmother for two weeks, they remained as amicable as possible. They divided the furniture, with

Nate getting most of it after he said, "I'm not giving up everything again. I've done that twice."

They promised they would help one another if either got in trouble.

At one point, during their packing, they brushed against one another and embraced for a long time; they said nothing. Each held back their tears. Then they continued packing as if nothing had happened.

They placed the furniture in storage. Lena moved into a spare room at Mary's house. Nate moved into a motel on El Camino Real.

Nate's illness returned and his wound reopened; it was draining again. A year before, a doctor in England had explained that his digestive system was the weakest part of his body.

Why now, when I'm a free man? When I can do all the things I've been putting off for so many years. I don't want to have another operation; not now. No telling what they'd find; I might be dying.

I better go ahead and do the things I want now while I still can.

Nate made a list, but didn't prioritize it.

- Climb Mount Whitney.
- Move to L.A. and party with Danny-Boy
- See all my kids again.
- Run the Gamma-Max experiment.

Every evening, Nate added more details to his plans. His memory of climbing Mount Washington, where he had seen a father and son hiking together, prompted him to call Darnell.

"Let's have lunch, tomorrow."

"Why?" Darnell said coldly.

"I'm planning something I think you'll be interested in."

"Another family thing?"

"No, nothing like that." Nate hesitated, "I'm going to climb Mount Whitney."

Darnell was silent. Then he said, "When?"

"No date yet, but I'm going to climb it. Just come to that restaurant at Jack London Square tomorrow and I'll show you my plan. Okay?"

"Yeah. I'll be there."

The next day, after a lukewarm greeting, they sat by the window and ordered seafood. Nate dug into his attaché case for maps and notes as Darnell stared out at San Francisco Bay. It was early and the restaurant was empty.

"I made a copy of everything for you, here's a map of the mountains."

Nate began describing his plans. Darnell examined the map, looked at Nate and asked, "You really feel you're up to this?"

"I will be in a month. I know how to build myself up." Nate said smiling, "The question is, are you up to it?"

"Don't I look like I'm up to it?" Darnell said, "I exercise for an hour and a half every morning before I go to The Base."

The food arrived and they began eating.

"Dee", Nate used the term fondly, "This is something I've wanted to do for over twenty years."

"You mean, ever since you left us?" Darnell kept chewing and didn't look up."

"This has nothing to do with that. And I didn't leave, I-"

"I know what you did." Darnell said loudly, "I know much more than you think I know. What I don't know is how the man I called my father could be like that."

"Whatever way I was then", Nate spoke softly, "I'm not that way now. I wish you could see that."

Darnell held up the map, "You still want to climb mountains."

"Just this one, while I still can. Do you want to come along?"

Darnell looked at the plans again, "You're going to go either way, aren't you?"

"Yes."

"I can't decide right now. I'll let you know." Darnell finished the rest of his food.

Nate's hopes of the two of them spending the day together vanished when Darnell said, "Is that all?"

"Yes, Darnell, that's all I had."

Darnell gathered up the papers, stood and then said, "I've got to get back to the base, there's an inspection today and they expect me to be there."

Nate was amazed that he could still tell when his son was lying.

"Sure, Darnell. Just let me know soon, if you're going."

"Yeah, I'll do that." Darnell started reaching for his wallet.

"I got this", Nate said.

"You want me to leave the tip?"

"No, I got it. Go ahead, don't be late for your inspection."

In the days that followed, Nate ate as much as he could, to gain weight before the climb. He remembered losing as much as ten pounds during previous climbs. He exercised each morning and evening and tried not to worry about his health.

He found a camping store that had all the equipment he needed. The modern paraphernalia were lighter in weight and more expensive than before. The dehydrated foods were so delicious Nate cooked some in his motel room - after disabling the smoke detector.

His digestive wound was taking an unusually long time to close and he found himself thinking, 'What if I never come back from Mt Whitney?'

On Tuesday, Dennis paged Nate with a message saying: 'Call Mario at this number after 5 pm'.

"Hallo, Nate?" the Italian voice said, "This is Mario."

"Hey, man, what are you doing in my country?"

"I'm here for training, for two months. Laura is with me. We want to see you and Lena and Brandon."

"Me and Lena are not together any more, Mario. We have broke up."

"Oh, I'm so sorry to hear that. How is Brandon?"

"He's okay. He's with Lena, I think."

"Well, anyway I hope we can get to see you before we leave."

"Oh, for sure."

"How have you been?" Mario asked, "What are you doing these days?"

"You remember how we talked about mountain climbing."

"Yes, are you thinking about going again?"

"As a matter of fact, I plan to climb Mount Whitney soon."

"No! Really?" Mario exclaimed, "Maybe I can join you."

"That would be great!"

"Anyone else going?"

"My oldest son Darnell may be."

"We should talk more about this. I will need to get equipment."

"You can rent everything, Mario. It will be really great." Nate opened his day-planner, "Where are you staying? I plan to come down to L.A. and, maybe, drive to the mountain just to see it."

Mario gave Nate his motel's address and they met that weekend.

Time passed fast and the adventurers gathered the equipment for the climb. Darnell, agreed to come and then said he had everything he needed. He didn't attend the trip-planning meeting that Nate and Mario had.

Their work schedules allowed only three days for the climb. Nate assured the others it could be done if they started early on a Friday morning. So, one crisp Thursday evening they met in L.A. stuffed their heavy packs into the back of a rented van and headed east.

The following morning found them sleeping outside the ranger station in Lone Pine, California. It was chilly and thirteen people were ahead of them in line. Nate entered the station and approached the ranger, who told him there were only two climbing permits remaining.

"But, there are three of us."

"I can't help that." The ranger stared at Nate.

"My friend came all the way from Italy for this."

The ranger didn't blink, "I told you, there's two passes left."

Nate stepped aside, in total despair, as the next two people in line got the passes. He came outside and told Mario and Darnell, "There were only two passes left."

"What?"

"The ranger said there's a limited number of passes for each day."

"Did you tell him we were three?" Mario asked.

Darnell looked toward the cabin door, as all the other dejected climbers were turned away, and then said, "Let's wait a while."

"What for?" Nate said.

"Just wait until the crowd dies down." Darnell repeated. They went to a coffee shop across the parking lot.

"I can't believe it." Nate said, "What difference does one more person make? I even told him my friend came from Italy. This is so cruel; that asshole is on a power trip."

Darnell stood up and then said, "Stay here."

"What are you going to do?" Mario asked.

"You'll see."

Fifteen minutes later, Darnell returned with three climbing passes.

"How'd you do that?"

"I gave him a sign."

"A sign?" Nate asked as he stood and grabbed his pack, "What kind of sign?"

Darnell showed them a ring on his finger and then said, "With this, and the right words, I can get into most any place."

"It's still not right." Nate said, "Just because I didn't belong to some organization, he denied me the passes. Now we're starting three hours late."

"We can make up the time." Darnell said as they headed for the van.

Nate put the car into low gear for the last part of the drive up to the base of the mountain.

"The tallest mountain I climbed back east was 6,000 feet. Now we're driving up to 6,000 feet just to start this climb."

"We don't have mountains this tall in Italy." Mario added.

They parked and adjusted their packs. Nate said, "Okay, remember what we agreed. We will stay together and will all turn back if any one of us has to turn back. No one will try to go on by themselves. Right?"

"Yeah, yeah." Darnell said.

"Right." Mario said.

But, the actual climb was different from the agreed plan. Nate and Mario paced themselves and were virtually marching up the narrow, switchback trails. Darnell sped ahead, often being out of sight of the others. Initially, he'd wait at predetermined checkpoints and they'd regroup. But, soon Mario and Nate didn't find Darnell when they arrived at a checkpoint.

At one rest stop, Mario and Nate drank water and looked out at the scenery. Mario said, "Darnell seems angry."

"He gets like that sometimes."

"It's not safe for him to be alone up there."

"I know, Mario. I think he's trying to show how strong he is."

"He can get sick if he goes too fast."

"I tried to warn him; that's why we had the planning meeting."

At the next rest stop, Mario and Nate were panting and their legs ached; their breathing was labored.

Mario asked, "Do you think we will make it in time?"

"I'm not sure Mario. Once we get above the tree line, we'll see how it goes. If we can get to the top by dark, then we'll come down tomorrow."

They asked a descending climber if he had seen Darnell and he said they were separated by about 500 meters. He also said the rangers were warning everyone about the predicted weather at the top tonight.

"There's a plateau about 800 meters up, where everyone is camping for the night." he said, "You can't miss it."

Nate was totally exhausted when he reached the edge of the plateau. Mario breathed heavily and paused often. At one point, Nate dropped to the ground and lay there, exhausted. A moment later Darnell hoisted him up, by his belt, and carried him to a small clearing nearby.

"That ... was the hardest ... climb ... I've ever ... done." Nate said.

"Me ... too." Mario said.

Darnell was setting up his stove, "I have a headache, that's all."

"I told you ... not to ... climb ... so fast." Nate said.

"We have to, if we're going to get to the summit before dark."

Nate shook his head, "A climber told us the weather is going to be bad up there this evening. We'll have to go up in the morning."

"I'm going on after I eat." Darnell said.

"Darnell, that would not be safe." Mario said, "We should stay together."

A moment later, a ranger approached and asked to see permits. He advised them to make camp where they were, for the night.

"It's expected to be clear and calm tomorrow."

Nate asked, "Can the average climber make it to the summit from here and all the way back down in a day?"

"If someone's in excellent shape," the ranger said, "it can be done. You might want to lighten up those packs though." He started off, came back, "And be sure to tie any food you have up in a tree tonight. Bears come out onto this plateau sometimes."

The climbers looked at each other. "Anybody bring rope?" Darnell asked.

"Let's borrow some rope from the other climbers."

By the time they pitched their tent, Darnell's headache had became severe. Both Mario and Nate used meditation techniques to ease the pounding in their heads.

"You guys don't have headaches?" Darnell asked.

"We know how to meditate and make them go away." Mario said.

"Meditate, huh?"

"I can show you how." Nate said.

"Nah, I'll just take some more aspirin."

That night, they marveled at the brightness of the stars. Mario preferred pitching his sleeping bag outside the small tent, while Nate and Darnell bedded down inside.

Before he dozed off, Darnell stuck his head outside the tent and then said to Mario, "Wake me if you hear anything. I brought my gun."

"I thought that was against the rules."

"It is." Darnell said, "And it's against my rules to get ate up by some animal too."

There was no wind that night and their fire lasted for hours.

Darnell was soon snoring, with his head uncovered. Nate reached over and pulled the sleeping bag's cover over the back of his son's head. *Eva would be pleased that I'm still taking care of our son.* He dozed off surprised that he had had such a thought about his ex-wife.

They slept later than planned and awoke, sore and with splitting headaches.

"I took four aspirin already", Darnell said, "and they didn't help."

"I took two myself," Nate said, "and mine got worse. Maybe, once we get moving, our heads will clear up."

"Thought you two could meditate your headaches away."

"We thought so too."

"Let's eat and see if we feel any better."

They ate and lightened their packs by hiding nonessential items in the bushes. Then they headed across the rock field. They began ascending a bolder field and Mario called out, "Hey, ... look at ... your watch." They did and immediately realized they were too far behind schedule to continue upward. They plopped down hard.

"I don't have to go back to work on Monday." Nate said.

"We agreed to all turn back together." Darnell said.

"Look whose talking. After you charged up ahead of us."

"Next time, we'll have to plan for more time."

Nate looked up at the peaks and, for a moment, thought about going on without them. He was fifty years old and he knew there would be no *next time* for him. He got up slowly and followed the others back toward the plateau.

On the way down, Nate's knees ached and he was reminded of how difficult a descent can be. After several hours and rest breaks, they were at the base of the mountain again. They threw their things in the back of the van and started down to town. Their brakes overheated and the last three miles down hill were more perilous than the climb had been.

*   *   *

Nate returned to San Jose and discovered his wound had reopened. He was thankful there hadn't been any leakage. He knew it was time to get it taken care of. He meditated for week, before going to a doctor. The surgeon examined him, drained the wound and scheduled him for an operation. Nate returned to his motel, called Darnell and explained he was going in for surgery.

"How long will you be in the hospital?"

"Only two or three days. The doctor says its not a big deal."

"They always say that."

"Well, that's the way I'm going to take it."

"Call me when you know the day you're coming out and I'll drive you home."

"Ok. And Darnell, if, for some reason, things don't go well, I-"

"You'll be fine. Call me when you're ready to go home."

"All right."

Nate awoke from the operation, remembering the nurse telling him to count backward. Everything was quiet and peaceful. He lay in bed, on his back, and felt wonderful. The lights in the room were soft. He wondered if he had died. He turned his head and saw a man lying in the bed next to him. Their eyes met and Nate said, "Hello."

The man's eyebrows formed into a frown and he grunted at Nate. *I know where I am now.* Nate thought, *back on earth.*

Darnell called that afternoon.

"You okay?"

"Yeah, I feel great. Must be the medication. You should try some."

"No thanks. I get high exercising."

Two days later Darnell took Nate from the hospital to the motel.

"This is going to be perfect." Nate said looking at his private Jacuzzi tub, "For the next three months, I need to sit in warm water three times a day,"

"Three months. Can you stay off work that long?"

"No. After a month off, I can work and come here during lunchtime."

"What about your immediate needs? Is a nurse coming?"

"Yes, it's all been arranged. I'll be okay." Nate said, "Thank you son, for being here."

Darnell turned back and stared at Nate for a moment, then he left.

Nate's recovery was both strange and frightening. Strange when he used a mirror and saw the wound from his surgery. Stranger, still, when the visiting nurses dressed his wound and gave him kind attention. One nurse told him he was taking painkiller too often and they laughed together when he described some of the vivid dreams he'd been having.

"In one case, I heard the devil whispering in my ear. We were making plans together. Evil, sinful plans." Nate said, "I wasn't the one initiating the plans, but I wasn't disagreeing with the suggestions either. Suddenly, I realized I was awake and someone had been speaking into my ear. It was really scary. I got down on my knees and then said The Lord's Prayer five or six times."

The nurse said, "So, you were going be like Flip Wilson and say 'The Devil Made Me Do It' huh?"

"No. The Devil slipped up that time and I actually heard his voice inside my head."

The doctor insisted Nate exercise by walking every day. He was weak and felt totally vulnerable to anything and everyone. He knew he couldn't defend himself. He looked in the mirror and decided he'd walk around the nearby shopping center every night. And so, he did – for four weeks.

Nate recovered quickly after Dennis Lyons told him there was a promotion waiting for him in Los Angeles. His surgeon, in San Jose, was reluctant to release him from weekly visits, but Nate insisted.

There was one thing Nate felt he had to do before moving to LA. It necessitated a trip to New York City and a reunion with his kids and his sibling's children. He wrote his kids explaining that he was coming to give a family meeting. He was pleased that his brother Douglas and sister Claudette agreed to participate. He was equally surprised when Claudette and her daughter, Daria, didn't come.

Even before the plane ride, Nate felt an inner warmth.

I've got to put my personal feelings of anger about the past aside. This is about family, not me. Our kids need to know about the health problems in our family and somehow they need to know the Devil is real. It doesn't matter if he's just in our minds or not. The influence is real and evil. So long as they don't even believe that, they don't have a chance of beating him. You can't defeat an enemy that you don't know exists. I've got to let love be in my heart to get the message across to them. I've got to!

Nate was surprised at how easy it was to call Eva and talk with her. Either he calmed her suspicions or piqued her curiosity by saying he wanted to meet and speak with her.

"About what?"

"Nothing special. I'm not coming to start any trouble. Just thought we could have a drink or something and talk about the kids."

"Okay", she said. He could hear the hesitancy in her voice. "I'll meet you at the coffee shop on Supthin Boulevard. You remember it?"

"Yeah. Seven o'clock."

Eva was waiting in a black SUV, by the train station, when Nate arrived. They greeted each other politely and entered the coffee shop.

Before the drinks arrived, Nate said, "I want to compliment you on the kids. Three out of four isn't bad. You did a good job."

Still suspicious, Eva frowned and then said, "Coming from you, that's a real compliment."

"It's a compliment you deserve. I remember you were the one that didn't want to have kids."

"Thank you. And how have you been?"

"I got separated recently." Nate wished he hadn't said it that way. "Anyway, I'm going to meet with the kids and Douglas's kids to tell them about my family. There are things they should know. Things like health problems and their history."

"Why now?" Eva said, "I mean, why are you doing this now?"

"I just know it needs to be done. I've come to realize what's going on is bigger than me."

Eva sat quietly studying Nate's face. Then she asked, "What are you going to tell them?"

"I told you what I'm going to discuss. Nothing more. Only if they ask questions about other things will I answer them. Eva, this is not about you and me. That's what I'm trying to show you."

"They might not all come to your meeting."

"I'll take that chance."

The next day, when Nate arrived at the house in Rosedale, Eva opened the door looking dejected. Determined to keep the light in his heart, Nate said, "You look like you could use a hug." He hugged her; she didn't hug him back.

He came into the living room and then said, "Who's going to dinner?"

Charlene got up and gave him a hug, "Hello, Deddy."

Malcolm shook his hand and smiled.

Kelly remained sitting.

"Kelly, say hello to your father." Eva chided.

"Hello, Nate."

"Hello, Kelly. Good to see you all. Let's get going; your cousins will be waiting for us."

* * *

The cousins dominated the conversations at the restaurant. Topics ranged from which New York teams were the best to which rap artists were the best. Douglas and Nate sat at one end of the table and ordered drinks. Nate ignored Douglas' excuse when it was time to pay the check.

After the dinner, the group went to Liller's house and gathered in the basement. Nate tried to give the message of the family's health history, but was interrupted by questions from Douglas's kids about Douglas. Meanwhile, Douglas got questions from Charlene and Malcolm about Nate.

Nate feared he was losing control of the conversations as Douglas sat on a bar stool, beer in hand, and told his kids, "I don't owe you a damn thing. I gave you life, isn't that enough?"

Kelly sat on a sofa looking bored until Douglas said something negative about women. That set off a gender debate that lasted for more than an hour.

As it got later, the music got louder and people drifted in and out of the room. Kelly and her new found cousin, Mary, approached Nate, and asked, "What really made you decide to have this meeting?"

"I wanted to give you all a chance to know about your family."

"Yeah, but why now?" Kelly asked.

"Well, if you really want to know, I had a dream and I saw that you needed to know certain things if you were going to have a real chance in life."

"What kind of things?" Mary asked.

Nate looked around the room, at the activity that was going on, and then said, "That evil exist. And if you're not aware of it, you will suffer."

414

"Is that it? Evil exists?"

Nate felt defeated, "Yes, that's it."

Kelly and Mary frowned at him and walked away from Nate.

It was after midnight when Nate dropped his kids off at home. He didn't go in. He got out of the car and Charlene gave him a hug. Malcolm shook his hand, and Kelly said, "We only came to meet our cousins, we didn't come to hear about all that other stuff."

"That's all right." Nate said, "You heard it anyway. Good night."

Douglas called Nate the next morning, "What time is your flight?"

"Hey, man, you caught me just in time; I was on my way out the door."

"I wanted you to know, I'm glad you came and I'm glad we had the meeting."

"Yeah, me too. Guess what Kelly told me when I dropped them off."

Without hesitation, Douglas said, "That they only came to meet their cousins?"

Nate laughed, "Exactly those words!"

"Then our real mission was accomplished."

"Yeah, I guess you're right. Take care of yourself."

"You too and call me sometime."

"I will."

On the plane home, Nate heard the thought in his mind saying, *now I can get back to being my self.* He said softly, "Get thee behind me, Satan," and he looked out of the window at the clouds going by.

*   *   *

Nate got his promotion to Macgillan's research department in L.A. and got an apartment in Northridge, California. He was welcomed by all but one of his coworkers; Claude had expected to get the research tech job. He glowered at Nate until, one day, Nate pulled him aside and then said, "Look, I heard that you wanted to get this job and you must be disappointed, but it's not my fault. You don't know me and I don't know you. But, we both work here and I don't see any reason for us to be enemies or something. Do you?"

Claude was so surprised, he blurted out, "Of course not. We're not enemies."

"Good!" Nate smiled and shook his hand.

Nate returned to San Jose, rented a U-Haul and paid a couple of guys to load his belonging from storage. He was careful with the boxes containing his Gamma engine parts. He drove back to L.A. and, again, paid to have his belongings carried into his apartment.

The following Saturday, Nate went to Bodhi-Tree bookstore, in West Hollywood, to restart his library of spiritual materials. Approaching the bookstore, he met his wife Lena.

"Hi, what are you doing here?"

"I could ask you the same question?"

"We don't believe in coincidences."

"No, we don't."

"Come on; want to have some tea and a sandwich across the street?"

"Okay."

They sat outside, under a canopy. Nate wondered what this coincidence meant. He decided there was no reason to tell her he had moved to L.A.

"So, what are you doing here?" he asked again.

"I'm attending a seminar on prosperity and healing."

"Who's giving it?"

Our old friend, Bert Goldman.

"He didn't send you here, to the book store, did he?"

Lena laughed, "Not consciously."

The food came and they ate in silence until Lena asked, "Why didn't you answer my letter?"

"What letter?"

"I sent you a letter two weeks ago."

"Where did you send it to?"

"To where you're staying", she smiled "the Granada Inn motel."

"I moved from there two weeks ago."

"Oh?"

"What was in the letter?"

"I don't have time to discuss it now, I've got to get back. This was only a lunch break."

"At least tell me what it was about."

"Aren't you getting your mail forwarded?"

"Actually, no. Nobody was writing to me."

"If you call them, I'm sure they'll forward it to you."

"I'll have to do that", Nate said, "How's Brandon doing?"

"He's fine. He told me how the two of you had talked and he said he knows you love him."

"Good." Nate resisted saying how he wished things had turned out differently. He also resisted asking about the Ross Perot campaign.

"And you?" Lena asked.

"And me, what?"

"What are you doing here in LA?"

"Macgillan Research brought me down to do some research work. Also, I had an operation."

Lena looked surprised. "That must be what I felt. You all right?"

"Yeah. I'm still healing. That's the reason I'm working in L.A."

Lena looked at her watch, and reached for her purse.

"No, no", Nate picked up the check, "I got it."

"Nice seeing you."

"Same here."

"Take care."

He watched her cross the street and walk away from the bookstore. For a moment, Nate felt anger, as if Lena had said "Ta-ta". He hated the fact that they could be so civil and intelligent, but couldn't work out the problems with their marriage.

He called the Granada Inn in Santa Clara and was told they had no mail for him.

"Are you sure?"

"I looked around, sir, there's nothing here for LaChae."

*   *   *

All Nate's hopes of running around Hollywood with the Jet Set were thwarted when he discovered his cousin Danny was nowhere to be found. Myheir and Danny hadn't spoken to each other for months. During that time, Danny moved from his boathouse and left no forwarding address.

Myheir left a message on Nate's machine that her mother, his Aunt Lil, was coming to L.A. for two weeks. Nate was elated. He brought her flowers, the Sunday after she arrived and they had a joyous reunion. Aunt Lil cried and so did Nate.

"This came for you just before I left."

She handed him a letter from Jeanette.

He put it in his pocket.

"Aren't you going to read it?"

"Not now. I'll read it later."

"It must be important, Nate." his aunt said, "You should read it."

"Aw, Aunt Lil, I don't want anything to spoil my time with you."

"Now, Nate, you know nothing will do that, you go on and read it."

When he did, he stared at the paper in disbelief.

"What's it say?" Myheir asked, "Is anything wrong?"

Nate looked up, "Daniel has been arrested for car jacking."

"Daniel?" Aunt Lil exclaimed, "Oh, my lord. Not little Daniel."

"What else does it say?"

"Jeanette wants me to contact her and help pay for a lawyer."

"Is she still here in L.A.?"

"Yes. Can I use your phone?"

"Of course. Use the one in the bedroom."

Nate dialed the number from Jeanette's letter and got her answering machine.

*   *   *

Nate arrived at the address on the letter and recognized Jeanette's son Derrick, stepping out of a black Mercedes. He called to him.

"Hey, Nate!" Derrick grinned.

They hugged and shook hands.

"What's going on?" Nate asked.

"We took Mama to the hospital; she passed out after she heard your voice on the answering machine."

"Is she all right?"

"They're running some tests. I just came to get some clothes for her."

"I'll go back to the hospital with you."

Nate followed Derrick into the house and sat on the couch. He could hear Derrick going through drawers in the bedroom.

"How's your brother?"

"Dikeba is fine; he's at the hospital, with mother, now."

"And Daniel, what's going on with him?"

"I'll tell you about it on our way to the hospital."

"Nice car." Nate said as Derrick drove the Mercedes along Crenshaw Boulevard.

"We gave it to Mamma for Christmas. She always wanted one."

"So, what about Daniel?"

Derrick's eyes darted back and forth, as he navigated the traffic.

"Daniel hooked up with some older boys and they got arrested for car jacking. When the police got them down to the station, they tricked Daniel into confessing and they let the other two go."

"How'd that happen?"

"You know, they played that old game of telling him that the others had already ratted on him and that they said he was the instigator. Then they told him they'd let him off if he confessed."

"He should have been smarter than that."

"There's more to it Nate. The three of them beat up a man after they forced him to withdraw money from an ATM. He had to get stitches too. So, when they told Daniel they'd drop all the other charges if he'd confess to the car jacking, he did."

"And they let the others go?"

"Yeah. They're older and knew how to play the game."

"At least Daniel is a minor, that should be in his favor."

"Not really. They're going to try him as an adult."

"But he's only fourteen."

"I know." Derrick shook his head, "They didn't even take him to juvenile court."

"Doesn't he have a lawyer?"

"Yeah, I'll give you his number and address when we get to the hospital."

Nate stared out of the window, and then looked at Derrick. "How have you been doing?"

"I'm fine. I'm an assistant manager at Walton's in Woodland Hills."

"I always knew you'd do well. Any kids yet?"

"No. But, MaryAnn wants to get married soon."

"MaryAnn, huh?"

Derrick turned into the hospital parking lot. "Yeah, and Mamma says she wants me to get married and give her some grandkids."

"Pressure from both sides, huh?"

Dikeba stood and greeted Nate in the dimly lit hospital room. Nate looked pass him and saw Jeanette lying there. The first thing he noticed was her hair wasn't in a huge Afro any more. She was bigger and wore glasses.

Jeanette's eyes widened, "You came." She said.

Nate took her hand in both of his and sat, "Yes, I'm here."

"I didn't know what to expect." She squeezed his hand.

"You can expect me to see this thing through. I'll help as much as I can. But, how are you doing?"

"They said my blood pressure is up, otherwise I'm okay. I'm exhausted from all the running around because of this mess Daniel got into."

"I'm going to talk to his lawyer as soon as I can. We'll get it worked out."

"Oh, Nate. I'm so glad you're here."

A nurse came in and announced visiting hours were over.

"I'll have some news for you tomorrow." Nate said, "Try not to worry." He kissed her on the forehead and left.

Nate waited, at the lawyer's office, until almost lunchtime. Finally, Harold Silverstein arrived and the secretary introduced Nate.

"Sorry, you had to wait. Come on in." Silverstein dropped his overstuffed briefcase on his desk and pulled out a folder full of papers. He sat, examined the folder and shook his head.

"Your son should have never signed that confession." Silverstein spoke in quick bursts. "There were other options available, but, not now."

Silverstein took out a pack of cigarettes. "Do you mind?"

"No, not at all." Nate shifted pensively in the hard wood chair.

"He could be looking at fifteen to twenty-five years."

"What!" Nate sat forward in his chair, "just for car jacking?"

"There are ancillary charges because of the beating they gave the victim." Puffing his cigarette, Silverstein added, "It's a difficult situation, Mr. Raleigh-"

"LaChae." Nate corrected, "My son uses his mother's last name."

"I see."

Nate leaned forward, putting his hands on the edge of the desk. "Mr. Silverstein, don't take this as an insult or anything, but is there some amount of money that can make all this go away?"

"No. And I'm not insulted, Mr. LaChae." He snuffed the cigarette out in an ashtray. "Car-jackings are a big thing in the current political climate in L.A. They're making examples out of every case that they can."

"Even so, fifteen to twenty-five years doesn't seem right."

"It's the maximum. I'm going to do my best to get a lesser sentence. I don't want to get your hopes up, but there are some procedures they used that may let me get the charges dismissed. The case will not be tried by a jury. It's going to a judge."

Nate slumped in his chair.

"What can I do?"

"Right now? Nothing. Just be there for him."

"I'll write a letter to the judge."

"I think you should know, the judge is Asian, like the victim."

"Can't we get another one?"

"I'm afraid not." Silverstein lit another cigarette. "Not at this stage, anyway."

"I want to thank you for your efforts Mr. Silverstein. Please help my son."

They stood and Silverstein walked Nate to the door. "I'll do everything I can. Keep in touch."

That evening, Nate composed a letter to the Judge:

Honorable Judge Fugi,

I am writing you concerning my son Daniel Raleigh whose case will be before you soon.

The circumstances and details of his crime have been described to me by his lawyer. His crimes are inexcusable. Of course, such behavior should not be tolerated in any society.

My appeal to you is that you give my son more humane treatment than he gave his victim. I beg you to consider the fact that he is only fourteen years old and was influenced by older boys, all of whom have been set free.

Surely, the fact that I have not been a daily factor in his life contributed to his state of mind. That crime belongs to me and not him. I have recently moved to Los Angeles to be closer to him and to be a part of his life. This I will do, regardless of the outcome of his trial.

If your wisdom permits, please give Daniel a chance to pay for his crime in a way that will show compassion and forgiveness. If he can be released in my custody, I will take responsibility for seeing that nothing like this ever happens again. I will do this by giving him love, a sense of responsibility and religious beliefs that abhor harming other human beings or taking their belongings.

Whatever your decision will be, I trust in your honor, humanity and judgment.

Thank you for reading this letter.

There was no acknowledgement or reply from Judge Fugi.

It was days before Nate got to see Daniel. At the jail, he went through security checks and gates with iron bars. He was directed to a large room with tables and benches. All the inmates wore grey jumpsuits. One was walking toward him with a book in his hand. The young man stopped in front of Nate.

"Daniel?" Nate asked.

"Yes."

"Daniel Raleigh?"

"Yes, dad. I'm Daniel."

As they hugged, their eyes teared, but neither cried.

"Come on", Daniel said, "we can sit over there."

Nate pulled a photo out of his wallet.

"My aunt gave me this picture and then said it was you."

Daniel smiled, "That's Derrick."

"Yeah, I see that now."

Daniel watched Nate's every move.

"Are you okay?" Nate asked.

"I'm alright. I'm learning how to avoid the troublemakers in here."

"What are you reading?"

"This book by-"

"Krishnamurti!" Nate exclaimed, "He's one of my-. I'd call him a guru, but he doesn't like that term."

"Yes, I read about that. He says we should each find the truth for ourselves."

"Daniel, if you read books like that, how come you're in here?"

"I only got it from the library yesterday. I never heard of him before that." Daniel looked at the book and thumbed the pages. "I think you know by now, how I got here."

"I wish you hadn't signed that confession."

"They tricked me."

"I know. I know." Nate said, "I've spoken with your lawyer. He's going to see if he can get the charges dismissed because of the way things were done."

"The guys in here tell me there's not much chance of that because of judge Fugi."

"We can still think positive."

"That judge gives me the creeps every time he looks at me."

"Don't stare at him or anything."

"He hates me. I can tell."

"He is still bound by the law, Daniel. He must follow the law."

"I might get twenty-five to life."

"They're not going to give you that, Daniel. Mr. Silverstein says, if he can't get the whole thing dismissed, you might get as little as five years plus probation. Just keep thinking positive, no matter what."

"I've been doing that. In fact, since I been in here, my head is so clear that I wonder why I did it in the first place. That wasn't me, I'm not like that."

"Were you high?"

Daniel sat upright, "I don't do drugs. I'm not a weak person."

"I didn't say you were."

"I've been seeing things clearer now." Daniel said, "And the fact that you're here makes me know things are changing."

"Yes, they are. I'll be here for you. You can count on that from now on."

They sat quietly and glanced around the room. Then Daniel said, "That guy over there tries to beat me at chess."

"Oh yeah. You think you're good?"

It warmed Nate's heart to see his son smile.

"I can hold my own. Momma says I inherited that from you."

A voice boomed over the PA system, "Visiting hour is over."

When the announcement came a second time, they hugged and looked at each other. Then Daniel joined the other inmates forming a line at the back wall. Nate waved as he walked pass the thick glass window to the exit.

Walking down the hallway, Nate peered through one of the small square door windows that lined both sides. Inside he saw a cot and a washbasin. Sandals were arranged neatly by the cot. Bars were on the little window. Nate's heart was in his throat. Inwardly he wanted to scream "NO-o-o-o!"

In spite of Silverstein's best efforts, Judge Fuji sentenced young Daniel to eleven years – without parole. Jeanette fainted in the back of the courtroom and Nate shouted, "WE WILL APPEAL, DANIEL! WE WILL APPEAL!"

*　　　　　*　　　　　*

Months later, Nate and Daniel were playing chess in the inmate's lounge.

"You've improved your game."

"Yeah, I been playing Professor." Daniel said, "He's the best player in here. They say he had a rating with the American Chess Federation."

"Sounds like the man to beat."

"I stalemated him once and the brothers said he was losing his touch. After that, he wouldn't play me for a while."

"Be careful."

"What? Prof is not the kind of guy to get angry over something like that."

"Daniel", Nate hesitated, "Prof's reputation may be all he has going for him in here. If you take that away, he'll have nothing."

"That's why I only stalemated him."

Nate and Daniel looked at each other, and laughed.

"Let's go out into the courtyard."

"Do you ever wonder what your brothers and sisters, in New York, are like?"

"I figured you'll tell me about them."

"I was waiting for you to ask about them in your letters."

"My letters are screened. Besides, I want you to tell me."

"Well, your oldest brother is named Darnell. He's been in the Coast Guard for a long time now. He's tall, and a disciplinarian kind of guy. You two look alike too. He's married and lives up near Oakland."

"You and him get along?"

"Things between me and Darnell run hot and cold. Sometimes he won't communicate and other times he does. Maybe he inherited that."

"I mean are you two friends?"

"I don't know." Nate admitted, "I think we are right now.

Then there's your other brother, Malcolm. He's a lot different from Darnell. It always amazes me how someone can grow up in the same household and yet be so different. Malcolm has been in jail for drugs. He came out and lived with me once. He stayed to himself most of the time. Then when he ran my phone bill up to hundreds of dollars, I sent him home to his mother. Last time I was in New York, he came to a little family reunion I gave. Everything was cool between us then."

"Are my sisters older or younger than my brothers?"

"The girls are younger. Charlene is a year older than Kelly. They're both sweet young ladies. They came out and visited me, in Sacramento.

Charlene discovered she was pregnant and went back home after a week or so. She has two kids, now. We talk on the phone from time to time.

Kelly stayed long enough to get a job. Then me and Lena broke up and Kelly went back to New York and continued college. I think she was mad with me because I had bought her an airline ticket when I knew me and Lena were going to break up. But, I was just *castling*, so she would feel secure when the breakup came."

"Why didn't she stay with Lena?"

"I guess they weren't that close."

"Did all of them come to the family reunion you gave?"

"No. Darnell said it would be a step backward for him. I was surprised when my sister backed out too.

"Do they know about me?"

"Yes. They have known about you for a long time. And when they ask, I told them I didn't know where you were – and I didn't at the time."

"That's what I've always told people when they asked me where you were."

"What about the rest of your family, in Chicago?" Daniel asked. Before Nate could answer, the announcement came that visiting was over.

"I'll write to you about them, Daniel."

For Easter, Nate brought a large bag of soul food – sweet potato pie, collard greens, fried chicken, potato salad and corn bread dressing.

Upon arrival at the prison gate, a voice on the intercom said,

"There's been a fight in Block-D and there's a lockdown."

"So, can I just leave this food for my son?"

"No. Nothing comes in or goes out."

"But, it's Easter and this is just food."

"I've told you, sir. Block-D is under a lockdown."

Nate stood there at the gate, in the dessert, looking at the intercom. He looked to his left and his right and saw only electrified fencing. He turned and stared up at the video camera.

Tears welled up inside of him as he walked back toward the parking lot. He threw the bag of food into a garbage can and he cried. An approaching couple avoided him as they headed toward the entrance.

He shouted to them, through his tears, "Those sadistic bastards are not gonna let you in. You'll see."

Daniel's letters became shorter and fewer, while his conversations became deeper and more philosophical. He said he was reading books by Gilbran, Krishnamurti, Casteneda and Jane Roberts.

Conversations between Nate and Daniel centered on chess and psychic phenomenon. Finally, one day while playing chess, Daniel said, "So, I chose this reality?"

Nate moved his Queen's knight and then said, "I didn't say that."

"No, but that's what Castaneda's writings imply. Even the Seth books say we make our own reality." Daniel moved a pawn, threatening Nate's knight.

"Daniel, I think all possibilities become reality at some level. It's like we choose which reality we experience from moment to moment."

Nate moved his black bishop, "Check."

"Well dad. I'm not choosing the reality that you've got planned for this game. I'm choosing this one ... " Daniel made a move that blocked Nate's check and simultaneously exposed a Queen threat to Nate's king.

"Checkmate in two." Daniel said.

Nate studied the board, then said slowly, "O-o-o-oh, shit."

Daniel smiled and then said, "You were talking about reality?"

"Very good, Daniel. You got me that time, Very well done."

"I beat Prof seven games out of the last ten we played."

Nate sat back in his chair, looked at his son and then said, "You think, maybe it's time you turned some of that brain power toward your education?"

"I'm ahead of you, dad. I've been studying already."

"Good! I didn't want you to think I was putting pressure on you to do it."

"Why?, Did you think I might rebel?"

"No." Nate lied, then added, "Well ... yes."

"One thing I've learned, since I been in here, is that an education is the most important thing. I'm going to use my time in here to get my GED and some college credits."

"All right!" Nate exclaimed, "You know I'm with you 100%."

At the end of visiting hours, they hugged and Daniel said, "Have a happy father's day."

Nate paused and looked into Daniel's eyes, "Thank you, I'll try."

*   *   *

Meanwhile, at the Walsh Senior Citizens Home, Miriam Streisand spoke softly to Colonel Abrams, "Nate LaChae has built another teststand, sir."

"Good work, Miriam." Colonel Abrams said. "Have we duplicated it?"

"Not yet. The design is almost identical to his previous one."

Abrams pounded his fist on the bed, "We must build the devices", he started coughing, "if we're ever going to understand them."

"Yes, sir." Miriam put her hand on his.

"I'm sorry, Miriam. I should thank you for believing me. The others think I've gotten senile, but I tell you Nate is one of the Indigos. Their minds can alter material objects. What we call reality can be changed by those like him." Abrams raised up from his bed and grabbed Miriam's arm, "You must protect him from imbeciles like Taggart. They see everyone as a threat."

"I understand, sir. I'll see that no harm comes to LaChae." She stood to leave.

"And thank you for the cigarettes", Abrams said, "I smoke only one a week. It's my only vice now."

They smiled at each other and Miriam said, "Take care of your self, sir."

"Shalom." Abrams replied.

She closed the door quietly as she left her father.

*   *   *

428

After weeks of borrowing and carefully assembling all the equipment he needed, Nate's Gamma-Max teststand was ready. He secured his engine into the metal frame he'd built in his closet. The computers and electronics were on a desk nearby.

One by one, he successfully conducted all the preliminary tests. Each component was checked and rechecked, measured and calibrated. There would be no margin for error this time. Nate knew everything would be happening too fast for him to intervene. He hoped the force on the gyro-disks wouldn't tear the whole device apart.

He lay down and meditated about the upcoming test, right to the point where he would switch the controls to automatic. His upgraded Simon program would then take over and automatically adjust the parameters to get the maximum Gamma effect.

At 3:47 AM, January 17, 1994, Nate switched the recorders on and ran the Gamma engine up to its resonance mode.

The new design didn't have the clanging, vibrating gyros of previous tests. Instead, there was only a smooth, deep, humming sound, which was reduced by Styrofoam inside the closet.

Nate typed the command that would let Simon take over, but paused before pressing the Enter key. He smiled as he imagined his engine ripping a hole through the ceiling and shooting through the two floors above.

Surely, that's not going to happen, he thought.

He pressed the Enter key and watched the video monitor and computer display. He tried to follow the frenzy of Simon's activities, hoping to see some indications of a lifting force.

Seventeen minutes later, Nate LaChae's Gamma engine began emitting an invisible, pulsating, beam of entropy energy deep into the earth … and the quake began.

Report of the SCEDC

TIME January 17, 1994 / 4:30:55 PST
LOCATION 34 degrees 12.80 minutes North, 118 degrees 32.22 West,
20 miles west-northwest of Los Angeles, 1 mile southwest of Northridge.
MAGNITUDE M 6.7
TYPETYPE OF FAULTING blind thrust
FAULTS INVOLVED Northridge Thrust (also known as Pico Thrust)
Several other faults experienced minor rupture, rupture during large
aftershocks or triggered slip.
DEPTH 18.4 Km

At 4:30 am, on January 17, 1994, residents of the greater Los Angeles
area were rudely awakened by the strong shaking of the Northridge
earthquake. This was the first earthquake to strike directly under an urban
area of the United States since the 1933 Long Beach earthquake.

The earthquake occurred on a blind thrust fault, and produced the
strongest ground motions ever instrumentally recorded in an urban
setting in North America. Damage was widespread, sections of major
freeways collapsed, parking structures and office building s collapsed, and
numerous apartment buildings suffered irreparable damage. Damage to
wood-frame apartment houses was very widespread in the San Fernando
Valley and Santa Monica areas, especially to structures with "soft" first
floor or lower-level parking garages. The high accelerations, both vertical
and horizontal, lifted structures off of their foundations and/or shifted
walls laterally.

FEMA Technical Rescue Incident Report

The Northridge Apartments was a three-story wood frame stucco
exterior construction apartment building. The initial earthquake
caused the building to collapse. Because of the first floor "soft story"
construction, the second and third floors "pancaked" down onto the
first story apartments. On initial drive-through by LAFD units, it was
not even noticed that there had been a collapse of the building. The

complete collapse of the first floor made the structure look like a two-story building. When first responders finally did realize there had been a collapse and many victims were involved, they requested additional resources and began rescue operations.

THE END

Made in the USA
Middletown, DE
19 April 2020